To S

Best Wishes

David T Applegate

CRISIS
AN EMPIRE OF THE ELVES NOVEL

DAVID T APPLEGATE

BALBOA.
PRESS
A DIVISION OF HAY HOUSE

Copyright © 2017 David T Applegate.

All rights reserved. No part of this book may be used or reproduced by any means, graphic, electronic, or mechanical, including photocopying, recording, taping or by any information storage retrieval system without the written permission of the author except in the case of brief quotations embodied in critical articles and reviews.

Balboa Press books may be ordered through booksellers or by contacting:

Balboa Press
A Division of Hay House
1663 Liberty Drive
Bloomington, IN 47403
www.balboapress.com.au
1 (877) 407-4847

Because of the dynamic nature of the Internet, any web addresses or links contained in this book may have changed since publication and may no longer be valid. The views expressed in this work are solely those of the author and do not necessarily reflect the views of the publisher, and the publisher hereby disclaims any responsibility for them.

The author of this book does not dispense medical advice or prescribe the use of any technique as a form of treatment for physical, emotional, or medical problems without the advice of a physician, either directly or indirectly. The intent of the author is only to offer information of a general nature to help you in your quest for emotional and spiritual well-being. In the event you use any of the information in this book for yourself, which is your constitutional right, the author and the publisher assume no responsibility for your actions.

Any people depicted in stock imagery provided by Thinkstock are models, and such images are being used for illustrative purposes only. Certain stock imagery © Thinkstock.

Print information available on the last page.

ISBN: 978-1-5043-1060-4 (sc)
ISBN: 978-1-5043-1061-1 (e)

Balboa Press rev. date: 10/05/2017

CONTENTS

Dedication ix
Acknowledgements.. xi
Foreword.. xiii

PART ONE: THE BOYHOOD OF KAEDE

Chapter 1:   A Boy Is Born 1
Chapter 2:   Opportunity 44
Chapter 3:   Just Asking 77
Chapter 4:   Progress 112
Chapter 5:   Champion.. 129

PART TWO: LOSS

Chapter 6:   Research 165
Chapter 7:   Dust 202
Chapter 8:   Action Stations 231
Chapter 9:   Homecoming...................................253
Chapter 10: Reactions 285

INTO THE ELVES' MOUND

Chapter 11: Kicked Out 313
Chapter 12: Awakening 344
Chapter 13: Acquisition 371
Chapter 14: Seventeen 409
Chapter 15: Last Week of Freedom 440

Glossary 513
    Aquatic Elves 513
    Archon 513
    Beast-Men 514
    Blood Witch 514
    Cat Sìth 516
    Centaur 516
    Cù Sìth 516
    Coven 517
    Daemon 517
    Dark Elf 518
    Demon 518
    Dragon 519
    Dwarf 521
    Elf 521
    Field Elf 526
    Flower Elf 526
    Forest Elves 527
    Free States 527
    Giant 528
    Goblin 528
    God 528

Hakama..529
Jötunn 529
Kazoku 529
Kimono 530
Kiseru 530
Kizami Tobacco................................ 530
Magic... 530
Makura..532
Mana Pool 532
Mountain Elves.................................532
Night Elves 533
Naruko 533
Oni...533
Ogre 534
Orcs 534
Púca...535
Pureblood 535
Ritual Casting 535
Silver Elves.. 536
Tabi 536
Titan... 536
Trolls 537
Unicorn 537
Wild Cat Sìth....................................537
Wraith 538

DEDICATION

For my son, Daniel.

ACKNOWLEDGEMENTS

I want to thank my sister Kelly for her support, encouragement, and assistance.

FOREWORD

The first people stepped out of the light whole. On top of the world, they built the great kingdom of Hyperborea, the land beyond the north wind. Hyperborea was the first civilisation, the birthplace of philosophy, art, technology, and magic.

When the Giants appeared, they were welcomed, educated and given a home. The Giants worked timber and farmed the land. A hardworking, honest, and caring, people, the Elves shared the bounty of Hyperborea with them.

When the Dwarves appeared, they were welcomed, educated and given a home. The Dwarves worked iron and polished gems. Hardworking, honest, and caring, the Elves shared the bounty of Hyperborea with them.

When the Goblins appeared, unlike Elves, Giants or Dwarves, they stepped out of the dark. Yet they were welcomed, educated and given a home. The Goblins were lazy and worshipped gold. The mischievous and greedy Goblins preferred to take, not make. They lied, used emotional manipulation and stole. The Elves expelled them from Hyperborea.

The Orcs stepped out of the dark. They were welcomed, educated and given a home. At first, the Orcs were peaceful and protected animals from hunters who killed for sport. Strong and proud, but they would bully those smaller and weaker than them to work the land while they got drunk. Eventually, the Elves expelled them from Hyperborea.

The Ogre stepped out of the dark, they were welcomed, educated and given a home. Like the Dwarves, they were a diverse race.

Land and resources were limited. Most of the world was covered in ice. They Ogres did not respect borders. They did not respect laws. They did as they pleased. They raped, they stole and killed.

The first ice war cost many lives before the Elves finally expelled the Ogres from their lands and driven them south.

The Ogres created the beast-man to make their armies more powerful. The second ice war destroyed many cities, but unable land on well-fortified Hyperborea, the war ground to a halt.

Aided by Dark Elves, the Ogres rebuilt their armies. They created homo sapiens and Dragons.

The end of the ice age was near, a slow melt had begun. Keen to control the world, the Ogres launched The Third Ice War. Again, the Elves were pushed back to the Northern edge of the ice. Using Unicorns and Pegasi as mounts on land and in the air. The Elves were unable to defend most of Hyperborea and forced to retreat.

West Hyperborea was cut off from Central Hyperborea and East Hyperborea. Near defeat in the West, the fortunes of war turned against the Ogres when the Elves in the East freed the Dragons, destroying the control collar and offering them their own lands.

Facing a humiliating defeat, the Dark Elves blasted the ice caps and accelerated the melting of the ice.

The Elves could not stop the ice from melting, so the Elves built ships, as many as they could. But they build ships not just themselves, but all races.

After the flood, the world was in ruins. The Elves look to the stars.

The Exodus of the Elves began, and by the end of the twelfth century, there was no pure-blooded Elf, Giant, Dwarf, Goblin, Orc, or Ogre left on Earth.

Those left behind soon forgot about the first people.

PART ONE

THE BOYHOOD OF KAEDE

CHAPTER 1

A BOY IS BORN

August 31, 11562, New Imperial Calendar.

Sub-basement Twenty of the Imperial Palace, Imperial City, Proxima Alcyone Three.

In the dark, three figures wove their way through the hawthorn bushes around a round white marble pool. They were Blood-Witches, masters of the healing arts and magic. Their uniform was a black double-breasted tunic, with red trim and a high Asian collar, with a black pleated skirt with red trim. On the left sleeve of the tunic was the symbol of the Empire, a black round patch with a gold rope edge and the seven stars of the Pleiades inside, and on the right sleeve was a white kite shield patch with a red Rod of Asclepius inside.

Each had a wide red patent leather belt, which had a mobile phone clipped on. Each wore red pantyhose and black knee-high boots. Each Witch had an ankle length black robe with red trim and a large hood with red cord. The robe had had the red Rod of Asclepius on the back.

Each Witch had the hood over her head, with her face

concealed by a red medical mask. The Blood-Witch in the lead carried a staff and a medical bag, the second was pregnant, and the third carried a small basket that contained a blue wrap.

They stopped in front of a pool at a quarter-circle marble bench seat. At the back of the pond stood a marble statue of a Flower Elf maiden, holding a vase that poured water into the pool, with the overflow and filter at its feet.

In silence, each Blood-Witch removed all her clothing, except for the medical mask. Each of them was a young Flower Elf. They each folded and placed their robes, clothes and underwear in a neat pile on the marble seat and then put their boots on the ground in front of the bench. Wearing only a medical mask, they entered the small pool in the dark.

Three more Blood-Witches arrived, each had three small gold bars on their collar. They stood silently on the edge of the pool and watched the trio in the pool.

The pool was behind a two-storey wooden Japanese Quadrangle house in the middle of the island. A palisade, with a walkway near the top, surrounded the house, it had high guard towers on the corners and either side of the single gatehouse.

The island was on a lake inside a dark, massive cavern. A low, flat, wooden bridge with stone pillars. Small pagoda lanterns were on the top of pillars. It ran from large round stone pillar in the middle of the cavern to the south side of the island. On each end of the bridge was guard hut. In the central column was two massive iron sliding doors that had 21 on them.

The lake was large, deep and it covered most of the cavern. A six-metre long Green Eastern Water Dragon came close to shore and rose out of the lake to peer over the palisade, it watched the Witches. At first, none noticed it.

The Hashimoto House Guards who stood guard on the walkway at the top of the palisade around the compound. They saw the Dragon and gave it occasional glances. Each guard was well armed and armoured. Over their uniform, a dark grey shirt with black pants was a black combat vest and a helmet. On the left sleeve of the tunic was the symbol of the Empire and on the right sleeve was a grey kite shield with crossed long swords inside the shield.

Each had a 9mm handgun, stun baton, torch, a mobile phone with microphone and earpiece on a cord and cuffs on their belt and carried a 7mm caseless, 30-round, Viper 1, bullpup assault rifle on a three-point sling. Over the vest was a green tabard that bore the symbol of House Hashimoto, the profile of an Eastern Green Winged Dragon inside a solid yellow circle on red.

Inside the house, Emperor Takahiro Hashimoto, a 155cm tall Flower Elf with gold eyes and a long, thick, pink hair cut like a samurai, sat on a Japanese wooden stool with a red cushion and smoked a kiseru. Beside him an ashtray on a stand with a small table with a tin of Kizami.

Takahiro has a long, thin moustache and long chin hair. His was hair is not discoloured, there were no wrinkles or age spots on his body. He wore a red silk kimono with green trim, with the symbol of his house on his back; his hakama was green. On his head was the crown of the Empire, seven platinum oak leaves, joined tip to stem, to form a circle.

His son, Prince Hiro Hashimoto arrived, a 167cm tall Flower elf with pink hair and gold eyes. He was wearing an Imperial Navy Uniform, a light purple collarless shirt, a dark purple double-breasted tunic with high Asian collar that had five vertical gold bars pinned on his collar. The symbol of the Empire was on the left sleeve, on the right sleeve was the Symbol of the Imperial Navy, the head of a trident with seven stars around it. He also had on dark purple pants with black boots. A mobile phone was clipped to his black leather belt beside a wand holder, inside of which was a wand that looked like a bamboo stalk with an onion bulb on its end. He has a holster for a sidearm, it was empty.

Hiro bowed low, "Father, I apologise for being late. I came as fast as I could. Has she given birth?" Hiro asked.

"Have you reported to Admiral Niemi?" Takahiro asked.

"No, I haven't submitted my reported yet," Hiro replied while still bowed.

"Hiro, relax and sit, they entered the birthing pool an hour ago. We can talk about your mission to Algol while we wait."

Hiro removed his tunic and placed it on the rack by the door to the inner courtyard.

The 600-metre-long ship drifted in space, a huge long gash down its side, bodies lay in their cabins. The Ogres went room to room, shooting, looting, raping and pillaging.

One of the Ogre's held the captain up by her neck, "Where is it?" he bellowed.

"What?" she replied.

"The sword!" the Ogre snarled.

"I have no idea what you are talking about."

The Ogre in a rage snapped her neck and turned to the Ogre beside him, "Find it."

The second Ogre went to the computer, pulled the dead operator off her chair and tapped at the controls, no response.

The Ogre in charge went over to another terminal, the cargo manifest was empty.

"Search the containers until the sword is found," the leader growled.

The Blood-Witches watched and waited until the pregnant Witch gave birth. Just on midnight, the púca was born with a full head of pink hair and teeth. The Dragon sniffed the air.

All Elves are androgynous; thus, even those with the male chromosome are born female, but they do not have ovaries, and they grow their male organ as a teenager.

The Witch washed the púca and lifted it out of the water. The púca opened its eyes and took its first breath. The Blood-Witch carried it up the stairs out of the pool and placed a tag on the púca's wrist. She looked her smart-watch resting on top of her clothes and wrote 'Hashimoto púca, 12:01 AM September 1, 11562' on the tag. While another bagged the placenta, clamped, and cut the umbilical cord. The púca did not cry; instead, it looked around.

The púca was wrapped and placed in the púca basket. The first Blood-Witch then handed it over to the first Witch in the second trio. The third Blood-Witch helped the second out of the pool. As the first trio dressed, the House Guards escorted the second group of Witches to the house. The Dragon looked at the guards, then slid back into the water and disappeared into the darkness.

The second trio of Blood-Witches was escorted around the house to the east wing of the house. Inside was a medical clinic. As one Witch washed the púca, another sat at the computer. On the screen was the red Cardecus, soon replaced by Birth Records, she selected create. The computer prompted her for an Imperial Identification Number. She copied sixty-four pairs of hexadecimal numbers from a message on her phone.

The clinic computer was connected to a hand-held scanner, a camera, DNA Sequencer, a scanning booth and network. She titled the record Hashimoto púca and imported prenatal scans and other records.

The second Witch took a mouth swab from the púca and placed it in the DNA Sequencer, and then she made a second swab. She sealed that one in a zip lock bag and handed it to the lead Witch, who labelled it and put it in her medical bag. Then the second Witch took the hand-held scanner, and scanned the palms and soles of the púca, after that, she used the camera to photograph him.

The third Witch took the púca and placed him in the scanning booth, which imaged him internally and externally from head to toe. The pictures of his body, layers of his brain, muscles, and organs, were added to his record. The DNA Sequencer finished the chromosome test and updated the display on the computer, gender changed to male.

The printer was not loaded with paper, but a slightly green sheet of plastic she removed from a box marked 'optical paper'. The printer loaded each sheet, and then a soft glow emanated from the papers slots as each sheet passed through the machine.

Each sheet had his identification number on top. While they waited, the trio of Blood-Witches fussed over him on a púca rug and dressed him in a blue rabbit suit. When the printing finished, the first Witch placed the first stack of plastic sheets into a folder in her medical bag, then printed a second batch.

While the trio in the clinic took turns hugging the púca and rubbing noses with him, House guards escorted the first trio of witches down the granite walkway around the house, to the iron double-gate.

On both the inside and outside of the gate, Imperial Knights were on guard. Each wore solid white full-body armour with three gold bars on their collar. On the left sleeve was the symbol of the Empire and on the right sleeve was a white oval patch with gold edge with the outline of a male unicorn's head inside. Each wore a white helm with a clear faceplate. On their belt was a 13mm handgun, stun baton, torch, a large combat knife, a mobile phone with microphone and earpiece on a cord and cuffs. A backpack and claymore sword on their back. They were alert, holding their Viper 2 10mm bullpup assault rifle, on a three-point-strap. The gun had a 30-round magazine. Like the Hashimoto House Guards, they all were female Flower Elves.

Two Knights lifted the bar, while two more pulled the large, heavy, gate open. It had the symbol of House Hashimoto on the outside. They closed the gates as the house guards escorted the first trio of Blood-Witches through the garden. The guard escorted them over the wooden bridge to a pair of doors set in the massive stone column in the middle of the cavern. A camera over the doors looked at the group, and then the doors slid sideways open to reveal an elevator. Inside was a touch screen, it showed an outline of the tower, they were 21 levels below the palace.

As the three Blood-Witches rode up the shaft, a pair of guards entered the main room to take away the kiseru and the ashtray stand. The trio of Witches with the púca waited in the walkway, they caught a glimpse of the inner courtyard, it had Knights in a white double-breasted tunic with high Asian collar and dark purple pleated skirt, with white pantyhose and white knee-high lace-up boots, doing drills with claymore swords.

The guards returned to the Blood-Witches and escorted them into the main room. The first carried a green book; the second had a púca bag; the third brought the púca, wrapped in a yellow blanket with blue stars on it. Together they stood before and bowed to the Emperor. Hiro stood beside Takahiro, who stood and returned the bow.

"Emperor, the púca is extraordinary," the first Blood-Witch said.

"Something not in the results of the first DNA tests?" Takahiro asked, his gold eyes narrowed.

"No Emperor, it is the púca, only an hour old, he crawled," the Witch replied. She turned to the one with the púca and nodded. The Blood-Witch placed the púca on the floor, then stood back. They all waited, looking at the púca, who looked around.

"Well?" Takahiro asked as he walked over and sat beside the púca on the floor. The púca giggled and looked at him.

"Are you joking with us?" Hiro asked, with raised eyebrows.

"Blood-Witches are not known for their humour; they take their duties seriously," Takahiro replied. He faced Kaede, knelt and held his hands out. Kaede looked at him and crawled over. Takahiro lifted Kaede and stuck a finger in his mouth, then pulled it out quickly. Then said, "What a fine boy, he already has hair and teeth." He looked at the Witches and asked, "You have confirmed the púca is a boy?"

"Yes, Emperor Takahiro, the púca has one X and one Y chromosome. I assure you he is pure-blood Flower Elf in perfect health. He has all the Hashimoto genes, he is Hiro's son," the first Blood-Witch replied.

"Excellent," Takahiro replied, he handed the púca to Hiro. "The charter guarantees every law-abiding citizen, one child." He turned to the Witches, and added, "Of course, with the Witches' permission."

"Yes, Emperor. It is our duty to enforce the population control law and preservation of blood-line act," the first Blood-Witch stated. "Should you or the crown prince require a bride, we can—" She was cut off by the Emperor, who raised his hand and spoke.

"Like me, my son has chosen to have a púca with a surrogate. I am aware of how keen the Blood-Witches are to see my son and me married to many females, but also like me, my son has chosen to remain unwed," Takahiro said.

"My apologies, to you both," the first Blood-Witch murmured, she bowed and said, "I meant no disrespect to you or your son, my Emperor."

"Consider the matter forgotten," Takahiro said bowing slightly.

The first Blood-Witch looked over to the one with the púca bag, who then stepped forward, removed a bottle of milk, and then handed it to Hiro. She placed the púca bag near his jacket. "We will be delivering to you mother's milk daily until either he is weaned off on his own or he turns twelve years old," she said.

The second Witch detached her phone from her belt under her robe and asked, "Prince Hiro, what will be the official name of your son?"

Hiro looked at Takahiro, "Kaede?" Hiro murmured. Takahiro nodded, Hiro turned to the Witches and replied, "Kaede."

"Prince Kaede Hashimoto," Takahiro said.

"It will be entered into his Imperial Identification Record shortly. We will print and send you a copy of the report along with his birth certificate, identification card and his medical record to the palace clinic in seven days, along with your updated Family Book. By law I must inform you that it is the parent or guardian's responsibility to renew the identification card for their púca every year on the week of their birthday until they are eighteen, then renewal will be his responsibility every five years," the first Blood-Witch said, putting the green book into her bag.

"Thank you, Blood-Witches. The guards will escort you to a waiting van to take you back to Blood-Tower," Takahiro said.

Two Knights then entered with a squad of guards. The trio of Witches bowed and left with the guards, the Knights bowed to the Emperor and closed the door on their way out.

Takahiro turned to Hiro and said, "Son, Kaede will have the best of care."

"I know, Father," Hiro said.

"The *Night Owl* will be space dock for at least three

months while it undergoes inspection and maintenance. Except for emergencies, let the quartermaster, engineers, and your executive officer take care of the ship. That is what they are there for," Takahiro said.

"Yes, Father, I shall," Hiro said rolling his eyes.

"As for your green-haired companion...make certain your son never calls her *mother*. If she does, not only will I ban her from the palace, I will pass the ring to your child. Around the clock, a squad of Knights will be guarding him," Takahiro said.

An Ogre entered a galley, Cadet Fukuhina, 18, was a 167cm tall Flower elf with pink hair and gold eyes. She wore an Apron over her Imperial Navy uniform and had one bar on her collar. She was unarmed, cowering and crying behind sacks of rice, in the pantry. An Ogre dressed in long brownish pants, a grey top with a combat vest raped, then strangled the chef.

The Ogre pulled up his pants, then searched the cupboards, he found Fukuhina unarmed and crying. Laughing as her dragged out, the Ogre then went to rip her top off. Fukuhina looked around, over the bench hung pots and pans. She kicked the Ogre in the testicles, then grabbed a frying pan, and hit the Ogre over the head. The Ogre stumbled, and as blood trickled down the side of his face, he laughed and took a step forward.

Fukuhina swung again, this time hitting him on the side of the face, he took a step without facing her, one eye fixed ahead, the other eye twitched, then he fell to his knees.

She hit him again and again until blood trickled down the side of his face. The top of his skull caved in, the Ogre fell face down in a pool of his own blood.

Fukuhina took his knife, handgun and ammunition. She then dragged the corpse into the pantry. Fukuhina looked at the dead crew member by the door. Her eyes were bulging, her tongue out, and her head was not on straight. Her panties down around her knees.

"Sorry," Fukuhina mouthed as she closed the chef's eyes. She then laid the body face down in the pool of blood. Fukuhina lifted one of the floor panels and climbed into the crawl space.

Fukuhina crawled beneath the deck on her belly. She heard screams, gunshots and laughing. In tears, she continues until she came to the supply closet. She lifted the floor slowly and looked about. The room was a mess, everything had been tossed off the shelves, boxes ripped open, the weapons rack empty, light bulbs smashed, and even some of the cleaning products spilt on the floor.

In the dark, she searched the boxes and shelves. She found a 4L plastic bottle of 'Industrial solvent'. The warning read, "Pure Alcohol: A deadly poison. Seek immediate medical assistance if ingested'. She unscrewed the cap and took a smell of the pure alcohol.

Fukuhina screwed the cap back on tight and opened the floor panel. She crawled to a vertical shaft and went down several decks to the deck between the cargo hold and living quarters. In the hold, she saw Ogres searching boxes, spilling contents out, piling valuables into a large cargo cart. In the living quarters, Ogres went cabin to cabin, looting, raping and killing. Passengers barricaded had themselves in.

Fukuhina went to the utility room behind the ship's reactor, behind the tools, fuses, pipe sealers, inspection hose, and welding equipment was an alcohol still made of copper pipes and used a washing tub as a keg. Fermented honey was dripping into the half filled tub. She took a mug off the shelf, took a swig, bowed and made apologies, then poured most of the solvent into the keg, then left.

Fukuhina climbed into the floor, almost forgetting the empty solvent bottle. She made a couple of trips from another supply room, dropping the empty solvent containers into the ship trash chutes after she had emptied the contents into the tub.

Fukuhina entered the crawl space.

"Happy thirty-sixth birthday, son and congratulations on your first mission as captain," Takahiro said smiling. He clapped his hands, and a guard entered from the door on the west side, carrying a tray with a silver pocket watch. Takahiro took the watch and placed it on Hiro's jacket. The guard bowed and left. "Son, I want you to have this."

Hiro's mouth dropped open. "Your watch?" Hiro asked staring at the silver time pieces covered in ornate swirls.

"Yes," Takahiro replied.

"But this is the watch Lilith gave you!"

"Relax Hiro and control your emotions. The original stopped working thousands of years ago; I made a copy for you in my workshop," Takahiro said standing by Hiro, looking at Kaede.

"I apologise, Father." Hiro bowed slightly, "Thank you."

"Look, son, I know I told you to never ask any immortal, especially me, about the old Empire. So, if I choose to tell you something about the old Empire, do not repeat it to anyone. Lilith gave me the original watch just after she finished build the first spaceship. She came to see me, and it was the last time I saw her alive. It was painful losing her," Takahiro sighed, then composed himself, sat down and asked, "Do you still use the sextant I gave you when you joined the Imperial Navy?"

"Yes," Hiro replied, then added, "Sometimes I use it when we disengage the ultra-drive to refuel."

"I did the same when I was in the First Fleet. We had such hope when we founded the new Empire."

"Father, I don't know what has you so worried, but we should go, I have to report in," Hiro said taking a step towards Takahiro.

"Hiro, why were you a month late returning?" Takahiro asked shifting his position in his seat.

"The ship we went to resupply did not arrive."

"I read the report you sent from Algol. As of three days ago, they haven't found it. There was nothing else?"

"No, we took part in the search, but there was no sign of the ship, so we left."

"I do hope they find it. An Exodus Transport is carrying 3000 passengers and 720 crew, and they have been travelling for centuries. Half of the passengers were born in space."

"When I left, many fear the ship broke up at light speed."

"We had that problem with the first ship. We upgraded ships with an additional shield facing forward," Takahiro said looking at Kaede. Kaede appears to look at him.

"Father, I do hear complaints, but they are few. Most I meet at Algol knew there is a small chance of not making it, but I have heard from them how our people were treated on Terra. I hated the stories you told me when I was young, but now, I understand, and I feel better knowing the truth about our home world and how the other races, especially the homo sapiens treated our people."

"Was there much fear or tension?" Takahiro asked looked up at Hiro.

"Those that I meet are not afraid, they are in good spirit. There was some talk of fear for the safety of those who didn't come," Hiro replied studying Takahiro.

"Yes, but it was me who convinced our people to make this journey 5,000 years ago. Many, not just Dain, are itching to depose me. This is the last and biggest Exodus fleet assembled."

"Father, relax, all but a few of the ships thus far have made it."

"Yes, but not all," Takahiro said looking at the wall.

"Father, you have often told me not to bear the weight of your burdens, or they drag you down."

"Son, the Empire has many problems," Takahiro said in a soft voice standing. He tapped the bottle of milk, Kaede had a grip on the bottle and was looking at him, "The biggest is a shortage of hydrocarbon fuel, we have too few ships to defend all 114 worlds and labour shortages. Despite my concerns, the Senate approved Dain's proposal to begin another terraforming project. This now makes ten worlds. He seems to think that spreading our current population out over more worlds will reduce crime."

"I know not why you are worried, but we have over

50,000 armed ships, of the hostile races, the Ogres fleet is the largest, and they only have 10,000 ships, the Goblins have only two thousand and the Orcs only a thousand."

"Yes, but half of our ships are dedicated to protecting the Exodus Fleet. The rest are spread thin. But son, for so long most of our resources have been dedicated to the evacuation from Terra. Many of the people now resent the fact we helped other races leave Terra, especially now that they plague us with piracy and petty squabbles. The Exodus was the only way to prevent a fourth global war, and it was the right thing to do, each of us post-flood began to spread out, populations grew rapidly. A great evil arose in Babylon. We had to decimate them to achieve victory, but the homo sapiens spread out in great numbers, they disrespected our borders, our forests, our people. Dain gave them land, but they always wanted more. Now, in our own, rumblings of discontent. Czar Petrov was attacked last month while investigating a group of Ogre spies posing as rare metals dealers."

"I heard about the fire, how is he?"

"He recovered, many did not make it, one got away," Takahiro said, he put his hand on Hiro's shoulder, "Many have come to resent the Exodus."

"I doubt most of the ground born have no idea what it is like for the Exodus fleet. Their idea of a long trip is the thirty hours it takes to get to the edge of the system, once there it is less than a day to the next star at FTL seven, but as fast as that is, it took us 140 days to get to Algol. Those on the Exodus fleet do not complain harshly about better technology. Nor with conspiratorial tones like the electric car lobby, who themselves do not make anything, they do not even try."

"Yes, the same journey here you took, will take an Exodus Class Transport is 127 years."

"Yes, I know, and we have many bases between Algol and the Pleiades. More outside than we do inside the Empire."

"But without those bases, the 3,720 onboard an Exodus ship would face a horrible death at 500 days. Those ships are only able to carry 500 days of food, so even with those bases, the Exodus Fleet needs the Imperial Fleet to find them and keep them resupplied. Each ship is floating exposed, along in the night."

"Father, when Admiral Niemi saw me off two years ago, he let slip that the fleet has always had stealth ships. I know official policy is to deny the existence of the distortion field generator, but during training, they call it our most modern ship."

"Yes, it is our most modern ship, and officially we do not have stealth ships," Takahiro replied. "but when Lady Toshiko and I completed building a copy of Lilith's ship, we needed to hide the existence of ships. Therefore, I invented the field generator to hide the ship not only from scans but from sight. In 1600 New Calendar, a Lilith-Toshiko Transport took us to Mars. A hundred years later the Phantom Class took the first trip to the Pleiades, and then in 2600 I united the seven kingdoms and began the Exodus."

"Nothing really prepares you for a journey of 300 days on a ship. Days melted into each other. You get used to the hum of the deck, the hard bunk suddenly is a soft bed, you look forward to the sticky food and squeeze pack drinks. I don't know how they stay sane during the Exodus?"

"The waypoint stations. Just getting off the ship, even if it is one tin can to another. Did you stay on the station?"

"Yes, we docked at the Algol shipyards. They are vast. Thousands of the Exodus ships are being used as stations around the three stars. When I first saw the Night Owl ten years ago, at 120m long, it was huge. But when we docked with a 600 metre Exodus Transport, it was like being a trainee shuttle pilot docking on a space station."

"Did you bring any of the Exodus crews back with you?"

"Yes, part of the mission was to swap crew. Given we didn't meet with the ship we expected to meet, we swapped some crew with those from another ship at Algol."

"There are nearly a million Elves at Algol, not shortage passengers. As long as they on the list."

"I am told only a quarter are waiting for a berth on a fast ship home. Many passengers and crews are helping break up their old ship to build a new Exodus Class Transport."

"Emotional attachment was a concern, but we cannot make them leave their ships," Takahiro said, he paused to look at Kaede, who been watching them talk and move his lips. Takahiro shook his head and looked to Hiro, "Did they socialise?"

"I am not sure you call it socialising. When the passengers first came aboard, they wanted to see everything. They did express some disappointment the fleet had not created the next generations of Ultra Drives that was promised to them 300 years ago. Once they saw our technology was not much better than theirs, they were quiet. On a personal note, they are rather frisky, more so than the nymphs of Merope."

"Yes, they have been in space for over 300 years. Nothing but routine for all that time."

"They are odd, much like Merope, they find the idea of any personal attachment funny. Even to their púca, they are happy to have them, so long as they get paid, and someone else raises them."

"Yes, because most sexually transmitted diseases don't affect our race many are extremely promiscuous. I am told syphilis is high on the ships."

"Yes, some of those we brought on board were infected."

"Hiro, what happens in space, stays in space. Over time most lose the desire to self-indulge. What is the status of the Exodus Fleet?"

"This is the last fleet. The lead ships are twenty years away from entering the Pleiades, with the spread out over four hundred and twenty-two light years. Since they only do light speed, most are between Aldebaran and Siris. The Imperial Fleet is trying to persuade those at Algol to build fast transports. However, the Pakkuraba may be much faster, it is much smaller."

"Yes, the Pakkuraba Class III Freighter was not designed to carry many passengers. Even if we stripped down the Exodus and added a second reactor, we don't have the computing power to build a more powerful ultra-wave generator or use more than one. For now, the Exodus fleet can only move slightly faster than the speed of light," Takahiro said, he paused, looked at Hiro, who was not paying attention. Takahiro tapped his shoulder and asked, "Son, what about the rest of the ships?"

"Yes, the lead ships are twenty years away from entering the Pleiades, with the Exodus fleet spread out over four hundred and twenty-two light years with most between Aldebaran and Siris."

"What are the chances of a lost ship been found?"

"Father, you should ask Admiral Niemi that. I don't know."

Takahiro paused, stood and took the empty milk bottle from Kaede. "Son, I will not tell the Admiral."

"Very slim, since they're travelling just over the speed of light, any number of failures would lead to complete destruction of the ship. A few have been found before they run out of food. A few were found adrift, we don't know how, but the pirates found a way to stop a ship. They often leave no survivors."

"Yes, which is why we execute pirates."

"Most run soon as fired on."

"Yes, the sad fact is Hiro, we do not have enough starships to give full-time protection to every transport. Nor do we have the workforce available to double the construction of more cruisers."

"The shipyards at Algol are amazing. They are nothing like our shipyards here. There were hundreds of docks in orbit around the three red stars. With thousands of Exodus ships, upright, covered in solar panels. They orbited the stars in a ring like a school of dolphins pirouetting around a large fire. These are not for scrap, but as homes, storage units, small factories, and even small farms."

"Yes, more ships are built there than in the Empire. But most of the yards will be repairing or salvaging Exodus ships."

"Yes, I took a tour, our orbiting shipyards are far more impressive in real life than reading the corporate holdings statement."

"Yes, *The Night Owl* was one of many built at Algol."

"I know we own all the stealth ships, the question to you is why?"

"I was only Emperor of the East when I built the first ship, the Kage, our clan has been the only clan to make them. It was a thousand years before I took power, so I would only lease my ships to the other kingdoms, but with my crews."

"Oh."

"Son, one day, we don't know when, yet. But one day we need to search for, and again move to a new home; because all worlds have a finite life. But to do so, we must be united and have a mighty space fleet. We need to learn everything we can from this Exodus to do better next time."

"Yes, Father."

"Son, time is the most precious commodity in the Empire. I gave you my watch as a reminder," Takahiro said. He extended his hands, and Hiro gave Kaede to him.

"Father, do not worry what they say in court or the media. I have heard only a few complaints inside the Imperial Fleet. The loss of ships is less than one percent, far less than projections."

"Yes, we all knew we were going to lose some ships. Each Exodus ship left Mars on a trip that could take 600 years knowing some might not make it. It would be an impossible journey had gone ahead and first built bases. We build a path to the Pleiades, it took a thousand years to prepare the first worlds so we could provide enough food and build a vast fleet of fast ships to provide the transports with everything."

"What will happen to Algol and the outposts, given this is the last fleet?"

"Dismantled like we did with the Mars settlement, we plan on keeping the outpost Algol."

"You sent me to specifically meet that one ship, I wasn't expecting you to tell me why, but will you tell me now?"

"That ship was carrying relics from before the flood."

"Relics?"

"Son, between you and me that missing ship is important to the Empire. It was carrying the last known light sword, technology lost to us when its creator, Lilith, was killed."

"Why wouldn't you put it on a fast ship?"

"Sending a ship all that way would draw attention. So, they boarded one of the preservation ships."

"Preservation ships?"

"Yes, they carry Blood-Witches from Mars with a dozen uterine replicators, a genetic editor and complete database of all the known genetic sequences. Each is very expensive and will take a long time to replace. Fortunately, we have a copy of the database."

"A uterine replicator; as in an artificial womb?"

"Yes. Fortunately, we can replace it and the other lost equipment. We can replace the lost passengers and crew. However, we prefer the ship found. I know chances are slim, but I want you to take a large supply fleet and go to the last known stop and try to find what happened."

"Just like that?"

"Yes, the Blood-Witches primary duty is the preservation of our people. That is why we built a much larger population and spread out on many worlds so quickly. We will mourn the loss. There is still hope that the ship will be found. I know chances are slim, but I want you to take a large supply fleet and go to the last known stop and try to find what happened."

"But Father, the size of the search area, and time are

against us. Ion Trails are hard to find after a year, and that is if nothing interferes with them. It is true that the Ion Trail is radioactive and has a half-life of just over twelve years, but space is neither empty, not still. Everything is moving, it hard to distinguish from background radiation after a week."

"I know about Ion Trails. I created the dispersal system on the stealth ship to scatter them."

"It would make more sense organising the search from Algol."

Takahiro stepped closer to Hiro. "I am hoping they find the ship, but if they don't, I am hoping you find them. I know it is a grim task. You leave in three months. Until then I want you to enjoy your leave with your son. I know you been hot and heavy with your companion. Don't you even dare think about getting her pregnant."

"Father." Hiro paused. "I know you do not like her. But if she offends you, then I shall keep her away from you. But I will not stop seeing her.

"I do not mind the fact that you did not marry. I never got married. My concern is not about your companion being a Giantess. I have a few Dwarven companions. Did you think I would notice you ordering new furnishing for your room?"

"But you and Masako have been together since before I was born."

"Yes, and I care deeply for Masako. She understands our bloodline and population laws and understands that I will not pay her more than the wage of a private assistant."

"Those same laws permit me to have a son. If you can have a prostitute that fits your sexual fantasy, then I can have a giantess girlfriend to keep me company when I am on leave."

"This is about you having Freya move in just as you get a púca. You must know how it looks. Besides, you only meet her a few weeks before you left for Algol. We cannot appear to be above the law or the already hostile Senate will turn against us."

"Her name is Freya Evergreen, Father. She is not a prostitute. Unlike you, I did not hire her from an agency to be a companion. She is my girlfriend, and she works as a translator for the Imperial Fleet. I will have her move in with me."

"Just make sure your son does not call her *mother*."

"Fine," Hiro snapped.

"Oh, don't be like that Hiro. You're not ten. It didn't work on me then, and it will not work on me now. It has cost me a fortune to have the Blood-Witches produce a Pure-Blood son for you after donated sperm without consulting me. I am all for you having a son. But the population and blood-line laws are there to must ensure our people never face extinction due to intermarriage or low birth rates again. Yet you let a girl you hardly know decorate your son's room. You must know how it looks."

"It looks like I am screwing my son's babysitter and I doubt you paid for anything less than a pure-blood Hashimoto with all the genetic tweaks."

"If Freya ever raises the topic of having a child, I expect you to explain to her the population control laws."

"Will you let her at least take care of him while I am away?"

"Of course, I had Lady Toshiko check her out thoroughly.

I already setup a trust fund for Kaede's care and education. When he is eighteen, legally, he will be required to earn his title. I expect you to take steps to prepare him for that but given you have no desire for court or business, I will be encouraging him to consider running the company for me when he has finished service."

"What if he doesn't choose to captain a starship?"

"It was your choice to be a starship captain. To retain his title, he could choose to serve as a Knight, a Medical Officer or as an Agent of the Inquisition instead."

"We should go. I arrived only a few hours ago, and the media was already waiting to see my son."

"We will, just in time to be live on the sunrise news. I won't say anything, just place Kaede on the lawn and let him crawl. You have a beautiful boy."

"Thank you, Father."

It was a few hours later when High Lord Dain, a male Field Elf, entered the dining room of a large mansion on the south side of the lake. He brushed his long blond hair off his rounded ears which came up to a point near the crown of his skull. He adjusted the jacket of his expensive, tailored, blue wool suit, complete with square gold cuff links with a stag's head embossed on the face and an electronic watch on a gold band.

His twin sister, Abel, wore a Knight's uniform. Like Dain, she had long blonde hair, blue eyes and high cheek bones. They were the same height.

Abelard, a slightly shorter Field Elf, wore a polo shirt

with casual pants, he and Abel were already seated. Abelard had a maid by his side, and as he passed her, Dain's nose itched from the girl's excessive flowery perfume, and he frowned at Abelard. Another servant stood near Abel, and one stood near the empty chair at the head of the table. "Son, must you?" Dain remarked as he walked past. Abelard ignored him and rubbed the girl's bottom.

High Lord Dain sat and studied the sumptuous meal of bread rolls, eggs, various jams, sliced fruit and fruit juices with coffee and tea on the table. A maid stood behind Abel, and another was waiting for at the only other empty chair.

"Any major events?" Dain asked, tapping his cup.

The maid beside Abelard leant over, pouring Abelard a coffee. His eyes fixed on her ample breasts. She wore no bra or panties under her uniform.

"The girl Hiro impregnated gave birth; they are holding the press conference in a few minutes," Abelard said without taking his eyes off the maid's firm nipples.

"You don't know that, so be careful what you say in public. Last year I witnessed Hiro take a green-haired Giantess to his room. The Blood-Witches have stated publicly many times that an anonymous surrogate carried Hiro's púca," Abel said.

"Sister, you are always defending the Emperor," Dain said as the maid poured tea. "Do you champion me just as vigorously when advising our dear Emperor?"

Abel was sipping her tea. "Despite your hostility, the Emperor does like you. You're his rival, not his enemy. That said, he is aware of your growing wealth and your efforts to rally support from the other major houses to replace him." She set the cup on the saucer.

Dain grabbed the arm of the maid near him and said, "Put Hashimoto news on."

Worried, the girl looked at Abelard.

"Father, you blocked that network," Abelard said.

"Oh, yes, I did," Dain said. He released the maid and looked at Abel. "Where was I?"

"Accusing me of being the Emperor's lap dog because you are upset that your spies have found nothing on the birth mother," Abel replied.

"My father should be king, and not earn back his birthright," Abelard said.

"See sister, if only those words rolled from your lips, instead of you parroting those of the Emperor," Dain said.

"You forget your father passed the title of crown prince to Abelard," Abel said.

"Abelard is my son, not his. Eve used magic on me to impregnate her, then she replaced my mother as Queen, and my father claimed my son as his púca," Dain growled.

"Long ago dear brother, that was a very long time ago. Abelard let his title lapse when Takahiro took power, and you were never king, only High Lord of the Senate. That lasted for a thousand years. Takahiro has been in office for over ten thousand years," Abel said.

Dain stared at Abel, who was holding a salt shaker. She held it up to him and smiled. He gritted his teeth, then a beep from Abelard's phone cut the tension. Abelard removed his phone from his belt and started messaging. Dain snorted then returned to his tea. Abel watched Abelard who had sprang to his feet and went to the large wall screen.

"I just received a message from our news crew at the palace; the Emperor, Hiro and the púca are coming out.

I replied to them to first adverts for our off-road four-wheel drive and the Dain Personal Desk computer. I added the slogan to the computer, the computer for the next generation," Abelard said as he put his phone back on its belt holder.

Abelard took a remote from a small table against the wall, under the large white wall panel, pointed it at the wall and clicked on. The Hashimoto Palace appeared.

"Where are my adverts?" Dain asked.

"You wanted the Hashimoto Network," Abelard replied.

"I changed my mind, switch it to our network," Dain said.

"Don't be petty, just once I liked you to thank Abelard," Abel said.

Dain snorted and stared at Abel.

Abelard sat and drank his coffee. "You're welcome, Father," Abelard said.

"Silence," Dain said. He stood in front of the screen and watched.

The scene on the television was the lawn in the front of the entrance to the Imperial Palace with a female Flower Elf on camera. "Prince Hiro is now on his way out of the Palace," she said.

The camera panned to the steps of the palace entry. The seven Knights on guard parted as one of the eight red iron doors opened. Hiro wore a red kimono with green trim, the symbol of House Hashimoto on the back, with a green hakama, white tabi, and wooden shoes. He carried Kaede, dressed in a full-body red púca suit with his ears out of slits in the sides of the hood.

Hiro crossed the driveway around the statue of Takahiro,

to the lawn east of the palace. He set Kaede down on the grass, faced the camera and said, "This is my son, Prince Kaede Hashimoto."

Dain watched as Kaede rolled over and crawled towards the camera. Dain paused the broadcast, then as he spoke, he pointed to Kaede's pink hair that protruded from under the hood, then to Kaede's teeth.

"No wonder we cannot find out if Hiro broke the bloodline law by getting the Giant pregnant; his púca appears to be two years old, the old fox has had years to bury the data, erase minds, and buy off the Blood-Witches," Dain snarled.

Abel stood, walked to the screen, and tapped the screen at Kaede's wrist. "If you bothered to look, the púca has a birth tag," Abel said.

"Why is that important?" Abelard asked behind her.

"The Blood-Witches would never fake birth records," Abel replied.

"Then in a week we will know if Hiro broke the bloodline laws," Dain said.

"No need, look at his pale-yellow skin and the almond eyes. His ears are long, thin, pointed and horizontal, and his hair the same shade of pink as both his father and grandfather. I have no doubt he is a pure-blooded Cherry Blossom Flower Elf. As for buying off the Blood-Witches, the only one who has been trying is you," Abel said.

Dain smiled and asked in a sweet voice, "Oh, whatever do you mean, Abel?"

"I know you sent agents to Blood-Tower to try to buy information on the púca's mother. You're lucky the

Blood-Witches came to me instead of reporting you to Patya," Abel replied.

"Czar Petrov is a friend," Dain stated.

"Patya does not tolerate corruption. I get it; you want to replace Takahiro so much that it hurts, but I urge you to find a legal way," Abel said.

"Do you have a suggestion?" Dain tapped his cup. The maid filled it.

"Drive to the palace in your new four-wheel drive, give Hiro and the Emperor your congratulations in person. As a first tooth gift to the púca, give him the Dain Desk Computer you had flown in this morning. That will give you free publicity and buy you some much-needed goodwill," Abel replied.

"Very generous of you Abel," Dain said.

"Also, from now on, you keep your mouth shut about Takahiro and Hiro having relationships with non-Elves. Not just because many nobles hire non-Elves as companions, but because the Emperor is aware you keep company with a certain male Dwarf for the last couple of years that you think I don't know about," Abel said.

Dain pondered this, and then he looked at the paused image of the happy púca reaching out. He drank his tea in haste, handed Abel the empty cup and left the room in a hurry. Abelard watched him leave.

Abel gave the cup to the maid and sat. "Do you have a birth gift for Hiro or a first tooth gift for the new prince, Abelard?" Abel asked. "There will be a line at the palace."

"What about you, Aunt Abel?" Abelard asked.

"As a Knight, I will drive past the line in the transit lane and show my identification at the gate," Abel replied.

She laughed as Abelard ran out of the mansion on the phone.

"You can join me. I am sure Dain and Abelard will be stuck in traffic before they remember they haven't eaten," Abel said.

The maids joined Abel in eating.

Fukuhina was inside the hull of the ship, on the maintenance walkway over the coils of the hydrogen intake. She looked at the release value.

"Open the value, fire the gun and the fuel will ignite, and the misery will be over," she pondered to herself.

Crying sat for hours in the dark, shaking, holding the Ogre's handgun in her hands, staring at it. The screams in her head stopped. She checked the gun, a bullet was in the chamber, she clicked the safety off, then headed down the narrow passage between the inner and outer hull until she was over the airlock, she looked down, the vents open and she saw an Ogre on his own inside the airlock.

Fukuhina holstered the gun, took a long breath, and drew the knife. The Ogre was bored and was staring at a video on a bright orange tablet that had flowers on it. Fukuhina opened the hatch, the Ogre looked up as she dropped down with the knife in both hands aimed down at his head. He went to turn and grab his gun as the knife was rammed it into the back of the Ogre's head.

The Ogre dropped to the floor, Fukuhina pulled out the knife and took the Ogre's sub-machine gun.

Fukuhina checked the door, no one outside either

airlock door, the transfer tube was extended and connecting the two ships. She ran down the passageway and found the Ogre's ship unlocked and unguarded. A couple of carts with tablets, jewellery, and weapons was in the Ogre's airlock. She pressed the open button, the door unsealed, she pulled it open and stepped in.

Masako, a Koropokkuru, was dressed in a short, low-cut, short black dress with round, white collars, white trim on the short sleeves and hem. Over that was a large frilly white apron. She had black stockings with a seam and flat black shoes. She exited the elevator and walked down the hall to a door in the north wing, on the floor just below the Imperial residence, near the top of the tower. She stopped at the door and knocked.

Freya, a Caucasian giant, 185cm with green haired and large emerald green eyes, answered the door. Freya was twenty years old, with soft, youthful skin and large perky and bouncy breasts. She wore a plain blue dress with white slippers.

Freya looked down at the 95cm tall dwarf who stood silently at the door. She had large round brown eyes with very long lashes. Her long brown hair was in a tight bun held by two chopsticks. Her head was slightly large for her body, and her face was youthful with rosy cheeks. Her handbag was large and orange, it was the kind of hard leather handbag found locked behind glass in the kind of store that had a doorman who knew the customers who can afford to shop there, it had no brand, but the zipper and studs were gold.

Crisis

Freya realised she was looking down Masako's top and saw that Masako was not wearing a bra. Freya looked away. Masako's hair was dyed and had grey roots, with her face heavy with makeup, making it hard to tell her age. But she had no age spots.

"I didn't send for a maid," Freya said.

"Hello, I am Masako."

"Sorry. I am Freya. If you're looking for Hiro, he is with the Emperor."

"I know, I just came down to meet you."

"Are you one of his maids?"

"Yes, well, sort off; can I come in?"

Freya stood back. "Sure."

Masako entered the unit. She smelt of chocolate, honey, tobacco, marijuana, sake, and orchids.

The Ogre's ship was small, boxes of tinned food, ammunition, fuses, and machine oil were stacked in the halls. Dirty clothes and empty bottles of alcohol littered the floor.

Other than two sleeping crew, no guards were posted throughout the ship, not even the bridge, it was empty. She looked at the helm, the display indicated were in orbit near some star with no name. She crept about, checking the crew quarters. Two of them in separate bunks. She stood over the Ogre nearest the door, and she took a breath, put the gun to his head, and paused. The Ogre opened his eyes, she pulled the trigger, the other Ogre jumped up, revealing he was naked with a battered Elven female in his bed. The

Ogre's captive screamed, and Fukuhina raced up, he looked around for a weapon.

Fukuhina put the gun to the Ogre's penis and pulled the trigger, the Ogre doubled over, bleeding. Fukuhina found the girl's clothes and handed them to her, the girl spat on the Ogre. Fukuhina put the gun to the Ogre's eye and pulled the trigger.

Fukuhina wrapped the girl in a blanket and left her in the ship's galley. Fukuhina opened a tin of peaches, then left. She checked the ship twice. Counting the beds, the ship had one room with thirty-six bunks and four beds in another. Finding no one in the reactor room or hold. The ship's armoury was open.

Finding no one else on the ship, she took a large bag from the Ogre's room, then went to the airlock. Elven sub-machine guns, handguns, stun batons, knives and ammunition clips, were piled into one of the carts. Fukuhina loaded sub-machine guns, some handguns into one bag. Then went and found a couple of backpacks and loaded them with ammunition.

Fukuhina went to the Gallery and left the bags with the puzzled girl. Fukuhina got one more backpack and went to the bridge.

Fukuhina looked about on the floor, found the panel and opened it. Below the bridge was the ship's computer, a collection of processors, data storage and network hubs, much of the roof and walls were covered with various power and data cables.

Fukuhina went to the main console, she was about to pull the wires out, then noticed some of the drives in the hot swap rack on the wall behind it. Navigation logs, communications logs, video library, music library, and video games. She ejected the drive marked navigation data. The computer beeped, and a warning appeared on the console. Fukuhina saw on the shelf a couple of the same drives, she took one of those and put it in. The lights flashed briefly, but no alarms sounded, and the warning that was in Germanic had disappeared. She slid the drive she had removed into the backpack. Tempted to pull the cables marked reactor out, she gritted her teeth and left.

Fukuhina raced past the girl and got two more bags, then after filling those, she returned to the girl, and loaded her up. Together they raced down the connecting tunnel back to the Exodus transport and into the crawl space.

A short time later, Fukuhina and the girl had crawled down the living area and handed out handguns and combat knives to two dozen members of the crew. They were barricaded in a gallery. They had only knives to defend themselves. Mostly frightened, they jumped when Fukuhina dropped a bag of weapons then jumped out of the ceiling. She held a finger to her lips and pushed them the bag of guns and passed them a bag of ammunition. Retrieving the rest of the bags and helping the girl down, Fukuhina took a sub-machine gun and loaded it.

Fukuhina gave the crew most of the weapons, Fukuhina entered the ceiling, crawled flat to behind the Ogre's outside the galley. They were trying to cut their way in with a blow torch. She dropped down and shot the two Ogres in the back with a sub-machine gun. She walked up and turned off the blow torch.

Fukuhina listened. No one came running.

Fukuhina banged on the door, "It's me," she yelled.

The crew opened the door, armed to the teeth and angry. Fukuhina reached over and unclicked the safety on one of the guns pointed at her.

"I need a group of four to guard to the port airlock, so they don't get back to their ship, the rest of you liberate the ship," Fukuhina said and stepped aside. "Oh, and capture an officer if you can, she called out."

The crew hunted down the Ogres, most of whom were now in the hold of the ship and drunk, having found the still. Most of them too weak to fight back and sick from alcohol poisoning. Many were stabbed many times and left to bleed to death.

Fukuhina tried to find the Ogre's officers, but she was unable to prevent the crew and passengers from revenge. Without mercy, they had killed the remaining Ogres. Many of the survivors used knives on the last few Ogres, cutting off their genitals and left them to bleed to death.

The Ogre captain was found collapsed against boxes, vomiting, too weak to stand, the crew stabbed him until he was crying and bleeding on the cold metal floor.

Masako lifted her feet and pulled off her shoes one at a time and placed them on the shoe rack in the small entry, then went inside to the main room and sat on the sofa, followed by Freya, closing the door to the entry behind her. Masako removed a gold cigarette case and lighter out of her large orange handbag, she looked at the tea table, and then looked around.

"Where is the ashtray?"

"Hiro doesn't want anyone smoking in his room," Freya replied sitting on the easy chair.

"Oh? Kaede has his own room."

"It is for me, please do not smoke in here."

"You do know there is a cure for lung cancer?" Masako asked as she put her case and lighter away.

"Yes, I am aware of that, I was born in the Empire."

"Oh, so was I," Masako said cheerfully.

"What can I do for you Masako?"

"I came to meet you."

"I'd offer you tea, but I don't know where everything is yet," Freya asked looking around.

"I do," Masako replied, jumping off the sofa and went to the kitchen followed by Freya. "Hiro keeps his tea in the pantry, pass me the step ladder behind the door," Masako said as she dug out a kettle from a cupboard.

"Cups?" Freya asked as she opened the pantry.

"The tea set is in the cupboard the sink."

"I don't see tea bags."

Masako came and showed Freya the boxes of tea leaves. "Hiro liked to pretend he is easy going, but in fact, he is very fussy, so never use a tea bag. He likes only green tea; these leaves are from the Hashimoto Plantations in New Ceylon."

"Sorry, I am used to tea bags."

"How did you meet? I hope you don't mind telling me?" Masako asked as she put water in the copper kettle. Then moved the stool to the stove and put the kettle on the glass covered hot plate and turned it on.

"Two years ago, I bumped into Hiro at the Founder's Day Parade. He was on the Navy's float. He was so cute in his uniform, I thought he was female, and we got to talking. We had tea and walked around the mall. I was embarrassed, but he took me to dinner then a week later he was off on some mission and told me to wait for him. Then one day I got some messages and videos from him, so when he returned I accepted his offer to move in. How did you meet the Emperor?"

"I thought everyone knew that. It isn't a secret. I am a prostitute. My first day at Hashimoto Tea House was nothing like I expected. It was clean, well-lit and luxurious. Not a smoke-filled den of iniquity filled with opium smokers."

"You're trying to tell me they don't sell opium?"

"They do. Lots of it, but mostly as opium tea. Yes, there are smoke rooms, those are monitored by Healers."

"How long were you in the Tea House?"

"You can say brothel. I was only there for a day. I was taken to meet my first client. It was a dark room, and the madam told me to strip naked and make green tea while wearing an apron for an old male elf who sat in the dark. Easy for him, since Elves can see in the dark. When I got close, I saw the long moustache and thought my first time was going to be a disappointment. It was not, he is well hung and very young for his age. I didn't even know who he was until I was brought to the palace. So, over a hundred years, I have been a live-in companion and personal assistant to my only client ever. When Hiro found out, he was embarrassed around me for a long time, as I bathed, changed him, and I was the one who taught him about sex. We are good friends."

"Why are you dressed as a maid?"

"I do many things for the Emperor. I make his tea,

clean his room, hire, and fire the other working girls. If he doesn't get off at least six times a day, he is grouchy. I don't know how Hiro can make do with only one girl," Masako said making the tea.

"Hiro is well, nice."

"Oh, yes he is. But most male Elves are like a young bull when it comes to sex. I found most Males want sex three to four times a day," Masako said facing Freya, who was blushing. Masako started swirling the tea pot and said, "You are going to love living in the palace. You will never need to go to a shopping mall again. Not only are there so many meals to choose from the menu, but there are so many little cafes and eateries scattered throughout the tower just for the staff. Get used to wearing your identification around your neck as security is fanatical. The last place you want to be is at the wrong end of an angry knight. They don't let anyone, even me, get away without having identification. They will put you in the palace dungeon."

"What about shoes? Clothes? I didn't see any shops."

"The palace has a huge workshop in the sub-basements, there are many small different work areas there with a variety of artists and crafters. There are the most exclusive collection of the finest dressmakers and cobblers in the empire work down there."

"That does sound great."

"Oh, it is. The workshop is huge, it is spread over three floors, it is the size of a small town. They can make almost everything there."

"Thanks, but-"

"Oh, you rather go shopping in a mall?"

"Yes."

"I envy your massive breasts, you probably need handmade bras, and I know a mountain elf who makes oversized bras and corsets out of silk so soft you think you were wearing your mother's breath," Masako said pouring the tea.

"Where is it?" Freya asked, she was blushing, but leaning forward.

"The Palace Workshops are in the fourth basement, but as for directions to, you go crazy trying to remember, it is the size of a small town. Just use the Palace Map on your phone, just search for something, and if you have access, the application will show you where it is. If you want extra food, wine, shoes, or clothes, you need to pay, but the Palace even has a jeweller. Of course, you must pay, and the Palace staff even deliver for a small fee."

"But, I don't have access to many areas, Hiro didn't even tell me there were levels below the kitchens in the basement," Freya frowned.

"Relax, Hiro was following the rules. I will ensure that you have access. I hope you join us for the fourth meal, we usually go down to the kitchens, Takahiro makes Turtle soup, I must warn you, he will offer you sake, not the soft drink he sells, but the rocket fuel he brews."

"Oh, does the palace have pickled herrings?"

"Trust me, the Palace has everything, Apples to Picked Herrings to Zucchini. The kitchens cook meals from over a hundred cultures. Most of the foreign ambassadors find an excuse to come at least once a day for a meal. Even the goblins."

"What about Hiro's tea?"

"Items like tea, daily meals, are part of the food package residents get delivered."

"No wonder taxes are so high," Freya said taking a sip of her tea.

Masako laughed and said, "The Hashimoto Clan provides the meals, not the taxpayer."

"Sorry."

"Don't worry. Are you going to remain working?"

"For now."

"You know it isn't personal."

"Pardon?"

"You know, the Emperor's concerns about you moving in. You should know Hiro stood up to him. I swear they are so alike, they even turn their head and huff at the same time."

"Hiro warned me about his father."

"Surely you understand it is about perceptions. Most, but not all, Elves are highly rational. Takahiro is rational, but there are those who do get emotional if Hiro's Púca called you mother in public."

"It isn't as if I am his real mother," Freya said, her voice was soft, a quiver in her lips as she spoke, she watched the tea poured into the cup then wiped her eye.

"Don't take it personally. Elves have strict population laws. The head of the clan must have an unbroken lineage of pure-bloods. It is hard, but not impossible to have a púca, having a mixed blood isn't illegal, and now that Hiro has a son, it is easier."

"Really? But Hiro said his father made a huge fuss."

"The Emperor is worried how it appears having you move in with him on the same day his son was born.

Inquiries and media attention about lineage will take the focus off major issues and could stall important projects such as liquid fuel plants. The Emperor is trying to prevent a major fuel shortage."

Freya sighed. "Hiro tried to explain that to me. I do get to play with Kaede after I return from work."

"I know, do you have any experience with Púca?"

"No."

"Don't worry. I helped raise Hiro. I will help you."

"Did Hiro call you mother?"

"All the time. Hiro lived his life in this room. When he was learning to walk, he walked to me in this very room. His first word was 'mother'. For years he called his father, Emperor," Masako said. Then after a long pause, she said, "If Kaede calls you mother, in public, politely correct him and have him call you Ms Freya. You watch, Hiro will call me mother in private and Takahiro's moustache will twitch, but he will not say anything."

Freya laughed. "You're nothing like Hiro described you."

"How did he describe me?"

"He called you a tough old lady with a baby face."

"I am not that old. I am 120 in December."

"Wow. I am twenty."

"I have a feeling we are going to be good friends. You should come upstairs with me. There is no reason the boys get to have all the fun drinking and smoking."

"I don't have anything to wear."

"Relax, no need to put on anything fancy."

"I don't like sake."

"Do you like wine?"

"Yes."

"I have a vast collection of wine, and it would be nice have someone to drink with," a very happy Masako said handing Freya a cup of tea.

Fukuhina with six crew members met with a dozen passengers in the galley.

"What is the condition of our ship?" an elderly female flower elf amongst the group of passengers asked.

"The ship is adrift, off course, badly damaged, most of the crew dead and over half the passengers," Fukuhina murmured in reply.

"We should take the Ogre's ship and go for help," someone yelled out from the crowd.

"No. We going to take everything we can off the Ogre ship and we going to use its systems as parts to repair our ship," Fukuhina said.

"Is that possible?" someone behind Fukuhina asked.

"Yes," the engineer replied, her yellow uniform was covered in blood.

"We have enough suits, we refresh our air using the tanks on the Ogre's ship, we can salvage what we can, then close off and shut down the badly damaged areas," Fukuhina said.

"What about the dead?" someone asked.

"We will put them in the empty freezers," Fukuhina replied.

"Even the Ogres?" someone hissed.

"Yes, we need evidence for the Inquisition," Fukuhina replied.

CHAPTER 2

Opportunity

December 1, 11562. Imperial Palace.

Hiro entered Kaede's room, and saw Kaede, in a nightdress and diaper, standing in his crib. Hiro raced over to him. Kaede lifted his arms and clearly said, "Father."

Hiro picked up Kaede and ran out of the room to the Knights outside. "Has the Emperor left yet?" Hiro asked them.

"Operator, what is the status on Green Dragon?" the first Knight asked. She had an earpiece with a microphone connected to her phone.

"Green Dragon is in the top of the Tower," the operator in the palace security room replied in her ear. The Knight repeated that to Hiro.

Hiro headed down the hall, carrying Kaede, followed by the Knights. "Delay him, but don't tell him why. I want to surprise him. I know you must call ahead, but please only inform him that I need to see him," Hiro instructed.

"Yes, Prince Hiro," the first Knight replied. "But you

have a car waiting to take you to the airport for a flight to the New-Ghana Space Centre."

"Cancel the car and give my seat to someone else. If necessary, I can ride in one of the company's cargo flights out of New-Singapore," Hiro replied.

"Yes, Your Highness," the first Knight said.

Hiro carried Kaede down the hall to the central column with the Knights to the large bank of elevators. He pressed the call button. Kaede was watching quietly. Soon one arrived, and they entered it. Hiro placed his hand on the screen, it was scanned, then the outline of the tower appeared on screen, he selected the floor below the flight deck, the go button appeared, and he pressed it.

The Knight whispered into her microphone as they went up three floors. In the ceiling, a security camera focused on each of them. In the security centre, an operator spoke with the Knight in the elevator and one of the Knights outside the kitchen on the top floor. While another operator had images of the passengers on screen. Facial recognition run, it was fast to place names on Prince Hiro Hashimoto, and Prince Kaede Hashimoto.

Emperor Takahiro had a large residence top floor of the two-kilometre tall tower. It occupied five floors. The first three were mostly bedrooms. The Emperor has a massive bedroom, he had rooms for his security detail, his companions, personal staff and guests. Masako and five other female Dwarfs had a room connecting to Takahiro.

The fourth floor of the residence was a flight deck with three hangars and repair area for three large luxury 30-passenger helicopters. As well as security rooms with combat ready guards on duty. The fifth floor was a large dome that was three storeys high. It had dining tables around the top of the shaft with stairs to more tables on the roof of the shaft with a spiral staircase up to the top of the dome to a balcony with an easy chair, ashtray stand and a screen. The dome was not one piece, but sections, each section was made of a thick plastic that could to turn from clear to white connected by a robust metal frame.

The residence of the Emperor had marble floors. Inside the central column was a pair of large red iron doors with the symbol of House Hashimoto above the metal ring knockers set in the middle of each ornate door. Beside the doorway, inside the shaft, was a security desk. When the elevator doors opened, Hiro saw two Knights already standing, and they bowed as the doors to the residence, opened. He looked at the first Knight with him.

"Prince Hiro, your father is waiting for you in his kitchen," the Knights said smiling.

Hiro nodded and walked through the iron doors into the huge foyer. He headed to the door on the north side. The iron doors closed fast and loud behind Hiro and Kaede. A camera over the doorway watched them. The metal bolts inside the door slid into their slots with a loud clang. The two Knights who had come up with him stood inside the central shaft. A knight stood beside the door and opened it for Hiro.

Hiro entered the kitchen, his father was in a house robe, sitting on a stool, at the bench, and was eating a bowl of ramen. Masako was dressed as a maid, she stood behind him.

"Son, you know I am heading to Shanghai soon and

shouldn't you be on your way to the *Night Owl* to prepare to depart?" Takahiro asked.

Masako waved, and Hiro smiled at Masako. "Yes Father, but I have something more important to show you," Hiro replied as he placed Kaede on the floor.

"I have already seen him trying to stand, son. I know how proud you are of Kaede, and now you know how I feel about you, son," Takahiro said smiling. He handed the empty bowl to Masako and stood up. She went to the sink and washed the bowl as Takahiro came out from behind the breakfast table in the middle of the kitchen and stood in front of Kaede. He leant over and held his hands out to Kaede.

Kaede stood and held up his hands. Takahiro, stood erect and took a step back. He pulled out of his sleeve a long thin bamboo wand. It had a walnut-sized bulb on its end and a Green Dragon on the side. He pointed it at Kaede.

Takahiro looked at Hiro.

"I am not using magic," Hiro said.

"Yes, I see Kaede is standing on his own. I detect no magic, not even residue," Takahiro said bent over closely examining Kaede, using *Aether Vision*. Kaede was bright yellow.

"Just before I came to see you, I saw him stand, and he spoke his first word."

Takahiro blinked, the spell ended, and he returned his wand to its pocket inside his sleeve and lifted Kaede. "I want you to come with me, and take part in my press conference before we board my flight to New-Shanghai."

"What about your flight?" Hiro asked.

"I am taking my private jet."

"Still, I don't want you blaming me for been late for your meeting."

"I already know what the research director will say. He will tell me how they have not found a way to reduce the size, increase power output or increase the efficiency of a fusion reactor. I have already read the advice he received on how to ask me for more funds and more time. I have already decided to keep the facility open and have them find ways to put some of the research to use," Takahiro said looking at Kaede, who was watching him. "What about your flight?"

"I already gave up my seat, the backup pilot will take the shuttle from the New-Ghana Space Centre. I can take a ride in a supply shuttle from The New-Singapore Space Centre, and the ship can send a shuttle to collect me in space," Hiro said.

"You can come with me. You can show off Kaede to the media. You can fly with me to New-Shanghai. I will call Viktor and explain to him why you are not racing to your ship and I will have my jet take you to New-Singapore," Takahiro said.

"Thank you, Father," Hiro said.

"Masako, send for the púca carrier, then notify my transport we are bringing Hiro and Kaede with us. Also, send Hiro's bag and spacesuit to the VIP terminal at the Imperial Airport," Takahiro said.

"Yes Emperor," Masako said.

"Father, would you object if Freya stays in my room while I am on deployment?" Hiro asked.

"No," Takahiro replied. Kaede touched Takahiro's moustache.

Kaede giggled and wiggled about, then grinned.

Takahiro then sniffed the air as Kaede held out his hands to Hiro.

"Father, nappy," Kaede said as Takahiro, looking sour, held Kaede out to Hiro.

"I am impressed. The last púca to speak before a year old was Dain's son, Abelard, and that was a very long time ago."

"Speaking of Dain, I can hear him bellowing, *he must be two years old*," Hiro said.

"Just ignore him, son. I have put up with his petty jealousy for centuries. The price of our freedom is not just lives lost fighting our enemies, but the home front must battle against the fools who abuse the very freedom we fight to protect," Takahiro said.

"Dain is no fool. He knows his supporters will believe him and help him erode our market share."

"I know that, but a rash response will only add fuel to that fire. That is why you must dismiss it. I have been defending against Dain's rants for centuries, leave him to me. I have dared him to prove his accusations; they're jealous you have an incredible son."

"You're a public figure, daily attacks are part of the position, my son should be off limits, any attack even ones disguised as questions about his age. It is not so rare to be born with hair and teeth," Hiro said holding Kaede out, his nose twitching.

Takahiro put his hand on Hiro's shoulder.

"You have nothing to worry about, the surrogacy contract with Blood-Witches was witnessed by Patya, and he is undisputed to be most honest Elf. You have a license to have a púca from the Blood-Witches. We have his DNA report stating he is a pure-blood and confirmation you are his father. The best thing you can do for him is express your desire to do your best to shield your son from malicious gossip from fools and bullies who go so low as to attack a púca for attention. Just do not name names when asked and then show the Empire Kaede walking and talking; that will take the cameras off Dain," Takahiro said.

Hiro brought Kaede to the east door of the kitchen, followed by a Knight with the púca bag. They went to the mothers' room between the toilets. Hiro removed the soiled diaper and placed it in a disposal bag, but when he tried to put a new diaper on him, Kaede squirmed and kept moving his legs away from it. "No," Kaede said.

"Son, you need to wear a diaper," Hiro said.

"No," Kaede said.

"I am your father, and you will do as I say," Hiro said.

Takahiro stood in the doorway behind him and laughed. "Son, remember the time you were thirteen and obsessed with getting a motorbike?"

"This is not the same thing. You refused to buy me one, so I saved my allowance and bought one," Hiro replied.

"The next day you broke your arm in three places trying to jump over the swimming pool."

"The following year I won the dirt-bike championship," Hiro said smiling.

"Milk," Kaede said holding out his hands to the Knight with the púca bag.

Hiro held the diaper up and said, "Diaper."

Kaede looked at Hiro, then he stopped moving his legs and held them out. Kaede watched Hiro put a diaper on him, and once the diaper was on, Hiro handed Kaede to the Knight, who bottle-fed Kaede.

Kaede started working the tabs on the diaper.

They took the elevator up one floor to the flight deck. Kaede undid his diaper and tossed it off as they left the elevator. The Knight turned, but the doors closed.

They entered Hangar One. Inside each hangar was a luxurious thirty passenger helicopter. In Hangars Two and Three, Knights and staff boarded a similar helicopter. Each had the symbol of the Empire on the tail, and the symbol of House Hashimoto on the sides and piloted by Sky-Force Officers, their uniform was a light blue top and dark purple. On the left sleeve of the tunic was the symbol of the Empire and on the right sleeve was a blue round patch with a white edge with the profile of a Pegasus on its hind quarters.

A Knight put a new diaper on Kaede and then dressed him in a púca suit. The Knight placed him in a púca carrier and strapped that into a seat beside Hiro, who watched Kaede squirm, trying to see out the window.

The outer door to the hangar lowered onto arms that extended from the tower to form a deck. Kaede giggled with excitement as the helicopter started its engines and the inner shutter rolled up. The powerful turbine engines roared to full power as it rolled out onto the deck and the helicopter took off.

One by one, the three helicopters rose. Once there was sufficient clearance, the roller doors lowered as the outer doors raised, and the arms retracted. Each craft circled the two-kilometre tall tower until all three were airborne, then they formed a 'V' formation and headed east.

The three helicopters swapped places in the formation until they landed at the 100,000-ha civilian airport, 50 kilometres from the eastern shore of Imperial Lake. It was south of the Imperial Command and Imperial Office buildings, separated by the Eastern Highway. The car park had a transit tower between the ramps to and from the highway.

Behind the wide five-storey entrance were five terminals, with the first three connected directly to each other by two concourses with both a walkway and light rail inside. The first, second, and third were public passenger terminals. Each had three small helipads on the roof. The fourth terminal to the west was a cargo terminal. It had one large helipad on the west side. To the east was the fifth terminal, only for VIPs; it had three helipads on top.

There were six runways south of the terminals, five of which were traditional flat concrete with blast shields at one end. Four were 4,000 metres long, and the fifth was 6,000 metres long. The six and the farthest runway from the terminals was a 1,000-metre-long electromagnetic aircraft launch system.

Waiting at the fifth terminal was a huge suborbital. It was a V tail craft with thin, curved delta wings that did not protrude far, with thrust outlets along trailing edge instead of ailerons. The wedge-shaped craft was fifty metres long with a long nose, no visible cockpit, with an airlock either side of the body near the front. The body had four breaking thrusters around the nose, with more thrusters around the body a third and two-thirds of the way down the body. At the rear was four huge rear rockets, while two long jets run against the body under the wings. It was truly a cross between jet and spacecraft. It was painted red with a large Green Dragon painted on the both sides of the nose.

Inside the fifth terminal at the departure lounge, a

group of reporters watched the helicopters land on large screens. Inside the helicopters, the passengers waited after landing for the ground crew to secure the rotor blades. The Knights were the first to depart, followed by Takahiro, then Hiro carrying Kaede. Masako and the staff came out last.

When they came down the escalator from the roof, Takahiro waved to the reporters, who watched from behind a group of House guards. Hiro with Kaede, the staff and Masako went past the reporters into the departure lounge, while Takahiro gave a press conference.

A Knight placed a small blanket on the floor; then Hiro placed Kaede on it. Kaede stood, ripped off his púca suit and his diaper, then he ran naked to a female Knight, who was carrying the púca bag. Kaede stood before her with his arms up. "Milk," he said.

One of the camera crew was filming Kaede. The others pushed past each other in a rush to get Kaede on camera. Czar Petrov arrived to see Hiro and Knights as they tried to capture Kaede.

In the first floor of the seven-storey palace around the base of the tower, Dain drank apple juice as he watched the interview with Emperor Takahiro at the Imperial Airport.

He spat out his juice when Hiro appeared onscreen with a diaper in hand as he chased Kaede around the VIP Lounge.

"There is no way he is three months old!" Dain exclaimed.

A group of Knights headed off Kaede, as Emperor

Takahiro and Czar Petrov, watched on and laughed at them. Kaede stood facing the Knights as they advanced on him. He turned to see more Knights behind him, with Hiro in the middle, holding a diaper. "No!" Kaede said.

"High Lord Dain, care to comment on the fuel program?" a reporter standing behind him asked.

Dain turned to see a female Flower Elf reporter with a camera crew. He smiled at her, then walked away, she turned to Maharajah Desai behind her.

Smiling, she asked, "Do you have any comments, Maharajah Desai?"

"Yes," Maharajah Arjuna Desai replied, smiling back, "Proxima Alcyone Three is one of many worlds with little or no oil or gas deposits. We have relied on plant oils for centuries to produce various hydrocarbons. But as demand for resources grows while natural deposits, dwindle, the Empire needed a new energy program. I believe the new fuel program has the right balance between meeting the demand for hydrocarbons and maintaining a high air quality."

"Maharajah Desai, do you have anything to say about High Lord Dain's comments on Prince Kaede's age?" the reporter asked.

"Dain is entitled to his opinion. The Charter of Rights and Responsibilities guarantees freedom of speech. The answer to any speech we disagree with is more speech. I remind everyone that the first floor of the palace is public space and in public, Lords should choose their words with great care. Saying that I believe his accusations to be false; he has raised his doubts many times before, and the Emperor responded to him every time, it is about time he moved on," Arjuna replied.

"So, then you are not of the opinion Prince Kaede is older than the official statement?" the reporter asked.

"I see no reason as to why the Blood-Witches, the Emperor, or so many others would tell a lie. I believe the Prince was born three months ago. We Elves are exceptional in longevity, health, and intellect. We have seen extraordinary púca before, just not this young," Arjuna replied.

Inside the suborbital, Hiro placed Kaede inside a púca-sized capsule with clear lid. Crew strapped him in and sealed it. The capsule was strapped tight to a seat, and then the air supply was connected. Hiro wore a light-weight spacesuit and sat beside him.

Once everyone was aboard and strapped in, the sub-orbital craft was towed to the sixth runway, a kilometre-long high-speed magnetic catapult. The plane's front wheel was lined up with and slotted into the launch cradle.

The pilot and co-pilot waited for the ground crew to perform the final external safety check. The ground controller gave a thumb up and left. The pilot closed the external shutters on all windows, including the cockpit. The tower made announcements, "Clear the area", and once the ground crew was clear, "Runway activation.". When the runway was active, the cradle rose slightly.

The blast shield behind the sub-orbital craft was raised. The tower the announced, "Clear to launch."

The pilot brought the engines to full power, while to co-pilot activated the gravity stabiliser. The pilot said, "Go for launch."

The tower activated the electromagnetic rail. It took seconds for the craft reach the end of the short runway, and the craft accelerated to just under the speed of sound and nosed up as they raced south. Soon they were ten kilometres above the city.

Hiro looked at Kaede, who was excited and he clapped as the ground raced past. Kaede was in awe as they raced over the city. Within minutes they crossed the coast and were out to sea.

The craft nosed up again, this time to near vertical and as the rockets fired, the craft's jets shut off. The craft went hypersonic and climbed fast, yet no one inside was pushed back into their seats. Nor could they hear the loud roar of the rockets. It was a smooth ride as the craft continued to climb until the sky turned from blue to black. As it left the atmosphere slowly, they levelled out. Then the pilot cut the engines. "Successful orbital insertion," the pilot said, everyone heard it via the speaker in the helmet. The gravity was turned off the gravity, and they were weightless. The external shutters then snapped open.

Kaede looked out the window, he looked out over the world below, he looked up and saw the stars and reached out with his hands. For twenty minutes, they were in zero gravity as the plane turned to face its destination. Hiro released Kaede's capsule from the seat and held it to the window.

"We are approaching re-entry point, the gravity stabiliser will soon be engaged, please return to your seats, place your tray in an upright position and strap in," the co-pilot announced. The exterior window shutters were closed. A member of the cabin crew came and checked everyone was strapped in.

The plane fired its rockets, nosed up and began its descent. Until cloud level the plane was in free fall, gliding over New China towards the coast. Once at cloud level, the craft fired its braking thrusters. It engaged its jets and began level flight. They landed at New Shanghai airport like a conventional jet, only it was on a six-kilometre-long runway. It was taxied to the terminal.

Hiro carried an excited Kaede on his shoulder as they left the plane. Meanwhile, outside Blood-Tower, a group of old Blood-Witches held a press conference to confirm Kaede's age and condemn any challenge to their integrity. The video of Kaede naked and running around the VIP lounge went viral.

Takahiro followed Hiro as he carried Kaede with him to the departure lounge and sat with him.

"Son, I love you, but I have to go soon," Hiro said.

Kaede looked at Hiro and Hiro hugged him.

Kaede lifted his arms to Takahiro, who hugged Kaede and picked him up.

"Son, you have twenty minutes while they refuel and ready my plane," Takahiro stated, then looked over the Toshiko and the other knights. They backed away. Then he turned back to Hiro, "I know it is difficult and it will take a long time, but check as many star systems near Algol as you can. Check every scan for signs of debris. If you find evidence of the destruction of the ship, make detailed scans, collect samples if you can and return."

"I will."

"You have a dozen Pakkuraba Class III Freighters; the Phantom Class IV Scouts, Whisper and Silent Death, with you, as well as a dozen Mercury Class I Couriers."

"I don't think I will need that many ships."

"Plan ahead, so you can spread out around the known course, if one of you finds them or wreckage, then you can send a courier ahead of the known course of the other groups."

"I am going to miss his early years."

"I know son, and nothing will get them back. But that ship is carrying important artefacts vital to the Empire, and whoever possesses them could achieve great power and wealth. It is vital we have them."

"May I know what I am recovering for you?"

"A mirror of far seeing, an orb of power, and the sword of light."

"All the history books state that the sword of light was destroyed in the Battle for Tir Na Nog thousands of years ago. I have never heard of the other items."

"I had agents swept Terra for everything. They found the artefacts in the hands of homo sapiens. Fortunately for us, none of them works. The Orb of Power, like The Sword of Light, are once off items made by Lilith before she married King Adamos. She never shared with anyone how they were made and left no record."

"Do you think there was a leak?"

"I don't know, yet, I have Toshiko investigating, at some point, I must tell the others, but I prefer you recover the items and have them in my vault. I have artefacts I can distract them with."

"Are sure that is why the ship went missing?"

"Yes, the chances of any ship to go missing is astronomical."

"Then why don't you send cruisers?" Hiro asked.

"Lilith told me whoever discovered her secret could run or ruin the Empire. I do not know if Eve knew, she was Lilith's assistant after she left Toshiko. But Dain killed her, along with Adamos for treason. They started the third ice war and conspired with the Titan Atlas. Part of their plan was to keep the war going for centuries to keep our people afraid, dependant on, and be virtually their slaves with high taxes and mandatory service."

"Yes, a twisted plot to unite the seven kingdoms under one king. Prince Abelard almost was our king, but you held out, Abelard had no real support other than Dain, so they comprised with a council of seven."

"Well, the Empire still today is technically seven kingdoms, and I expanded the Senate five thousand years ago to thirteen to include leaders of biggest factions to make sure Dain could not just vote me out with his friends. Still, do not underestimate Dain, he is brilliant, it took me thousand years to get him out of office. Every day he and thousands of others seek to remove me, they would succeed not for the others all keeping the factions from uniting. Dain is well known to have once wielded the sword of light, in his hands again, that would be a powerful symbol to the old guard like Adalwulf Feygold. But Hiro, I should have told you sooner. I have a dozen factions within the New

Tokyo Council who are unhappy. Not enough of them to oust me, yet."

"Why are they unhappy?"

"They are no longer satisfied with the wealth and power I have provided them. The Lords want to be promoted to Planet Lord. I cannot break the rules of the Senate, we each get to pick in turn the lord of a planet and once appointed Clans will cling to that office for generations."

"Yes, and if you had your way you marry me off to their daughters. They are not better than whores, they only bleed us of our wealth. You need better friends and allies," Hiro said, looking around.

"Son, don't be so cynical. I would never force you to do anything. Say the word, and I will ask someone else to take this mission."

"No, father, I understand, it is too important to trust an outsider. But it will take about five months for us to reach Algol. You know the fleet is searching?"

"Yes, but they assume the ship is dead. Algol has sent ships along its plotted course, and yes, they adjusted for time. Most of the scans are the same as when the course was scanned. I looked over the information, and to me, the only conclusion I have is the ship was attacked and is not far from its last rendezvous point, likely close to a star, making it hard to see on long-range scans. I was hoping you come to the same conclusion."

"I already planned to stick in a tight group and follow the plotted course, stopping every eight hours, the scouts will go last, given they have the best long-range sensors, they can both avoid and catch up with ships ahead and find those off course. We have 1,500 days of food. I have studied the course the ship was assigned at Aldebaran. I have the studied all long-range scans from the fleet at Algol. We know where the ship is not, and I am sure the ship must not be too far from its last rendezvous. There are some small stars near its last known position, they make huge shadows in long-range scans. But it will take about 30 days to reach that area."

"If you need another scout, or support ships, now is the time to ask," Takahiro offered, smiling.

"That would take too long to organise, I would like another scout, but that would mean more support ships."

"I can ask Admiral Niemi to allow you to draw some from the search and meet you at Algol."

"Thanks, father."

"Anything else before you go?"

"Yes, send me lots of videos of my son."

A humiliated Dain issued a retraction in a phone interview. He said, "I was referring to the belief by some that life begins at conception."

An hour later, he was again under fire, this time from his clan and supporters who believed in life at birth. Dain appeared on a late-night talk show on the Dain Network.

"I received unfair criticism today. I want to be clear about Prince Kaede's age. I do not doubt the Blood-Witches. I made observations about how advanced Kaede is."

As Dain left the studio, his phone rang. He looked at the Caller I.D. "Yes Abel?" Dain asked when he answered his phone.

"Do you need help removing your foot from your mouth?" she asked in reply.

"You are hysterical."

"Again, the Emperor has poked you in the eye. You should have expected him to have reporters from the Hashimoto network to follow you around in court. You only have yourself to blame; questioning the integrity of the Blood-Witches to get at Takahiro was a bonehead move," Abel said.

"Reporters should not be in court, it is not dignified."

"For over a thousand years, the public has had the right to be there, and that includes the media. If you want privacy, then go hide in your office. Oh wait, you think Takahiro has it bugged," Abel said then laughed.

"Did you call me just for your amusement?"

"Also, to inform you that you are three points down in the polls."

"You could not wait for me to return home to tell me?"

"True, I could, but since you did not go with the Emperor to represent Dain Corporation, despite the fact we own the carbon processing plant that supplies Petrov Oil's plant, I have boarded a flight east to go in your place. My flight will soon descend into New-Vladivostok. If you want to know what happened to those three points you lost, they went to the Emperor," Abel replied. She ended the call.

As her plane began its descent, Dain entered his mansion, Abelard was waiting. He stood and said, "Father, Abel left a few hours ago, and didn't say where she was going."

"Relax, she called me," Dain said. "I told you to put a tracker in her car and have a team follow her with drones."

"I did, she drove west and took the exit into camp Bravo,

I am not sure how she knew, but when Aunt Abel stopped, she stood at the gate and looked back in the direction of the drone, then it went offline. The car following her remained on the highway, but a roadblock with Knights was waiting for them. After entering the base, she said some rather insulting things about you, then the bug inside her car went silent," Abelard said.

"I take it you want me to call General Feygold to have him release my House Guards from detention?" Dain asked.

"No. Lady Toshiko has your guards," Abelard replied, "She has sentenced them to kitchen duty for thirty days in Camp Bravo for being out of uniform and Adalwulf will not release them. Also, she has billed you for cleaning Abel's car, and for the interceptor missile used to shoot down the drone. She also issued you a fine for flying a drone being in restricted airspace."

"One of these days I will hit that witch," Dain said, as tightened his lip and formed a fist.

"Is that before or after you invent your magic Quantum computers, shields, deflectors, ultra-drive, ion-gravity drive, gravity beam and hundreds of other products we licence from the Lilith Foundation, of which she is CEO?" Abelard said.

"They belong to me; my mother invented magic and built the first spacecraft, I was there, Toshiko was just her assistant," Dain replied.

"Father, may I remind you that your mother was—"

"Watch what you say, son," Dain interrupted, taking a step towards Abelard.

"—Tragically lost in an accident and that she left everything to Lady Toshiko," Abelard said.

"Still no reason to charge me, her son, a licence fee, to make technology designed by my mother."

"I am sure the Emperor will gladly let you get in the ring with Lady Toshiko today if you like. She is an active Knight, and it has been a long time since you were in active service. She is too popular. Any public feud with Toshiko would cost you; the public adores her," Abelard said, then with a grin, asked, "Shall I renew your gym membership?"

"No, I will not give Takahiro the satisfaction. He has been smug ever since the First Ice War. He sat nice and cosy in his mountain fortress for centuries, then he spent five minutes on the front lines, and everyone called him a hero," Dain grumbled his reply.

"He did tame the Dragons; he still has them still wrapped around his little finger, and they come to him like a Cat Sìth begging for cream."

"Yes, because he gave them eight large, tropical worlds. There are vital resources locked away just so Dragons can frolic in the meadows."

"The Dragon Treaty granted them the same rights as other higher life forms, which enabled us to defeat the Giants, Ogres and Titans, and end the Third Ice War. He saved millions of lives. We could have been caught in the flood. Instead, we had time to build ships."

"What victory? He retreated to Mars, which led to millions leaving terra, allowing Sapiens to rise. Then when he seized power from me, he and the founders build an amazing fleet, only to go into space instead of retaking Terra," Dain said heading down the hall.

"Why are you so obsessed with ruling one overcrowded planet that freezes over? The ice age lasted over one hundred thousand years? We now have 114 systems, with terraforming on ten underway."

"Terra is our home world. I did not object to sending the Dwarves, Giants, Orcs, Titans, Goblins or Dragons away, nor to establishing an Interstellar Empire; I object to leaving our home world to ungrateful, treacherous, barbarians," Dain said entering an office.

"Father, Terra is old, look at how quickly Mars decayed without constant attention. As immortals, we will live to see a day when Sol expands and engulfs Terra and all the other planets. Leaving Terra was inevitable," Abelard said following Dain in.

"Yes, but we should have first mined Terra, Mars, and the other planets of everything, not left behind tens of billions of tonnes of carbon, iron, methane, gold, oil, uranium and other resources. We should have left those ungrateful barbarians with nothing. We saved those mud-hut dwellers from the ice and floods, taught them fire, speech and farming, only to have them repay us with rape and war," Dain said going to the desk. He swiped the top of the black desk, a screen appeared with the words Dain Corporation in gold gothic lettering over a stencil of a Stag's head in gold.

"One day we will return, Father," Abelard said sitting. "I hope you have a defence plan. The Ogres with their Orc, Goblin, Titan, Oni, Troll and Black Daemon allies will attack us for violating the Dragon Treaty."

Dain glared at Abelard, "Abelard if I wanted the Emperor's advice, I would call Abel."

"Father, was you who leaked the information about the Stem Cell Program?" Abelard asked.

Dain pointed to the door without replying. Abelard left the office.

In New-Vladivostok, Emperor Takahiro followed by a team of four Knights was on a tour of the massive oil plant with Czar Petrov, a 195cm tall, stern looking field elf, who wore a tailored white shirt, with black pants, boots, three-quarter coat and officers cap. He had five stars in a cluster on his collar, a 9mm on a shoulder holster under his coat and a wand in an open holster on his belt. His wand was a white rod with a pommel. The symbol of his house, the outline of a standing growling bear.

House Guards with the symbol of House Petrov patrolled the plant, stationed at the gates, jeeps each with a team onboard patrolled the area around the plant.

Following Takahiro and Patya were Elves in technical services uniforms, they wore dark purple pants, yellow shirts with a long white coat and yellow hard hat. On the left sleeve of the coat was the symbol of the Empire and on the right sleeve was a white square patch with a yellow edge with the outline of a grey upright double ended open spanner inside. The group with Patya had 'Petrov Oil' on the back of their coat. The group with Takahiro had 'Hashimoto Resources'. The third group had the profile of Stag with 'Dain Minerals'.

"This is where powdered carbon is dissolved in distilled water then hydrogen is added under high pressure and cooked. Each tank produces a different batch of hydrocarbon products. If you'd like a detailed explanation of the chemical processes and how the different hydrocarbons are produced, ask my engineers and chemists," Patya said, nodding to the group of Field Elves in technical services uniforms.

Abel arrived, in Knights Uniform, and stood in front of the group from Dain Minerals.

"Emperor. Czar. I apologise for being late. There was a mix-up in communications and transport arrangements. So, I hitched a ride on a cargo flight from Camp Bravo when I found out my brother was unable to attend. I am told that my company's carbon dioxide extractors are required to meet a higher daily target met on how much carbon dioxide they must scrub and inject as carbon into the process," Abel said.

"Yes, the Ministry of the Environment sets those targets based on monthly readings," Patya said.

"No need to worry Lady Abel, we already toured your carbon processing plant; I am impressed, and we know the new targets are higher than expected. Your engineers have assured us your facility can meet the new targets and the construction team says new extractors will be ready before the plant reaches full production next year," Takahiro said to Abel.

"Of course, it can, the plant is state of the art; not only can it process the carbon we mine in space, but many sources of carbon such as timber, coal, as well as carbon dioxide. It produces pure graphite in solution."

"What about the more valuable forms of carbon?" Patya asked.

"Yes, before the crushing process any diamonds and Lonsdaleite are separated," Abel replied.

"This is a crucial project. This project is not just to reduce local dependence on hauling liquid crude but to avoid an Empire-wide fuel crisis," Takahiro said.

"I know how important this plant is. I am sad to report we are a month behind on building spaceships designed to collect carbon dust with a modified fuel scoop," Abel said.

"We cannot comprise on quality, all spacecraft must use the best technology, be made with the best materials, to the highest standard and construction itself must be as safe as possible," Takahiro said looking to Abel then Patya.

"My Emperor, I am not my little brother. I am not suggesting that you reduce any standards; I am saying we need to increase industrial output and have more space docks building ships," Abel said with a smile.

"Lady Abel, I know you are not your brother. I am glad you and he are not here at the same time, for he would start arguing with you over who is the older twin. Fortunate Patya's planning team took such delays into consideration. We are all aware of the shortage of engineers. I have already spoken with Árni about increased training. I know your brother would rather see more immediate results by increasing the work day from six to eight hours but keep the working week six days long and no pay increase. He has called for a reduction in the number of inspections during construction, reduced hull thickness and a dozen other measures he calls cost-cutting. I fear he would have existing ships fly longer between maintenance checks," Takahiro said.

"Dain would reduce the number of holidays to just Yule and then reduce Yule to one day," Patya grumbled.

"I know my brother, he would keep Founder's Day, not that he would ever admit to looking forward to September first, given it is also your birthday Emperor," Abel said.

Takahiro laughed and said, "I haven't celebrated my

birthday in centuries. But I get to celebrate with my son and grandson."

"We had too many deaths this year in the construction industry, not just in starship construction. We must work harder to reduce this. As head of the Inquisition, I have held many inquiries into workplace deaths; we must not sacrifice safety to meet demand. Let us not forget that six workers died while building this plant. I am sure Dain is not here because of that," Patya said.

"I am aware four of those deaths were on our carbon dioxide extractor. Dain's response is well known, he wants to increase robotics," Abel said.

"Robotics has a significant level of opposition. I learnt a great deal from my inquiry into robots. I was sceptical when many workers' groups claimed it would cost far more jobs than would be created in new industries because to build better robots you need robots build and eventually repair robots. It would create a permanent underclass of service workers. Robotics can weaken society with low morale as more workers wait to be replaced. Eventually, no one will work because once robots can build and repair robots, they will not need us at all," Patya said.

"Yes, the increased level of robotics in manufacturing, clothing, automotive and consumer products a century ago was a mistake. It took half a century to decrease unemployment to below five percent. The cost of retraining workers to re-enter the workforce in the food, service, construction and agriculture industries has cost the Empire more than the revenue increase," Takahiro said.

"Emperor, I am aware of the problems the Empire has. The main problem with the unemployed is they gather in cities and will not move to small towns to work. They are used to the services found in a city," Abel said.

"Yes, only a few see the lack of services in a small town is an opportunity for small business, we must review the economic model and encourage more small business in small towns," Takahiro said.

"Proxima Alcyone Two has a shortage of farm labour, and Proxima Alcyone Four has many vacancies in factories, but their youth would rather come here hoping to become lawyers or accountants," Patya said. "But we should discuss methods of getting people to return to those worlds without force tonight. Abel, we have already inspected the second stage filtration process, we need to proceed, next is the main hydrocarbon pressure cooker." Patya turned and headed towards the group of thin tanks towering over the plant.

"Emperor, do you still plan on sending the crude to New-Singapore for processing and distribution?" Abel asked as they walked below the maze of pipes connecting the various tanks.

"Not just New Singapore, this facility provides fuel to the local market and has a natural gas to the pipeline to New-Moscow. Once we increase production, we will supply gas via pipeline to New-Beijing, with a third pipeline is planned to New-North Pyongan," Takahiro replied.

"I don't recall seeing a fuel quality report; how does the fuel compare to other fuels?" Abel asked.

"It is high quality, as good as natural or biomass fuel; I can provide you with a copy of the report," Patya replied.

"I am not against biomass, alcohol or plant oil fuels. Nor against the electric cars. Chief Belaúnde is producing fuel from sugar. Prince Vlasov is producing fuel with biomass, but artificial fuel has only met 20% of the demand for small vehicle fuel. Most Methane fuel is used by suborbital planes to carry shuttles to and from space," Takahiro said.

"Once this plant is operating at full capacity, it will produce 1,500,000 barrels of oil a day. We need to build 80 of these plants to meet global demand, more if any sugar or biomass fuel plants close, which may happen as we need the land for other crops," Patya said.

"Abel, carbon and sulphur space mining is short-term. Once the plant is fully operational, in twenty years, we will have atmospheric extractors globally to capture and process sulphur dioxide and carbon dioxide," Takahiro said.

"I understand. What about those who worry about the environment?"

"Yaotl assured me if we keep the global level of sulphur and carbon dioxide well below dangerous and the air quality is good, then he will not shut down the plant. I have already increased the size of all my kelp farms," Takahiro said.

"If only he let us reduce the size of the Sahara Desert with tree farms," Patya said.

"The environment is his portfolio; Mine is treasury and internal trade, Dain had agriculture, and you have Business, Finance and Economics. Not that you cannot suggest, but you know as well as I do, that he will tell you even a desert has its place. I took us centuries to get him to agree to have the Gobi an inland sea as it was in the pre-ice age era," Takahiro said.

Patya stopped. "Lady Abel, my apologies, do you need my engineers to explain to you these high-pressure tanks?"

"The pipes deliver pure carbon in the form of fine graphite dissolved in purified water from your desalination plant. The tanks first heat the carbon; steam is collected and recycled; then the carbon is super-heated under extreme pressure with hydrogen," Abel said.

"Correct, then it is filtered to remove any carbon and hydrogen gas, returning them to the boiler. We have many tanks to simultaneously produce various hydrocarbons, depending on heat and hydrogen levels. Last, some products have sulphur, and other chemicals added," Patya said.

"I understand the process, and the product is good. I know you are running the plant at low power. The decision today is to bring the plant to half power, but the plastics recycling plant is behind schedule," Abel said. "Patya, I would like to know why you reduced the sulphur content."

"That is one of the legal requirements from Yaotl to reduce acid rain," Patya replied.

"I am aware low sulphur diesel fuel is the cause of engine damage in older engines. Dain was in Senate when we voted to approve Yaotl's changes to the Clean Air Act," Takahiro said.

"My brother feels these regulations target him," Abel said.

"Yaotl is targeting pollution; he does plan to increase the number of electric vehicles produced and have cities improve public transport. Your brother has no excuses; he was present when Yaotl tabled his plan to fight pollution," Takahiro said.

"Dain feels his regulations are targeting his new four-wheel drive," Abel said.

"Lady Abel, I did not appoint Yaotl as the Environment Minister, he chose to be when Dain was our ruler. Nor did I demand him to find fault with everything, he does that on his own. Dain has known Yaotl for over 15,000 years;

he should be aware by now Yaotl's level of commitment to the Environment, and these laws should not be a surprise to him," Takahiro said.

"You should have designed it to the new standards," Patya said.

"I didn't design the Stag, Dain did," Abel said.

"Then he should have had you design it; the last decent car made by Dain Automotive was the Model 101," Takahiro said.

"I agree with you, but Dain ceased production of the Model 101 500 years ago, and I have not designed any vehicles since," Abel said.

"We can discuss this back at the hotel tonight," Patya said.

"Yes, when do we start construction of the second plant?" Abel asked.

"Arjuna wants it in New-India and Takis wants it in New-Alexandria. Naturally, Yaotl prefers we build more sugar ethanol fuel refineries, like those he built in Amazonia," Petrov replied.

"Yaotl knows we cannot sacrifice any more peanut oil, sugar, soy or corn, to produce fuel," Abel said.

"If Takis and Arjuna do not budge, then we have them fight each other to see who gets the next plant. As Emperor, it will be my duty to host and referee," Takahiro said.

"You mean you will make sure they don't kill each other," Abel said.

"That too," Takahiro said.

They all laughed.

Late at night, in the hotel room of Emperor Takahiro, he was sitting with a gō of sake by the fireplace with Czar Petrov, who was drinking vodka. In front of them was a drinks trolley with sake, vodka and a decanter of Germanic raspberry brandy on top with a tray of snacks. Underneath was a púca bag.

Prince Kaede was on a rug, in a nightdress in a diaper. He was playing with a puzzle cube. Abel removed her large 13mm handgun and knife from her vest, then handed them to the Knight on guard before entering the room.

"Abel, what is Dain really upset about, surely it isn't the little one," Takahiro said looking at the fire.

"You know my brother is always angry. He still is upset how you deposed him and then made him Minister of Agriculture. He plans to create and have you run the department of waste management when he takes over," Abel said. She sat on the rug, took the cube and showed Kaede how it was solved, then she scrambled it and handed it to him.

"I played by his rules and won. Since then had made no secret of his desire to take back the crown. I have not dramatically changed the rules," Takahiro said.

"Abel, you and Dain are my dear friends, but he lost Tir Na Nog by refusing to destroy the invading Celts at sea. We still do not know how he made the dead walk, we lost thousands of our finest Witches. He let sentiment get in the way of our survival, which is why we made sure no one can make a decision without consequence," Patya said.

"He died that day, and I don't regret casting revive on him. He stands by his decision, the Celts had woman and children on their boats. He didn't expect them to use their own as shields."

"I don't fault you for bringing him back to life, Abel, but he took precious artefacts, and they were lost or destroyed. We are still unable to replace them, I am not blaming him entirely, we allowed wizards to keep secrets, but he would not let us examine the sword, armour and shield Lilith left him," Takahiro said.

"I cannot tell you what he was thinking then. He is angry his mother went to live with you. He is not happy with me. I carried the lifeless body to a cauldron of everlasting. I believe most of his anger is the peace deal with the Celts. Our females forced to mate with them, but he directs that at you because you came with stealth ships and took us to Mars," Abel said.

"I never said I told you so to him," Takahiro said.

"You don't have to," Abel said.

There was silence.

"I noticed you handed in your weapon," Patya said.

"Yes," Abel said.

"But as a Knight, you are trusted to remain armed in my presence," Takahiro said.

"True, Emperor, but I wanted to play with the púca," Abel said.

They all heard Kaede cheer, they turned and looked at Kaede. He was standing and holding up the solved puzzle cube, with no diaper on.

Lady Hitomi was a 155cm tall flower elf with gold eyes, long lashes and long pink hair in two buns with tails down to her waist entered the room. Aged thirty-six but looked to be sixteen, she had large perky breasts. She wore the uniform of a Blood-Witch and carried her cloak was over her arm. She placed her staff and medical bag by the service trolley, then placed her robe on the rack by the door. She came over to Kaede.

"Emperor, it is time for his feeding," Hitomi said.

"Look," Kaede said, holding the puzzle up to Hitomi.

Hitomi knelt, smiled and said, "Well done my little prince." She took the puzzle and handed it to Able.

"He is big for three months," Abel said.

"Yes, but his height indicators are around 155cm," Hitomi said as she picked him up. Kaede hugged her.

"You can use the bedroom, Lady Hitomi," Takahiro said.

"Milk?" Kaede asked.

"Yes," Hitomi replied.

Kaede hugged her.

"Hitomi. Thanks for coming on short notice, we have run out of breast milk, and he refuses formula," Takahiro said.

"I don't mind," Hitomi replied.

Hitomi carried Kaede, he leant on her shoulder, to the bedroom and closed the door.

"I need to find a better Diaper," Takahiro said noticing Kaede's diaper on the floor.

"Save yourself a lot of trouble and test them on him," Patya said.

CHAPTER 3

JUST ASKING

September 1, 11563. Imperial Palace.

In sub-basement six of the Palace, was a Japanese garden, with orchids and sun lamps hung from the three-storey vaulted roof. A row of cherry trees, with bright red leaves, stood tall under sun lamps on either side of a path that led to a koi pond, west of the central column. The path was made from assorted polished pebbles that crunched underfoot, it continued to a wooden bridge over the pond, and continued to an open area, surrounded by cherry trees, up to the steps of a small two-storey teahouse, with a children's play area behind it.

The teahouse was entirely wood, unlike the modern concrete and plastic houses of the Empire. It had a large balcony and wooden shutters over glassless windows with wooden slats in the void. Its design was a pre-industrial style and was held together not by nails, but joints. The roof was irregular handmade terracotta tiles.

Inside the púca change room, Kaede sat on a rug on the floor, watched by a Knight. As he removed his soiled diaper, despite her efforts not to, she screwed up the face. Kaede, holding his breath, placed the diaper in a disposal bag. He raced to put it into the waste receptacle chute in the wall. Kaede wiped himself with wet wipes as the Knight sprayed air freshener.

The Knight watched Kaede dress. He put on padded underpants, pulled on his clothes, shoes, and socks. He tied his laces. The Knight held the door open for Kaede, he bowed to her and raced out of the change room to Takahiro, and the Knight followed him.

In the teahouse the Senators Czar Petrov, a Field Elf; Lord Argon Agrovar, a Mountain Elf; General Kenta Yoshida, a Flower Elf; Sky Marshal Rudolf Reinhart, a Field Elf; Maharajah Arjuna Desai, a Night Elf; Lord Takis Alexandris, a Silver Elf; Prince Georgi Vlasov, a Night Elf; Lord Árni Tikkanen, a Forest Elf; General Siegfried Feygold, a Mountain Elf; Admiral Viktor Niemi, an Aquatic Elf; Chief Yaotl Belaúnde, a Forest Elf; and High Lord Dain, a Field Elf were seated at a large table on the top floor. Takahiro introduced Kaede to them.

There were three other tables, two covered with an assortment of food and drinks, and one with a stack of gifts. Emperor Takahiro went a sat in the middle of the main table with a high chair and an empty chair beside him.

"Where is my father?" Kaede asked as he climbed onto a high chair beside Takahiro. The Knight who followed him pushed him to the table.

"Your father is on his way," Takahiro replied.

Lady Toshiko and Lady Abel arrived together. They placed gifts on the table in the middle of the room, and then they came to the main table. They both bowed to the Emperor.

"Happy Birthday, Prince Kaede," Toshiko said.

"Happy Birthday," Lady Abel said.

"Have you seen my father?" Kaede asked.

"You thank them for the gifts," Takahiro replied, the whispered in Kaede's ear. "What did I tell you about manners?"

"Just asking," Kaede replied.

"Prince Kaede, your father's shuttle arrived at the Space Centre in New-Ghana only a few hours ago. However, due to a storm here, his flight here was diverted to New-Constantinople," Viktor said.

"Is he safe?" a distressed Kaede asked.

"Of course," Toshiko replied.

"Why don't you use magic to make the storm go away now?" Kaede asked in a high-pitched shrill.

"Kaede!" Takahiro exclaimed.

"Just asking," Kaede replied.

Takahiro leant towards Kaede, but Toshiko stepped between them. "It is all right, my Emperor. He doesn't understand. Let me explain it to Kaede," Toshiko said. She knelt, face to face with him, and said, "Prince Kaede, magic has limits, and a storm is too big, even for me, the witch of the east, to just blow away."

"My father is trapped by the storm. Shouldn't you rescue him?" Kaede asked.

"He is not trapped; he is safe, and the storm will soon be over," Toshiko replied as she placed her hand on his shoulder.

General Yoshiko leaned over. "Prince Kaede, perhaps you like to go outside and play with my daughters?"

"Yes, that is a good idea Kenta. Kaede, go play with the twins and the other púca," Takahiro said, standing. Kaede looked at Toshiko and blinked.

"I shall take him outside. Kenta, where are they?" Toshiko asked, grabbing Kaede by the hand.

"They are playing in the park behind the teahouse," Kenta replied as Kaede tried to pull away from Toshiko.

"I don't want to play with púca. I want to read!" Kaede said, stamping his foot.

"You are a púca, and it is time you went outside to play," Takahiro said. He nodded to Toshiko who picked him up.

"He has no diaper on under his hakama. I can fix that," Toshiko said feeling his bottom.

"I do not need one. I can change myself," Kaede said proudly.

"Do not worry Toshiko, I let him go without one. He promised to use the children's toilet, and so far, he has not soiled himself," Takahiro said.

"What a big boy," Toshiko said to Kaede.

Kenta stood and said, "I want to introduce him to my daughters."

Toshiko held Kaede tight as he tried to wiggle his way out of her grip. She followed Kenta out the rear of the teahouse to a park with swings and a large climbing hill that had slides. Mako and Miko, dressed in the same yellow and black striped yukata, sat at a children's table and poured juice from a teapot into teacups, watched by Freya.

Toshiko placed Kaede on the ground in front of Mako and Miko, aged six. Behind them, came Sora and Akiko, aged four. They were pushing a stroller with Izanami, aged one, inside screaming with joy.

Kaede looked at Izanami. "Who is she?" he asked.

"I am Izanami," Izanami replied.

"She is small," Kaede said.

"Kaede, behave," Toshiko commanded.

"I am the same height as you," Izanami said. "I know who you are; you are Prince Kaede, and today is your birthday. It is also my birthday, and I am one, like you."

"Are you from Lord Kenta's clan?" Kaede asked.

"No," lzanami replied in a soft voice.

"These are our friends," Mako said.

"Izanami, Sora and Akiko are from Hashimoto House," Miko said as she pointed to each girl.

"Oh?" Kaede asked.

"Don't you like abandoned púca?" Izanami asked standing.

Kaede looked at Toshiko. "That is not a nice thing to say, Izanami," Toshiko said.

"He started it," Izanami mumbled.

"Tea," Mako said loudly, handing Izanami a cup of juice.

"Thank you," Izanami said. She drank it down and held out the cup.

"To your liking?" Miko asked as she took the empty cup.

"Yes," Izanami replied, "To my throne, please ladies," Izanami pointed at the swings.

Sora and Akiko pushed Izanami to the swing, and Mako and Miko followed them.

"Why would anyone abandon púca?" Kaede asked Toshiko.

"Kaede, that is something to ask when you're older," Toshiko replied. She leaned over and said to him, "Now, be nice and go play," then looked over at the girls.

Kaede ran after them and asked them, "What are you doing?"

"We are playing-" Mako started.

"Princess," Miko finished the reply.

"I am the princess," Izanami said lifting her nose.

"I can walk," Kaede said, and he ran ahead and got on the swing.

When the girls arrived, Kaede just continued to play on the swing. Izanami unclicked the restraints on the stroller, left the stroller and climbed on the swing beside Kaede.

"So, can I," Izanami said.

"I can change my diaper," Kaede said.

"That is so easy," Izanami said, rolling her eyes. "I can read."

"I can read and write Kanji," Kaede said grinning.

"No way!" Izanami exclaimed.

"Yes way, Grandfather taught me," Kaede said.

"Well, Mako and Miko have been teaching us to read and write common, I can do cursive," Izanami snapped back.

"You are so cool!" Kaede exclaimed as he swung. Izanami stopped and looked at him.

"Yes, I am cool," Izanami said, nose up, looking ahead as she swung.

"My father promised me I could make a wish on my birthday. I will ask him to send us to school." Kaede said hopping off the swing.

"You must be," Mako started.

Crisis

"Six years old to go," Miko finished.

Kaede facing Mako and Miko as Hiro came out of the tea house. Hiro raced up behind Kaede and lifted him up.

"Go where?" Hiro asked.

"Father!" Kaede exclaimed.

"Hello son," Hiro said as he put Kaede down, "Is everything all right?"

"I have missed you, Father," Kaede replied.

"Good, now tell me, where did you want to go?" Hiro asked.

"To school," Kaede replied.

"You are too young," Mako started.

"You only just learnt to write," Miko finished.

"I am smarter than you," Izanami said hopping off the wing.

"Prove it," Mako and Miko taunted.

"I made Sora and Akiko push me in a stroller, while you served me," Izanami said.

Sora and Akiko ran off, crying. Mako and Miko huffed, and then walked to the tea set got the juice and poured it over the stroller. Then walked to their father, who was standing on the porch around the tea house.

Kaede laughed and said to Izanami, "You're not very clever."

Hiro took Kaede's hand and said, "Come, let us open your presents," then to Toshiko he said, "I think it is best if I take him inside while you sort the girls out."

"Yes, Your Highness," Toshiko replied, then went over to Sora and Akiko who sat crying under a nearby cherry tree.

"I want to watch," Kaede said then leaned over and

poked his tongue out at Izanami, but Hiro carried him back to the tea house and inside. Not putting him down until they got to the top of the stairs. A knight and sailor waiting by the stairs followed them.

"Son, when and how did you arrive?" Takahiro asked when they entered the top floor.

"I hitched a ride on a patrol boat to New-Odessa, and I caught the tube train to the city, then I rode the subway to the Island," Hiro replied.

"On your own?" a concerned Takahiro asked.

"No Father," Hiro replied, he then turned to a Knight holding a small folding scooter, standing behind Hiro with Ensign Fukuhina. Hiro reached out, and the Knight came to him and handed Hiro the scooter, who then handed it to Kaede. "Sorry son, I didn't have time to wrap it," Hiro said.

"Awesome Father, thank you," Kaede said.

"No riding it until we get you a helmet. I will take you once the storm passes," Hiro said.

"Can I go to school?" Kaede asked.

Many laughed at Kaede, including Hiro, who looked at him, confused.

"Sorry son, you are too young," Hiro replied, placing his hand on Kaede's shoulder.

"Mako and Miko are going," Kaede said.

"General?" Hiro asked.

"Yes, they are, but they are already six," Kenta replied.

"Kaede, you need to be six before you can start school," Hiro said.

"What if I use my wish for Izanami and me to go to school?" Kaede asked.

"She will go to school when she is six," Hiro said.

"But you promised me a wish," Kaede said.

"Son, what did you promise him?" Takahiro asked.

"Father, Kaede sent me a message, in which he asked me if wishes were real. I send back a message trying to explain how on your birthday you get to make wishes before blowing out the candles on the cake. It seems he has taken it literally," Hiro said.

"I see, in that case, until he is eighteen, you owe him a wish. A reasonable wish. That will teach you to be more careful what you say to him," Takahiro said.

"Yes Father," Hiro said, "I brought Ensign Fukuhina with me. Her story is incredible. She organised the survivors of the attack, killing all the pirates, and captured an Ogre pirate ship."

"You did well."

"Not really, we found them in the outer orbit of a star trying to repair their ship using parts from the Ogre's ship. We resupplied them. They lost most of the crew and over 2000 colonists."

"What happened?"

"The Ogre's pushed an asteroid into the path of the ship and followed it towards the transport. It triggered a collision alert, the transport ultra-wave field turned off, and the crew changed course to pass the asteroid. The crew in the transport didn't see the Ogre's ship, and they stopped and turned off the shield to check for hull damage. The Ogre's pushed the asteroid into the transport and opened fire on the crew outside the ship. Hundreds of passengers were killed as the asteroid ground against the hull and tore the hull open. More were killed when the midsection was depressurized. The Ogre's were able to then board and commit rape and murder," Hiro said with a clenched jaw.

"We cannot arm every transport, but the crew had weapons," Takahiro said.

"The Ogre's knew the layout, had heavy armour, and most of the crew scattered over the ship trying to deal with the loss of atmosphere, most didn't even know they been boarded," an angry Hiro said.

"We must issue a warning to all ship," an alarmed Takahiro said.

"Will the Navy attack the Ogre's? I have seen the pirate ship, it was no converted freighter, it was a purpose-built class four cruiser, I took photos and scans of the ship," an angry Hiro said.

"That I cannot say," Takahiro replied in a hushed voice then looked around and put his hand on Hiro's shoulder. Then said, "I am proud of you son."

"I didn't really do anything. I just guessed the right search zone. The fleet from Algol will take care of them now."

"The cargo?"

"In the vault."

"Unopened?"

"Only by me. The agent died protecting it. It doesn't look like they knew she had the items, as they questioned everyone. I found her locked trunk in luggage. I found the items and removed them."

"Enjoy your son's first birthday," Takahiro said, then headed to Admiral Niemi.

"Who died?" Kaede asked.

Hiro turned to see Kaede. "Kaede, don't listen in on adult's speaking."

"Father, do I tell you my wish and then blow out the candles?" Kaede asked.

"It does not work like that," Hiro said. Kaede about to say something but Hiro put his hand on his Kaede's shoulder and said, "Son, the wish must be something my father would approve off, and choose carefully because you only get one each birthday until you are 18."

"That is easy, I want to go to school."

"But, Kaede, I do not think you are ready for school," Takahiro said behind Hiro.

"But—"

"Kaede! You respect your elders and do not answer back," Hiro said in a low tone. Kaede looked upset but didn't cry.

Izanami sitting at the table poked her tongue out at him.

"Kaede, when you are ready for school, you may go, so don't waste a wish on that," Takahiro said, in a soft voice.

Kaede asked softly, "Can my friends come?"

"Lady Abel?" Takahiro asked.

"If they pass the entrance examination. But seeing how smart Izanami and Kaede are, I am sure they would qualify to attend school with Mako and Miko," Abel replied.

"Kaede is a boy," Mako said.

"The Imperial Academy is for girls," Miko declared.

"That is true, but the Academy for Exceptional Students does accept male students," Abel said to Mako and Miko.

"But -"

"-."

"You go to the school I sent you, you will make new friends, like Kaede," Kenta said.

Kaede looked up at Hiro. "Do I still get my wish?" he asked.

"You are not ready for school, but if you do well, you will go to school with Mako and Miko," Hiro said.

"Izanami?" Kaede asked.

"If she behaves," Takahiro replied.

"Can I have a wand?" Kaede asked.

Everyone gasped. Toshiko knelt beside him, "Sorry, but you need to be eighteen to own a wand."

"But Grandfather can change the law. I heard him say so."

Everyone laughed. Hiro looked Kaede and said, "Only with permission of the Senate."

Kenta and the others laughed.

"But anyone can use magic," Kaede stated.

"Yes, and when you're old enough, I will teach you," Toshiko said behind Hiro.

"Yes, Lady Toshiko," Kaede replied.

"Think of another wish," Hiro said, "No rush, I have time," he added, looking at his father, who nodded.

"Yes, take your time," Takahiro said stepping forward.

"Son, time to go open your gifts. Think what you need, not what you want," Hiro said.

"Yes, Father," Kaede said.

"Good, now go open your other gifts and don't forget to thank everyone," Takahiro said.

As Kaede unwrapped his gifts, Toshiko went to Takahiro. "He has found his red shirt," she said.

"Pardon?" Takahiro asked.

"His rival, someone to challenge and inspire him," Toshiko said.

"So, you think he is the blue shirt? What makes you say he is the gentle one?" Takahiro asked.

"I have seen him sit for hours in your office in awe of you," Toshiko said.

"He is well-behaved."

"You did not invite those girls because you have a soft spot for abandoned púca."

"Am I that obvious?"

"I have known you my entire life, I know you better than you know yourself."

"The Blood-Witches selected them, not me."

"Yet, Sora and Akiko do not appear to be that intelligent."

"They have potential; I am told their genetic disposition is sports. You know Abel's school program is exceptional in everything except sports. I am sure someone could convince her to have a sports scholarship program," Takahiro said, then looked at Toshiko.

"Am I in the way of your plans?"

"No. Kaede is not ready for school. I hope one day to pass the company to him. Since Hiro never went to business school, I want to prepare Kaede myself."

"Kaede is only one, shouldn't you wait and see what he wants?"

"I know he has a little growing to do. But he must learn he cannot have everything," Takahiro said walking over to watch Kaede open gifts.

Kaede opened a gift box and pulled out a tablet. Without looking, he placed it on the table beside another. He looked at the card and said in a dull, flat, tone, "Thank you High Lord Dain."

Hiro came and said, "Kaede, don't be like that."

"It is all right, my mistake, it appears the Emperor had already gifted him a tablet; however, young Prince, this is the model used in school," Dain said.

"Is it loaded with the learning application?" Kaede asked with excitement.

"Yes, you will need a qualified teacher to monitor any exams if you want to add the results to your Academic Record," Dain replied.

"Thank you," Kaede said, with a smile, and he picked it up and walked over to Hiro. "I wish to have a teacher."

Hiro looked at Takahiro, Abel said, "Emperor, I know someone."

After the meal, Takahiro places a medal, Star of the Empire, a large silver seven-pointed star, with seven diamonds in a circle, around Fukuhina's neck.

"For bravery above and beyond the call of duty, our highest medal, the Star of the Empire," Takahiro said.

Many stood to clap and cheer. Then Hiro took Kaede to his room.

Many gathered around Fukuhina to talk to her. Admiral Viktor Niemi, a tall Aquatic Elf, with a short crew cut. He wore the Imperial Navy dress uniform, gold trim on his jacket, a gold strip down his dark purple pants and had five stars in a cluster on his collar came and took off his officer's cap, put it under his arm, and shook Fukuhina's hand with his gloved hand.

"Well done young lady," Viktor said.

"Thank-you Admiral," Fukuhina said.

"What will you do now?" Viktor asked.

"Pardon?" Fukuhina asked.

"You're on mandatory leave for the inquiry into the loss of your ship," Viktor replied.

"Oh, I don't know what I will do yet," Fukuhina replied.

Takahiro came with Patya Petrov.

"Lady Fukuhina, this is Czar Petrov, he will be conducting the inquiry," Takahiro said.

"Lady?" Fukuhina asked.

"Yes, those who achieve our highest order if they are not already members of the nobility are given a title for life. As a member of the nobility you will be allocated land, given a modest reduction in tax, have access to the levels of the court above level one, and the more service you do, they higher office you are eligible for appointment," Patya said.

"Even the throne room?" a surprised Fukuhina asked.

"No, just levels two to six," Takahiro replied.

"When you return to duty you will be promoted, for now, you have my apologies, it must have been very a difficult situation to face on your first deep space training mission," Viktor said.

Before Fukuhina could say anything, Patya said, "It could be some months before you face the Inquiry. We must get the whole story on record and await more crew members and evidence to arrive," Patya said.

"How did you end up on an Exodus transport," Takahiro asked.

"I entered the Imperial Navy after leaving Hashimoto House, I volunteered to be relief crew on an as part of my training," Fukuhina said.

"Emperor-" Patya growled.

"Natural curiosity, my apologies," Takahiro said.

"Sorry," Fukuhina said to Patya. Then turned to Viktor and asked, "If I may ask, what will happen to that ship?"

"The Inquisition has officers gathering evidence, the surviving passengers and crew are on priority to be brought here for questioning. The Navy will then salvage the ships where they lay," Viktor said.

"A memorial service will be held for the dead, I would like a memorial using the ship's name plate will be used as part of a memorial to the crew and passengers," Takahiro said.

"Yes, we can talk about that later, the ship's name was Seizon-sha," Viktor said nodding.

"How poetic, it means Survivor," Takahiro said.

"Lady Fukuhina, do not to talk about the incident before the inquiry," Patya said to Fukuhina.

"Yes, Czar Petrov," Fukuhina said.

"You on leave, it will be many months before you appear before the inquiry, what will you do with your time?" Patya asked.

"I-" Fukuhina started to speak.

"I was going to offer her a position with my staff," Takahiro said to Patya, then turned to Victor, "While I have your attention, I am putting your daughter on special duty to teach my grandson. It will mean two shifts a day."

"Oh?" Viktor asked.

"I know Emi is your daughter, but she graduated top of her class, and she is the only Knight with a púca," Takahiro replied.

"I remain hopeful she will transfer to the Navy, but since you pay the Knights twice that of a senior officer per shift, I am sure she will welcome the extra income to help with the cost of raising her púca," Viktor replied.

"Emperor, I like to offer Lady Toshiko a place in the Imperial Knights, when she isn't training, she can help with Kaede," Takahiro said, then turned to Patya, "Any problems?"

"I rather Lady Fukuhina wasn't someplace close to her rescuer," Patya said.

"Hardly her rescuer, he found them, gave them food, comfort, sent for help and gave her a ride back to the Empire to report in. You need to interview Hiro soon, as he will leave in a few months. Patya, you might as well interview them both tomorrow," Takahiro said.

"Yes, it will take time to bring you all the survivors, in the meantime, the media will do everything they can to talk to her," Viktor said.

"Lady Fukuhina, your only comment to the anyone, especially the media, on the loss of your ship, is no comment," Patya said, "Clear?"

"Yes Czar," Fukuhina replied.

"Good, Lady Toshiko will find a room in the barracks, arrange your security pass and in the morning, first will meet Lady Emi Hagihara, a Knight. You will train with her to take care of and train Prince Kaede. When you are not with the prince, you will be in train, eating, or sleeping in the palace. Until the Inquiry you will not leave the palace without orders from Lady Toshiko," Takahiro said then nodded to Lady Toshiko.

"Yes Emperor," Fukuhina said. Lady Toshiko took Fukuhina's arm and escorted her away.

"Now Viktor," Takahiro said turning to Viktor, "We need to increase patrols between Algol and Aldebaran."

"I would need to removed ships off other areas," Viktor said.

"We have unarmed starships located between twenty and four hundred years out, millions of lives are at risk. I know it is cold comfort to any small freighter attacked, but each Exodus transport lost is thousands of Elves dead," Toshiko said with emphasis on thousands.

"You think crime is bad now, there will be riots of shipments of fuel don't arrive, and local lords will turn against us," Viktor said in a low voice.

"I know it will slow down interplanetary trade, but have freighters travel in a convoy, followed by a pair of frigates," Takahiro said.

"I will consider your proposal," Viktor said.

"Easy for you to say, you have your own fleet of armed ships," Patya grumbled, "I need the Navy to guard my freighters. Need I remind you they are carrying the oil needed to keep the people from dragging you off the crimson throne?"

"I am not asking Viktor to send every cruiser," Takahiro said.

Late at night Takahiro and Toshiko entered a metal room and closed the door behind him, it was cold, but he did not shiver. He walked to the metal bench, there was a metal box, he opened it, and pulled out the contents.

Toshiko stood and watched as Takahiro unwrapped the items, wrapped in soft leather.

The metal ball was the size of a tennis ball, it was tarnished, it looked like an eye. The sword was a Celtic leaf blade and was 42cm long. It had no leather on the hilt, the pommel was crushed, and the guard was round, and had broken open. Inside of the guard was hollow, except for gold mesh inside. The mirror was the side of a dinner plate, and once was polished silver, but now was tarnished, buckled, and badly scratched. It was framed in bronze.

"I doubt we learn anything from them," Takahiro said as he held up the sword.

"We know Lilith used solid state memory, we still have the workshop. Even if I can recover a portion of the spell I could run every combination on a charged aether chamber and if changes form, then we will test it," Toshiko said.

"I need you to look for the leak," Takahiro said.

"I can have a team at the Foundation pull them apart, study them, and try to recreate them," Toshiko said stepping forward, "All loyal members of the Hashimoto Clan."

"Worth a try. The sword could burn as bright as the sun. So sharp it could cut through bone and steel armour with ease. The wielder could cut down a foe, at a distance with a mere slash of the blade," Takahiro said admiring the blade, he turned to Toshiko, "The best we can do today is a stun baton."

"Lilith didn't record the spell, and the old weapons could not be interfaced with to transfer data from the weapon," Toshiko said.

Takahiro wrapped the sword in leather and said, "Good thing you kept the recreation of her workshop. You can take them with you, find out what you can. Last time we succeeded in studying one of her creations."

"Yes Emperor," Toshiko said bowing.

The next day, at 6am Lady Toshiko, bashed the gong in the shrine in the middle of the group of barracks. The barracks was a huge octangle Japanese style compound north of the central column in sub-basement 14, a three-story high cavern beneath the Palace.

Inside the eight large buildings with red terracotta roofs like spokes around the shrine, most of the Knights already making their bed, stripping off their tank-top and shorts, or washing in the group showers.

On each floor of the two-story barracks, an officer with four stars on her shoulder went room to room checking the Knights, Squires, and Cadets have risen.

Fukuhina was slumbering peacefully, the officer flipped the bed over, sending Fukuhina tumbling. The officer was armed with a naginata and a 13mm pistol. Fukuhina jumped up.

"Drop and give me twenty," the officer barked in Erufu, the language of the flower elves.

After doing twenty push-ups, Fukuhina stripped and washed. After that she put on the purple underwear, then a white tunic, white silk tights, then a purple pleated skirt. Over her top she put on a white double-breasted jacket with a high Asian collar, then a thick black belt with wand holder and phone holder. Last, she pulled on black knee-high boots. The whole time the officer watched her, and when finished, she handed Fukuhina a box and phone. Fukuhina clipped the phone on her belt and opened the box. It had a wand inside.

"Cadet, your wand has been checked, and it has been loaded with the spells we use. After the first meal, you will be issued a Viper 2, a 13mm pistol, a combat knife, and vest," the officer said.

"Yes ma'am," Fukuhina responded.

Lady Emi Hagihara, an Aquatic Elf with light blue hair and violet eyes, woke in her room, she noticed the room opposite was empty, she looked, the double bed still made. Emi left her room, went down the hall, woke her son and breastfeed him.

Emi bath and dressed her son. She left him in a playpen and returned to her room, stripped off and washed in a cold shower, then put on her Knights' uniform. She removed her wand from a box in her drawer and opened the Velcro flap of her wand holder and slipped it in. Her holster was empty.

Grabbing a black backpack, then a blue shoulder bag, on her way out, she carried her púca, went down the hall and took the elevator down to the second floor and went into the open door of the day care centre.

"Hello Nori," the blood-witch, a flower elf, cooed as Emi handed her púca over.

Emi left, took the elevator down to the garage and took a remote out of her shoulder bag and pressed it at a dark grey four-seat cruiser. The large four-door car beeped twice, she went to the rear and clicked the trunk button on the remote.

The rear opened. She removed and put on her vest, then took out a 13mm gun and put it into the shoulder holders, then put two 7 round clips into the other side, then slide a knife into the sheath in her combat vest.

There was a gun rack with a Viper Mini, Viper 1, Viper 2, and Viper 2L. Each was a bullpup weapon that used caseless rounds. Each the Petrov Bear on the side of the weapon on the lower receiver.

The Mini was a 9mm, a sub-submachine gun with a 100-round casket magazine. The Viper 1 had a bayonet attached. The Viper 2 had a 60-round casket magazine. The Viper 2L was 13mm caseless, 10-round sniper rifle with a large scope.

Emi checked the sword rack, she had a 42cm leaf blade, a large claymore, and a katana. Last, she checked the smoke, concussion, and HE grenades. Then she got in the car, drove out of Hashimoto Apartments, on the East shore of the massive lake, soon on the ramp, joined traffic on the Eastern Highway, going over the bridge headed to the Imperial Palace.

Kaede woke to see Lady Galené, a half Night Elf, Half flower elf. 150cm tall, black, with gold Flower Elf eyes, with pink hair. She was watching him. She bathed him, struggled to get him into a diaper, then dressed him.

Galené handed him over to Freya

"Good morning Mother," Kaede said.

"Good morning your Highness," Freya sang, "We have a big day today."

Freya bottled feed Kaede. She then picked him up and carried him to the elevator, followed by Galené. Inside the elevator Galené scrolled the panel down to the Palace, selecting the first floor. Kaede wiggled, Freya held on tight, but Kaede did not stop, and she eventually put him down.

Kaede followed Freya and Galené to the Emperor's office, was one of thirteen office centres around the outer wall, each was between the outer wall and the inner palace wall. Each had offices on either side and a security desk and waiting area with bathroom. Galené stayed on the elevator.

Emi and Fukuhina sat in the waiting area. Lady Toshiko was at the security desk.

"Lady Emi, Lady Fukuhina, I present Prince Kaede," Freya said.

Lady Toshiko came to them, "This way," she said and lead them to an empty office. She opened the door and said, "You will use this as a classroom. Lady Abel provided the teaching materials."

A week later Kaede was in the Emperor's office wearing a painter's smock covered in paint. He held a painting. It was a Japanese tea house, Kaede Hashimoto in Kanji was written on the bottom right.

"Amazing," Takahiro said to Toshiko.

"Emi and Fukuhina assure me, he did it himself," Toshiko said.

"I see the evidence all over him," Takahiro said looking at all the paint on Kaede. Takahiro went to the bookshelf at the rear of his office and removed a book. Then he went over to the Japanese style sliding door in the side wall and pulled it open.

"At least a week Kaede, I will teach you, starting today, in my tea room."

Kaede gasped.

"Go inside and wait for me," Takahiro said placing the book on the tea table in front of the sofa just inside the door. Kaede raced and sat on the couch.

Takahiro went to the sliding paper door at the rear of the tea room and slipped inside, then a short time later a groggy Masako came out wearing a bright pink kimono and pink fluffy slippers. She went to the middle of the side wall and pressed on it. The wall slid apart in the middle and revealed a little kitchen area. She and started to make a pot of tea.

Takahiro went to Toshiko. "Any progress with the sword of light?"

"None, the memory sustained too much damage. It could take years to figure out how Lilith moulded the blade around the casting device and I have no idea what the mesh in the guard does," she replied in a soft voice.

"The mirror and ball?"

"Like the sword, they used state memory. It is known the mirror of truth was used to reveal any illusion. We recovered the spell Truesight. But I discovered it was also a scrying and two-way communications device. We only have fragments, but the communications device is technological."

"Very handy, would be good to have those all over the Palace."

"We are working on a prototype," Toshiko smiled.

"What about the ball?" Takahiro asked smiling.

"It does appear to be the ball from the aegis shield."

"The Aegis Shield?"

"It was a large full round shield that was able to withstand spells and the Dragon's acid attack. The wielder could hide behind it, yet see what was in front of them because of the eye. The eye was a magical drone that could detach from the shield and levitate ahead to look around corners."

"Can you recreate this?"

"In time. There are gaps in the ball's memory, but there are large sections intact, including a basic flight program, some of it matches the one in the broom. Most of the spells used, we already have. As for the shield, I am sure it was just a display device."

"Are you sure?"

"Lilith's last journal gives few details of what she intended to achieve, not the method of construction or the spell formula."

"She wrote some rather personal things in that diary," Takahiro blushed.

"Yes, she wrote fondly of you, but I haven't revealed the diary's existence or contents to anyone."

"When you're done with them, place them the vault on the third floor," Takahiro said and then bowed slightly to her.

"Yes Emperor," Toshiko said, as she bowed, then left.

Takahiro returned to Kaede, who was looking at the thick unopened book on the table, Masako was waiting with a tray of tea.

"Pour me a cup, please Masako. Then wait in the outer office until we are done, you can then dress and arrange for someone to hang Kaede's painting on the wall of my office. I want it facing my desk," Takahiro said to Masako.

After pouring a cup of tea for Takahiro, Masako left.

Takahiro grabbed the book and said, "This book contains the 1001 secrets of my success. How to get the best out of every deal, how to be successful with females, the rules of wealth and power. How to win influence others. Now, many things you are too young for, but you need to understand this. Titles are paper, power comes from wealth."

"But you are Emperor, are you not the most powerful?" a puzzled Kaede looked at the book.

"In the Empire, the wealthiest thirteen rule the Empire, and no one in the Empire is wealthier than me."

"Grandfather, can I have my friends to come to class."

"You had your birthday wish."

"I know, but Lady Hitomi says traditional dance it is better in a group."

"You don't need to sing and dance to be a leader."

"Lady Toshiko told me they do Yosakoi in the Tea House, and adults play games in the Casino."

"I see," Takahiro said trying not to laugh.

"Can I go see the dancers in the tea house?"

"No, it is for adults," Takahiro said, frowning.

"But children learn Yosakoi in school," Kaede said.

Takahiro looked at Kaede, then opened the book, "Yes, but entertainment is only a small part of our wealth. It is an amazing distraction, you can watch it on your screen in your free time."

Kaede sighed.

"Now, wealth creation starts with self-control," Takahiro

said picking up the book, Kaede was staring at his feet. "Kaede, if you don't pay attention, I will not teach you."

"You never let me do anything fun," Kaede mumbled, "Everyone calls Lord Dain the gay lord, I looked in my dictionary, and it means happy. What is a sour-faced old goat?"

Takahiro closed the book, looked at Kaede and asked, "What will it take for you to pay attention?"

Later Takahiro took Kaede outside, Toshiko was waiting in the outer office with Masako. Kaede raced over to Masako and held up two milk candy balls.

"Grandfather gave me a milk chew and told me if I didn't eat it, he will give me another one," an excited Kaede said.

"That is nice," A puzzled Masako said, she looked up at Takahiro.

"I am going to save them all, so he will give me the whole packet," Kaede announced looked around.

Takahiro was talking softly with Toshiko by the office door, his hand on the knob.

"Kaede told me what you said about the tea house and casino," Takahiro said.

"He caught me off guard, I couldn't tell him you run the biggest network of opium dens, brothels and casinos. Technically you do sell fun and games," Toshiko said.

"Yes, but he is more interested in Yosakoi than learning to control his emotions."

"What did you expect, your idea fun of fun is to hide piles of gold from Imperial Revenue. You need to make learning fun for him, or like Hiro, he will run away to join the Navy."

"Hiro worked hard to earn enough money to buy the bike."

"But only to get away from you. You of all people should know repeat a mistake only gets the same results."

The next day Emi arrived at the office, Lady Toshiko was waiting with Kaede.

"The Emperor thanks you for taking on the extra work," Toshiko said.

"No problem," Emi said.

"Kaede, class is noon until four, if you behave, then from four until six you will get dance and music lessons from me," Toshiko said, then left.

Emi took Kaede's hand and led him into the classroom. Inside Fukuhina was handing out tablets with a stylus clipped to them to Sora, Akiko, and Izanami who were wearing pink sailor uniforms and sitting at desks in the classroom. Yukata hung on a rack, a range of musical instruments on the side bench. Kaede sat at his desk his tablet and stylus on his desk. Toshiko puts down one the Yosakoi clackers on the bench and came over to Emi and Fukuhina.

Kaede raced to his desk, sat down and got out his large red tablet.

On September 1, 11566, Sora, and Akiko, aged six; Kaede and Izanami, aged three with Mako and Miko, aged eight, were flown north over the lake by Hiro in a large, 30-passenger, luxury helicopter, with Lady Toshiko as co-pilot. The Knights, Lady Yuki and Lady Galené sat with Kaede between them in the front with House guards in the back sitting with each girl.

They flew over two rows of large estates on the north side of the lake. Northern most point of the lake was an estate that took up four blocks, surrounded by a high wall made of granite, on the short with a large Japanese gate with a road heading north through the park, past Abel mall to the large campus.

"The large estate we are passing is mine," Toshiko said over the speaker. Kaede looked out the window at the massive mansion, it was a three-storey quadrangle house with red terra cotta roof. A large dock with a large power cruiser docks. The many gardens had many workers.

Mako and Miko waved and pointed at the large Japanese style estate on the east side with a three-story castle in the middle of Japanese gardens. It had yellow banners with the profile of a tiger's head growling.

They passed over the Founders Park. Divided by a road, the west side was larger, with a memorial of thirteen statues south of a large lake. On the east side was seven large black granite walls. North of that was Abel mall. The mall was massive, it covered nine city blocks with a two-story convention centre on the east, that which covered six city blocks.

North of the west side of Founder's park was a Transit Tower. On top was a helipad where the helicopter landed.

On the top floor, a white passenger van and an SUV were waiting with Hashimoto House Guards. Hiro loaded

Kaede and the girls in the back. Toshiko got in beside Hiro. Yuki and Galené got in the SUV with a squad of guards, the rest guarded the top floor and helicopter.

Hiro drove the van into the car elevator and went down to the bottom floor. The tower, owned by The Hashimoto Group, Hiro showed his identification at the booth, the gate was opened. They drove down Main Street to The Imperial Academy.

The campus was five separate schools the size of a large university that shared two aquatic centres, six small ovals, three large ovals, and six dormitories.

They drove through the gate. Hiro looked at the sign. First School and Second School was to the left, Administration and Third School straight ahead. Fourth School and the School for Exceptional Students to the right. Hiro turned left.

"Father, you said we going to the School for Exceptional Students," Kaede said as Hiro headed to the First School.

"Yes, but first we delivery Sora and Akiko to First School," Hiro replied.

"But you said we going to school with them," Kaede said.

Hiro parked turned off the engine. He turned to Kaede. "Son, it's the same campus, only a different group of buildings to you. You will see them every day on the main oval."

"Father, why are there different schools?" Kaede asked as Hiro got out of the car.

"First School is for six to eight-year-old púca, Second School is for nine to eleven-year-old púca, Third School is for twelve to fourteen-year-old púca, and Fourth School is for from fifteen to seventeen-year-old púca. The School for Exceptional Students is for Púca too smart to attend regular classes," Hiro replied, he went to close the door.

"Why?"

"Kaede, what have I told you about questioning adults?"

"Just asking," Kaede replied.

"There are rules, and even the Emperor must follow the rules," Hiro said.

"Why?"

"Honour. A good leader never asks anyone to do something they are not willing to do themselves, especially a starship captain," Hiro replied.

"Is that why Toshiko made Izanami push Sora and Akiko around in the stroller at my first birthday?" Kaede asked.

"Must you always bring that up?" Izanami asked, arms folded, with a sour face, looking out the window.

Sora and Akiko giggled. Hiro closed the car door and got Sora and Akiko out of the back of the vehicle.

"Girls, this is the first week of school. Now, this week, you will finish at 3pm, because it is only commencement week. This week, you get your books, uniform, load your tablet with your class program, class and sports schedule, you meet your teachers and class. I collect you here in three hours," Hiro said.

The girls nodded, behind Hiro, Toshiko stood with Lady Yuki.

Lady Yuki was twenty-one and had two bars on her collar. She adjusted her jacket to cover her 13mm handgun. She checked her belt. She plugged a wired earpiece into her cell phone on her belt, then put it into her ear, and attached the microphone to her collar. The whole time Kaede watched her.

Yuki came up and said, "Hello girls, I will be your escort today."

"Her first day," Toshiko said to Hiro. He smiled and nodded.

Lady Toshiko and Yuki lead Sora and Akiko to the school while Hiro drove back down the road, all the way around to The School for Exceptional Students.

"Must I have a Knight with me all the time?" Kaede asked as Hiro drove.

"Yes," Hiro replied.

"You don't."

"That is not true. I always have at least one Knight following me, I even have knights on my ship," Hiro said.

"What about when I pee?"

"Kaede, don't be embarrassing, you know they wait outside the toilet for you."

"You said I am a boy, but why am I the same as Izanami?" Kaede asked.

Mako and Miko giggled.

Hiro was shocked.

"Silly, a púca does not have a thing," Miko started.

"Boys grow that when they are twelve," Mako finished.

"Why?" Kaede asked.

"All Elves are born girls, and boys develop in their teens," a red-faced Hiro replied.

"What if I don't get mine?" Kaede asked.

"Then you will be a beautiful girl, like me," Izanami said.

Mako and Miko giggled.

"Son, do not worry about that. As a Hashimoto, you always have a place in the clan so long as you respect the clan elder and are a good law-abiding citizen," Hiro said.

"Why are there so many girls?" Kaede asked as Hiro parked.

"It is our genetics, son. Accept who you are, be hardworking and cheerful," Hiro said, getting out of the car.

"Why not change it," Kaede asked.

Hiro went around the vehicle and opened Kaede's door, looked him in the eye and said, "If your grandfather has not said it yet, you going to hear him say it often. Having power means using said power wisely and accepting responsibility for your actions. I am telling you, your life will be easier if you accept who you are and be yourself."

Lady Galené got out of the SUV parked beside them, bowed slightly and said, "I will take him from here, Prince Hiro."

"Thank you, Lady Galené," Hiro said, returning her bow.

"Where is your big gun?" Kaede asked.

"In a locked box in the back of the SUV," Yuki said.

"Why?" Kaede asked.

"Forgive him Lady Galené; he asks many questions when nervous," Hiro said to Galené.

"I do not," Kaede protested.

"Kaede do you want me to take you home now?" Hiro asked, staring at Kaede.

"It is all right Captain Hiro. Prince Kaede, in a closed area, a large assault rifle is not the best weapon to use, we are in school, and a stray bullet could hit a student," Galené said.

"What if they have machine guns?" Kaede asked.

"I will use magic to move fast and use my magic to create armour and a shield," Galené replied.

"Have you ever killed anyone?" Kaede asked.

"Kaede!" Hiro said.

"Not today; but it is only 8:55 am," Galené replied looking at the band on her wrist. "Now I need to get you in line to collect your uniform," Galené said as she took his hand.

Hiro coughed and held out Kaede's school bag. "You forget something," Hiro asked.

Izanami jumped out of the van and grabbed her school bag.

Galené blushed, took it from him, as their hands touched, Galené winked at Hiro, he shifted his feet and waved to Kaede, who was trying to pull out of her grip.

"Hey, hands off, he is mine," Izanami said trying to get between them.

Hiro sat in the vehicle and waited with Mako and Miko. Hashimoto Guards stood outside. Another van arrived and delivered a couple of Yoshiko house guards. Their tabard had a profile of a growling tiger on the front and back. They escorted Mako and Miko to class. The girls had the same black and orange striped school bags with the symbol of house Yoshiko on the side of the bag with their names in both Kanji and common.

"Are we stupid?" Sora asked Yuki.

"No," Yuki replied.

"Why aren't we in Kaede's class?" Akiko asked.

"Just do your best and do as the other instructors tell you," Toshiko replied.

"Yes, Lady Toshiko," Sora and Akiko both said.

"Good," Toshiko said. "Now girls, unlike Kaede and Izanami, you are in the regular school program, you have four stages of school to attend. Each is three years long."

"Toshiko, a pleasure to see you," Abel called ahead of them as she approached.

Abel wore a blue skirt suit, she walked up to and hugged Toshiko.

"Girls, Lady Abel, owns the school, she will show you to class today," Toshiko said.

Abel walked up to Sora and Akiko. "I heard you girls like football. I used to play for the Galaxy Girls, and I will be your football coach," Abel said.

"Lady Abel. The Emperor hopes he has not made things too difficult for you?" Toshiko asked.

"No, my brother will stop whining like a schoolgirl as soon as the team wins; once we have a few trophies on the shelf and he will be telling me the scholarship program was his idea," Abel replied.

CHAPTER 4

Progress

August 29, 11569. The Academy for Exceptional Students, Imperial City.

Kaede and Izanami, aged seven, were seated on the stage in the school hall. Takahiro was in the front row. The seat beside him was empty. Abel came on stage and went to the podium.

"Prince Kaede with a score of 125, the highest possible, has graduated all four stages of schooling in record time. As you know, each school program is usually three years. In the advanced learning class, we engage, nurture, and challenge each young genius to do their best. Congratulations Prince Kaede," Abel said.

Abel started to clap; Takahiro stood and clapped, followed by Mako, Miko, Sora and Akiko. Then Izanami, beside him, joined in. Soon he had a standing ovation. Abel waved him over and handed him his graduation certificate.

Kaede smiled as he saw Hiro enter the hall. Kaede held up his graduation certificate and raced off stage to Hiro, who picked him up. "You are getting heavier, son."

"Yes, Father."

Abel held up her hand; the hall went silent. "Izanami scored 124, the second-highest score. Both Prince Kaede and Miss Izanami broke the academic record; the previous highest test score was 123, set by me. Congratulations Miss Izanami," Abel said.

As they walked to the van, Hiro said, "Sorry I was late, I came from the Airport."

"We can bend, not break the laws of physics," Kaede said looking up at the stars.

"Son?" Hiro asked.

"We must bend them further," Kaede said.

"I warn you, son, don't push me, I came as fast as I could," Hiro said.

Kaede looked at Hiro. Smiled and said, "Sorry Father, something Lady Toshiko told me about how starships go faster than light."

"Oh yes," Hiro said, relaxing, "We bend time space around us, but that is hard to do inside the star's sphere of influence."

"Father, Navigation is a requirement of a starship captain?"

"Yes son, it is one of many subjects you need to master; before you can command a vessel, you need to be a starship pilot first, in fact, know how to operate every station on a ship," Hiro replied.

"But Izanami wants me to do computers with her," Kaede said.

"Do you want to be a starship captain?" Hiro asked.

"Yes, Father. I want to study navigation," Kaede said.

Hiro opened the door to the van, Kaede got in, and

Hiro strapped him in and looked Kaede in the eye and said, "Look her in the eye and say no."

"It is not easy, she is very loud."

Lady Yuki and Lady Galené stood not far behind them, they giggled.

"My father told me you have Football on Monday, Judo on Tuesday, Kendo on Wednesday, play Go on Thursday and then compete in the talent quest on Friday nights," Hiro said.

"Izanami and I are good at football. In Judo and Kendo, we mostly do stances and learn the names of the moves and equipment. I play at the Go Guild Hall, most of the time with the Yoshida twins, Mako and Miko. Their father General Yoshida is the Grandmaster. Izanami and I won the talent quest last year. Grandfather said I am a natural at dancing," Kaede said.

Hiro got in the driver's seat.

"I see no problem if you get enough sleep and behave," Hiro said.

"Yes, Father."

"I have some images from my last trip," Hiro said. "Father told me I could show them to you. But you must not tell anyone about them."

"Why?" Kaede asked.

"They are secret, and you need to learn to keep secrets."

Hiro took his bag from behind the front seat and removed his tablet. Unlike a regular tablet, it had a screen protector and a large, orange, rubber edge with an easy grip surface with a large round loop on a corner. He sat beside Kaede and showed him an image of an Exodus Ship in close orbit of a star.

"What is it?" Kaede asked in a shrill voice, leaning in.

"You tell me?" Hiro asked. "You should know which ship this it is."

"Is that a colony ship?" Kaede asked.

"Yes, it is called an Exodus Class Transport," Hiro said.

"Why is that photo a secret? I have seen pictures of them in the history books."

"Yes, and there is a fleet comprised of a hundred thousand Exodus Transport and are bringing the last Elves from Terra and Mars to the Empire. Now, the reason as to why this and other pictures are secret is that a good navigator could position the ship from the stars in the background."

"I read these ships carry not just Elves, but also animals. But how? Animals do not live a long time."

"That is why the Founders of the New Empire first built a faster-than-light fleet; they went ahead of to build and expand the seven colonies. They built a whole network of stations. Then the Imperial Fleet unloaded the animals and púca from the Exodus ships and brought them to the Empire. It is a slow process because our fast ships are much smaller than one Exodus ship."

"How do you put an animal in a space suit?"

"No," Hiro laughs, "They are caged and loaded into shuttles. Every Exodus ship has a docking bay, and each Exodus Fleet makes regular stops along its assigned course where there are space stations established ahead of them where they replenish their food and medical supplies, obtain replacement fuel rods, make repairs, transfer crew and cargo. The Imperial Fleet operates these space stations."

"Is that what you do?"

"No, The *Night Owl* is for secret missions. But most of them are mundane, such as taking pictures of ships."

"Secret Mission? Is that why you have a cloak?"

"How do you know about the cloaking device?"

"Mako and Miko told me."

"It is a secret, and we do not discuss secrets in public."

"We didn't. We were playing in the gardens in the sub-basement and grandfather says that is a secret place."

"Yes, it is," Hiro said, then changed the image, to a cruiser alongside an Exodus transport, "This is a Lightning Class IV Cruiser escorting an Exodus Class XX Transport to one of the docks."

"Why are the faster-than-light starships so small?"

"The cruiser is not that small; it is 120m long, but it is the largest faster-than-light ship we can build. Before you ask why, the bigger the ship, the more power it takes to move. Just like how a truck needs a bigger engine to do the same speed as a car. But we don't have bigger starship engines to make stronger ultra-wave bubbles. The Exodus Transport has the same Ultra Drive as a cruiser."

"What is an ultra-wave bubble?" Kaede asked, looking at the picture. The two ships side by side is like a pilot fish following a large shark.

"The field is a compressed gravity field created by superheating Negative Matter suspended in a vacuum inside superconducting coils; the field is so powerful that it can bend time. We move inside the bubble at a tenth of the speed of light. Inside the bubble, each second lasts for 349 seconds, thus in a day, my ship will have moved approximately one light year. End of each run we adjust course and use the fuel scoop."

"Have you been on an Exodus ship?"

"Yes, and one day I take you the Exodus ship museum. In the New-London Docks is an Exodus ship open to the public."

"Why do pirates attack them? Everyone calls Lady Fukuhina Ogre Killer."

"Not everyone is good. The Ogres think we are transporting gold and precious gems from hidden asteroid mines."

"Is that why you go out to? To Exodus ships safe?"

"Yes."

"Why is it a secret from the people. Surely, they will not tell the Titans, Black Giants, Jötunn or the Ogres?"

"Not everyone in the Empire is good, Kaede, and not all Ogres are pirates. Various pirate groups are known to have spies amongst the foreign traders. They monitor our information networks. Like I said they believe the Exodus Fleet is carrying gold and gems because the ships are so precious to us."

"Didn't you tell them the cargo is animals and púca?"

"Son, one day you will understand. They are judging value from their perspective. Our enemies do not understand us; all life, but especially our people, are far more valuable to us than gold or gems. We do prize gold and gems, just look at my father. But he values you more. We also value art, knowledge and hard work."

"Why not just give them the gold and gems? Then they will go away."

"It doesn't work like that. When you give someone something, they keep expecting it. It only makes them desire more, and when you run out, they will attack you wanting more. It is not charity to give. Real charity is to teach another to fend for themselves. We did that. We gave them a new home; we taught them to build better homes, farms, and factories and even starships. Then we gave them their freedom. That was over 5000 years ago, and even today they still expect us to keep providing for them. Learning to fend for yourself is a hard lesson, but the hardest lessons are the ones we remember for the longest time. Which is why you are expected to earn your title."

"Grandfather says he doesn't want me to be lazy like Abelard, but many ladies in court say he is very hard and vigorous."

"That is a topic for when you are older, but learn to stay away from those ladies. They will be the death of you."

"Have you ever killed someone?"

"Yes," Hiro said. He paused and looked at Kaede. "Son, ship to ship fights are rare; most pirates would rather flee as soon as they detect us."

"Why?"

"Their officers know they face execution. Most times the crew are held in cells and put them on a prison farm. We sometimes trade them to their homeworld in return for cattle. Pirates do not fear us, but they do fear retribution from the criminals who gave them the starship if they lose it."

"So, kill the criminals who supply the pirates."

"It is not that easy son; one day you understand. We don't want a super cunning enemy lean and hungry attacking us at random from unknown places. We want them to be fat and lazy, so we know who they are and where they hide."

"Why?"

"So, I can come home to you instead of doing long-range patrols hunting for them."

"Father, can I go do navigation at university?"

"What did my father say?"

"I haven't asked him yet."

"We ask him together when we sit to Third Meal."

Kaede saw Izanami escort to a car beside them by Lady Toshiko. As they drove off. He smiled and waved to Izanami. She smiled and waved to him.

August 28, 11570. Kaede was backstage of the meeting hall on the Imperial University campus. He peeked out and saw Takahiro in the front row with an empty seat beside him.

"My Emperor, Lord and Ladies, ladies and gentlemen, I present to you, the youngest graduate of the Imperial University, Prince Kaede," Abel said.

The audience clapped, and Takahiro stood to applaud when Kaede came on stage.

"One year ago, aged seven Prince Kaede, started a three-year degree in Navigation, which he completed in a year. During his studies, he designed a high-speed ultra-wide-angle digital telescope to map the night sky, called Sky Scan. The Imperial Fleet will build the new telescope on the top of New-Roman-Kosh mountain. At the Imperial Observatory, he conducted a detailed study of Proxima Alcyone Prime, with an ultra-wave detector. Proxima Alcyone Prime was the original destination of the First Exploration Fleet, believing it had many planets. Instead, they discovered Proxima

Alcyone Prime was a twin star system generating a very high gravity field with many asteroid belts and clouds. Prince Kaede conducted a detailed study of the system, calculated orbits and confirmed that several large asteroid fields appear as planets from a distance. He then created a new method to distinguish dense asteroid fields from planets using area sampling. His scans support the astrological society's theory that the fields are failed planets, broken up by the high gravity of the twin stars," Abel said. She stopped reading her notes and looked at the audience.

Many professors in the first row nodded and murmured in agreement, then Abel continued, "Thus, a degree in Astronomy and Astronavigation is awarded to Prince Kaede with honours. Also, along with his degree, Kaede is awarded a lifetime membership of the Imperial Astrological Society. I present to him this sextant, a replica of the one used by the First Exploration Fleet," Abel said.

As he accepted his degree and the sextant, the audience stood and applauded. After that, Kaede posed for pictures with Abel, then Takahiro, and then professors. Many came to congratulate him.

After the ceremony, they went to the Palace Banquet Hall, one of seven wings around the base of the Imperial Place for a meal in his honour. It was three storeys high, with the main table in the middle of the first floor. The second and third floors were only balconies, but each was wide enough to fit a table for eight.

Kaede sat beside Emperor Takahiro, while Sora, Akiko, Mako, Miko and Izanami sat at a table at the back with other púca. An empty chair was beside him.

Hiro arrived late, missing the dessert. He took Kaede

to the outside balcony and kept the door open while two Knights stood at the door on guard. He sat and held his arms out. Kaede took a few slow steps, then raced over, and climbed on his lap.

"I am sorry I am late, you know a captain's duty is to his ship, and many depend on us to protect them. To return to port a ship must either complete its mission or be damaged," Hiro said.

"Yes, Father."

"This time my ship had to go a long way. Each patrol usually enables me to return in time for your birthday. But missions usually have set goals to complete, not a fixed time," Hiro said.

"When can I see your ship?"

"I need clearance to bring you aboard."

"I have been in space before."

"You remember that?"

" You took me in a suborbital, I was inside a púca capsule, I saw the stars out of the window, and you sat beside me," Kaede replied.

"Is this your wish?" Hiro asked.

"I wish to build a balloon and race Izanami around the world, but she is still at university," Kaede said.

"Tell the truth son. I know you already asked my father and he said no," Hiro said.

"Yes, Father. Sorry, Father, he caught me climbing down the Central Shaft," Kaede said.

"Son, what were you thinking? You know that is dangerous."

"I wanted to see the Dragons."

"You know that is forbidden," Hiro said.

"Each ladder inside the shaft is only one storey, each had a safety line, and there is a landing with safety rails. They are not near any fuse boxes, power junctions and it is easy to avoid the cables and pipes," Kaede said.

"Once when I was nine, I wanted a unicorn. My father said no, so, I hid in the crawl space under my room for a week. Instead of coming in or sending the guards in after me, my father sat in my room with a plate of Uirō," Hiro said.

"What happened?" Kaede asked.

"I came out, he finished eating the Uirō; then he spanked me. A year later he had the stables built by the maze garden, and we now have a herd of Miniature Unicorns, and as a boy, I had to clean out the stables," Hiro replied.

"Then what happened?" Kaede asked.

"I learned my lesson. Son, you need to obey your elders and learn that you cannot have everything. Nothing is free in life son, you have to earn them."

"Are you going to spank me?" Kaede asked.

"Not this time, I think my father spanked you for the both of us," he replied.

"He said next time he will take away one of my projects," Kaede said.

"Well, you better learn to behave. I need to talk to my father. Despite your disobedience, I am proud of your hard work and dedication. I promise I'll find out about taking you up to see the ship, but what is your next project?" Hiro asked.

"A captain needs to know a little about everything on his ship from engineering, magic, computers to weapons, not just piloting and navigation so I will do a course on computers and another in general engineering," Kaede said.

"Son, a captain, also needs to be a good leader and a role model to his crew," Hiro said.

Takahiro came to the balcony and sent Kaede away. Kaede ran to Izanami and crawled under a table with her. "I need your help," Kaede told her.

"To do what?"

"To close a vent behind me, then wait for my return and open it for me," Kaede said. He pulled open the vent located at the base of the wall. The air duct went down and under the floor. Kaede jumped in, crouched, and crawled inside the cross-shaft that ended at the air duct near the balcony door where his father and grandfather were talking.

When he got near the vent in the wall beside the balcony, he saw the Knights' polished black boots. He settled to listen.

"Father, I double checked, there are no signals from the location beacon, no other ships been in the area. I was unable to find any trace of that ship," Hiro said.

"But they cannot go FTL, and they leave a massive Ion Trail," Takahiro said.

"Every ship is built to last for centuries; they can travel for nearly four-hundred years before all their fuel rods are exhausted. Once the fleet is underway, starships are unable to communicate because of the temporal distortion field. The ship likely changed course years ago," Hiro said.

"Those ships are not just carrying a few families, sheep, cattle and hogs. They have a genetic database and a uterine replicator," Takahiro said.

"You told me that before, and you said we could replace it."

"Yes, but what I didn't say before is every ship carried part of our entire database of knowledge. That ship also had a copy of the master directory and every file's checksums," Takahiro said.

"The Fleet has delivered to the Blood-Witches the other six uterine replicators and to Technical Support the entire database already," Hiro said. "Father if our enemies have it, our spies will locate it."

"Yes, I will speak to Yaotl about that," Takahiro said. He stepped closer. "I am worried Dain may exploit the loss."

"What will do you do, Father?" Hiro asked.

"Only a few in the Senate know of the disappearance, but I must inform the rest. There will be an inquiry, but we lost ships before. Without evidence, it will go down as lost with cause unknown. They need to know the Fleet did all they could have done to find them. I can hear Dain on the talk shows whining about them lost and abandoned," Takahiro said.

"They will not be happy you did not tell them sooner," Hiro said.

"Those who need to know already know," Takahiro said. "Now, about Kaede hang gliding off the palace roof?"

"I told him if he repeats it you will spank him twice as hard for twice as long and then take away one of his wishes," Hiro said.

"Good. Kaede reminds me of you. The palace is full of temptations for púca to go exploring and playing, so keep a close eye on him," Takahiro said.

"You know he wants to be a starship captain; I told him

he needs to learn to fly. It might help if I show him my ship, only for a day. It would best if I take him soon, while the work crews are busy running diagnostics, so he knows what is involved in running a starship," Hiro said.

"That will be good for him. I told him no more flying, and he needs to be sixteen because of the danger of other púca trying to be the youngest to flying," Takahiro said.

"Yet you let him have an electric racing kart," Hiro said.

"He bought two with the gold he is making on his Sky Scan Telescope. He has a multi-million gold contract with Hashimoto Defence. We going to incorporate Sky Scan and his ultra-wave analysis program into ground stations, satellites, every space station, and every starship. He and Izanami can race them around the car park, the Knights will keep an eye on them, and they have been speed limited. I let him buy a car, and he chose a Hashimoto Off Road. I told him Lady Yuki must drive it for him until he is sixteen," Takahiro said.

"I remember my first car, a Hashimoto Two Door and I thought it was fast as the wind until Abel flew past as if I was standing still," Hiro said. "Speaking of Abel; when I was over at Imperial Intelligence, I heard you have them investigating Dain Research."

"Dain Medical is working on something seemingly significant by how much it costs them. It could be a distraction; he might be funnelling those funds into his high-energy research project. Whoever develops a more powerful fusion reactor, therefore producing larger fields, will make a huge fortune. He knows if I lose the reactor contract with the fleet, it brings him close to taking my crown," Takahiro said.

"Why not just ask Abel? She knows covert research is illegal. Do you think he is developing weapons of mass destruction?"

"Patya is the only one licenced to produce nuclear warheads, but Hashimoto Defence does manufacture the coils for EMP warheads. The Inquisition will make sure Dain doesn't violate the arms limits in the Dragon Treaty," Takahiro said.

"Are you using the fact Patya is head of the Inquisition to have him spy on Dain for you?" Hiro asked.

"Dain has banned Abel and Abelard, as well as most of his personal staff, from his medical research centre. That it is suspicious and Patya and Yaotl agreed with me," Takahiro replied.

"I know the focus in the past was on space travel. Thus, we have serious gaps in levels of technology in other fields. You should encourage, not shut down, research to avoid situations like the current fuel crisis in the future," Hiro said.

"Magic, terraforming and space travel until recently was the focus of all research. But some advanced technology is not efficient; take the flying car, for instance. A helicopter is cheaper and is more fuel-efficient," Takahiro replied.

"I agree with that. A flying car is dangerous. So many are unable to drive without crashing, I would hate to have them flying, especially all those who run out of fuel," Hiro said.

"That is why I shut down the flying car program years ago. Dain took it personally. He is brilliant, but not always forward-thinking. Dain did not understand the dangers and inefficiency of the flying he proposed. It used far more fuel than an ordinary car does, with increased difficulty, with a dramatic increase in risk. It was only able to carry two passengers, and it had a smaller range than a helicopter. He is aware of the danger in them falling out of the sky, but he thinks he is so exceptional, that he is immune from any disaster," Takahiro said.

"Can you do that?" Hiro asked.

"What can go wrong, will," Takahiro said. "The Senate under the charter has the authority to ban dangerous technology. If Dain can find a way to counter the danger, he can develop a flying car. But what he developed was a device to makes a car into a plane. It was a frame with wings, a tail and a small push propeller engine on the back; it was an attachment to go on existing cars."

"Speaking of flying, I might get Kaede a flight simulator program. A few crashes might be a good lesson," Hiro said.

"Just be clear to him if he can wait until sixteen to fly, you can take him with you to the base to use the flight training simulators," Takahiro said.

"He will like that; he likes flying," Hiro said.

"Kaede is obsessed with flying. First, it was trying to get the Dragons to take him flying, then tying balloons to a chair; he even attempted to use Toshiko's witch's broom, and last month he made a hang glider in the workshop. If he tries one more time to fly before sixteen, I will punish him severely," Takahiro said.

"Maybe I should get him a flight simulation booth," Hiro said.

Takahiro smiled and left.

Kaede scurried under the floor back to the panel and tapped on it many times. Izanami was slow to open it.

"What took you so long?" Kaede asked.

"Look at how dusty you are," Izanami said.

"Go distract my father," Kaede said.

"How?"

"Tell him we are going to dance Yosakoi and ask for some paper umbrellas for you, Sora, Akiko, Mako and Miko," Kaede said.

"We are not ready to perform," Izanami said.

"Yes, we are," Kaede said. He peeked out from under the tablecloth, then headed for the door to the place. He ran straight past Lady Toshiko, but she grabbed him.

"Look at you," Toshiko said. "You need a bath."

"But—"

She picked him and carried him off to the central shaft and up to the residence.

Toshiko later returned to the ballroom with Kaede in a colourful Yukata, with traditional socks, and shoes. The girls with paper umbrellas waited on stage in a line. She went to Hiro and said, "My mistake, he told me he was going to perform Yosakoi, so I assumed the others would also get dressed up," Takahiro said.

"No harm done, he looks cute," Hiro said.

Kaede sang on the stage with Sora, Akiko, Izanami, Mako and Miko behind him in a line. They danced with naruko. Freya recorded them on her phone. When the dance finished, everyone clapped and cheered.

Lady Yuki, clapping, came to them, and Kaede bowed to her. "Sensei, how did we do?" he asked.

"Wonderful," Yuki replied with a big smile.

CHAPTER 5
CHAMPION

August 29, 11570. Imperial City Airport.

Hiro, Kaede and Lady Toshiko, were flown by helicopter to the VIP terminal at the Imperial Airport. In the departure lounge, they changed into spacesuits and went downstairs to a six-wheel open buggy that took them to the sixth runway.

On the runway, a light grey suborbital, much like Takahiro's suborbital, except it had a docking cradle, holding a 20-metre shuttle, on its back. Ground crew with blowers and small six-wheel electric street sweepers cleared the runway. The craft was already in the launch position.

Two sets of stairs stood by the craft, one large set to the shuttle's airlock, and another to the airlock in the front of the suborbital. The shuttle, unlike the suborbital, had a visible cockpit. Another buggy stopped near the stairs at the front, and a pilot and co-pilot boarded the suborbital.

Kaede tried to walk up the stairs in his space suit. He found it hard walking up the stairs in the suit, each step was like lifting a bag of bricks. They didn't have air tanks or helmets on. Kaede stopped and looked up and saw his father. He moved just as slow in the heavy suit. Toshiko caught up with him.

"Are you all right Kaede?" Toshiko asked.

"It is too hard," Kaede replied.

"I'll carry him," Toshiko offered.

"I got you, son," Hiro said as he took two steps back. Hiro reached down and lifted Kaede and carried him up to the airlock on the side of the shuttle. Where he put Kaede down, opened a panel beside the door and keyed a code into the concealed keypad. The door popped open.

"Can I sit in the front?" Kaede pleaded as Hiro opened the door.

Hiro looked at Toshiko, she nodded, "Sure son," Hiro replied.

Hiro lifted Kaede and carried him to the co-pilot's seat while Lady Toshiko took the helmets and air tanks from the ground crew.

"Remember son, you may look, but don't touch," Hiro said as Lady Toshiko secured the hatch. Kaede smiled and nodded.

Toshiko attached the air tank to Kaede's suit, attached his helmet and tested it while Hiro put on his air tank and helmet.

Hiro sat in the pilot's seat and took out the checklist. As he performed the systems checks, he spoke to the suborbital crew and control tower.

Toshiko put on her helmet, and air tank then checked Kaede's harness and pulled it tight.

"Hiro, I know normally you prefer not to use the Lilith-Toshiko Time & Gravity Stabiliser during launch, but I hope you are not going to expose him to three gravities?" Toshiko asked.

"I thought you and Lilith invented magic?" Kaede asked.

"We did, but she left me designs for a spacecraft, and I finished it with help from Emperor Takahiro," Toshiko replied, then looked to Hiro, "Well?"

"Of course not. But in orbit, I will turn it off," Hiro replied pressing a button on the console, he then checked the status screen on the left.

"Why?" Toshiko asked while looking at the same screen as Hiro.

"While my ship is being serviced, it has no gravity," Hiro replied as he checked the screens on the control panel. Hiro looked at Kaede, "Lady Toshiko, we going to orbit a couple of times in zero gravity, if Kaede panics in zero gravity, I will have the suborbital raise the transfer tube and have you take Kaede back, I will deliver the supplies in the cargo hold."

"Go back?" Kaede asked with a high-pitched voice, "I have been in orbit before."

"You remember?" Hiro asked.

"Of course, it was just like swimming," Kaede replied.

"Hiro, he cannot walk properly in his suit, what if something goes wrong?" Toshiko said.

Hiro turned to Toshiko and smiled, "I know these new suits are heavier, but they block far more radiation," Hiro said.

"So, did your father make you test the new suits in return for bringing your son into space?" Toshiko asked.

"We only made the undergarments and lining of the suit, everything else is Niemi Industries," Hiro replied.

"Why do I have to wear a nappy?" Kaede asked.

"We all do," Toshiko replied.

"Are you wearing a nappy father?" Kaede asked.

"Yes," Hiro replied as he watched the results of the system's self-check.

"Why?" Kaede asked.

"Everyone in a space suit is," Toshiko replied.

"At least this one is comfortable," Kaede said.

"It should be, it took us months of testing on you to get a nappy you could wear, but by then you were toilet trained," Toshiko said.

"Nappy is for babies. I could walk and talk. Not a baby," Kaede said with a firm nod.

"Hiro, why are wearing Kaede's diapers?" Toshiko asked.

"You know my Father, had the material for a couple of years' worth of diapers purchased. They have mostly been used in Hashimoto House," Hiro said.

"Kaede helped develop them, maybe you should market them as Kaede Diapers," Toshiko said.

"I will when we get back," Hiro said.

"Will I get paid?" Kaede asked.

"Yes," Hiro said.

The suborbital's pilot said, "Ten minutes to launch."

A countdown clock appeared on the screen in the middle of the bank of three screens on the control console in front of Hiro. Outside the craft, the stairs and the ground crew withdrew. The magnetic rail was activated, and the cradle hovered on the kilometre-long magnetic rail.

Kaede as the seats folded back, looked at Hiro, he was calm, arms crossed. Kaede listened to the countdown. Then

Crisis

came the roar of the massive jets under the Suborbital's wings. The craft didn't shack as the suborbital raced down the runway. The craft at first slowly rose, then it nosed up and rose above the city. In a short time, they were high over the southern coast.

On the roof was a screen, it displayed the forward view. Kaede watched as the land disappeared as they flew out over the sea. Then as the craft nosed up to near vertical, they saw the clouds. The craft's jets stopped, as all four rockets fired. Soon there was a sonic boom, as the craft rose fast. Kaede exclaimed as the sky went from blue to black.

The suborbital levelled out and cut its rockets. They were in orbit. Hiro pressed a button on the panel beside him and the seats adjusted to a relaxed position. Hiro reached forward and turned the gravity off, then unclicked his hardness and rose from his seat. He floated over to Kaede and grabbed his seat, reached down and pressed the release on his harness, then pulled him up and let him. Go, Kaede smiled and looked down.

"Father, why cannot shuttles fly into space on their own?" Kaede asked as Hiro pushed off the seat over to the side window.

They floated over the window. Hiro looked down, Kaede was excited and looked out the window.

"Shuttles use a gravity-ion drive, and they don't work as good as rockets in an atmosphere," Hiro replied.

"But Grandfather keeps saying how he needs long-range shuttles that fly to and from on their own."

"Yes, he does."

"Why?"

"Suborbitals use most of the fuel we obtain from

methane, but first we need a better engine for shuttles and one that doesn't use liquid fuel."

"Why doesn't he make one?"

"Many have tried to make a shuttle engine that didn't use liquid fuel and is as powerful than the current peroxide thrusters in an atmosphere, but to date, none have succeeded."

Hiro looked over to Toshiko, who remained in her seat.

While they orbited on the back of the suborbital, Kaede was in awe of the view. They orbited past satellites, then saw another suborbital, carrying a shuttle on its back. It fired its nose rockets, then nosed up. At first, the fall was slow, but soon it was blazing its way towards the ground. Kaede silently watched in amazement, then as it disappeared, he faced Hiro's seat and pushed the wall with his feet. Hiro gasped and turned.

"Kaede!" Hiro exclaimed.

"Wee," Kaede giggled as he floated over.

Toshiko was in the pilot's seat, she stood and saw Kaede. She grabbed him.

"Can you show me the re-entry of the other ship?" Kaede asked.

Toshiko sat Kaede down, then sat in the pilot's seat and worked the controls. "Yes,", she replied as she tapped the view icon on right screen, soon the re-entry appeared on the right screen.

"This is from the nose camera of the suborbital," Toshiko said.

Kaede was excited as he watched the other suborbital blaze towards the ground, then it fired its forward rockets and manoeuvring thrusters embedded around its main body, it flew to the and landed on the long runway in New Ghana.

"Awesome!" Kaede said.

After a few orbits, the suborbital disconnected the shuttle and Hiro piloted the shuttle. They rose, the gravity was still off. When away from the suborbital, Hiro inverted the craft and slowly flew forward. Hiro tapped the view on the rights screen.

"Look," Hiro said, pointing to the screen to his right on the console. Kaede saw the suborbital as the moved away from it, another shuttle was approaching it from behind. The shuttle was above and descended slowly towards the suborbital.

"What is the other shuttle doing?" Kaede asked.

"The Fleet plans each launch to space is timed, so each suborbital will carry a shuttle up, then return with another, to make the most efficient use of fuel," Hiro replied.

"Speaking of the Fleet. They frown on giving its officers going on joy flights and civilian passengers. What did you tell the Admiral about your son?" Toshiko asked.

"Nothing. We're on a civilian flight. The shuttle and the suborbital belong to the Clan, we are on a supply run," Hiro said.

"What about the Night Owl?" Toshiko asked.

"It is currently docked at one of our docks and while not on active duty is the property of The Hashimoto Clan," Hiro replied.

"What is a supply run?" Kaede asked.

"We are carrying fresh fruit, MAGs, and electronics components," Hiro said.

"MAG?" Toshiko asked.

"The Maximum Absorption Garment," Hiro replied.

"What is that?" Kaede asked, looking puzzled.

"The padded underpants," Hiro replied.

"Why don't you call it a diaper?" Kaede asked.

"Adults don't wear diapers," Hiro said.

"But you're wearing one now," Kaede said.

"I am wearing a MAG, not a diaper," Hiro said.

"Adults are so confusing," Kaede said.

Hiro piloted the shuttle to one of the many space docks that were in high orbit around the planet. Kaede sat beside Hiro looking in awe. Hiro past close enough to see satellites, switching views on the external monitor for Kaede.

It was not long before they saw the space station come into view. Kaede stared at the one-kilometre-diameter space station as they approached.

Kaede was confused, when near, Hiro strapped him in. Toshiko strapped in, then himself. He took the controls, and the shuttle flipped, then performed a serious of burns, then as the shuttle was almost past the station, it turned and performed a slow orbit of the station.

"I am impressed, Captain," Toshiko said.

"Thanks," Hiro said, then turned to Kaede, he was staring at the space station.

The main body of the space station was hexagonal with a flat-topped dome on the top and bottom with six one-kilometre long docking arms around the middle of the main body. Each arm was a U-shaped frame with tunnels in both sides with adjustable transfer tunnels attached to spaced out airlocked. On the top, bottom, the sides of the hexagonal body, on the sides and ends of the docking arms was the symbol of House Hashimoto.

Inside each dock was a 120-metre-long starship nose facing the station. Each ship had no name on the exterior hull. Nothing distinguished the ships from each other. On the side of each dock was a number. Each dock was mostly a frame with a series of hydraulic adjusted cradles on rails, on the bottom so it could fit a range of different-sized and shaped ships.

"Which is your ship?" Kaede asked.

"Arm three."

Kaede looked out, each arm had the number on its side, end, and over the top.

"They all look the same."

"Yes. The *Night Owl* is only one of a hundred Phantom Class Scouts, and all of them belong to the clan. You tell a ship apart by its interstellar identification transponder."

"Wow."

They passed over the top of ships in each arm. All were 120 metres long, 35 metres wide and 30 metres high. All the ships same dabble grey coat with an assortment of hatches and exhaust ports. The shuttle approached the ship in arm three from the rear.

"It is huge! Is your ship bigger or smaller than the Lightning Class cruiser?"

"They are the same size, they have the same basic hull design, but the scout has two dishes in its nose, is painted with darker shades of grey and the exhaust ports have a dark trim."

"Why?"

"The scout is low visibility and has fewer weapons. It was built to be hard to detect, with a very small heat signature. It is a scout, not a warship."

"Because of the cloaking device?"

"Yes. Inside the hull is the distortion field generator, when on it makes it hard to see, part of the system are field emitters around all exhaust ports to disperse the heat and ion trail."

The shuttle came to a stop, and the largest hatch situated in the top-rear of the *Night Owl's* hull, split in the middle, popped up and slid apart. Then the shuttle was brought inside by a gravity beam from inside the landing bay and deposited onto a cradle. The beam turned off, as the outer hatch closed and sealed.

"Father, why don't we land craft like this?" Kaede asked.

"I don't know. I will ask my Father about it later," Hiro replied.

"It would make landing easier on the tower," Toshiko remarked.

"I agree," Hiro said with a nod.

Kaede looked around, light passed over the ship, but then nothing happened.

"Why are we waiting?" Kaede asked.

"They are pressurising the bay, checking the hull seal and scanning the shuttle before opening the inner doors."

The inner doors opened, and a six-wheel open buggy entered. Two crew got out and attached the cradle to the buggy, and then hauled them into the hangar.

The shuttle was towed in, then the crew opened the hatch.

"Captain on deck," an officer called out, then she saluted Hiro as he left the shuttle. Hiro had a black armband with five vertical gold bars on the left sleeve of his spacesuit, and his identification card was in a clear pocket on the chest.

The armband on Kaede's spacesuit was black with the word 'Visitor' in orange letters, with his identification card also in a clear pocket on the chest of his suit.

Lady Toshiko also wore a spacesuit, and the armband on her sleeve had a platinum star. She followed Kaede out.

Hiro and Toshiko turned off one another's air tanks and removed their helmets. Hiro then turned off Kaede's air, removed his helmet and carried it for him.

Hiro took Kaede on a tour of the ship, and the whole time Kaede was wide-eyed and interested. They went from the hangar to the main hall, where he showed Kaede the medical centre, the ready room, the captain's office, then entered the bridge. After showing Kaede the helm, he took him upstairs to the living quarters, crew dining and recreation room.

All over the ship, some wall panels had been removed by the crew. Inspection cameras on cables snaked their way down pipes, and other had consoles opened with test equipment attached to the electronics inside.

They went down the spiral stairs two decks, then to the rear. Outside the bulkhead door to engineering, Hiro made Kaede outside wait with Toshiko while he went inside and then came out after a few minutes. He took them to the control room. Kaede went to the window to look. In the middle of the section was a small fission reactor in front of the large spherical fusion reactor with many pipes.

"Are they on?" Kaede asked.

"No, they are both off. The crew have removed the fuel rods from the fission reactor," Hiro said.

An engineer entered, wearing a Technical Support uniform with five stripes on her sleeve.

Hiro turned to face her. "This is my son Prince Kaede. Son, this is my chief engineer. When the ship is in a dock, she is in charge. It is her job to make every system is inspected and passes inspection."

"How goes your tour, Captain?" the chief asked.

"Good, Chief," Hiro replied.

"Captain, the reactor rods are at reprocessing. The inspection team has passed engine one, and I have a repair team working on engine two," the chief said.

"What is the problem with it?"

"I didn't like the results of a test on one of the magnetic accelerator rings, so I am having it replaced."

"Speaking of results, Viktor didn't like the quality of photos from our last mission, so have the auto-focus on the primary sensor pod checked," Hiro said.

"I will assign a work team to that soon. We may have a problem with the main computer."

"Oh?"

"I called HQ and filed a request to have someone come and figure out what is wrong with the main board," the chief said.

"What is the problem?"

"We do not know; the system is 0.001 percent slower

than it should be. Three teams have checked, and they have not been unable to find a reason."

"Did they swap processors with the secondary system?"

"That was the first thing we tried."

"What was the result?"

"We run tests on the primary and secondary systems. The primary board was still slower," the chief said. "I had the crew take the mainboard, with its original eight processors, to the repair bay in the space station. They couldn't find the cause, so I put in a request. But it is a low priority, so could be weeks before we get an answer."

"Is it within specification?" Hiro asked.

"Borderline, on a long mission, you going to notice."

"Yes, we cannot afford calculations taking longer every day, we going to lose hours repositioning to catch up to the fleet."

"Did they check the secondary data storage unit for file fragmentation?" Kaede asked.

"Kaede, I told you to listen and not talk when adults are talking; you can ask questions after I am done speaking with the chief," Hiro replied.

"Yes, but in a quantum computer, file defragmentation of secondary storage is not automatic, and while negligible, it can the cause of performance reduction," Kaede said.

"It couldn't hurt to check," the chief said.

"I agree. Go ahead and check if that is the cause," Hiro said.

The chief saluted and left. Hiro turned to Kaede and knelt before him. "I told you to behave."

"If I said nothing the ship could be in dock longer," Kaede said.

"True, but if the computer had a fault, then it needed to be replaced," Hiro said.

"Yes, but a hardware test does not check for data fragmentation in the file system. The assumption is the file system was first defragmented," Kaede said.

"What makes you sure speed reduction isn't due to a faulty component?" Hiro asked.

"It ran slow when connected to the computer, but fast in the space station, so I assumed the secondary storage unit was not connected the second time," Kaede replied.

"We shall find out soon," Hiro said, taking Kaede by the hand and moving on.

"Why do you take photos of other ships?" Kaede asked.

"Hull inspection. Experts will examine the photos to help determine if a Lonsdaleite coat is more effective than the traditional armoured outer hull with the inner hull made up of five kinds of radiation shields."

"Why?"

"No deflector system is perfect."

"Why do you have an inner hull?"

"Under the outer hull are plasma conduits to the engines, two ram scoops to the fuel tanks and various field generators," Hiro said.

They entered the top weapons room. Kaede looked in the small room. There was an ammunition rack with a chain feed against the wall that went into the hull; a computer console facing it, it was off; a large hook and a locker by the door.

"Where is the gun?"

"Above us."

"Where is that?" Kaede asked pointing to the rack.

"That is the ammunition feed, a drum with 500 projectiles inside would be on the rack, the drum ejects a 10cm round into the feed, which then carries it up into the chamber."

"No missiles?"

"No. We have three railguns. One on top, one on the bottom left and the third on the bottom right, with four anti-missile guns, one under the nose, one on each side of the ship and another to the rear under the engines."

"Why don't they break off in flight?"

"The whole ship is protected by the main deflector in front of the ship and a shield around the whole ship, as well as the gravity and time stabilising field. In theory, you could stand on the outer hull even when the ultra-drive is engaged, and the is ship moving faster than light, if not for the shields needed to prevent impact."

"Why is there a weapons console here? I thought the weapons officer was on the bridge?" Kaede asked as he pointed to the console that had two screens, keyboard, and a joystick.

"The Chief Weapons Officer can control all Weapon Systems, but normally the Chief would assign targets to each gunner and allow them to operate independently. Each station is crewed full-time, and it takes two to move an ammunition drum and connect it to the magazine feed," Hiro replied taking Kaede's hand.

Hiro took Kaede back upstairs to the living quarters, to the crew recreation room where a few off-duty crew relaxed, watching a movie on a wall-screen. They paused the movie and stood as Hiro and Kaede entered the room. Toshiko arrived with a trolley with three trays. On each was six mounds of different mashed food, with a spoon and juice in a squeeze pack.

"Prince Kaede, this is a typical meal served to crew. Enjoy it," Toshiko said.

Kaede looked at it, sat at the table, then started eating with Toshiko.

"At ease, I am showing my son around," Hiro said to the crew, then he sat opposite Kaede. "Son, this is where off-duty crew come to eat, relax and watch a movie from the ship's video library on the screen."

"Thinking of entering the service?" one of the crew asked.

"Yes Miss," Kaede replied.

"Don't join because you have to, join because you want to," she said.

"I want to be a starship captain like Father," Kaede said.

"Then you need to study hard because only the best graduates from the Fleet Academy become bridge officers," she said.

Hiro had a meal with Kaede and Toshiko. Afterwards, in the hall, Kaede asked, "Father, why are all the rooms so small when the ship is so big?"

"The ship has many systems, not just weapons; also, we need to store fuel, food, waste, and medical supplies," Hiro replied.

"Why are most of the crew not wearing a spacesuit?"

"Only in some areas of the ship do the crew need to

wear a suit; for example, engineering and the hangar. The rest store their spacesuits in lockers," Hiro replied.

"Why?"

"To work at our best. See son, we know the risks and accept them; we are aboard a ship for months, and that is too long to be inside a spacesuit full-time," Hiro said.

As they headed to the hangar, Hiro thanked the crew.

The chief came up to Kaede and said, "It was fragmentation. You have my thanks, your Imperial Highness."

"You are welcome ma'am," Kaede said.

"Chief, I am not an officer," the chief replied.

"Thanks, Chief, keep up the good work, and that will be all," Hiro said.

"Aye Captain, enjoy your leave," the chief said. She saluted Hiro, and he returned the salute. It was a proper salute; he stood to attention, thumped his chest with his left hand, in a fist, then straightened his arm out, then dropped it to his side.

She smiled at him as she left.

Hiro looked down the see Kaede salute. He looked tired, so Hiro picked him up and carried him to the shuttle.

"Let me get you home before grandfather calls to see where we are."

"I will be getting my black belt soon."

Hiro placed Kaede's helmet on him, and asked, "Do you want me to stay for that?"

"I was hoping you can at least help me prepare?"

"I can help you, but I cannot delay my ship's departure."

Kaede sat beside Hiro in the shuttle with Lady Toshiko in the back. A six-wheeled kart towed the shuttle into the outer hangar. The vehicle left, and a turntable turned them around as the Inner Hangar doors were closed, then sealed.

They waited inside the shutter as outside the atmosphere was evacuated. The exterior doors were unsealed, raised, then slid apart. The gravity beam operated by an officer in the hangar's control room lifted them into space.

Hiro piloted the shuttle back to Imperial City where a pilot waited at the airport to take it back to the *Night Owl*.

At 7 pm, Kaede had Third Meal with Hiro and Takahiro in the dining room, on the top floor of the Emperor's residence. After the meal, a Knight took Kaede down the elevator, to his room, beside Hiro's room, on the level below the Emperor's residence. Takahiro and Hiro went into the sitting room beside the dining room; Takahiro closed the door said, "He saved the empire a few million gold notes today."

"I didn't want to encourage him to interrupt, but I'll let him know tomorrow what a good thing he did pointing out the possibility the problem was file fragmentation," Hiro said.

"He is going for his black belt in Judo soon. If he is successful, he will be the youngest black belt."

"I am worried he is trying to overachieve to please me."

"I have Lady Cherise monitoring him for any signs of exhaustion. He even beat Kenta once at Go; one day he might be Grandmaster."

"My advice to him, do not play like you."

"What did you say, son?" Takahiro leant over to Hiro.

Crisis

"I said I hope my son beats Kenta," Hiro said, he got up and poured two Sake into flat saucers. "Father, I almost forget, Kaede asked the oddest thing, maybe it is nothing, but he wondered why we don't use gravity beams on ground ports. I'd like to have some engineers to do a cost-benefit analysis. Even if landing on building like the Palace."

"In your name?" Takahiro asked as Hiro handed him a Sake.

"No, it is Kaede's idea."

"For a start, the problem could be an issue of power. Even just launching the ships will need more reactors to power the beams. Each reactor will need tankers to supply them fuel and transport the waste plasma. I think it will create a loop that may never close."

"What about emergency supply pods or landing in difficult weather or places like the tower?"

"I will do a study, and if there is any benefit, I will create a report and table it in Senate. I will crease Kaede as the originator of the idea. But the reward for cost-saving is small."

"He is happy for the attention. But today he went all day wearing a MAG, I never thought I see the day he wore a nappy. I think you should market them, with his name on them, again for a small fee, but I really think the MAG will become a popular diaper, even if Dain has the fleet contract, still lots of private ships out there," Hiro said looking at Takahiro.

Takahiro pondered then said, "It costs twice the price to produce. We only use them because they last so long and we use fewer of them."

"I am sure if you feature Kaede on the cover and adverts,

even at twice the price of the most expensive diaper, you will sell much more with him bouncing around one in zero-G than have you talking about cost-benefit."

"I will consider it, what about the space trade?"

"Why not both? More than once I have traded a shipment of MAGs for tinned peaches. You cannot give fleet diapers away."

Takahiro smiles and sips his sake.

On the last Thursday night of September; Hiro took Kaede, Sora, Akiko, and Izanami in an SUV around the lake, to the north side of the lake, to a hall near Abel Mall. It had Go in Kanji and common Elven over the door in neon. Long lines of Flower Elves went in the main door.

Kaede was followed by Izanami, with Sora carrying the Go board and Akiko the vase with the pieces. They entered via the side door guarded by Yoshida House Guards. Once inside, Hiro looked up at the leaderboard. He saw Kaede Hashimoto was ranked second, with Kenta Yoshida ranked first, and Takahiro Hashimoto ranked twenty-fifth.

Kenta placed his left hand on Hiro's shoulder. "So, your father didn't tell you how your son beat him seven times in a row, last month, twice?"

Hiro turned to see General Kenta with Mako and Miko. "Nice to see you, General," Hiro said.

"Hiro, in Go, we do not use our titles, so you may call me Kenta. Kaede is a very keen player, at times brilliant, a tough opponent and an intense competitor. He has risen the ranks fast with smart challenges; he even beat me once," Kenta said.

Kaede smiled and said, "Kenta you honour me with your praise; I see you brought lucky charms with you tonight."

"Kaede, it is Lord Yoshida to you. I apologise, Kenta," Hiro said.

"No, in battle, we address our adversary by their first name; all are equal in the arena, even the Emperor forgoes formality inside the hall, because, in combat, a title had no meaning. However, since he didn't come tonight, he will drop in ranking," Kenta said.

"My apologies, I didn't know. I have never been to a match before," Hiro said.

"I encourage players to respect their opponents and when in battle you treat your opponent as your equal, even in a competition," Kenta said.

"What are all the numbers alongside each name?" Hiro asked.

"The first is rank, the number of wins and losses, how much a player has won and what a ranking match will cost," Kenta said.

"I see, Kaede has won more games than he has lost, but if I am reading it right, he has won over twenty-four million gold?" Hiro said.

"He has earned every coin," Kenta said.

"Kenta, I want a seven-match duel," Kaede said.

"You know the price, but since you lost last week, I advise against it," Kenta said.

"I am prepared to put up seven million," Kaede said.

"Kaede, we should talk. Sorry, Kenta, I had no idea the boy was gambling," Hiro said.

"Your father knows. Kaede is a professional player. I earn ten percent when I win, and the rest goes to the Go society," Kenta said.

"If you win. If I win, Kenta pays the fee, and I get ten percent. Relax Father; most matches are only one-hundred gold," Kaede said.

"I did come to see you play, so go play," Hiro said.

Mako and Miko stood behind Kenta, who sat on a Japanese wooden stool and set up his board on the table in the middle. Kaede stood and watched while Hiro sat with Izanami. Sora and Akiko stood behind Kaede. Kenta drank sake during the first game with Kaede.

Kaede won the game, and Kenta stood and bowed to him.

The audience cheered, and they chanted, "Kaede!"

Hiro, beside with Izanami, asked her, "Why are they chanting?"

"Kaede has a following, and many believe he will defeat Kenta," Izanami replied.

"The second match is about to begin, quiet on the floor," Kenta called out.

They played an intense game, which Kaede won. The third was faster, they both placed their pieces quickly, and Kaede's win was by a narrow margin. The crowds around them cheered. Kenta took a short break to drink some water.

Kenta won the fourth match, and in the end, Kaede pondered the board as Kenta, with a broad grin, cleared the board.

"The tiger had only scratched the Dragon," Kaede said.

"Isn't it time for the hatchling's nap?" Kenta asked.

"After I make a tiger skin rug," Kaede said.

Crisis

The crowd laughed. Mako poured a glass of water and Miko passed it to Kenta. Sora handed Kaede water, then took the empty glass. Akiko held out a hand towel; Kaede returned to the board.

Kenta pondered each piece as he placed it, and each studied the board as they played. At the end of the sixth game, with three wins each, Kenta looked intense, Kaede relaxed.

They started the seventh game, and each placed his pieces fast. The crowd was silent as Kaede and Kenta raced to the corner, then Kaede spread to the side, then a short time later he took the corner. The game was close, and in the end, Kenta had a narrow lead. Kaede placed the last piece. Kenta stood and bowed low to Kaede.

"Grandmaster Kaede," Kenta said.

Mako collected the pieces into the vase, with Miko holding the lid. When they finished, Kenta handed Kaede the ancient vase.

Kaede bowed slightly then accepted it. He slowly handed it over to Sora, then took his jar from Akiko and gave it to Kenta. They bowed and then exchanged boards.

Kenta said, "I will have the Emperor arrange a formal ceremony next week to confer title."

Kenta saw Mako and Miko bow to Kaede.

"Well," Mako said.

"Done," Miko said.

"Thank you," Kaede said, and he bowed to Mako and Miko.

Kenta noticed Mako and Miko had red faces with big smiles.

"Now I see, he had inside help," Kenta said, as he looked at Mako then at Miko.

"Sorry Father—" Mako said.

"But we want to marry him," Miko said.

"Settle down girls, that is a topic for another day," Kenta said. He took Hiro aside, "Hiro, can we discuss arrangements tomorrow?"

"I will discuss it with my father tonight and get back to you," Hiro replied.

The next night, Hiro went with them to the studio for the talent quest.

Kaede had a dressing room to himself where he put on his makeup, suit, and tie. Izanami had a dressing room opposite his. She came out of hers in a tight, red, sparkling dress, with a black belt. The lower half of her dress comprised seven pieces shaped like leaves, overlapping and down to her knees. White pantyhose covered her legs, and she wore black patent leather shoes.

The producer came to Hiro. "Prince Hiro, your son is such a talented púca. We are so happy to have him on. The show's ratings are huge thanks to him."

"I hope my father didn't pressure you to give him a dressing room?" Hiro asked.

"No, he and Izanami are the stars of the show. The audience loves them; the phone poll runs hot all night with votes for them," the producer replied.

"What about the claims from a rival network my father rigs the contest?" Hiro asked.

"I assure you they have won every year on merit. The Inquisition monitors the voting," the producer replied.

"Good, he will never strive hard if the red carpet is always laid out at his feet and I don't want you to cater to his whims, such as having a dressing room," Hiro said.

"Your son is no demanding diva. They are both well behaved, and they each have a dressing room because they are our top performers," the producer said. Then the light at the end of the hall came on, over a door marked 'studio' and a buzzer sounded.

"Sorry, I must go, that is the first call," the producer said before he left.

Kaede and Izanami followed the producer on stage.

Hiro watched from the wings as the producer placed them in the middle of the stage. Other contestants lined up in the wings. An usher came and showed Hiro to a seat in the front row.

Hiro watched Kaede and Izanami dance. They were fast and graceful. He spun her, dipped her, then lifted her over his head, carried her around the dance floor, then ended with a slide to the judges. They bowed their heads. The audience stood cheering and clapped when the sign over the stage changed from displaying 'silence please' to 'applause'. Hiro stayed and watched the whole show, and realised none of the dancers, even the adults, were as good.

Backstage, Kaede showered and changed into his red kimono with green trim and black pants. When he came out, he saw Hiro waiting outside the room, smiling.

As Kaede approached, his father bent down on one knee, looked him in the eye and said, "I am proud of you, son."

"Sometimes Grandfather comes to watch, but I didn't see him tonight," Kaede said.

"I am sorry I said you were wasting valuable study time," Hiro said.

Kaede reached out, and Hiro hugged him.

In the palace dojo, Hiro practised Judo with Kaede, watched by Lady Yuki.

Hiro found himself on the mat with Kaede standing over him.

"Well done son," Hiro said, standing.

The following Tuesday Kaede was awarded a black belt after a couple of Demonstrations of defeating the other black belts.

The next night in Kendo, Kaede won every match and advanced his ranking. An impressed Hiro took Kaede to a restaurant. During the meal, he said, "I must leave soon; have you considered your wish?"

"One day I would like to serve as Emperor. I know Grandfather must appoint you as Emperor first. I have read the Charter; any noble may designate their legal heir as their representative in court," Kaede replied.

"Sorry son, that is not a reasonable wish. I do not have the power to make my father step down," Hiro said.

"If you are appointed, I'd like you to consider standing down, in your own time, for me," Kaede said.

"We shall see. Do you have another wish?" Hiro asked.

"I do. I want a few research teams. I have projects in the fields of physics, quantum computers, electronics, medicine, and energy. I can show you a list of the projects and my ideas," Kaede replied.

"I will first read your proposals and then give you my answer," Hiro said.

After the meal, they returned to the palace. Kaede went to his room and handed Hiro his second tablet, then sat with his Dain Tablet and opened the textbooks folder. Hiro took the proposals with him to his room.

After reading a few, he went to the top of the tower to see his father.

Takahiro came out of his room, and Hiro got a quick glimpse of scars from a Dragon bite on his side as he put on a robe.

"What is it, son?"

"Sorry to interrupt your evening, Father, but I have a proposal from Kaede I think you need to look at it," Hiro replied, as he held out Kaede's tablet.

"He had done some amazing things I grant you, but is it so important that you interrupt my personal time?" Takahiro took the tablet and looked at it. "I already know he wants a research team."

"I am prepared to fund his proposals."

"Good, then we speak in the morning." Takahiro moved to leave.

"Father, it cannot wait until then. I found something in Kaede's proposal for redevelopment of the island. Your lease on the land around the palace expires in a few days."

"It does?"

"Yes, I checked, your ninety-nine-year lease on the land around the palace will soon expire. Yesterday, Kaede accessed the land registry. A week ago, Dain did. He has filed an application to take over the lease."

"I am not worried. Hashimoto Industries will have

received a renewal notice and will pay it on the due date. Dain cannot take it over because the land is in use; I have the marina and the people's park."

"Yes, but Dain is going to challenge your lease."

"When?"

"He filed a claim just before closing time today in the civil court, his claim states you are land banking to artificially drive up the value of the land on edge the lake."

"The park is for security and all lakeside property has always been overpriced."

"Do you want to take the risk that Dain hasn't paid off the judges?" Hiro asked. "I rather see you on the morning news announcing the largest mall, hotel and casino in the empire; you still have a park. I called the lawyers, and they told me if you file the development notice and extend your lease then Dain had no case because most of the land will be in use for commercial purpose. You can try to claim the park is for security, but as Kaede wrote in his arguments for the development, there are cheap portable missiles with a range of over 60 kilometres."

"What does Kaede propose?"

"The largest mall with a one-kilometre tall hotel-casino, surrounded by hotels, units, offices with underground parking and a cruise ship terminal on the north side of the palace. On the west side, a large fun park with an aquatic centre. As for the southern shore, a beach, and a dock for a high-speed ferry service."

"If the project is profitable, I will gladly poke Dain in the eye."

"Good, then get dressed, Father. I already arranged with

head office to wake the real estate development team and the legal team, then come with them to the palace."

"Did you call Alard?"

"No. Alard would tell Dain."

"That is my problem. I need Alard to arrange deals with the other houses for the supply of the building materials as well as arrange private enterprise partnerships. Once Alard is here, I will jam his phone, and have some prostitutes keep him busy in a room out of the way."

"Why do we need him?"

"Alard is not just the owner of the largest private bank. He is the go-between for the thirteen houses. To get a project this big built, I need cooperation from the other houses."

"But he is an influence peddler, a greedy middle-man with his hand in your pockets."

"Yes, that is another reason we use him, we keep an eye on him. Alard, like me, is immortal. That makes him our problem, not yours."

"Yes Father," Hiro said. "Before I go, Kenta wants to discuss arranged marriage."

"Good, I will talk to him tomorrow."

In the morning, Dain turned on the news, went to sip his tea, and dropped the cup.

Abel looked up and asked, "What is wrong?"

"Look!" he cried out, pointing at the screen. He grabbed the remote and unmuted the news.

On screen, the Emperor was turning soil with heavy

machinery behind him, and the west wall of the palace in the background.

"What started as my grandson's desire to have a new play centre in the park has expanded into the fun park," he said to a hovering reporter. "It will feature a large púca play centre and an aquatic centre. Another part of the redevelopment of Imperial Island is Hashimoto Plaza, featuring a collection of hotels and office buildings, around the palace. It will have the largest entertainment centre on the north side of the Palace with a casino, mall, and large underground parking. The largest will be known as The Grand Hotel and Casino; it will be the biggest in the Empire at 1km tall. Hashimoto Mall will have underground parking, and it will be the largest mall in the Empire at 1,800,000 square metres. We will also expand the docks to include a cruise ship terminal. Some open space will remain. To offset the reduction in people's park, we will make sure other nature parks around on the peninsula are protected from any future development, ensuring the city meets the minimum green space, especially the shoreline," Takahiro said.

Furious, Dain turned off the screen.

"Oh dear, didn't you have plans for that land, brother?" Abel asked.

"You told him?" Dain asked.

"Of course not. You are not the only one who just lost gold; I just don't get worked up about losing. It is part of the game," Abel said.

"This development was big, not just in scale, but in prestige," Dain said.

"It was symbolic," Abel said.

Crisis

"I would have had our new head office, right in his backyard," Dain said.

"As much as I like you to move out, a one-kilometre tall office tower would see him still looking down on you. Patya already started construction a tower in New-Moscow, so I suggest you use the land in central New-Berlin," Abel said.

"Why?" Dain asked.

"If the Emperor does know of your plan, then change your submission, and make sure it was dated a few days ago, or just hand the deed to central New-Berlin to the Empire as a gift, before it is turned it into a park. You know if the emperor asked Yaotl to, he would gladly do that," Abel replied.

"Wait until I get my hands on Alard. I saw him holding the little prince," Dain said.

"The last thing you want to do is upset the Elf who is holding most of your gold," Abel said.

"Father, you know they would have kept Alard busy all night, and Aunt Abel is right, the Emperor only needs to plant the idea, and Yaotl will be personally counting the number of trees on every property, with you in tow. If I were you, I would be breaking ground in New-Berlin before sunset today," Abelard said.

"Just don't sit there, do it," Dain said.

Abel sipped her tea as Abelard left, then came back into the room and grabbed an egg and bacon roll.

Without looking up, Abel said, "Dain, you are more like him every day. If I were you, I would be very careful. Or one day he might execute you for being a tyrant. After all, Abelard does want to be like you."

"I am not my father," Dain said.

"Not yet," Abel said.

"What was that?" Dain asked, banging his fist on the table.

"You heard me," Abel said, then she sipped her tea.

Takahiro was in the elevator with Hiro and Kaede. "Kaede, why didn't you tell me sooner?" Takahiro asked.

"I was going to tell you at First Meal this morning," Kaede replied.

"Next time, you tell us as soon as you find out. We worked all night," Hiro said.

"I am sorry."

"How did you find out Dain was planning to take control of the land around the palace?" Takahiro asked.

"Oh, I heard Dain gloating to Patya in the palace," Kaede replied.

"They would not talk business in front of you; they know you would tell me," Takahiro said. He reached for his wand.

"Father, no need to threaten him, especially with magic," Hiro said.

"I was in the crawl space playing," Kaede said.

"You are both very naughty and very brave Kaede; I told you many times not to go into the sub-basement, and you know what that means, loss of all your projects," Takahiro said.

"It was only the vent under the floor, not down the Central Shaft," Kaede said.

"It is the same thing," Takahiro said.

"I will get lawyers and sue. You said, *don't let me catch you going near the Dragons or down the shaft,* and I didn't. You always say to keep your word," Kaede said.

"He has you, Father; do I need to remind you what you told me about being careful what I say to him after my mistake explaining birthday wishes?" Hiro said.

"Very well, Kaede you are not to go into any crawl spaces or air vents. Not just in the palace, but in any building. The only thing you can climb is approved play equipment, and if you continue to undermine my intentions then I will confine you in your room, and you will do what I say when I say as punishment," Takahiro said.

"Son, you know the crawl space is not a play area," Hiro said.

"Yes Father," Kaede said.

"You are permitted to work on your projects, but instead of play time, you will go to your room and study. When the girls are over to play on Sunday, you will not go out to eat, you will not have dessert with your Third Meal, and must always carry your phone, with location turned on. Grandfather must be able to always know where you are. If you are without your phone or your assigned security, you will be punished further, starting with your racing karts," Hiro said.

"Father!"

"You can play hide and seek in the garden maze with the girls on Sunday. But for talking back, I am taking your scooter away. Answer back again, and I will punish your further," Hiro said.

Kaede bowed low and said, "Yes Father."

"Father, I will leave the scooter with you; you will decide the duration of Kaede's punishment," Hiro said.

"Kaede, I will read over your projects, have them evaluated, and next week you will pitch them to me. The island redevelopment will cost 4.1 billion gold. You and Hiro will each receive ten percent of the shares in Imperial Island Development Corporation," Takahiro said.

They bowed to the Emperor who placed his hands into his sleeves. They rode the elevator to the dome top of the tower.

Masako had laid out a meal for them, and they sat down to eat.

"Kaede, I have been thinking about your punishment," Takahiro said.

Kaede gulped, "Yes, grandfather?" he asked softly.

"You will come with me to the Founder's Day parade. If you behave, we will have your birthday party after," Takahiro replied.

"Yes, grandfather," Kaede said.

PART TWO

LOSS

CHAPTER 6

RESEARCH

September 1, 11570. Imperial City.

In the middle of Main Street, opposite the main entrance to Able Mall, was a park with a stadium with many rows of seats with a row of small marquee tents on top.

Takahiro was on the top row, in the middle. Kaede was with him. Behind them, a pair of Knights in a solid full-body plastic armour stood on the walkway. The faceplate of their helm was down and one hand on the Viper 2 that was on a three-point sling over their shoulders.

Takahiro looked at his pocket watch as he sat waiting.

"When does the parade start?" Kaede asked.

"Soon," Takahiro replied

Exactly at noon, he stood and walked to the microphone at the front of the box. As Takahiro spoke Kaede went to the front of the box. He looked out at the people watching and waved. A few waved at him.

"Welcome to the 11571 Founders Day Parade. Today we celebrate the founding of the new Empire. On behalf of the Senate, to those about to start school, we hope you enjoy commencement week," a very animated Takahiro said.

Kaede was clapping. Takahiro stopped speaking and looked at Kaede, the crowd was hushed. Takahiro then said, "Everyone, this is my grandson, Prince Kaede."

Kaede went to the microphone, Takahiro took it off the stand and pointed it at Kaede. Who looked at the microphone and said, "Hello Empire," in a clear, upbeat, voice. Then looked at Takahiro who nodded. "Everything looks so much fun, especially the cotton candy in the park. Save some for me, please."

Many laughed, and the media took photos. There was a hush as Takahiro looked down at Kaede. He smiled and said into the microphone, "My grandson is right, enjoy the parade."

A whistle blew, and the parade started at the top car park of the mall. At the front of the parade was a marching band, which was led by a baton twirler. They wore a similar uniform to Imperial Navy, a pleated skirt on females, pants on males, with a button shirt, double breasted jacket with a high imperial collar. They had a yellow top over a dark purple bottom. Their boots were white lace up, they had a white peaked cap, except for the baton twirler who had an officer's cap.

Followed by that was a float with a model starship surrounded by female Imperial Fleet officers waving. On the side of the float was written 'Imperial Navy'.

Following that was a float with a model of a Banshee with female officers in a light blue tunic with a dark blue skirt, around the plane, with 'Sky Force' written on the side of the float.

Then came a float shaped like a tank, without the torrent, and had 'The Guard' written on the side. On top were different officers in the grey and black uniform. At the front of the pack was a female with a round cap, white gloves and a stop sign with a yellow safety vest. A pair with 'Public Safety' on their sleeve over a white shield stood either side of her, they had a 9mm sidearm and a baton. Behind them stood more guards, they had 'Port Security' and 'Park Patrol' on their sleeves. Unlike the Guard who stood along the parade route, and in patrolled in groups around the parade, none on the float had a Viper rifle.

The next float had a statue of an Elven female holding a sword and scales. Around it stood six females, their uniform was a black shirt, black pleated skirt with a black double-breasted tunic with a high Asian collar and black gloves. On the left sleeve of the tunic was the symbol of the Empire and on the right sleeve was a black round patch with a white edge, with a pair of yellow eyes over scales of justice inside. Each held a white rod. On the side of the float was written 'The Inquisition'.

Knights mounted on large male unicorns followed them. Then came a float with the Medical Bureau, their uniform was light green tunic over dark green pants. On the left sleeve of the tunic was the symbol of the Empire and on the right sleeve was a red round patch with a white star of life inside.

The next float was the Blood-Witches, three witches carrying staffs and a basket stood around a large pram.

Then came Technical support, the centre of the float was a representation of the planet. The six young females wore yellow hard hats and had tool belts. They wore yellow t-shirts and dark purple shorts and carried power tools. On the left sleeve of the shirt was the symbol of the Empire and on the right sleeve was a white patch with upright double ended open spanner. The banner read, 'Technical support.'

Following them came various groups of Elves in native costume. Behind them came the various floats with sporting teams; the first being the Galaxy Girls Football team. A team of mostly female Field Elves in a pink top with white shorts, wearing pink socks and black football boots with pink laces, stood around a huge gold cup with a red one on the side and *Petrov Interstellar Football Federation Champions,* on a banner. Behind them was the Hashimoto All Stars, a group of female Flower Elves in a half pink, half white top with green shorts, they had black boots with green laces. Then came a couple of floats representing volleyball, tennis, badminton and water polo.

In the park were many vendors set up, Lady Toshiko took Kaede from stand to stand, a dozen Hashimoto house guards kept the crowds away. They visited a stand with a Germanic sausage sizzle, a Japanese noodle stands, more than once to the cotton candy stand, and many other stands with food, bags of candy, and fairground games from different cultures. When over Kaede carried a pinwheel, followed by Toshiko with a large stuffed unicorn and the guards carrying bags of candy.

September 5, 11570. Imperial Palace.

Lady Toshiko, in a suit, escorted Kaede to the throne room, located on the seventh floor of the palace. Takahiro was inside on the throne. Toshiko closed the double doors behind them and escorted Kaede to the throne. They bowed.

"Your father told me you applied to do a multiple discipline science degree at the Imperial University," Takahiro said.

"Yes, Grandfather, with some courses in engineering," Kaede said.

"Kaede, I have spoken with Toshiko about your proposal to start a research centre focused on the Artificial Cell, Fusion Reactor and a new Quantum Computer," Takahiro said.

"I hope you don't mind," Toshiko quickly added.

Kaede turned to look at Toshiko. "I know you are the top advisor to the Senate," Kaede said.

Toshiko smiled and said, "I am."

"Kaede, Lady Toshiko is not just an advisor to the clan and the head of the Imperial Knights. She is one of the top engineers in the Empire, and owns the Lilith Foundation and," Takahiro said.

"Yes, Grandfather," Kaede said, then looked at Takahiro and asked, "Am I in trouble?"

Toshiko laughed and said, "No Kaede, not since Lilith have I been so excited. Your compact reactor design is amazing."

"Really?" Kaede asked. "I am confused. I thought you and Lilith created magic."

"Lilith and I discovered Aether together, then we created the Orichalcum device to harvest it, and then we created a Quantum computer the size of a walnut," Toshiko replied. Then she huffed and said, "However, we had a disagreement and then we each created our own casting devices separately;

she created the wand, and I the staff. Lilith created the first spell, Heal, a week before me. But she had used my spell program to do so. So, we share the credit of First Witch. She was titled The Witch of the West, and I was given the title Witch of the East."

"Why?" Kaede asked.

"Well, the staff took longer to build because I had created the mana battery after discovering it was not unlimited. But apart from a few illusion spells create by Arjuna Desai, I created most of the spells, the flying broom, and cauldrons because Lilith left to have children."

"Wait, but Lilith built the starship," Kaede said looking puzzled.

"Lilith returned to the workshop after having Dain and Abel. She invented the fusion reactor and the first spaceship. A few years later she returned East, then as you know died a few months later when her ship exploded. They never found her body."

"Kaede, Lady Toshiko inherited every invention, together she and I made the first starship," Takahiro added.

"Really?" Kaede asked.

Toshiko knelt and put her hand on Kaede's shoulders. "Yes, and for a long so many, not just me, have tried to improve on her ideas, and until now, none succeeded," Toshiko said.

Takahiro stood and said, "You're not in trouble, far from it, we want to do a deal with you."

"Really?" Kaede asked.

"Yes, a 100-kilogram fusion reactor will give us more room on a starship, and it is brilliant, but my interest is the 3D printer that uses lasers to stack atoms. For thousands of years, no one has even considered atomic manipulation for anything but fusion power. But it will need a lot of power," Takahiro replied.

"Yes, but the 3D Printer is needed to build my reactor," Kaede said.

"Yes, I agree, your reactor needs be very precise," Toshiko replied.

"Kaede, do you have a company name yet?" Takahiro asked approaching him. Takahiro sat in front of Kaede.

"No," Kaede replied smiling.

"You will need a company name," Toshiko said. "I thought you would have one ready, you planned the research, but not the company. You should be branding yourself. I am surprised you don't already. You have offers to do product endorsements and a dance exercise video. Takahiro, I am surprised you haven't had Izanami holding Pure Orchid up on billboards all over the empire by now."

"I choose Kaede Enterprise as the name of my parent company, and I propose we create subsidiaries for each partnership," Kaede said.

"I will have my lawyers create them for you," Takahiro said.

"Lady Yuki told me if I ever need legal help, to speak with her because she did law as her secondary studies when she did magic at the university. So, I will ask her to be my lawyer," Kaede said.

"We can discuss it with her later," Toshiko said. "Kaede, I am impressed not only with your theory, but your attention to detail to explain the theory. But I have questions before I commit to your projects."

"What would you like to know?" Kaede asked.

"What makes you confident that your method will increase the power produced?" Toshiko asked.

"Yes, all attempts have failed in the past," Takahiro said.

"I found school so easy. Grandfather told me if I am bored find something to do. So, I read his papers on engineering. Then to understand that I read Lady Toshiko's book on Science and Magic. Eventually, I used my access to the records library to study failed research. I wanted to know why technology has not progressed."

"One theory is we close to peak technology," Lady Toshiko said.

Kaede went to say something, then Takahiro said, "If he has read my notes, then he knows my theory is we raised generations of parrots who copy the past so well they cannot see the future. Kaede mind has not set in stone."

"Well, each generation is working with the same theory and same materials for containment. To them, more power means bigger. But containment consumes most of the energy produced and they don't even consider reaction rate or energy loss. I have designed an aneutronic fusion reactor, it uses the heat of the reaction powers to help power the containment field; the reactor should generate 100K in Standard Power Units per hour for twenty years. If you want to double to power, then add a second reactor to the grid," Kaede said.

"The reason for the current design is to generate plasma for the starship engines. Your design is not producing more, but according to your calculation less. However, we can replace one existing reactor with two of yours, but you are not generating enough plasma for the primary ion thrusters,"

Toshiko said, "Did you consider that and if so, how are you going to generator plasma?"

"My reactor uses hydrogen to cool the outer shell. The superheated hydrogen can be used to power the gravity rings. However, I am working on a fusion drive that will be more powerful than gravity-ion propulsion and work in an atmosphere," Kaede replied.

"Good," Takahiro said, "We should focus on the reactor project first."

"The current system doesn't produce a timing signal or handle the number of calculations per second needed which is why I designed a new processor," Kaede said.

"Oh?" Takahiro asked leaning in.

"Yes, and Izanami helped me design the processor," Kaede replied in a soft voice, looking down.

"Kaede, there is no shame in asking for help. You could have come to us sooner. But no harm has been done. I know how much Izanami means to you," Takahiro said.

Kaede and Toshiko looked surprised at Takahiro. "Really?" Toshiko asked.

"Of course, but before we start building a prototype, we will need to patent the designs. You will need to allocate Izanami some shares and have her sign an agreement with us," Takahiro said.

Kaede went to speak, "Don't worry Kaede, I will make sure her name is on the patent," Toshiko said to Kaede, who closed his mouth.

Kaede smiled. "Thank you."

"If Yuki becomes their lawyer, she will need to manage their trust fund," Takahiro said.

"Don't you trust me to control my money?" Kaede asked.

"Do I need to remind you that you are still a púca?" Takahiro asked.

"But I want to expand and build my own company," Kaede whined.

"Don't be like that," Toshiko said frowning at Kaede.

"Your own company?" Takahiro asked.

"Yes. I propose that I own 51% Kaede Enterprises and each project is a subsidiary company, of which Kaede Enterprises owns 51% of each," Kaede said.

Takahiro stood and asked, "What about us?" Takahiro growled.

Toshiko stepped between Kaede and Takahiro, "I remember hiring a particular engineer who then demanded 51% of the rights to his geothermal plant in an active volcano," Toshiko said as she poked Takahiro's chest.

"I remember giving a certain Witch everything, who ran off and became extremely wealthy without thanks, then a hundred years later you came crawling back for my help," Takahiro said.

Kaede gasped and asked "Everything?" from behind Toshiko.

"The ice age was a terrible time. When your grandfather was eighteen, his parents died from the cold, and he became Emperor. He found me in the snow near the Palace. I had been abandoned as a baby," Toshiko said.

"She was the first of many I took in," Takahiro said softly putting his hand on Toshiko's shoulder.

"Yes, he built Hashimoto house and took in thousands, including Lilith. He funded our education and research,"

Toshiko said in a soft voice looking down. A long pause, she looked at Takahiro and said, "Takahiro, we settled this argument long ago, I am sorry I run off, I know you felt betrayed. Now is not the time. You know Kaede is right; even if he didn't invent the original product, he owns his contribution. He has rights to commercially exploit his work, on the condition that he obtains a licence to do so from the rights owner."

"Who is rights owner?" Kaede asked.

"The Lilith Foundation, which I control. Takahiro owns 20%, but I control the licensing. Don't fret, I am prepared to invest in you," Toshiko replied. "Takahiro, you can either be an investor or get out of our way. If you are staying, then call Alard."

"Why do we need a banker?" Kaede asked, "You own a bank."

"Alard is a merchant banker, the Hashimoto bank is private banking. Alard does the banking, accounting, and taxation for corporations," Takahiro replied.

"Why not just pay him?" Kaede asked.

"Never pay Alard by the hour, you will regret it," Toshiko replied.

"How much will you invest?" Takahiro asked Toshiko.

"Three billion a year over three years; I will accept no less than 20% share;" Toshiko said.

"After 1% to the Banker and 1% to the lawyer, if Grandfather invests the same for 20%, that leaves 7% for Izanami," Kaede said.

"I consider that fair," Toshiko said.

"Lady Toshiko. I hope you are not insulted, but I want to hire Lady Abel to build my car," Kaede said.

"Anyone but Abel!" Takahiro exclaimed.

"She is a brilliant engineer, not only does she know electronics, computers, and reactors, she knows how to design and build cars, and she already has omega clearance. I trust her not to tell her brother anything," Toshiko said.

"Very well," Takahiro grumbled.

"I will talk to Yuki if she agrees to be his lawyer, then I think it is best that Yuki and I chat with Izanami," Toshiko said.

"I will provide you with a transcript of this meeting to help speed up the formation of the company and have the funds ready," Takahiro said.

"A transcript?" Kaede asked. "I do not see anyone taking notes."

"Palace Security maybe in sub-basement ten, but they see and hear all," Toshiko said.

"Why only three years?" Kaede asked.

"Kaede, three years is just a rough estimate on how long it will take to make and test every component while we test the theory. I hope by then we have built a working prototype of your reactor."

"I have broken down each project into key areas, and I have an extensive list of experts needed. We will need experts not just in fusion and fission, but in hydrogen capture and storage, heat-resistant materials, high-temperature superconductors, direct heat to electricity conversion, magnetic field, plasma conduits, gravity plates and beams, hot and cold lasers, megawatt batteries, electromagnetic bottles, plasma conduits, and particle accelerators. My original plan was to take over Fusion Two from Hashimoto Energy and hire you to oversee the project," Kaede said.

"His system is very complicated; how can it be that small?" Takahiro asked.

"His theory is sound," Toshiko said, she turned to face Kaede, "I am the better engineer, his speciality is geology and geothermal."

"Grandfather, current reactors lose 80% of their energy as neutrons; which does not happen in aneutronic fusion," Kaede replied.

"It still seems too small to provide the same power as an existing model," Takahiro said.

"If the fusion reactor does come in at 100 kilograms; which I am sure it will. Even with a gigawatt battery and new computer; we are looking at a reactor a third of the size of the current size," Toshiko said.

"Yes, and while that is under development, I help design a gravity engine to replace both the Gravity-Ion Engine and the liquid fuel rocket. Imagine a fighter with a gravity engine able to power a shield and a gravity stabiliser; one that can ground launch," Kaede said.

"Kaede, how will a smaller reactor produce the power required?" Takahiro asked.

"Takahiro, the only idea you and your teams have is to go bigger, but bigger the ship, the slower the ship, you know we haven't been able to synchronise ultra-drives to work together," Toshiko said.

Takahiro stared at Toshiko, then asked, "You know it isn't as easy as just having an idea? We both will have to reassign engineers, and that will slow down other projects."

"I know, but your grandson has practical ideas, and those other projects can wait. If you don't help, I will fully fund his projects," Toshiko said.

"I don't deny Kaede is brilliant, you know there are many things I must consider," Takahiro said as he looked at Toshiko.

"I know you are busy building ships because the Exodus has not finished. Thousands of ships need to be built over the next thousand years. You can have engineers dismantle incomplete reactors, then have them working on and testing the new reactor, so they have the skill to build and install them. But by slowing down now, later you can complete the ships with more power, better computers, and faster drives," Toshiko said, Kaede stood behind her.

Takahiro walked around Toshiko to Kaede. "Kaede, you said before If you want to double to power, double the number reactors, are you saying you can synchronise them?" he asked.

"Yes, I have heard you say how desperate you are for more power and-" Kaede said, he was interrupted by a laugh from Toshiko.

Takahiro glared at her, then said, "Please continue."

"The mathematics has always been sound, it has always been about timing and energy. I noticed in the past you always tried to produce more energy by building larger reactors. But large reactors need more fuel and laws of diminishing returns apply. I noticed the current reactors lose large quantities of energy as neutrons. So, I made the reaction chamber smaller, with a faster fusor, inside a high compressed gravity field to make use of the excess heat to power containment and absorb the radiation. It is low radiation, and with precision optical connectors, that are all the same length, connected to the same computer. Heat converters in the shell will charge a gigawatt battery. I

Crisis

designed a smaller, lighter battery using graphene and gold nanowire. Secondary power systems can be made smaller using materials and techniques from my projects. The computer, in theory, can have multiple reactors connected to a bank of batteries. You can use the same optical network to provide the field pattern, and a timing signal to multiple ultra-drives so the fields combine, not cancel each other. For timing, I replaced the cesium clock with an ytterbium clock. Existing ultra-drives could be upgraded by replacing the onboard field generator with one controlled by the main computer; once we have a test for synchronisation ships with a backup drive should be able to use both at the same time, resulting in an increase in their FTL speed," Kaede said.

Takahiro gave Kaede his complete attention. He smiled and nodded as Kaede talked. Toshiko smiled. Then when Kaede finished talking, Takahiro returned to the throne and sat. Toshiko took a step towards Takahiro.

"Takahiro, you have poured more gold a year into your Shanghai Research Centre than I am asking you to spend on Kaede," Toshiko said.

"It not a matter of gold, I need to keep the Shanghai Research Centre open because of the political support from Lord Wang who runs Shanghai," Takahiro said.

"No one is asking you to shut down Shanghai, just change their mission. They have a role to play, they can build the tools that go into space to build the tools that will build a 3D printer. Once we have the printer we use it to build the parts to the reactor," Toshiko said.

"I will fund the project," Takahiro said to Kaede.

"Thank you, Grandfather," Kaede said racing up to

Takahiro. Toshiko went to stop him, Takahiro bent over and held his arms out. Kaede and Takahiro hugged.

"The research will not end with just a better fusion generator, I want to produce engines to power bigger ships and increase the speed of existing ships," Takahiro said.

"Yes, before we can think of bigger engines, we need better tools. My device is going to need a large work area in zero-gravity," Kaede said.

"We have a station," Takahiro said.

"You do?" Toshiko asked.

"Yes, one of my stations was working on a large starship powered by two reactors. They had attempted to synchronise two drives, and are currently studying the wreckage. We can build the 3D printer in that station's zero-gravity laboratory, and they can build a ship to test the reactor, computer and use that to synchronise two ultra-drives," Takahiro said.

"Why did you keep that operation secret from me?" Toshiko asked.

"I don't have to tell you, I am only obligated to file a research notice with the Inquisition. I only told Patya so he can check the Inquisition for leaks," Takahiro said.

"We can discuss trust later," Toshiko said.

Takahiro stared at Toshiko, then looked to Kaede and said, "Kaede, tell me about the computer?"

"My next project started as a dual-core Quantum Computer. I am aware that a quantum processor is as fast as it can be. Abel and others have confirmed this. There are two ways to increase the number of calculations per cycle, one is to add a second core the other is shorter cycles. To date, no one has succeeded in either because of overheating. The processor is the size of a pin head making it difficult to work with. I plan to combat overheating by spiralling the two processors inside a boron nitride nanotube, connect them using gold nanowire and put them inside a cube filled with non-conductive liquid coolant. The new chip is the same size as a Quantum One. I replaced the atomic clock, which produces more timing signals per second, it will increase the speed, in theory of the current Quantum processor. The current operating system with need slight modification to it multi-processing code to use a Q2. We should be able to update an existing computer, but it will need to have the OS upgraded to recognise a Q2 processor before slotting in a Q2. The new liquid cooling system will replace large fans and heat sinks as it is non-conductive you can build large systems inside a pool, so we can get more out of existing systems and upgrade them cheaper than building new computers, but new systems will be smaller," Kaede said.

"Why boron nitride?" Takahiro asked.

"Obvious. It is used to make high-temperature bearings and various other products, including the heat-resistant tiles on the outer hull of Suborbitals," Toshiko replied.

"Heat reduction will not increase processing speed by much, but a second core will double the number of processes each processor can do per cycle. With each cycle counting, especially in a starship, I believe this project is vital, not just because the fusion plant needs a fast computer to control it, but if we going to use the atomic manipulator used to build more than just processors, it will need the processing power," Kaede said.

"I will fund the prototype of the processor and the new manipulator," Toshiko said.

"As will I," Takahiro said, "Toshiko, I think the research

and development for the computer should be done by the Lilith Foundation, and have Shanghai believing the manipulator is just to improve production of the current processor."

"Agreed, I have the office space and security as well as the required atomic scope and an atom manipulator," Toshiko said.

"Not in zero gravity?" Kaede asked.

"We need the tools to build better tools. The first Q2 will be used on the first Kaede atom manipulator in zero gravity to build its replacement, then we see if we can use it to repair, recycle or rebuild old systems into new," Toshiko replied.

"Oh," Kaede said.

"I am curious about your third project, I can see why you developed the computer, but I don't see any connection to artificial cells," Takahiro said.

"I didn't think there needed to be one," Kaede said looking around.

"Relax and pretend we haven't read your paper and tell us about the project," Takahiro said.

"I read Dain Medical was developing the cells and they officially they abandoned the project. As you know Lilith developed the cell as a way of targeted delivery of vitamins and minerals without poisoning. Dain planned to use the technology to create artificial stem cells. As you know the collection of these cells is vital but expensive and time-consuming. I think Dain and his researchers are close to success but don't have a commercially viable product, but only leaked rumours of the research closed," Kaede said.

"Why do we need artificial cells?" Takahiro asked.

"Stem cells are used to grow skin and treat a range of diseases. If we can mass produce enough cells, we could create organs for transplant and replace the mandatory organ harvesting from the recently deceased. Grown organs should not suffer rejection. Many failures in transplants occur, such as limb transplants and some skin transplants leave patients covered in patches of darker skin. Many are too embarrassed to go out in public and are living in seclusion," Kaede replied.

"Yes, burns are the largest injury to púca, and I see the need. While many fortunately regenerate within a year, some do not," Toshiko said.

"Yes, especially the very young and very old," Takahiro said.

"I see the need, the average population is three billion, with 114 worlds, the number is small, but signification, and we must remember non-Elves do not have regeneration," Toshiko said.

"Dragons have better regeneration than we do," Takahiro said.

"We are talking about the people," Toshiko said.

"Yes, now if Dain was looking for a way to produce skin, we should we invest?" Takahiro asked, "Especially if as you say, he is close and hiding his research from the others."

"I don't see how he could be close, the Lilith Foundation has had some success with collecting and cloning adult stem cells, but so far we have not been able to grow skin or cells in large quantity," Toshiko said.

"No other way of collecting the cells?" Kaede asked.

"We outlawed foetal cell collection, as it would lead to mass abortions. Many are too willing to throw away morality for themselves with no regard for who they hurt along the way. Just look at Babylon," Takahiro said.

"We should not give Kaede nightmares; we can discuss Doctor Moloch and her reign of terror over drinks and toast Dain for putting her to death, not that you ever tell him he is a hero."

"Dain did our people proud many times, I gave him the star of the Empire, that is enough," Takahiro said.

"What for?" Kaede asked.

"Kaede you are too young, just know that Babylon a successful military campaign led by Dain against the Goblins that helped end of the third ice wars," Toshiko said.

"Many history books only talk about him as the one who lost Tir Na Nog," Kaede said.

"Yes, he did. He led an army of Sorcerers, Knights and Blood-Witches. The Celts had woman and children on their boats, so he waited until they landed. He tried to separate the civilians from the soldiers, but It was a trap, Dark Elves flanked them and reigned fire on Dain's army. Three days and nights, none on either side survived. But there was no one to repel the Celts. So, Abel sued for peace and brought Dain back to life using blood magic. They destroyed the magic weapons and cauldrons that littered the battlefield. All we had left are wands, staves and cauldrons of spell casting. The only magic weapon we have is a stun baton, which is just a user powered, hard wired casting device," Takahiro said.

"Dain died?" Kaede asked.

"Yes. It is a secret; Not to discuss it with your friends," Takahiro said.

"I know about security," Kaede said.

"Relax Takahiro, we in the throne room, I will make

sure Kaede doesn't talk about anything we discussed here. Since these projects will need to have the highest secrecy rating of Omega, we can edit the transcripts to just business talk. But you need to change Kaede's security rating from Delta to Omega," Toshiko said.

"Kaede, few know Dain died. He was only supposed to be on Terra to recover magic artefacts and negotiate with the last Elves to bring them peacefully to the Empire. Tir Na Nog is something we never discuss openly, nor with Dain ever," Takahiro said.

"Why is he still in the Senate?" Kaede asked.

"Losing isn't a crime, the Inquiry found he wasn't negligent, just out played and his losses were punishment enough," Takahiro said.

"If Blood-Witches can raise the dead, why don't they do it often, so everyone has a long full life?" Kaede asked.

"It is true the Blood-Witches have spells to raise the dead. These spells are secret for a good reason. Magic does have its limits, such as you cannot raise the truly dead, only the recently deceased. Nor can you raise those who will die immediately. Always remember magic is not the answer to everything, and it is not perfect," Takahiro said.

"Spells? As in more than one?" Kaede asked.

"We not here to discuss the Blood-Witches and their secrets," Takahiro replied, he leaned over and growled, "Do you need another lesson in secrets?"

Toshiko stood between Takahiro and Kaede. "Enough! I am sure you drilled how and why he must keep secrets until his ears bleed," Toshiko said to Takahiro. Toshiko turned to Kaede and said in a mild voice, "Kaede, in your paper you mentioned Artificial Cells can be used in gene therapy. But Elves don't have naturally occurring genetic abnormalities."

"Yes, but there some caused by radiation damage and the current chemical treatments are hit and miss. Also, other races are not as fortunate as Elves. Artificial Cells can target the damaged are and encapsulate the damaged cell or deliver treatment. These cells have many uses, such as replace pills and deliver the contents into the blood stream, Hemoperfusion, Artificial Blood, targeting deadly viruses and cancer treatment. I know Elves all have the same blood type, but so many non-Elves work in the Empire, and they do not. Currently, hospitals need to collect and store many blood types. I think soon we will be able to make artificial blood. One day we will no longer harvest organs from the dead, but grow them in a uterine replicator, and to eventually printing them on demand," Kaede said.

"It is the most ambitious your three projects, and I think it a noble and worthy endeavour, but it is also costly. We must find a way to fund it," Toshiko said.

"I hope the first projects will help fund the others, the 3D printer is only basic. The aim is a Forge, a furnace that can turn anything into plasma and sort the atoms, then inject them into a construction chamber that is cooled by a blue wave laser, hydrogen and heat converters," Kaede said.

"I noticed you planned stages of tools, processors, upgrades, power plants, and using licencing to fund the Kaede Medical Research Institute, why stem cells first? Why not blood or skin first?" Takahiro asked.

"I plan to create a cell that will encapsulate a given cell, which we will use to harvest adult stem cells and the Blood-Witches will create a tissue bank. Once we can harvest, we move to growing skin, we make and clone stem cells to clone and grow skin cells. We need to be able to make blood, not just red blood cells. That will be complicated research, and the teams will get experience from early research into creating artificial cells. Once we can do skin, a separate team will work on cloning other cells, working to clone organ tissue for implants, to eventually cloned organs for transplant and then combine to create print on-demand technology for skin, blood, hair, organs, nerves," Kaede said.

"Impressive logic," Toshiko said.

"The Artificial Cell research team, how did you find them?" Takahiro asked.

"A mix of biologists, researchers and healers who are top in their profession and most, until recently, were employees of Dain Medical. I think Dain is continuing his project in secret. I do not believe he had reached a dead end. I suspect he had made a breakthrough and the leak of failure and closure came from him to justify terminating those he no longer needed and did not want to share profit with," Kaede said.

"If as you say he is close, then we should let him have his success then," Takahiro said.

"Should Dain develop this before us, he will dominate medicine and become wealthier than you in less than a hundred years," Kaede said.

"Two reasons why it will not happen. The first reason is the Wealth Cap. We are close to it now, any rise in his wealth faster than economic growth will trigger to Cap, all of us will be forced to sell corporate assets. The second reason is most medical facilities are government-run. I don't see how the profit margin will bridge the gap in annual earnings between us," Takahiro said.

"What is the Wealth cap?" Kaede asked.

"It is a limit on the wealth of the ruling houses. When the Dragon Treaty was negotiated between the seven kingdoms, we demanded the right retain our businesses. The people demanded free education, health care and guarantee we never take their land again. The lesser lords demanded a limit placed on how much we can own and a limit on the profit margin made by providing services to the government. We guaranteed their rights, so long as they make no attempt to remove us by force," Takahiro said.

"How will my projects affect the Cap?" Kaede asked.

"The first part of the cap is a limit on every corporation. No company cannot own more than a fifty-one percent of any market for more than a month. That is based on gross sales. It is a production limit. In that time, we will licence the technology to public companies to grow the wealth base to close to the cap without closing or selling off assets. I know it slows down research, but if the economy grows too fast, it creates a shortage of workers, too much wealth too soon creates mass consumption, which when combined with high unemployment leads to the collapse of the economy due to labour shortages and soaring prices," Takahiro replied.

"To overcome this, we develop the technology and limit production?" Kaede asked.

"No. The thirteen ruling houses are limited to how much they can own. The value of the top thirteen corporations cannot exceed fifty-one percent of the combined value of the top one thousand private companies, while that value is in the trillions, the thirteen currently stands at 50.2%," Takahiro said.

"How we do overcome that limit?" Kaede asked.

"We licence the technology to private companies to grow the market, and the cap is flexible. It is the value of the company based on the market value of its assets, not revenue. Also, the Senate can grant an extension. Know this, the lesser lords, even private companies can challenge an extension in civil court, and there are financial penalties. But we can use any challenge to extension buys us time to grow the market," Takahiro replied with a smug grin.

"If I understand you, we can develop the technology, build new factories and then sell them and licences and the gold doesn't affect the Cap, nor does licence fee?" Kaede asked.

Takahiro smiled at Kaede. "Correct! The aim is to maximise annual income not grow our assets," Takahiro replied.

"Why are our expenses so high?" Kaede asked.

"We employ so many members of the clan and relatives of the New Tokyo Council of Lords," Takahiro replied.

"You buy loyalty?" Kaede asked.

Takahiro growled, Toshiko laughed and replied, "Never tell a Lord his loyalty is bought. Without the support of friends and family, they will go to work for someone else, or favour other companies and your clan will lose its wealth and power."

"Kaede," Takahiro said, "We off topic. All the ruling houses are owners of the top thirteen companies listed the Imperial Share Market. I am only the Emperor because I am the richest male in the Empire. Dain was for the first thousand years. He inherited his wealth from his father. Though he did kill his father and step-mother, the rulers of the other nations and I had agreed it was self-defense."

"Why did Dain kill his father?" Kaede asked.

"King Adamos was a Sorcerer, and he was possessed by a Demon. When Dain was eighteen, Adamos replaced Queen Lilith, Dain and Abel's mother, with her assistant Eve, who was pregnant with Abelard. We didn't know until later, Dain was the father and that Eve used magic on Dain. Adamos and Eve past many unpopular laws over the next hundred years. They restricted magic to select nobles, increased taxation creating a huge number of poor dependant on the crown, kept the war against our people going for hundreds of years to keep power, but it was only when facing a huge flood and they refused to use Lilith's ships to save the people. According to Dain, Adamos had demanded he kill Lilith, or he would be killed, then Abel, then Lilith. He refused, his father went for his wand, Dain cut him down and Eve fled. A short time later Lilith's departed for Mars, her ship exploded, then Dain confronted Eve on the wall around the city. He beheaded Eve, then fled the city. A week later arrived at my Palace with Abelard and asked for my help. I was sceptical, but he submitted to Patya and allowed his mind to be read. With the Dragons as mediators, we got a peace treaty, that became known as the Dragon treaty and the year of the flood became the first year of the new calendar," Toshiko replied.

"What is a Sorcerer?" Kaede asked.

"They were powerful male magic users. Often, they had groups of three witches completely loyal to the death to them. They were so powerful they could fight Dragons. You will not find this in any book, but a Sorcerer could talk a female witch into almost anything, they were a secret society that only numbered in the few thousand. Under Dain, they served the crown alongside Knights. That was until the battle of Tir Na Nog, in the year 6500. The red, white and black Sorcerers fought each other. The red Sorcerers sided with the Celts. Not only was Dain defeated, but all 5,000 Sorcerers were killed. After that, there was no Elven nation left on Terra, no Sorcerers left. Dain and those who wanted Terra to remain part of the Empire returned to the Empire humiliated," Toshiko replied.

Kaede looked puzzled then asked, "If Adamos was so bad, why was he the king?" Kaede asked.

"Adamos lead the revolt against the matriarchy that enslaved males for twelve thousand years. The last Empress was Maria Hartman, his mother. The Imperial Knights used to be called the Amazons. The first hundred years of his rule was great, then he married Lilith," Takahiro replied.

"What happened to the Sorcerers?" Kaede asked.

"No Sorcerer has been born since Tir Na Nog fell," Takahiro said.

"Why?" Kaede asked.

"No one knows why. The members of the society had never shared their secrets with anyone," Toshiko replied.

"Now back to the topic of artificial cells," Takahiro said, he stood and asked, "Why should we fund this expensive project?"

"The computer project is not a processor. I am working on data storage."

"Where is the storage unit project?" Toshiko asked.

"First we need to develop a 3D printer. The printer will revolutionise manufacturing. I calculated that we can 700 MB of data in one cell. But we need to develop a small and inexpensive printer, then we need to develop the device to print and read the cell. With better, cheaper and smaller lasers will develop smaller, and better optical data storage units, but we need the power, computers and the first true 3D Printer," Kaede said.

"Print a cell?" Toshiko asked.

"Yes, not just to store data. Eventually, I hope to develop an Organic 3D printer that will print food, organs, blood, even an inexpensive and non-toxic organic fertiliser," Kaede said.

"Animals already print waste," Takahiro said.

"Not to an exact specification. Image food and cutlery that is edible or processing smelt organic waste into pellets easy to ship and be planted like seeds or a car printed in hours, not days," Kaede replied.

"It will need safety protocols, or else someone will print weapons," Toshiko said.

"But edible cutlery sounds interesting; more than once I've wanted to pin Dain's tongue with a fork to the palace dining table," Takahiro said.

"If we do not progress and develop the technology despite the danger eventually one of the other races will. We are not on Terra where you can eliminate dangerous technology with wars and assassinations. If I am not mistaken, the Fukuhina data revealed the Ogres had secret bases, which you had the Algol fleet destroy. The Ogres are angry but cannot say anything, else they admit to all they sponsored terrorism and committed an act of war. Under the Dragon treaty sponsoring piracy should triggering trade sanctions from the other members, and be a justification for an armed response aimed at removing their leadership. I am sure you have a list of possible replacements and plan to sponsor a coup inside the Ogre alliance," Kaede said.

"Takahiro, your grandson, knows you very well," Toshiko said with a giggle. She paused, as Takahiro only stared at her. "Kaede is right, we cannot stop progress. Already criminals in their basements can cook powerful bombs using only common ingredients. Our lid on crime is not as secure as you think, it is like a lid on pressure cooker, and the whistle is blowing."

"Kaede, why didn't you come to me sooner?" Takahiro asked.

"I want to develop it and other technology on my own. The printer can assemble but disassemble. It can be used to build, repair, or recycle. It can recycle anything. We will transform the economy from one based on mining, large fleets and large central manufacturing centres to one that is decentralised and based on resource recycling and food production," Kaede replied.

"I think you will find a lot of opposition to a decentralised economy," Takahiro growled.

"Takahiro are you worried Kaede is going topple you?" Toshiko asked.

"I am not," Takahiro said as he slid his arms inside his sleeves.

"I know Dain is trying too, he plans to dominate medicine, if he succeeds in wearing down General Kenta, you may lose a key ally, then he will go after Patya, Dain Resources is not going to stop at Carbon, they will go after Methane and other resources," Kaede said.

"I am aware of that," Takahiro said.

"That is no secret; I think he has asked everyone in court, not just his fellow Senators, for support on expanding Wealth cap limit from a year to a decade to allow his expansion into space mining. Currently, the only large private fleet is the Hashimoto Fleet. Dain plans on building hundreds of mining ships, that will push the combined wealth of all houses close to 51%. If he triggers a sale of assets, all houses end up selling. That affects the income of weaker houses like House Belaúnde the most, and they are a key ally of House Hashimoto," Toshiko said.

"If I lose anyone, even Yaotl, who is a swing voter, we lose revenue. I am invested in Patya, Kenta, Arjuna, Takis, Árni, and Yaotl. I am away Dain is looking for ways to chip away at my wealth," Takahiro said nodding.

"As Emperor, why not stop Dain from forcing Chief Belaúnde to sell assets?" Kaede asked.

"Kaede, the only power the Emperor has over the other twelve senators, is casting the deciding vote in the event of a tie. The only time he can order them is as supreme commander of the Imperial Security Agency, and that is limited to military action or procedural regulation changes to the Agency, not to only one agency," Toshiko replied.

"I don't see how we can risk funding the project, especially if Dain triggers the Wealth cap, the last assets and research projects are often first to go," Takahiro said.

"The cell will be worth billions, and that is just from growing skin," Kaede said.

"Kaede. The idea of Artificial Cells is not new. During the Ice Wars, research led to the manipulation of DNA. Ogres used that to create Dragons to be living weapons, there are many restrictions on that technology," Toshiko said.

"Yes, I am aware some Dark Elves changed their DNA to give birth to Daemons. Dain used selective breeding to increase the size of unicorns, giants created Centaurs and how you created Pegasi with Grandfather," Kaede said.

"Yes, we did. Later we freed the Dragons and other engineered races," Takahiro said.

"I am aware artificial cells could create new artificial life forms, but we not doing that. The reason I want to hire Abel is her desire to take over Dain Medical, Dain Automotive, and Burgers. Companies she founded," Kaede said.

"Dain only owns a third of his companies. Abelard and Abel each own a third. Abelard always sides with his father, but Abel has sort support from us before," Takahiro said.

"Why not help her?" Kaede asked.

"Should Abel buy out Dain it will give him a cash infusion, an increase in wealth that would trigger the Wealth Gap. For now, the Senate does not want Dain back in office," Takahiro replied.

"Why?" Kaede asked.

"He wants us to return to Terra, which could spark a war with the Dark Elves, the other free states, backed by the Orcs, Ogres and Goblins," Takahiro replied.

"I read it was because he wants to make you commissioner of trash in New Tokyo," Kaede said.

"Reading dossiers on my rivals is not why I allow you into my archives," Takahiro said. "I hope you do not intend on repeating that in public?"

"I know you want me to study business, but business and politics are both a form of warfare. Both are entwined, and the weapons are products, words, spies, and gold," Kaede replied.

"Clever and accurate," Toshiko said with a grin.

"What makes you think Dain is still working on artificial cells?" Takahiro asked.

"I know the uterine replicator is top-secret technology, but rumours of them exist in public records, and that the Blood-Witches control them. Dain Medical never announced this, but you have records of him hiring a group of Blood-Witches who make the replicators. Dain medical has not made any significant personnel changes since then. Even now while the same group of Witches are now former employees of Dain, there have been no other employment terminations from that centre. In fact, Dain's last three years reported costs for the centre have not changed, which means he is paying a new group of researchers," Kaede replied.

"The replicator is not made using artificial cells, but made using tissue taken from a dead female," Toshiko said.

"Yes, what has the uterine replicator got to do with artificial cells?" Takahiro asked.

"It keeps the womb alive in a tank, and the nutrient tank is the same technology used in growing cells in," Kaede replied.

"Kaede, you can teach my information researchers a thing or two. They have only rumours that Dain is still working on artificial cells. It is circumstantial, but Dain Medical Research only had stem cell research. Abel and Abelard don't have access to his research centre in Krasnoperekopsk," Takahiro said. "But what makes you think you can get his former employees, especially a group of Blood-Witches, to work for us?"

"For a share of the profit in the product," Kaede replied.

"What makes you think you can beat him to the market with a viable product?" Toshiko asked.

"I assume he has had some success before firing them, but Dain does not have a product. I believe he is using Lilith Foundation research without permission, in the form of the uterine replicator to make his cell growth tanks. My only evidence is the hiring of the Witches, then lodging no research papers. So, we talk to them, if they are willing, we co-publish research papers with the three of us as project leader," Kaede replied.

"Toshiko, I hope you will be wiping out the licencing fees on every product we improve?" Takahiro asked.

"I want my intellectual rights protected, my name on every project and a guarantee that my share of the company will not be diminished, I want no power struggle to force me out," Toshiko said.

Takahiro pondered.

"Grandfather, by lifting the wealth of the Lady Toshiko it increases the wiggle room in the Wealth cap. I am offering you both 20% of Kaede Enterprises, I will retain 51% of all rights and shares, but don't forget 20% of the profits from Kaede Computers is Izanami's before profits transfer to the parent company," Kaede said.

"These projects are very expensive, what if the company fails?" Takahiro asked.

"I am willing to take that risk and so should you, Takahiro, this isn't Hiro wanting a dirt bike or Lord Iti asking you to hire yet another relative," Toshiko said to Takahiro. She turned to Kaede and said, "Don't worry, Kaede, he loves you but is afraid you are going to depose him. Your projects are not small and will make you one of the top wealthiest Elves, making his rule dependant on you."

"Grandfather, just because you stockpiled gold in caves

and plotted against Dain in secret, doesn't mean I will stab you in the back. I will openly admit to you. I want to replace you," Kaede said.

"See, he admits it," Takahiro said.

"Oh please, the only one who doesn't want the throne is Patya," Toshiko said.

"Only because if there is a coup, he gets to stab me in the back," Takahiro said.

"Viktor is not planning a coup, he is genuinely worried about the number of ships leaving the empire for the free colonies," Toshiko said.

"Thank you for handing my admitted rival information to use against me," Takahiro said.

"Anytime," Toshiko said. "Now Kaede, tell me about your profit share plan?"

"Yes, the small percentage unallocated will go to an employee trust. It will be used to pay a bonus to key researchers. We will encourage anyone with an idea to register it on the company's internal network before going to their supervisor. Part of the reward system is how well they abide the terms of employments, especially secrecy," Kaede replied.

"Much like the foundation, only we share our profits by funding the education of those who have the talent, work hard, but cannot afford to get an education," Toshiko said.

"Yes, I will be dedicating a percentage of my income to the education fund for the residents of House Hashimoto," Kaede said.

"Not your friends I hope?" Takahiko asked.

"No, I pay for their education," Toshiko replied.

"Yes, Izanami is doing an electronic engineering

degree which covers the design, construction and theory involved in a Quantum Computers. Including a course in programming," Kaede said.

"These projects will cost billions a year, and we will not be able to keep them secret for long. Dain reads all the public reports we produce, another problem of public office is not only our wealth, but expenditure is public. The lords are touchy about poaching of projects," Takahiro said.

"Dain doesn't own Artificial Cells, and he claims the stem cell project is shut down. You can dismiss it as more provocation, just point out how Dain already provoked you recently by trying to build on your land," Kaede said.

"You have one year to produce results," Takahiro said.

"That is not fair. You know it could take years to find the right process. I have given Kaede three years just to show the theory is sound," Toshiko said.

"I know that, and I expect to see monthly progress reports. Do not fret, Toshiko, I will give him all the support needed to achieve success, but only if progress is being made. It is on you to make sure the researchers are doing as they are employed and not just learning as much as they can to seek protection and payment from another Lord," Takahiro said.

"Not everyone is devious or underhanded, grandfather," Kaede shouted.

"Assume they are, you will live longer," Takahiro said.

"Don't worry Kaede, we can do this," Toshiko said.

"Good. Now I am going to impose strict conditions, especially on security. I know you showed Kaede the sword of light," Takahiro said.

"Kaede has been to my workshop a few times asking questions and borrowing my books. He believes the

Orichalcum tree inside the blade was not just part of the casting device but provided cooling. We think the cores in the hilt were three separate processors. We found scorch marks on the inside of the mesh in the guard with a connection to one of the processors. It appears to be a trap used to capture incoming spells and was able to use that to mana to power the flame blade," Toshiko said.

"You have the spells?" Takahiro said.

"No, but my belief is magic takes more than trying every combination, it takes belief," Kaede said.

"Sounds like nonsense to me," Takahiro said.

"It may be nonsense to you, but we have a tiny fragment of the spell to the spell *Produce Flame*, the spell *Absorb Magic* is fragmented, and the spell *Slash* we only have the start and end. I have tried combinations and have not produced a spell. We need to go back to the original way we created spells. That is to study the forces of nature, then combine those patterns with the brain waves. I would like to record Kaede imaging the spells. I don't have someone to operate the equipment in the Lilith Lab to record mine," Toshiko said.

"You may bring him to that laboratory. But strictly for studying the technology and to record his brain waves. I do not doubt he has an excellent imagination, but you know the effect magic has on adults, he is too young for that," Takahiro said.

"What of the Artificial Cells?" Toshiko asked.

"I want supervisors to ensure the researchers are not biding time for Dain to resolve any problems he has. Or worse, they use us to do additional research for him. But, as for Abel, you may employ her a technology consultant on the computer project. She must not to tell her brother anything about the project," Takahiro said.

"My list of proposed supervisors has many clan members on it. I believe the profit share fund is a much better incentive than threats in the long-term," Kaede said.

Takahiro stood and went to Toshiko. "He must beat Dain to the market by a minimum of ninety days with a process different from his, and it must be profitable. If not, Dain could win a lawsuit," Takahiro said.

"I will ask special research to find out how far along Dain is, and make sure we can cross the finish line well ahead of him," Toshiko said.

"Good," Takahiro said to Toshiko, he bent over to Kaede and said, "You even breathe the words Sword of Light or talk about the other items in the special collections room to anyone, then you will be sent to a boarding school on the edge of the Empire and stripped of everything. Those items belong to Lady Toshiko and are an omega level secret. If you can create anything from them, you tell her or me only. Nothing is to be recorded about them, even on the nondisclosure agreement. Remember Kaede, honour before profit."

"Yes Grandfather," Kaede said.

"Relax, Takahiro, I do know what I am doing," Toshiko said.

"Good, I expect you both to do your best," Takahiro said. He placed his hands inside the long sleeves of his kimono and stared at Toshiko. She poked her tongue out at him.

CHAPTER 7
DUST

September 1, 11571, Abel Mall.

Kaede, aged nine, stood on a float in the large car park at the north end of Abel Mall. With him were Izanami, Sora, Akiko, Mako and Miko. Kaede wore an orange yukata. Izanami was in pink, with Sora and Akiko in red, Mako and Miko in yellow. Each had bright white flowers and white trim.

Abel, in uniform, came to the float. "You all look beautiful. Welcome to the Founder's Day Parade. Since this is your first in the parade, listen carefully. After leaving the car park, you will slowly go down Main Street, the full-length of Abel Mall, and into Founders Park. Your float will stop at the crossroad before entering the park, and you will get off the float there and head into the park with Yuki," Abel said.

"You're not coming with us?" Izanami asked.

"Yuki will be driving the float, and many Knights, House Guards as well as members of the City Guard, are on duty along the route," Abel replied.

Crisis

An organiser blew her whistle and drivers went to their floats and waited. Camera crews stood ready on the road and rooftops. Teams of four Knights with a Cu Sith stood in front of and to the rear of Kaede's float. The dog, the size of a bull, was not collared or on a leash, without any command, it followed the Knights.

In the middle of Main Street, opposite the main entrance to Able Mall, was a park with a stadium with many rows of seats with a row of small marquee tents on top.

Takahiro was in the middle box. He looked at his pocket watch as he sat waiting.

Exactly at noon, he stood and walked to the microphone at the front of the box.

"Welcome to the 11571 Founders Day Parade. Today we celebrate the founding of the new Empire. On behalf of the Senate, to those about to start school, we hope you enjoy commencement week.

In the years before the Empire, we were in a terrible ice age on Terra and fought three wars for survival against the Orcs, Goblins, Ogres, and the Naga. Then came the great flood.

During the great flood, we saved all life, including the primitive Homo Sapiens, only to be persecuted, hunted, and enslaved by them. Forced to live as a minority in our lands, persecuted and oppressed, we planned our escape. A thousand years after the flood we landed on Mars and began a long slow Exodus. Yule, 11201, the last Elf left Terra.

Never again will we give another race *our* land, *our* women, or *our* resources.

In the year 2,000, the First Fleet carrying 77,000 arrived

in the Pleiades. Since then we have grown to a thriving Empire of 114 star-systems, with no rival.

We will bend, but not break, we will be kind and merciful, but never again will we put the needs of another before our own. We will never again face Armageddon!" A very animated and loud Takahiro spoke into the microphone. Many stood and cheered.

Kaede, listened wide-eyed. Then a whistle blew. Izanami tapped Kaede on the shoulder. Motors started, Kaede tapped his naruko, and Yuki turned the music on. They began their dance routine while they waited, with Kaede at the front of the line of girls. They had a naruko in each hand, and they tapped, twirled, and spun to the beat of many drums and a large cymbal, backed by three different kotos and a flute.

At the front of the parade was a marching band lead by a baton twirler, followed by the Imperial Navy float. It was followed by Sky Force, The Guard, The Inquisition, Knights, Medical Bureau, the Blood-Witches, and then Technical support, floats.

Following them came various groups of Elves in native costume, with the Flower Elves was Kaede and the Yosakoi float. Ahead of him was Geisha Girls dancing with fans, with one at the back who played a shamisen, and behind him was a float with shirtless well-built male Flower Elves beating on Japanese kettle drums.

Then came the sports floats; the first being the Galaxy Girls Football team with a red one on the side and *Petrov Interstellar Football Federation Champions,* in bold on it.

Main Street was split by a roundabout at the entry to Abel Mall, the middle of the stadium lined up with the main entrance to the mall. The parade stopped just before the roundabout, while the marching band marched around, doing a peel off and merging back together.

Hiro, Freya, and Masako were in the box beside Takahiro's. They clapped and cheered loudly as Kaede passed them. Kaede saw them but didn't miss a beat. He danced in front of Izanami, Sora, Akiko, Mako and Miko. Kaede performed various dance moves such as twirls, windmill turns, and the girls repeated every move he made, all while using the Yosakoi Clackers in tune with the music.

Along the route, many fans of Kaede cheered and held up signs with 'We Love You.' and holding pictures of Kaede. One group of screaming fans followed them along Main Street. Many of them were young girls in kimonos covered in pink hearts with a red K in the middle.

Founder's Park was a large park divided by Main Street, crossed by the road that ran around the lake. On the east side of the park was seven large black marble walls with the names of the 77,000 founders on them in gold.

On the western side were thirteen statues of the first rulers of the New Empire in a ring. They were life-sized marble statues of High Lord Dain Hartman, Emperor Takahiro Hashimoto, Czar Patya Petrov, King Argon Agrovar, General Kenta Yoshida, Sky Marshal Rudolf Reinhart, Maharajah Arjuna Desai, Pharaoh Takis Alexandris, Prince Georgi Vlasov, Chief Árni Tikkanen, General Adalwulf Feygold, Admiral Viktor Niemi and Chief Yaotl Belaúnde.

Main Street ended at a large double gate in a white wall that lined the south side of the park. The gates opened as Toshiko approached. On the wall beside the gate was a sign that had 'The Home of the Witch of the East' on it. The driveway was of different coloured stones. The lawn was beautiful. The driveway ended in a roundabout around a garden with a statue of Lilith in the middle. To the east of that was an underground parking bay, and to the west, a small parking area. Staff stood on the steps and bowed, Toshiko waved and led Kaede past them. The estate was on the edge of the lake with its own beach, a large cabin cruiser at the dock. A helicopter approached the helipad south of the house.

Toshiko's house was a huge three-story mansion and was on four city blocks. Inside the double doors was the main entrance. It was two storeys with a domed roof and had two stairs, either side of an arch, to a balcony. They passed under that into the two-storey main hall that led to two sets of glass double doors at the rear. The rear deck was huge with four stone columns with a balcony over it. They walked down the steps towards the helipad east of the pool house.

Most of the pool house was clear, and inside was a large black marble pool with gold flecks. It had a diving board.

There was a hedge maze, with a two-storey pagoda in the middle east of the main house. East of the helipad was a two-storey guest house. To the west of the main house stood a hothouse, greenhouse, and a cold house.

The estate was on the edge of the lake with its own beach, a large cabin cruiser at the dock. A helicopter approached the helipad.

"Wow, your place is huge," Kaede said.

"Yes. It is as big as the Hartman Estate and the Yoshida Estate combined. They happen to be either side of me," Toshiko replied.

"You must have a lot of fun there."

"I spent most of my time at the Palace."

"Who takes care of it?"

"I hire former Knights and girls from Hashimoto House."

"That is so nice."

"That was exciting music, but I never heard it before."

"It is called Thunder Storm, and I wrote it myself."

"That is amazing. I noticed the koto sounded different."

"There are three different kotos, which I designed myself."

"Why didn't you tell me? I love the koto; can I see them?"

"Yes, they are in my storage."

"Could we play them?"

"Yes.

"Who arrange the other floats to play the music for you?"

"Lady Hitomi. She is a member of the Flower Elf Cultural Society. She was on a float playing the flute."

August 20, 11574. The rim of the Alcyone System.

Hiro, the captain of the *Night Owl*, sat in his office aboard the ship. The screen on his desk displayed a video of his son, Kaede.

"Hello Father, you have been gone a few years. Grandfather let me send you this video before he went away on business, and he has taken Toshiko, Yuki and Galené with him. Before leaving, Lady Emi brought her son, Nori, over to stay with me. Izanami is jealous of him; she says I am spending too much time with him. She says she is not jealous, but then she cried when I danced with Sora. I don't understand why, as it was for Sora's birthday. Czar Petrov and his wife are staying in the guest rooms. She is watching Nori and me. He goes back to school soon, but I hope Grandfather will let me have him over more. It is nice to have a friend who is not fighting over me.

I am doing well in the talent quest, but competition is high, so I am taking singing lessons. However, Izanami and I are in the lead. Oh, I found out why shuttles do not fly in an atmosphere. It is because ion engines do not work in the presence of ions outside the engine. My gravity-plasma engine does.

Do not worry about my studies with Lady Toshiko away. Lady Toshiko had me do basic medicine. She told me it was because of how magical healing works. I graduated with honours. Not sure if I want to spend the next eight years studying medicine.

That year, after I turned 11, to test the strength of the casing for the Fusion 2 reactor, I had a submarine made. I set a record when I took the DSV down. The depth of the dive was 10,912 metres.

Lady Toshiko has told me that I am magically active. A fancy way of saying I am better at magic than the average Elf. I am learning what I can about magic, but it is hard because it is illegal for me to use a wand. I asked Grandfather for a wand and magic lessons. Instead, he has permitted me to take flying lessons. Sky Marshal Reinhart is my instructor. He is cool; we started in his propeller driven biplane, and he let me call him Rudolf when we are flying. He has a vast collection of aircraft. I hope to have my pilot's licence a day before my birthday. I have designed a few aircraft; one uses four Kaede-Toshiko Gravity-Plasma Jets to lift off the ground. So, I am going on a solo flight in a balloon around the globe; I have already designed it; then Izanami and I are going to race them around the globe.

I have many companies now. I still make toys. But I have been helping Lady Toshiko in her workshop to learn what I can about magic. I have learnt how wands work and are made. We worked together on studying magical devices. I understand the technology commonly referred to as magic. I designed a microphone that projects sound equally over an area, a keyboard without keys that uses motion control to make music and I am working on using the same technology on drums and a guitar. I wanted to take guitar lessons, but Czarina Katerina is teaching me to play the piano.

Admiral Niemi is going to teach me to sail; he said it is a naval tradition that starship captains must be able to steer a sailboat without crashing. He told me you are one of the best sailors in the naval academy. I will do my best, so when you return, we can take a yacht and race him for the peninsular cup when you return. Maybe I will design one for us.

I have so many prizes now. My latest was the Imperial Award in physics for the semi-portable fusion reactor and another in biology for the Artificial Cell. Mako and Miko have joined Kaede Medical as students. Czar Petrov is sure Lady Toshiko and I will get an Imperial Award for a new electric engine for vehicles. But we don't have a battery yet.

Please don't forget you now owe me three wishes. I love you, Father," Kaede said and then bowed. The background was the Palace gardens, which then faded to a green room. Then the video ended.

Hiro sat with a smile. There was a knock on the door. Hiro closed the video, got up and pressed to open the door.

The door slid open, to reveal a Knight. Lady Galené was a short, young, dark-skinned female half Flower Elf, half Silver Elf. She had red eyes with pink hair with a long silver streak in her fringe.

"Lady Galené, my son, says hello," Hiro said.

"I think he has a crush on me," Galené said.

"You best not let my father hear that or he might assign you to the Ice Fortress," Hiro said.

"As a guard or inmate?" Galené asked with a giggle as she entered his office.

"From what I heard about the prison, the guards have it worse; at least inmates are inside," Hiro said, pressing to close the door.

"The Emperor heard we are an hour away from Alcyone Station Seven," Galené said.

"My father is the worst passenger I have had," Hiro said. "What is it this time?"

"Was it necessary that we sling-shot around the sun?" Galené asked.

"I already told him, the helm operator plotted both a sling-shot and direct route. That has been standard procedure for over a hundred years, and as with most times, the sling-shot was the fastest course," Hiro replied.

"Sorry, I thought a direct path was always the fastest, as it is the shortest distance between two points," Galené said.

"With a sling-shot, we gain speed, and the fuel scoops fill our tanks faster than in open space," Hiro said.

"He wants to speak with you before we dock," Galené said.

"Of course, he does," Hiro said rolling his eyes.

"I don't get it, we travel to an empty system, then all the

way back to a space station near the star, then we heading to the edge of the system."

"I think we picked up a package from one of our spies, then picked up the prototype space planes from one of our secret laboratories, and now we heading to test it."

"He isn't in a good mood."

"He probably wants to try again to talk me out of flying to the prototype of my son's engine."

She turned and headed for the door, then turned. "Is that it? Not because I ask that my brother to flying the stealth fighter?"

"I haven't seen him in years, and I believe you. I do not think your brother is involved in stealing information from you, but you know my father, always assume the worse and no one will disappoint you," Hiro replied as he followed her to the door. "You do know we were in flight school together?"

"I know. The same time I was at camp Bravo training to be a Knight," Galené replied. "I am sorry my twin brother doesn't keep in touch with you. You know how it is, it has been twenty years, and you are at the helm of a cruiser, and he is in Sky Force piloting cargo planes."

"We were twenty, young and foolish. Galen might be a better pilot than me, but a starship is about teamwork," Hiro said.

"He was angry as a child. It isn't just you. He has never made friends with any pureblood. I hoped by having him pilot the latest space plane would have shown him the Empire doesn't discriminate against the mixed-blood Elves."

"Despite the laws, some do, but that is not my father's

fault," Hiro said. "Surely he understands why we have blood-line laws?"

"No, he doesn't," Galené replied.

A few hours later a large black streamlined single-engine stealth space plane soared through space towards the enormous asteroid cloud that surrounded the system.

Inside the cockpit, the pilot sat, visually searching the asteroid field ahead of him on his screen. He checked the 3D radar screen. On edge behind him were two contacts, one the space station, the one beside that, the cruiser, the *Night Owl*.

Two Banshee One space planes were near the station escorting a civilian freighter to a docking arm. More space planes were in the area around the station; most were between the station and the tunnel in the asteroid cloud. One space plane was heading towards him.

"Galen, please return to the station. I promise they will let you live," Galené pleaded over the radio.

Galen changed the channel and set communications to passive.

The space plane was closing on him, but still too far away to fire missiles. The Banshee Two was cloaked, and that traded speed for stealth. He checked the engines; the field generator to disperse the ion trail was on. He checked the electronic warfare system; the craft was not broadcasting signals, nor was he being tracked by radar. He changed the view on his main screen to rear, and on screen, he saw a Banshee One.

The twin-engine Banshee One, unlike the sleek black single-engine Banshee Two, was dull grey, larger, longer, and faster than the Banshee Two. Also unlike the Banshee Two, the Banshee One did not carry missiles in an internal bay. Instead, they were in launch tubes under the wings, usually three under each wing. Galen saw the ship had only two. Each launcher had a large self-guided anti-ship missile inside.

The Banshee Two altered course. The Banshee One adjusted to an intercept course. Galen armed missiles.

"Operator, I have 'Red One' on ultra-scope. Over," said the pilot of the Banshee One. He waited ten seconds and counted to himself. In his earpiece, there was silence. "Operator, this is Star Dust, do you read? Over," the pilot said.

Like the Banshee Two, the cockpit of the Banshee One was inside an armoured ball, buried in the hull behind the forward manoeuvring ring, thus having no outside view, so they both flew by instrumentation.

Both had three large screens side by side that formed a panoramic view of outside with two more small screens below that. An assortment of buttons, switches, and dials was to the left and right of the pilot's seat.

Hiro turned a three-position switch from A to B on his communications panel to his right and listened for a few seconds.

"Operator, I am one light second from the station, on channel B. Do you read me? Over," Hiro said.

He tapped controls with his right hand, his left hand not steady on the stick. On the external view was mostly a field of black, with only a few dim stars. The right side was a grey cloud marked in red, "Alcyone Asteroid Cloud". In the centre was a gunsight tracking a target, with a "1" over the sight.

The left main screen displayed weapons status, showing rail gun with 500 rounds and two anti-ship missiles. The right main screen displayed ship status, with two wireframes in the box of the Banshee top and side with a fuel bar on the side; also, a network box top left which flashed off and on.

The message box displayed, "Executing systems diagnostics."

Then the message box slowly filled with a list of the craft's systems, which one by one displayed, each went from the status of 'checking' to 'okay'.

Hiro watched the wireframes of the ship turned white, then one by one they turned green. On the HUD over the primary display, the fuel bar showed just under 80%. The three solid rings around a green dot in the network box first marked "A" second "B" and third "C" each went from green to red.

Under the main screen, was two small screens. The one on the left displayed a 3D globe, and it showed the location of the Banshee Two, he was closing on its position. The one on the right displayed a message box, it was empty.

"I do not know if you can hear me. I am closing on target, going weapons hot, all systems green, yet I have no response from the operations on Alcyone Station Seven. I have run a system check, no warnings in my message box, yet no network connection, no error message," Hiro said.

Hiro switched communications from B to A then listened for ten seconds. He switched back to B, to hear only silence. The pilot turned the switch from B to C.

"Alcyone Station Seven, this is Star Dust, I have lost contact with my operator. Over," he said. Then he counted under his breath.

As Hiro counted, he heard static from his earpiece then on thirty he heard, "Star Dust, this is Alcyone Station Seven Space Traffic Control, please repeat your last transmission." Then came static.

Hiro's external view turned into static, and the 3D representation of radar contacts was blank. An alarm sounded, and the marked box sensors on the systems status screen turned red.

Hiro swore as he hit reset, and took a deep breath. He grabbed the throttle and pulled it back, steering a hard left away from the clouds.

As he approached the station, "Star Dust, this is Alcyone Space Traffic Control; please respond. Over," an operator said.

"Alcyone Station Seven, I found 'Red One'. He is heading towards the asteroid cloud ahead of my current location. I have lost communications contact with my assigned operator, and my sensors are reporting a fault. Over," Hiro said.

"Star Dust, return immediately to Alcyone Station Seven. Over," the operator said.

"Alcyone Control. I request you send immediate support to my location. 'Red One' has engaged his cloaking device; I am activating the seeking missiles. Over," Hiro said.

"Negative Star Dust, disengage and return immediately to Alcyone Station Seven. Over," another voice said, then there was static.

"Alcyone Station Seven?"

The only reply was static.

Hiro changed channels, but there was static on all frequencies.

"Go ahead; keep jamming me; soon I will ram my radiation seekers up each nostril," Hiro said, and he activated his missiles.

Hiro fired and yanked the joystick hard left while pressing in hard on the pedal. Suddenly on his display, he saw a glimpse of the Banshee Two, right behind him.

"Missile Alert, Missile Alert, Missile Alert, Missile Alert," sounded in Hiro's ear. He reached out and pressed the flashing button to his right. The alarm went silent. He launched decoys and spun the plane up in a loop and twist, then dived, a course that should have flown him towards the craft behind him and past the missiles.

On his 3D radar display, two dots appeared behind him and headed towards him. Then came two more, while his missiles flew towards an asteroid, where unseen by Hiro was a small jamming station fixed on him.

Hiro tapped decoys again. Four little irises opened around the rear of the hull behind the rear manoeuvring thrusters. Inside each was a launch tube that ejected a small canister propelled by compressed gas. Each canister shone a powerful light and broadcast electronic signals.

"Launching decoys, taking evasive action," Hiro said, he hit reset on his sensors panel. The external view came on, and the sensors went from red to green.

On his scope were four balls of static behind him, between him and the missiles. Hiro was slowly putting distance between himself and the cloud. He again pulled a hard turn. The four missiles headed for the cloud fast.

Unknown to Hiro, he was slowing down, his craft not responding. Inside the nose of his spacecraft, a black box with legs sat on his computer, taking orders from an unseen operator.

Hiro saw the missiles closing fast; he noticed he was still close to the decoys as they passed through the cloud. Hiro released the joystick and tried using the thruster controls. Two balls each had one to eight on the dial; in the arms of his pilot set. He spun them. He pressed reset on engines. The craft was not moving away from the decoys.

Hiro's external view came on, and he saw the Banshee Two in front of him; it sat watching him. The four missiles side by side slowed as they approached Hiro.

The first missile changed course in an arc. Hiro saw on his 3D radar the missile head for the belly of his spacecraft. Hiro launched more decoy canisters, but the incoming missiles did not change course.

"Alcyone Station Seven, this is Star Dust, 'Red One' attacked me with four anti-ship missiles at me. I am ejecting," Hiro said as he looked at his screen. His HUD displayed 0-0-0 as his location. He hit the eject button, and nothing happened.

He sat and listened to the static. Suddenly a soft female voice said, "Warning Impact Alert."

Each of the four missiles was a long flat black cigar, a flying engine with two sets of manoeuvring rings and a sensor pod in the nose. Each was designed to disable a starship by flying into and exploding inside the engine. One was enough to destroy a Banshee.

Hiro stopped pressing eject. On his radar the missiles circled him, and the Banshee Two just sat in front of him.

"Hiro, are we having fun yet?" Galen asked.

"Why are you doing this?" Hiro asked.

"Tell me, Hiro, who is the better pilot?"

"You don't understand; in a few years, you could have been captain of a new class of ship," Hiro said.

"Wrong answer," Galen shouted.

"Why are you doing this?"

No reply.

Hiro pressed eject repeatedly. Then all around his craft, the missiles exploded. Each sent a hot slug of metal smashing into his plane. The main body was torn open, the two fuel tanks ripped open, plasma vented from his rear engines. Hiro's thumb pressed hard on the eject button, and as the nose of his craft was ripped off, his secondary computer engaged.

As his spacecraft was torn apart by a series of explosions, his radiation-seeking missiles slammed into the asteroid, blowing apart the jamming station. Hiro was tossed about inside his suit, and a voice in his ear said, "Ejection engaged".

The plane shuddered with violent force; all his screen went blank, then Hiro found himself tumbling. Inside the hull, many explosions went off. Inside the cockpit, Hiro's seat inflated and reclined, the straps holding him pulled tight on his spacesuit and forced him back into the seat.

The first of two manoeuvring rings held the nose to the midsection. It exploded as small charges inside blew the nose off, exposing the cockpit. The rear manoeuvring ring held the engine section to the body. It was severely damaged; the internal explosions were enough to detach only the rear section.

As the various explosive charges blew the spacecraft

apart, the cockpit umbilical cord detached and its rocket motors fired. The cockpit was inside an armoured pod. The disintegrating space plane shot the pod out like a cannon ball. Two little irises in the hull beneath the cockpit opened, and each ejected a black box recorder, only they were in the shape of a small ball, in different directions.

Hiro, now a prisoner of his acceleration chair, had no control over the craft. The rocket motors stopped burning, the ball tumbled in space, moving slowly and broadcasting a distress beacon.

The twisted wreck of the Banshee drifted in space as parts flew off in all directions. Galen was caught off guard, his craft by debris.

Then Galen saw on screen the cockpit soar past him. He turned on LIDAR and turned his spacecraft around. He tracked the pod, then turned on the high-intensity lamp in the sensor ball under the nose of the Banshee Two.

Galen stared at the tumbling pod on screen.

He flipped another switch. Under the nose, a bay behind the sensor ball opened. Out of it came a large cannon on a gimble mount. Galen fired the gun repeatedly at the top of the pod, making it spin fast. He laughed.

Galen manoeuvred his craft closer. His engines did not fire a bright yellow, but a dull blue. Like most Elven spacecraft, this one had two sets of manoeuvring rings that divided the craft into three. These housed the manoeuvring and braking engines. Each engine was smaller than those on the Banshee One. Also, the Banshee Two had two smaller engines around the ring, a total of sixteen to the Banshee One's eight engines. The sleek craft danced in darkness as

Galen moved around the pod, with no bright flashes to alert those searching for him.

"Where are you?" a voice hissed in Galen's ear.

"Taking care of business," Galen replied.

"Hurry, we need to leave soon," the voice said.

"Relax," Galen said. He turned the lamp off and retracted the gun. Then the craft shuddered, an alarm went off, he hit reset and checked the status screen. An impact on the hull was displayed on the wireframe in the status window.

Inside the tumbling cockpit, Hiro tossed about inside his suit. He exclaimed loudly when his nose hit his suit's faceplate hard. That broke his nose and splattered blood all over the inside of his faceplate. A single drop of blood hung near one eye. All Hiro could do was look at this single drop floating near his eye. It was the centre of the universe, and he was slowly spinning around this single drop of blood.

Hiro felt intense fear. The harness holding him to his seat pulled on his suit tightly, and he was unable to move.

Unable to brace himself, all he could do was scream as he bounced around inside his suit. His internal organs ruptured, and he was in intense pain. There was no light. Hiro shivered and then as he gasped for air, his body convulsed, then he went limp.

Galen peppered the pod with more gunfire, this time from his fixed guns. That breached the hull. Bullets and shrapnel bounced around inside the tumbling pod, wreaking havoc. The bullets had popped the airbags, smashed the screens, and controls. The air was hissing out of the holes. Bullets hit Hiro, but the light was already gone from his eyes, and he was frozen.

The Banshee Two moved in closer to the pod and turned on the high-intensity lamp. A beam of light shone on the pod. On the outside of the pod the solid fuel rocket packs, already burnt out, were both smashed. The atmosphere was venting from various holes in the outer skin and the tanks in the base; the rear hatch marked *rescue* was distorted; a locker above it was smashed open, and its contents gone.

The Banshee Two moved sideways around the pod. Galen saw on his display a signal coming from Hiro's pod. Furious, he flicked the switch and fired the cannon at the source of the signal until he ran out of ammunition.

"Goodbye Hiro," Galen said.

The light was turned off, and the nose cannon retracted into its compartment. The rotary missile bay turned and sealed. Galen flew away and engaged the cloaking device. It generated a distortion field around the craft that scrambled light, radar and other detection methods, except one; it could not hide the gravity waves of its engines.

The Banshee Two resumed course for the asteroid field and entered. Galen flew the craft slowly down a snaking tunnel in the asteroids towards an enormous asteroid.

Nori, an Aquatic Elf, was playing laser tag in the underground gardens with Kaede, watched by Czarina Katrina Petrov. While they stalked each other in the lush gardens in front of the tea house, Katrina sipped her tea, looking at the tablet on the table. It had a tracking application open showing the boys' location.

Kaede crawled under a large bush, then climbed a tree,

and waited. Nori walked past the large bush, then saw the tracks. He looked under it, his toy laser pistol ready.

Above him, Kaede stood on a branch, holding onto the tree with his right hand, his pistol in his left. He watched Nori emerge from under the bush. Nori stood and looked around, and when he turned around, Kaede shot him in the back. Nori spun around as his alarm sounded.

"No fair," Nori cried out.

Kaede dropped down out of the tree, landed in front of Nori, and shot him in the chest.

"Yelling no fair in battle gets you shot at a second time. There is no such thing as a fair fight," Kaede said.

"You cheated," Nori said as he ran up to the tea house.

"Sorry, but Kaede is right. The only fair fight is one everyone loses," Katrina said.

Patya walked down the path. "How goes the test, Prince Kaede?" Patya asked Kaede as they walked to the tea house.

"Good," Kaede said.

"Why only two detectors on the vest?" Patya asked.

"They are the heart shot; I am going add smaller ones to a soft-padded helmet for the headshot; one on the forehead and then another one on the back of the head," Kaede replied.

"Some want to place a ban on your selling the device because it is military training equipment," Patya said. He kissed Katrina on the cheek and sat beside her.

"I am adding to the system a helmet, shin, knee and elbow pads, each with detectors. Let me market a kid's toy. I can sell the Imperial Security Agency a version where the gun is a training rifle. I can add a device to the vest that generates a mild shock when a hit is scored. I can make the detectors smaller, have a counter to require a set number of hits, or set a minimum time for laser contact on the detector to count as a hit. I could also add a hit point bar on the vest. Or a combination of those," Kaede said.

"General Feygold has enough support for a ban," Patya said.

"I will present him a better version, with simulated weapons with the right weight. Have you taken into consideration that Orcs give their kids rubber axes and mallets? Goblin teenagers carry real knives, and Giants take their children hunting with real guns?" Kaede asked.

"You can have a toy gun, just one that is not like a military training device," Patya said.

"But the guard has off-road vehicles," Kaede argued.

"Yes, they do," Patya said. "What has that got to do with toy guns?"

"You don't stop private sales of off-road vehicles. Anyone who can afford to can have armour and bullet-resistant glass installed by Alexandris Security, a company owned by Pharaoh Takis Alexandris, who sells you the same glass for all Imperial armoured vehicles," Kaede said. "Again, I ask you, can I sell the toy version?"

"Patya, he has you there," Katrina said standing. She walked over to Kaede. "You will make an excellent lawyer, but it is soon time you boys went to bed, so pack away your toys." She looked at Patya when she said *toys*.

"Did you come to confiscate my toys?" Kaede asked. "I warn you I have an army of lawyers on speed dial."

"No, I came with a proposal from Petrov Arms to licence your laser and laser detector," Patya said.

"I have proposals from Hashimoto Defence and

Reinhart Armaments; I will consider yours, then work out if one of your bids is high enough for an exclusive contract, sell you the product or licence manufacture to one group. Whichever proposal makes me the most gold, wins," Kaede said.

"Prince Kaede, this is for Imperial Defence," Katrina said.

"I want to be Emperor one day, so I need to be richer. Under the Defence Contractors' Act, the profit is limited, so I need the best contract possible and a civilian market," Kaede said. "You cannot just proclaim any invention is for Defence of the Realm and take it, there is a process of negotiations, bidding, an inquiry and audits."

"Are you sure you haven't been to law school?" Patya asked.

"I have read a few law books already, as I plan on going to law school," Kaede replied.

"A piece of advice for you, go with a lowest priced laser diode you can. Don't reduce the quality of yours and sell it to everyone. I am sure you will have many supply contracts all over the empire, even with some restrictions, you will make a pile of gold, and I will change my offer to a manufacturing deal," Patya said.

"Nori, why don't you take the toys and meet me in my room? One of my Knights will take you," Kaede said, he packed his gun and the laser tag vest in a box and handed the box to Nori.

A Knight stood behind Nori. "This way to the elevator," she said.

After Nori, had left, Kaede said, "You could have just placed a call to me, Czar Petrov. What is on your mind?"

"Honey, we can use some tea," Patya said as he walked up the stairs and sat at the table on the balcony.

"Yes please," Kaede said and sat opposite Patya.

"Remember the rings that we confiscated?" Patya asked.

"Yes, how could I forget? The next day after you took them Grandfather came and threatened to shut all my projects down," Kaede said.

"We know you were developing a smaller and cheaper cloaking device. In the interest of Imperial Security, we confiscated the field generators along with the data. Your grandfather will compensate you. eventually. He will licence the technology from you, Takahiro is the owner of the patent on the original cloaking device. He left me a licencing agreement and other contracts for you to sign," Patya said.

"What about my engine?" Kaede asked.

"As part of the agreement, strict controls are set in place, so your plant makes only the approved gravity containment rings for your fusors. We have for you a couple of supply contracts for fusion two plants, fusors, gravity rings and different engines. Strict conditions will be placed on your research centre as well," Patya said.

"That is the big secret; they are testing my engine now?" Kaede asked.

"You know I cannot tell you," Patya replied.

"I have the highest clearance," Kaede protested.

"So, do I, but he continues to keep secrets from me too," Katrina said as she placed a tray on the table.

Kaede looked at the teapot and three cups.

"Clearance means if you need to know, we will tell you what we think you need to know. The Emperor doesn't believe you need to know the details," Patya said.

"But I need to know the results. My team worked on many designs just as my grandfather asked. With the fusion plant, he had them test different fuels, different containment designs, and he informed me of the results then," Kaede said.

"Many are worried a semi-portable fission device is a bomb, not a power supply, especially since it weighs only one hundred kilograms and you mounted it inside an armoured contained to be transported by a large truck," Patya said.

"You can say his name," Kaede said.

"Dain is not the only one in the Senate who is concerned. Not all think it is a bomb, but there is a fear it could be made into one or used as one," Patya said.

"Everyone is worried because I designed a fifty-megaton bomb, right?" Kaede asked.

"Designing such a weapon aged nine has made a few worried. Worse you didn't tell anyone," Patya replied.

"I abandoned it, you hold the patent on micro-fission, fission and fusion devices, there is almost no need or profit for such a device, nor has one been built," Kaede said.

"We built, and I personally tested the trigger, I checked your calculations, and it is possible your design works," Patya said.

Kaede was excited, he jumped up and said "You set it off? Can I see the video? How big was the blast?"

"See, this is the why everyone is worried about you," Patya said.

"As if you sat straight-faced when you set off the device?" Kaede asked.

Katrina grabbed Patya's hand and said, "He giggled like a schoolgirl as we watched and waited in the command centre. They tested the bomb far outside the system, a drone was streaming live to us. The bomb looked tiny as it floated in space, ships cleared the area. Then when the bomb went off, he stood cheering like he just scored his first goal. He was so excited, he couldn't sleep that night. The main blast was over a thousand kilometres in diameter."

"I did not," Patya said.

"You did so. Patya, let Kaede view the video," Katrina said. "Viktor is worried because the blast was far stronger than defensive shields on a starship."

"Soon we will be able to power bigger and stronger election cloud shields and particle deflectors. It will take a long time to get a shield able to survive the blast wave from a fifty-megaton bomb. However, given the size and complexity of the device, it should be easy to detect. I am sure my team has enough time to develop better shields," Kaede said.

"Relax, drink your tea, and I will get some bread and cheese," Katrina said. She slid the tablet to Patya. "Go on, show him the videos."

"Yes, dear," Patya said.

Kaede watched Katrina leave and leant over. "I know everyone thinks a Demon possesses me," Kaede said. "You hunt Demons, right?"

"I used to, but we will not talk about that today," Patya said as he opened the Big Bang folder and added the videos to the playlist. "The first video is only of the trigger."

"Is it true that is the real reason we left Terra?" Kaede asked. "To leave all the possessed behind?"

Patya looked at Kaede. "Where did you read that?"

"Conspiracy pages on the dark web claim you arrest and torture anyone for talking about possession," Kaede replied.

"I do not torture anyone," Patya said.

Katrina put the tray down hard and looked at Patya. "Patya Alexandra Petrov, you are head of the Inquisition, and you are not supposed to lie."

Patya looked at her and with a smile said, "...who didn't deserve it is implied."

"His favourite is Mind Probe; he enjoys using forced magical extraction of information, it is well known to be a form of torture and illegal for civilians to even know the spell," Katrina said.

"I only use Mind Probe only in cases of treason," Patya said.

"Which include possession by a Demon, acts of terrorism, industrial espionage against defence contractors, conspiracy to harm members of the Senate, their families or attempts to steal military weapons," Katrina said.

"Yes, dear it does," Patya said.

"Kaede, for the Truth Analysis Spell to work the caster must be honest, but Patya frequently bends the truth," Katrina said.

"Cool," Kaede said.

"Thanks," Patya said.

"Why is his lying cool?" Katrina asked.

"The bending, not breaking the rules is a mental challenge. One needs to keep secrets without lying. It must be so exciting to be that intelligent and cunning," Kaede said.

"See, he gets it," Patya said with a broad smile.

"Your ego is over-inflated," Katrina said, she took a hunk of cheese and put it in Patya's mouth, then pressed play on the tablet.

Kaede leaned over and said, "Anyone can lie, it takes a genius to avoid telling a lie and not reveal a secret."

Patya with a broad grin, adjusted his position closer to Kaede holding the tablet up.

Nori sat in the bubble bath when Kaede joined him. Nori splashed Kaede, and Kaede splashed Nori back. Freya leant over and pulled them apart. "No fighting."

"We were just playing," Kaede said.

"Keep it friendly," Freya said and sat down.

"Watch this," Nori said and put his head underwater and floated face down.

Freya stood up and waited. After a minute, she pulled Nori out of the water.

"You be careful around water," Freya said.

"It is all right, I can hold my breath for a long time," Nori said.

"Not in my bath," Freya said.

"Yes Miss," Nori said.

The boys dressed, and got into bed, Freya wished them good night and tucked them in. She turned out the light and left. Katrina at the door nodded to Freya as she left the room.

"Goodnight Czarina Katrina," Freya said, she turned to leave.

"Freya," Katrina said.

"Yes?"

"Don't worry about what happened in the bath. Nori was showing off."

"He scared me. What was he thinking to lay on the bottom of the bath like that?"

"Aquatic Elves can hold their breath longer than other Elves can."

"He scared me to death. Worse they both laughed at me when I pulled Nori out of the water."

"Aquatic Elves are natural swimmers with their streamlined bodies, big lungs and webbing between fingers and toes."

"I hope you don't mind me asking. Are Aquatic Elves like a Daemon?"

"I don't understand. What you are asking me?"

"Nori said he can free dive to twenty metres and stay underwater for five minutes. It got me wondering if they are genetically altered like how a Daemon is a hybrid of Elves and animal DNA."

"Oh no, Aquatic Elves have always been natural swimmers."

"You don't alter DNA?"

"The Dragon Treaty forbids the creation of new races and the altering of the existing races."

"I see."

"Don't worry, I will talk to the boys, make sure they don't do it again."

"Thank-you Czarina."

"Goodnight Freya, see you tomorrow."

CHAPTER 8

ACTION STATIONS

August 20, 11574. The rim of the Alcyone System.

On Alcyone Station Seven, in the operations room, dozens of Console Operators were busy at their consoles watched by the station's executive officer. The noise from so many talking at the same time was loud, and everyone wore headsets with microphones, connected to phones on their belt. Operators plugged their phones into an interface slot in their console.

"Star Dust, this is Alcyone Station Seven, do you read? Over," a Console Operator said. She waited thirty seconds, then tried channels B and C.

The station's executive officer, Lady Commander Nadia Dvorkin, a Field Elf with blonde hair and blue eyes, sat at a console on a rotating platform top of a gantry in the middle of the operations room.

The Console Operator for Star Dust changed the channel on her console to the intercom.

"Commander, I have no response from Star Dust. I have both data links showing as green, I am receiving a data stream, but none of the video feeds," the Console Operator said.

"Standby. I will test the data link to Star Dust," Nadia replied.

She tapped at her keyboard and looked at her screen. Nadia listened to the audio link to Star Dust and heard only loud static in her headset. Then onscreen a message box stated, "Interference Pattern Detected."

Nadia opened a call to Admiral Fukuhina on her screen.

"Admiral, Star Dust is being jammed," Nadia said.

On screen, Admiral Fukuhina, a Flower Elf with pink hair and gold eyes, and two gold stars on her collar, was at her desk in her office at the end of the gantry.

"Commander, send a squadron to the last known position of Star Dust," Fukuhina said.

"Aye," Nadia replied.

The admiral reached over and tapped *end call*. She then placed a call to the *Night Owl* where it was docked.

While the Admiral was talking to the executive officer on the *Night Owl*, the console "Star Dust" messages flooded the status box. "Missile Warning" "Hull Breach" "Engine Failure", "Fuel Tank Rapture", "Reaction Chamber Rupture", then "Auto Ejection Engaged" and then "Self-Destruct Engaged."

The Console Operator paused, then she turned to face the commander. "Commander, Star Dust had been destroyed."

Nadia flipped open the cover of the alarm and pressed it. The room's lights turned red.

Admiral Fukuhina ended her call, grabbed a headset, and ran down the gantry to the executive officer's desk.

As she adjusted her microphone, she was on the walls the screens showing the docking arms. On five was the *Night Owl*. Its hangar was opening. Fukuhina leaned over and turned the camera to dock five off, then plugged her headset into her phone and set chat to Flight Control.

"Nadia, issue a Bird Down Alert to all ships in this sector and have the *Unicorn* investigate," Fukuhina said.

The admiral selected Flight Deck A and Flight Deck B on the chat application. "Deck Commanders, scramble all interceptors, send three flights to search the last known position for Star Dust and have them search for the cockpit pod," Fukuhina said.

"Aye," both officers replied.

Admiral Fukuhina ended the call. She set the chat to Lady Commander Nadia Dvorkin and called her.

"Nadia, I will be in my ready room, leave the camera to dock five off," Admiral Fukuhina said.

"Aye Admiral," Nadia replied.

The admiral ended the call.

Various Console Operators stopped to look when the door to the Operations Room opened. An officer in black entered. Lady Naru Inoue, a Flower Elf with light purple hair and violet eyes, was an Agent of the Inquisition. Two armed and armoured Knights entered the command room with her.

Commander Nadia left her desk and came down the spiral stair near her desk to Lady Naru. "Lady Naru," Nadia said.

"Do we have a second bird down?" Naru asked.

"Yes and no. 'Red One' and Stardust are both offline,

but it appears Senior Flight Officer Galen lied about having a critical malfunction," Nadia said.

"We can talk later, first show me to the console for the second lost craft, Commander."

"This way."

Nadia led Naru over to the console "Star Dust", where two Knights stood in guard position at the door.

Naru looked at the Console Operator's Identification and chose her on the chat application.

"Touch nothing, leave your identification card and phone in their slots, and go with them," Naru said. She extended her black gloved hand to the phone in the console and pulled the Console Operator's phone out, unplugged the headset and put the plug in the Console Operator's hand.

Naru removed an evidence bag from inside her satchel along with a black marker. She wrote on the evidence bag, then placed the phone inside and sealed it. A Knight escorted the nervous Console Operator from the stations Operations Room down the hall to the security office. Inside a cell, another Console Operator sat. She stood when the light came on. The Knight put the worried Star Dust Console Operator in a cell facing the other one.

The Knight closed the clear plastic cell door, and the light went off when the Knight left. On her way, back to Operations room, she stopped to check both Console Operators were on camera.

Naru, Nadia and Fukuhina were on a conference call. Naru sat at the Star Dust console, Nadia at her desk, Fukuhina at her desk, in her office.

"Admiral, I have sent you a copy of the data for Star

Dust, I request the data from the *Night Owl* from the time she first docked, until now, to be sent to my office," Naru said.

"Of course, Lady Naru," Fukuhina said.

"I would like the original data nodes from the two consoles to be removed. I want them sealed in evidence bags and transported to headquarters for detailed analysis. I will need you and the commander to appear at the inquiry. I find the loss of, not one, but two test craft on the same day both very distressing and extremely disturbing," Naru said.

"Naru, I will go aboard the *Night Owl* and ensure they send you the data before leaving. Commander, you will brief the third watch before joining me on the ship," Fukuhina said.

"Admiral, I have omega security clearance, so I am aware of the details of today's test," Naru said.

"I know you have my full cooperation and I will make sure all my crew will give the Inquisition their full cooperation. However, Lady Naru, Commander Nadia, please join me in my office," the admiral said.

"Yes, Admiral."

The Admiral was in her office typing fast on the wireless keyboard on her lap, as she talked. Her desk was a computer, and the desktop was the screen. The display was four windows. The one that was active was a report addressed to command.

Two comfortable chairs with padded armrests stood on the other side of the desk, not as big as her own. They were superior to the work chairs in the control room, though. A small square tea table with cushion seating for four to the left had a Japanese tea set on the table. A small terrarium on a stand beside her contained a Pink Orchid. A small gold plaque on the bottom said, "Congratulations on making Admiral, Lady Fukuhina, Regards Emperor Takahiro."

Nadia stood and walked down the gantry. She stopped to look at a couple of dozen Console Operators. All but two of the consoles were busy communicating with various craft in the area as well as parts of the massive space station. One of the six large screens on the walls showed a freighter lifting from the docking arm. Nadia felt the vibrations as she headed to the admiral's office. Naru was not far behind her on the spiral stairs to the gantry.

Two work details came, each accompanied by a pair of Knights. Each headed to one of the two unused consoles. Naru paused to watch as they disconnected them from the cable that rose from under the floor, unplugged them from the floor, then wrapped each console in plastic. A Knight tagged each and sealed them with black tape that had *Inquisition* on it in yellow. Naru waited until the consoles were loaded on trolleys and wheeled away before heading to the Admiral's office.

Naru came to the door to the admiral's office and knocked.

Fukuhina opened the door from her desk. Naru entered and sat beside Nadia.

"I received new orders. First, Lady Naru, you are to document your investigations and escort the data to the Inquisition Command in Imperial City aboard the *Night Owl*," Fukuhina said.

"What of my investigation?" Naru asked.

"The other Inquisition officers will take over," Fukuhina replied.

"You need authorization from the Inquisition to give me orders that affect my duties," Naru stated.

"They come from Emperor Takahiro aboard the *Night Owl*. I will show the orders soon," Fukuhina said.

"Oh," Naru said.

"Star Dust was Prince Hiro Hashimoto. We are ordered to recover the body and hand it over to three Blood-Witches from the *Night Owl*. Naru, you will go with Nadia to the *Unicorn*. If they recover the flight data recorders, take possession of them."

"Anything else I need to know before I go?" Naru asked.

"You should know this, but as a reminder, Blood-Witches refuse to transfer between ships in open space. They will travel by shuttle only so you will depart from the *Night Owl*. A shuttle will take you both with the Blood-Witches and their equipment to the *Unicorn*, and a second shuttle will follow you with Knights and containers to secure the two data nodes."

The station was a hexagon. It had two large domes on the body, and six arms over a kilometre in length reaching out from the middle from each side of the body. The top of each dome was flat, and inside each dome were two hangars. The Inner Hangar was a hexagonal room with six landing pads. Each pad had a landing tractor and was an elevator that lowered into the hangar below. Each had an outer armour hatch waiting to seal.

Outside the Inner Hangar was the vertical take-off rapid deployment tube. Each had armoured shutters to seal them off from the Inner Hangar, and on all six outer walls were launch-tubes, control room and a ready room for pilots and room for the crew. Each section had a rack able to stack four fighters. Only two Banshee remained in each rack.

In the hangars, above and below central deck of the station, Banshees were already sitting in cradles on prongs waiting to be made vertical inside the launch tube. Upon hearing the red alert, pilots rushed from the ready rooms to their waiting craft, and crews on deck followed them up the stairs to strap them into the cockpit. They'd seal the pilot in the cockpit and remove the stairs. The pilot rotated the cockpit into launch position.

As pilots left, others were made ready. Replacement interceptors had been removed from the rack and craned into the first position as the one ahead was made vertical inside the launch tube, then sealed in.

Once a craft was in a launch tube, it was sealed in. The pilot had only a short wait for the air to be evacuated. The outer hatch was opened first, followed by two iris hatches inside the tube. Console Operators in the control room monitored each fighter. When ready, each craft was catapulted out at high speed. Once far enough out, the pilot inside ignited the engines.

Most of the ground crew wore the purple Imperial Navy uniforms. The pilots wore the blue Sky-Force uniform, all guards wore the grey guard uniform, while the high-ranking ground crew such as the engineers working in the repair bay below, wore the yellow and black Technical Services uniform.

Four lifts in the floor around the hangar led to the repair bay. There was also an area for shuttle storage and the armoury holding various ammunition, including an assortment of missiles for the Banshees.

A navy officer on the flight deck speaking into her headset said, "This is not a drill, this is a red alert. I want all craft launched. I want all repair crews in space suits ready. I want fire suppression checked. I want all weapons lockers unlocked."

Guards evacuated civilians to the docked freighters. One by one the docked starships departed once the last ones had boarded. As each ship left its docking arm, the automated system fired engines around the main body to keep it stable. More fighters launched from the ninth planet. It was only the size of a large moon with a couple of large rocks for moons. It was host to an ultra-wave communications hub and a navy base with large anti-ships weapons at the ready.

All around the station's hull armoured hatches opened. Turrets with a collection of sensors, quad cannons, missile launchers and anti-missile defence systems usually concealed between the inner and outer skin were now active, controlled by remote from the command deck deep inside the station.

Sensor pods all over the station searched space. The long-range scan began slowly; it took thirty minutes to build a scan of the entire system. The scan displayed as views from different angles on the six screens around the main walls.

The *Unicorn* was a Crusader Class Frigate, smaller than a cruiser. It was on patrol inside the large passageway through the asteroid cloud on the edge of Alcyone System. It kept clear of asteroids by using the ship's forward deflectors to push them out.

Along the walls of the passage were small automated stations. These did more than relay communications signals, for they took scans of each ship and sent that data to Alcyone station. The station was located near the exit and moved position to keep close to, but never in front of, the passageway. For now, the ninth planet was nearby.

On the bridge were six female officers. In the captain's chair sat Lady Emi. She wore the light and dark purple Imperial Navy uniform. She had four gold bars on her collar. The other five bridge crew each wore the white and yellow Technical Services uniforms, and each had three gold bars on their collar. Like most of the ship's crew, they were a mix of different Elves.

"XO, Priority signal from Alcyone Station Seven. It reads, Priority Commander Override. Proceed flank speed to the following location for search and rescue of a cockpit pod. Set condition red and investigate any contact, even the intermittent. An unknown hostile downed a Banshee. Upon retrieval of the Pod, signal the *Night Owl* and then standby for additional orders. End of message. XO, the message was correctly formatted, coded, and I have verified the sender as Admiral Fukuhina. Included was a data file named 'search area', and a second message encrypted as 'Captain Only'," the communications officer said.

"Thank you, Lieutenant. Send the location data file to the helm and send both messages to the Captain. Helm, cancel the current course and prepare a new one, at flank speed. Weapons, cease asteroid clearance, secure weapons, reload, set deflector to automatic and sound red alert," Emi said.

The Helm Operator pressed stop on her control panel. Then she opened the message from Communications. Upon opening it, the system performed checks and added a navigation waypoint, named Star Dust, to the system map

Crisis

on the Navigation screen, which was to the right of her main screen.

The main engines ceased firing, then all forward facing ion-gravity engines on both manoeuvring rings pulsed, deaccelerating the ship. The atomic clocks around the ship detected changes in gravity and adjusted the gravity field to keep the ship inside one gravity bubble.

As the ship decelerated, the primary deflector field, projected from the nose, reduced size. The deflection field that surrounded the hull remained unchanged. As the ship came to a halt, the forward deflector fields merged into the bubble that surrounded the ship.

Most of the time, the Helm Operator did not pilot the ship manually; she programmed and monitored the ship's autopilot. Most of the ship's systems are automatic, though the Helm Operator was able the pilot the ship if necessary; she had flight controls in addition to the keyboard on an adjustable arm.

"Commander, we are ready to proceed," the Helm Operator said.

"Engineering, this is the XO, secure the ramscoops and prepare for flank speed," Emi said.

In Engineering Section, an engineer and a crew member monitored the reactor. They wore a Technical Services uniform. The Chief Engineer had 5 Strips on her collar, her assistant had 3 Strips. The Chief tapped the *run full system diagnostic* button on her console. "To be chief of the boat, you do not need to know the science of how these systems work, only how to keep them running and how to put them back together. On a normal patrol, we would travel in a pack, but we are close to home," the chief said.

"Yes Chief," the assistant replied.

The Chief looked at the console for hydrogen fusion reactor. On the screen was an image of the reactor with various temperature readings and a flow diagram of the plasma from the reactor to each ring, the gravity-temporal stabiliser and to the Ultra-Wave generator. All arrows were green with no alarms or warnings in the message box

The Chief checked fuel from another console. The screen displayed eight fuel tanks with the ramscoops either side on its screen. Above each ramscoop was an open button. It was green. Inside the scoop was a vertical status bar, full and green; with a close button at the bottom of each scoop. The Chief clicked *close*.

The next console was for the Lilith Gravity-Temporal Stabiliser System, the Chief engine said, "This system keeps the ship and crew from being crushed by gravity and altering the length of time."

"Does it alter the length of time?" the assistant asked.

"The ultra-wave drive generates a gravity field outside the ship that slows time. The Stabiliser counters that field, so that time and gravity inside the ship is what we normal," the chief replied while looking at the console. Internal gravity was showing as exactly one, and the readings from the two caesium atomic clocks in the ship were both 1.000.

A slide on the right side of the screen was labelled 'Engine auto shut-down', the reading was at seventy gravities with the maximum seventy-five gravities. "The ship can withstand seventy-five gravities, but we can only just tolerate three, and not for long. We normally would shut down engine thrust at seventy gravities, to extend engine life."

The assistant nodded, while the Chief checked the

Crisis

console for the engines. Both were green. She set ultra-wave field strength from zero to one.

"One?" the assistant asked.

"The maximum setting is seven, but within thirty AU of a yellow star, due to the natural ultra-wave field, one is the safest maximum setting. At one, we are going to travel at light speed, which is impossible to achieve with an ion-drive," the Chief said.

"Why don't we always travel at one?" the assistant asked.

"Inside a gravity bubble, we cannot use radar or radio. We fly by instrument, too fast to react, and must rely on computer course predictions and deflector fields to prevent a collision. Inside a system, especially one as crowded as Alcyone, the chances of collision are so high the system would shut down often," the chief replied.

The Chief went back to the main console. No warnings or errors displayed.

"Commander, all systems are green, we are good to proceed," the engineer said.

"Communications, send Alcyone Flight Control our new course," Emi said.

"Aye Commander," the communications operator said.

The Helm pressed accept on the course. The computers checked the course and then asked for an approval code. The communications officer sent the message. A tight beam sent a message to the nearest beacons inside the passage. The beacons relayed the message to Alcyone station. On the station, a flight controller and the station's computers reviewed the course. Finding no collisions, the Console Operator replied to *The Unicorn* an approval code that appeared on her display.

The Communications Officer saw the message. "Course change approved, Commander, forwarding you the authentication code," the communications operator said.

"Helm, engage auto-pilot," Emi said.

The helm engaged the autopilot. The ship fired its port thrusters in the first ring, and its starboard thrusters in its third, manoeuvring rings and turned the ship 180 degrees. The Helm Operator monitored the firing of the engines, with a top view and side view of the ship on her left screen. She followed the course of the ship with a virtual view of the ship in the passage in 3D on her main screen.

On display on the left screen, each thruster had a number that highlighted when the equivalent thruster fired. On the forward view was a HUD that gave details of speed, relative heading, and other readings. The Helm Operator kept a hand near one of the emergency stop buttons in either armrest of her seat; the XO at the captain's chair also had emergency stop buttons, and so did engineering console in the reactor room.

The Captain was in her office reading the message, a slight hum in the deck beneath her feet from the vibration of the two large engines as the ship accelerated down the passageway. She looked at the course, thinking flank speed for a short trip was rare, especially when a cruiser was closer.

The *Unicorn* sailed itself down the long passageway in the asteroid cloud; the forward deflector extended well ahead of the ship. All along the passageway, automated shuttles moved along the sides; each brought fuel to the navigation beacons and the small fleet of frigates and a cruiser at the mouth.

Around the entry and exit to Alcyone Passage, as well

as along the walls of the passageway, was a ring of beacons. Each was only ten metres round. Each beacon was a small space station with two docking arms for a shuttle, each had no crew, for like Alcyone Station Seven they automatically repositioned themselves.

Each ring contained sixteen navigation beacons, with many rings spaced inside the passageway. Each beacon had radar, LIDAR, and a communications array. As the *Unicorn* passed each ring, it was scanned by LIDAR and transmitted the image with course information to the Navigation Information Network. The nearest hub was Alcyone Station Seven.

Alcyone Station Seven regularly provided navigation information to all ships around it and inside the passageway, also those at the mouth of the passageway, via the navigation beacons. Flight Control at Alcyone Station Seven processed the data, Console Operators kept ships far apart. Not just to have a course to avoid a collision but one that that would not have them blasting the station, a planet or each other, with radiation.

The system had flaws. LIDAR had a range of one light second. Long-range scans used ultra-wave but took 45 minutes to scan 75 AU around them. They could not reveal objects hiding in the shadow of the star, planets, moons, or asteroids, or those hiding behind other ships.

It was hard to detect a small ship that did not broadcast its location. Thus, many frigates were on patrol. Pirates typically targeted automated supply shuttles and then hid in the asteroids, knowing where frigates were from the information network.

As the *Unicorn* sailed fast down Alcyone passage, as the

stealth plane flew deeper into the asteroid field, snaking its way around the larger chunks, the deflector field ahead of the ship pushed small objects, but large asteroids, the ship was moved to avoid them.

A massive circumstellar cloud surrounded the star. Its inner border started at thirty AU, with its outer edge at fifty AU. Most of this field was frozen volatiles with carbon and iron dust. The sheer number of asteroids and dust made both radar and LIDAR scans inside the cloud impossible at long-range.

As the only safe passage, Alcyone passage was busy and well patrolled. The passage was marked by a series of navigation beacons in rings through the cloud. But asteroids crossed into the area. Inside Alcyone, the fleet had many space stations. Over the north pole of the star was a ten-kilometre diameter space station, with five others in orbit between each of the nine planets, and one just past the ninth planet.

These stations were not for navigation and trade. They had shields and were armed with gravity beams, rail guns, and missiles. Alcyone was the busiest system in the empire with three inhabited planets, the second, third, and forth, from the star. Hundreds of ships sailed between the planets. The uninhabited planets were moderate in size. Under large clear domes were mining operations. Small ships had mining crews in space suits in the asteroid fields between the sixth and seventh planet, as well as the cloud of asteroids around the entire system.

"Now leaving Alcyone Passage," the Helm Operator said.

On her right screen, a detail of area showed a 100km

wide passage, with haze either side marking the cloud. Ahead was Alcyone Station Seven, below and to the left.

Once clear of the passage, the ship cruised towards and continued past the large station, it then slowed and turned starboard towards the cloud and headed to the waypoint marked 'Star Dust' on the Helm's navigation map.

As the *Unicorn* approached its destination, the ship automatically reduced the forward deflector field shrank back into the deflection bubble around the ship. The ship was facing the opposite direction it heads, pulsing the massive engines to reduce speed.

As the ship sailed to its destination, the Captain called the XO to leave the bridge and come to her office, with another officer taking the XO's place.

The Captain opened the door, and Emi entered and sat at the desk. "Did you remind the Admiral that the chances of recovering anything in space are lower than the chances of winning the Hashimoto Lottery?" Emi asked.

"Alcyone Station Seven did a long-range scan and sent me the details. I am sending the results to the Detection Officer. The data pods, the cockpit and even the downed craft, are slow moving and we will get to them well before they enter the dense outer cloud," Hilda said.

"Someone kissed a lucky fairy."

"After angering them, they ejected out of shuttle range of the station."

"I wonder why they didn't use the ship docked at the station?"

"They are bringing shuttles to us. I learnt long ago if you question command you will only go insane when they try to explain why their way is the right way. We need to launch our shuttles, catch the pod in our tractors and hold it until the shuttles have offloaded and departed."

"The craft didn't collide with an asteroid, did it?"

"I don't know. I will inform the crew once I know more, but the wargames have been cancelled."

"I was looking forward to seeing the fleet in action. Blasting drones is fun."

"They will reschedule the games."

"I am on loan for this month."

"I know. We patrol for a month, then the ship spends about the same docked, I've already missed a few exercises."

"I was looking forward to using the stealth space suit."

"Since it was made to fit you, I doubt it will go unused. We have a new radar and anti-missile system; you are not the only one who has a new toy to play with."

Once on the edge of the search area, the ship had slowed to a crawl and ceased deceleration. The Helm Operator alerted the Captain, while the Detection Officer began a search with LIDAR and active radar in the sensor pod in the flat nose of the frigate. It looked like an eyeball, and it moved fast left to right. It not only had LIDAR and radar, but also visual, gamma, x-ray, and infrared scopes, with a targeting laser.

The hull had various types of radar emitters and receivers built into it. An array ran down both sides of the hull where the top two decks and the bottom three joined, as well as another along the spine and another on the keel of the hull.

Nine hatches opened: four on the top of the hull, four on the bottom and one at the rear, between the two engines. From inside, a pod extended. Each pod had LIDAR, radar, a visual scope, and a targeting laser.

The two iris hatches on the side of the ship's hull opened. Two more iris hatches, either side of the hull, just below the midline of the hull, two-thirds down and facing the rear, opened. Inside were missiles ready to launch.

In the middle of the hull, on top, a turret with a railgun turned and faced forward. The ship had two more on the bottom sides of the hull. They swung around and faced out.

Another four small iris hatches remained closed; they were spaced out around the hull behind the third ring. Each had a decoy canister loaded.

Inside the ship, crew in guard uniforms stood ready in the main hall. Each had on combat vests, armed with a Viper automatic rifle, 9mm handgun, and a leaf blade. Officers inspected the airlocks, checked the crew quarters and recreation was empty, and that all consoles had an operator ready for action.

The kitchens kept cooking; the laundry kept washing, and in the medical bay, a medical team prepared a medical pod and a medical cart. In the hangar, an electric multi-purpose six-wheeled vehicle pushed a shuttle into position on a turntable in the Outer Hangar. Crew disconnected the cradle and retreated into the inner bay, the internal doors closed, sealed and the atmosphere executed into tanks in the inner hull.

At first, the LIDAR scanned a wide area, but as soon as the pod was detected, the rest of the lasers formed a box highlighting the pod. Slight adjustments were made to course, the *Unicorn* slowed and moved lower than the cockpit pod.

With the Inner Hangar sealed, the large rear hatch split as the seal deflated and the massive locks disengaged. The outer shell of the hull slid apart, and the second hatch on the inner hull slid open. As soon as both hatches were wide open, the internal tractor beam lifted the shuttle and slowly pushed it out of the ship. With the shuttle clear of the ship, the tractor turned off, and the hatches closed fast.

Soon after that, they launched the second shuttle. Each two-engine shuttle craft used an explosive chemical used to produce superheated gas to power its gravity-ion engines and was thus unable to fly in atmosphere.

The shuttles flew in opposite directions; each chasing down one of the relatively slow-moving black balls that were broadcasting a weak homing signal. Each shuttle opened the roof to deploy its cargo crane with a satellite net on the hook.

The pilot and co-pilot wore space suits. Each pilot headed towards a blip on their navigation screen while the co-pilots operated the cranes to catch the data pods, the capture net closing around the pod as the shuttle matched speed. With the net tight, they slowed before bringing the crane inside and closing the roof. The co-pilot then secured the data node in a cargo box.

Most of the crew inside the frigate did not wear space suits, only their uniforms. However, they all wore a headset with a speaker in each ear, plugged into their phones, which all had COMMAND NETWORK – *UNICORN* as status. In the small sealed control room in the heart of the nose, the Captain sat in the middle of the room, directly behind the Helm Operator. On the main screen was the view ahead. The Helm Operator had an array of three displays in front of her. The Captain went over various reports then flicked a switch on her chair, the screens retreated above her, and she clicked another button and the arm with her keyboard retreats.

"Communications, anything?" Hilda asked.

"Captain, I am still not receiving any signal from the escape pod on any channel. Not even the pilot's phone," the Communications Officer replied from the console to the left of the Captain.

"XO, where are we on the retrieval of the computer cores?" Hilda asked.

Emi was in the hangar's control room. Two consoles behind her faced the wall on either side of the entry, with another two consoles in front of her. Each console had a Console Operator.

On the wall in front of them was a large view screen. It displayed a four-split video feed. The first view was from a camera inside the shuttle bay. All the crew in the hangar wore space suits. The second view was the cargo lift to the storage area below the shuttle bay. The third was the inner door of the Outer Hangar, from inside. The fourth showed the outer hatch, from inside the Outer Hangar.

Emi turned to the two consoles behind her and looked at the screens, each displayed text of audio from the shuttles.

"Shuttle One has captured the first and is on its way back," Emi said, looked at the first screen. She stood behind the second console. "Shuttle two has matched vectors with the second data core and closing in with its satellite capture net."

"All right XO, carry on," Hilda said, then turning to face Console Operator on her right, "Detection, report?"

An officer sat at a console to the right of the Captain. The console had two screens, one displaying a 3D radar, range set 5km. There was a contract ahead of the ship, with another two slowly approaching from the rear, one approaching from above and one off in the distance below heading down and away from the ship. The second screen displayed a visual of the tumbling escape pod.

"Captain, I have a visual on Star Dust. We are 643 metres away, and we are closing at a rate of 1-metre per second. I am have not detected any power. I see damage to the outer hull, but the pod does seem to be intact," the Detection Officer said.

"Where are the two shuttles?" Hilda asked.

"Five minutes away," the Detection Officer replied.

"Hangar, prepare to receive company, refuel and turn the shuttles around," Hilda said.

"Aye Captain."

"I will be coming down. Helm, as soon as those shuttles have departed, I need the ship turned around. Hanger, as soon as the ship is in place I want the pod landed onto a shuttle cradle," Hilda said.

"Aye Captain."

CHAPTER 9

Homecoming

August 20, 11574. Imperial Palace.

Kaede entered the room in the palace workshops in sub-basement 5 that served as his office. He looked around. The room was clean, his desk organised with an inbox and outbox, and the inbox was full of manila folders.

Sora was supervising Mako and Miko as they filed papers in the cabinet.

"If I needed a filing cabinet, I would have one installed," Kaede said, looking around, "Where is my shredder?"

"Akiko has taken it to the workshops on sub-level four," Sora said.

"I need it," Kaede said.

"Shredding is not secure, and you should not leave important documents on your desk," Sora said, taking the last stack of folders from his outbox and handing them to Mako.

"Do you expect me to tear them myself?" Kaede asked.

"Use a—" Mako started.

"Burn bag." Miko finished.

"Akiko is on her way with one for you," Sora said. "Now, all your papers have been placed into folders, and filed by project name."

"Thanks," Kaede said looking around. "Where is Izanami?"

"Installing black wall on your private server," Sora replied.

"What is a black wall?"

"A security program," Mako replied.

"Our father's company designed it," Miko added.

"Now sit. I made you lunch," Sora said getting a bento from the fridge.

Mako and Miko raced to the hat rack to get and put on aprons. They brought him a jug of iced tea.

"You girls don't have security clearance to be below the kitchens," Kaede said.

"Czarina Katrina let us in," Sora said holding out the bento.

Kaede opened the black lacquered box. Inside was neatly arranged rice, fried skinless chicken pieces with hot sauce in a dipping bowl, prawns on lettuce with soy in a different dipping bowl, soft short rice in small balls and a skinless, sliced orange, pieces of mango and chopsticks wrapped in a silk napkin.

Kaede looked at Sora. "Thanks," he said with a smile.

Sora smiled, and Mako rushed to pour iced tea into a cup held by Miko. Izanami came running in and looked at Kaede as he ate from the bento, then she looked at Sora, stomped her foot and leant into her. "Hey! You said that was your lunch," Izanami protested.

"I gave it to Kaede," Sora said, turning the lid over to

display a big pink heart with *Kaede* in gold coloured Kanji in its centre.

"I like the heart. I might use it as my logo, but most Elves only know Germanic letters," Kaede said.

"How about a red K?" Izanami said.

"Good idea, 'Nami."

Izanami smirked at Sora and poked out her tongue.

"Now, if you're serious about replacing your grandfather, you are going need an Empress," Sora said, tapping the inbox.

Kaede looked at the inbox. It had a stack of folders with names and photo of girls' faces on each. The top folder was Sora's. He lifted it and saw Akiko's file underneath.

Izanami took the folder from Kaede and looked inside. "Hey, no fair," she said, looking at photos of Sora in a bikini holding a big red heart with '*Kaede-kun*' in kanji on it, over her head.

Izanami started looking for her file. "Where is mine?" a red-faced Izanami yelled.

"Oh, it is in there, somewhere," Sora remarked, "What is important is Kaede has a mix of wives with beauty, experience and intellect to suit him. Mako and Miko are obviously on the approved list, along with Akiko."

"We love you Kaede," Mako and Miko said together.

Kaede turned and saw Mako and Miko were smiling at him.

"Hey! What about me?" Izanami asked.

"Excuse me; I think I hear Nori calling me," Kaede said, and ran out the door.

Sora, Mako and Miko looked at Izanami and closed in on her.

Izanami, red-faced, backed away from them.

Akiko came in, pushing a large canvas bag on rollers. Izanami ran out past her to Czarina Katrina and hid behind her.

The black Banshee landed in the hangar built into the giant asteroid and waited as the rock-covered hatch slid back into place behind him. Two little figures in tight black space suits approached in the dark and hooked a steel cable to the landing gear.

A winch pulled the spaceship slowly inside. Galen rolled the cockpit pod to have the hatch behind him facing down. He pressed open on the missile bay, and nose cannon.

Once the cockpit stopped rolling, he removed his harness, got up and opened the exit hatch, and he opened that. He opened the external hatch, and a pole extended, prongs automatically sprang out. He climbed down the ladder and stopped to slide a Viper 2 and Magical Staff from a storage locker between the hull and cockpit.

Galen ejected and inspected the magazine and gun. He slid the magazine back in and chambered a bullet, then shouldered the Viper 2. "Thanks, sis," he muttered, as he grabbed the staff and climbed down.

Galené saw a group of Ogres on the gantry at the rear of the hangar. The one in the middle was black, not his natural skin colour; his skin was burnt. Unlike the other tanned, brown-haired, brown-eyed Ogres, his eyes were red, and he had no hair.

Goblins, each in wore a spacesuit, with a tool belt. A

Crisis

group had wheeled stairs to the plane, one stop was on top looked at the top of the craft.

"Touch my plane, and my cannon will cut you down," Galen said as stepped out from under the plane and he pointed his staff at the large nose cannon.

"Leave us," Shade shouted.

The 130cm tall Goblins retreated out of the hangar.

Galen removed his helmet. "Shade," Galen said, stepping out from the space plane, he removed a small bag from his pocket. "I come bearing gifts. 50 rare diamonds."

"I am sorry I doubted you," Shade said, "but you are late."

"I had to take care of business," Galen said walking to the gantry.

"Lot of guns for a plane that flies faster than a bullet," Shade remarked.

"Yes. The two rear facing guns cannons and rear fire missiles, I get. The nose cannon has an anti-missile mode. But it also has four forward heavy cannons," Galen said.

"I don't recall seeing forward guns in the original design," Shade said, taking a step forward, he held out his hand.

Galen put the bag in Shade's black hand. Shade emptied the diamonds.

"It was a last-minute change," Galen said, looked at a black box beside Shade.

"Nothing on the work orders," the second Ogre said, looking at his tablet.

"Then you need better spies," Galen said.

Shade looked at Galen. Shade slide the diamonds back

into the bag and slide with his foot the box to Galen. "All yours," Shade said with a grin.

"I know you hate questions, but where is your starship?" Galen asked, picking up the box.

The two Ogres started laughing but stopped when Shade rose his hand, then said, "Where the Imperial Fleet cannot find it."

"You owe me four nuclear-tipped missiles," Galen said stepping forward.

"Come," Shade said. He turned and headed along the gantry against the back wall of the hangar, to the metal stairs up to a door top left.

The asteroid vibrated, "You and your pirate friends are daring to try to steal from me?" Shade roared.

Galen picked up the box, then jumped over the side and ran for his ship. Shade fired dark bolts at him. They hit Galen but only removed layers of the invisible armour around him. Galen slid the box into the craft, and then climbed inside, put the box beside the pilot's seat and closed the hatch.

Goblins run after him. Galen pressed close quarter defence mode on. The nose cannon fired a burst at them. The Goblins ran for cover. Galen stowed the gun and staff then closed the inner hatch, then put his hand on the top of the box and closed his eyes.

Aboard the *Unicorn*, Emi sent the hangar crew out. Outside, in the main hall, Imperial Knights stood at the door. Inside were Naru, Nadia, Hilda, Emi, and Cerise. They cut Hiro out of his suit.

Crisis

Naru collected pieces of his suit, his identification card and phone, and placed it all into a small cargo box and sealed it with yellow tape with 'Inquisition' written on it. Hilda and Nadia put Hiro into a medical pod, Cerise closed the lid and pressed *start*. Hilda looked inside at his face, then stepped back, for blood was filling the chamber. She looked at Cerise.

"Lady Naru, I need you to leave," Cerise said.

"Yes, Lady Cerise," Naru replied. She put the box on a trolley and pushed it out.

"Your father is immortal. Surely you have seen this before?" Cerise asked.

"Renewal?" Hilda asked, looking at Cerise.

Nadia and Emi came and looked, and Cerise turned the lid from clear to white. "After we use Purge Death," Cerise replied.

"I never heard of Purge Death," Emi said. "Are you going to tell us what it is?"

"It is like a detox spell, only for the chemical process of dying," Cerise replied, checking the flow regulator on the tank on the medical pod.

"So why soak him with blood?" Hilda asked.

"For the Oxygenate spell I cast on him, I need to keep his cells alive until we can start his heart," Cerise replied. "All right, push him to medical."

Hilda moved the pod with ease, and Nadia and Emi followed Cerise. "How can you start his heart?" Hilda asked. "I never heard of anyone starting a heart after one hour."

"I know a revival spell will not work, and if casting force is seven, it can restart a heart up to seventy minutes after it stopped. I am using a resurrection spell," Cerise replied.

"Is that like a Rebirth Spell?" Emi asked she looked at Nadia. "My father told me about your father's death once."

"We will be trying that if the Resurrection Spell failed," Cerise replied.

"What is Rebirth?" Nadia asked.

"I trust you, but don't tell anyone. It is a spell that makes an 8-cell embryo from a body. The process is complicated, but what I can tell you is it is implanted into one of us, magically, during the ritual. The púca will be genetically Hiro, but with no memories," Cerise replied.

"At least he will be alive," Nadia said, she turned to Emi. "My father has never admitted to being killed. When I asked him about it, he replied all immortals eventually get reborn."

"It is true; the Anti-Aging process will eventually fail to work. But don't ask me if Czar Petrov has been killed and reborn. I could not tell you. I already told you too much," Cerise said. She stopped and turned. "I need your help. So please no more questions, just follow me."

The other two Witches stood and looked at Cerise as they entered. "Relax, this is Hilda Feygold, daughter of General Feygold; this is Emi Hagihara, the daughter of Admiral Niemi; last is Nadia Dvorkin, she is the daughter of Czar Petrov."

"So?" the second Blood-Witch asked. "They are not us. They should not be in here."

"Like me, they have better regeneration than the general population, and they can keep secrets. We are going to need their help," Cerise said.

"You are the daughter of Pharaoh Takis Alexandris; your blood is sufficient to provide the advanced regeneration until Emperor Takahiro arrives," the third Blood-Witch said.

"No time to argue and no time to explain. Hilda, Emi, and Nadia, I need you to lie on the beds. I am going to put you to sleep, it will last a week, and you are likely to remember you had dreams, but not details," Cerise said.

Soon after the ladies on the medical beds were asleep, Cerise looked at the Witches. "Hiro is in a hypothermia-induced coma. I have already cast oxygenate on him. Since we do not have a memory machine we are going to transfer memories his memories to them, so we can rebuild his mind later," Cerise said.

"I see," the second Witch said.

"We don't have a memory machine or time to transport him to Blood-Tower, so shall we begin?" Cerise asked. "The Emperor is coming, so you can report me. I accept all responsibility. If you have another way to save Hiro, then tell me now."

The two Blood-Witches looked at each other. "We need to make sure Hiro doesn't die when we try to resurrect him," the first one said.

"I will hook your friends to a drip," the second one said.

The first explosion exposed the metal plate beneath the rock. The Knights rushed into place more charges, but the hangar doors shuddered and began to open.

"Shield line!" Toshiko yelled.

A dozen Knights with large shields formed a line. The others got behind, some with bows, some with swords, and others with Viper 2s at the ready.

"Prepare for combat," Toshiko yelled into her microphone.

The Knights in armoured space suits, wands inside their suits, could cast spells on themselves. They first cast Quickness, a spell to make them think, and thus react, faster. Then they cast Haste, a spell to make them move faster. Next was the Armour Spell, which coated their space suits in an energy barrier.

The four shuttles shone lights from their sensors into the hangar. Beside them were two Banshees that concentrated on the hangar.

A horde of Goblins in the Outer Hangar of the asteroid fired heavy machine guns from nests around the cavern. Casters behind the Knights cast shield walls in front of them. The Knights behind the shields took aim. When the shield walls went down, they opened fire with bullets and spells.

Toshiko cast power ball, and the seven-metre ball of energy wiped out a nest. Then, like all magic-users, she needed time between castings to recover.

One by one the Knights advanced in a row of four, securing the outer hangar. The first of four black shuttles landed, and the Knights loaded the wounded.

Then the inner doors opened, and the Goblins charged the Knights.

Toshiko cast blast at a pack, sending them flying. Having no place to retreat, many wounded were desperately holding the holes in their suits.

The fight was quickly over. The Knights raced from Goblin to Goblin, the lead team disarming them, while others patched holes in their space suits. The backup team sorted the wounded and landed shuttles.

Galené raced up the gantry. She saw the door at the end, and ran to it, opening it to a dark empty room.

Toshiko raced up behind her. Galené looked at Toshiko and turned on her helmet light. The walls were solid rock.

"I don't understand it; we followed Galen here," Toshiko said.

"I am sorry," Galené said.

"He is your brother, so it is natural you doubted his guilt, but Czar Petrov is not the head of the Inquisition because he makes mistakes," Toshiko said.

"No one is going to trust me," Galené said.

"We can worry about that later. I am going to question every Goblin until one explains where the fighter went. A 20-metre long space plane just doesn't vanish," Toshiko said, shining a torch into the empty room. She looked over at Galené. "Even cloaked it is still a solid object."

"I don't get it. If the craft were above the Goblins, then the downforce would have scattered the group. If it had left, it would have distorted the light from the shuttles."

"Maybe there is a concealed lift. There is an airlock back of the hangar."

Galené nodded in her suit. She tapped the walls with the butt of her torch and shone the light on the large footprints in the dust. They walked into the wall.

Days later, the *Unicorn* approached Alcyone Three. It looked exactly like Earth at the end of the ice age. Emperor Takahiro sat in the captain's chair controlling the sensor pod as the ship entered orbit around the world with its rear exhaust facing away from the planet.

It was the first of many terraformed worlds. Imperial City was massive compared to any other city below. It covered the Crimean Peninsula, with an enormous artificial lake in the middle, with canals to the ports of Yalta, Feodosiya, Kerch, Sevastopol, Chornomorske and Yevpatoria. Then on screen, in the centre of the lake stood the 2km tall Imperial Palace on a large round, artificial island.

Hilda came to him, "Emperor, they ready to transport Hiro. You can leave with him."

"Thank you," Takahiro said, as he turned to leave.

"I don't understand. Did Lady Cerise do something wrong?" Hilda asked.

"She broke their rules, but the inquiry into the theft of the stealth ship is first," Takahiro said, as he left the bridge.

The base of Imperial Palace was a round flat top building with seven oblong wings. Around the palace was a large wall, with a gatehouse and entry on the east side. There was a second outer wall with a gatehouse, with many gardens between the walls and a large park on the outside.

At the west side of the Palace was a large three-storey Orchid and Butterfly house, with an even bigger ballroom to the north, and stables to the south. The gardens to the south had a large marble pool.

Here Prince Kaede, aged twelve, was swimming in the pool with Izanami, also aged twelve. Sora and Akiko, both fifteen, and the seventeen-year-old twins Mako and Miko lay on lounge chairs by the pool sipping orange juice.

General Yoshida sat at a table, sipping iced tea, watching the púca in the water. A couple of maids in red yukata waited

Crisis

with towels. Armed guards, in dark combat uniform with vests, stood watch, wearing tabards of house Hashimoto.

General Yoshida, in a yellow casual shirt and black shorts, answered a call on his large flip phone. The caller ID was the Emperor. He held the phone to his ear and listened for a few minutes, then stood. "You have my condolences, my Emperor," he said.

"Put Kaede on."

"Yes Emperor," Kenta replied.

Holding the phone, he went to the edge of the pool and yelled, "Kaede. A call for you."

"If it is Father, remind him tomorrow is my birthday," Kaede replied.

"It is the Emperor," Kenta said.

Kaede swam over and climbed out of the pool by the ladder. He came over, saw the video, and bowed. The Emperor in the captain's office of the *Night Owl* stood and bowed low.

"Grandfather?" Kaede asked, confused.

"Kaede, I have bad news. Your father has suffered an injury. I am not at liberty to go into details. I can tell you it is bad and that right now he is in a coma in a hospital," Emperor Takahiro said, still bowed.

"How bad?" Kaede asked.

"The Blood-Witches need to replace his heart, lung, liver and spleen, and he will be in the hospital a long time," Emperor Takahiro replied.

"I must see him," Kaede demanded, a tear in his eye, his body tense and his fists coiled.

"Kaede, how many times have I told you to control your emotions. You can see him later; right now, he is in surgery."

Emperor Takahiro put his hand on a large rock on the desk, as if for support.

"Yes Grandfather," Kaede said, bowing. "I apologise for my outburst."

"Good. Czar Petrov is coming to see you, but not about black diamond. I want you to tell him the truth about your relationship with Galené," Emperor Takahiro said, tapping the rock.

"You never like any girl I like. I am twelve and still have no formal fiancée. My friend Nori has a girlfriend," Kaede said.

"Galené is too old, and you are not alone. The Yoshiko twins like you. I am sure you can find a clear diamond in the vast field of diamonds in my vault, and you can make them your formal fiancée," Emperor Takahiro said.

Kaede looked at the rock, it was yellowish to brown and was the size of a football. Kaede was sure it was Lonsdaleite and had never seen a crystal that big before.

"I prefer Sora," Kaede said, looking at General Yoshida.

"Kaede, she has no clan," Emperor Takahiro said, looking angry.

"Sora is awesome, she is a natural leader," Kaede said, again looking at the crystal. Takahiro raised an eyebrow and put his hand on the rock. Kaede nodded.

"Trust me, when you are older you will want the twins," Emperor Takahiro said, putting his hands in his sleeves.

Does this mean more diamonds or so much Lonsdaleite the value will decrease? Kaede wondered.

"Kenta is right here, Grandfather," Kaede said.

"General Yoshida is my close friend and ally, and he tells

me Mako and Miko are keen on you," Emperor Takahiro said.

"I know that, and I do like them. I want you to approve of Sora, Akiko, Izanami, Mako and Miko. I know legally I can marry ten, but I have only five to ask," Kaede said.

"Your prime wife needs to have all the qualities of a princess. Remember you also need her consent before you can marry the others," Emperor Takahiro said.

"Sora is a good organiser and a champion footballer. She has been recruited to play for the Galaxy girls," Kaede said.

"Do you plan on wearing me down?" Emperor Takahiro asked.

"Yes, Sora is popular with the public, she is one of them and has many fans," Kaede said.

"I see," Emperor Takahiro said. "Has it grown out yet?"

"If you are referring to my manhood, I am still a girl," Kaede replied with a red face.

"You are not a girl. Your father was fifteen when he grew out. I am not worried. All males go through this. You're young and will not lose your title. There is always next year's penis festival," Emperor Takahiro said, tapping the rock on some words, then he put his arms inside his sleeves.

Kaede bit his lip.

"Can we discuss my next project and wish?" Kaede asked.

"Can it wait?" Emperor Takahiro asked.

"I have a project which could even be more profitable than artificial cells," Kaede said.

"I have a shuttle waiting for me. I must go now and suit up, so send me your plan on the internal clan link, and I will decide tonight," Emperor Takahiro said.

"Grandfather, I want to schedule a meeting," Kaede said.

"Why?" Takahiro asked.

"I want you to announce my official engagement. Please accept Sora, please, my Emperor?"

"I will consider it Kaede," Emperor Takahiro said.

The call ended.

A shuttle took Hiro in a medical pod with the two Blood-Witches and Takahiro to a space station, where they transferred to a chemical-fuelled shuttle and landed at the Imperial Airport. A helicopter took them from the roof of the fifth VIP terminal to Blood-Tower.

Dain rushed into the palace, and as he left the lift on the seventh floor, Sora stepped in front of him.

"Lord Hartman," Sora said, bowing.

"Miss Sora, you should not be here," Dain said. He attempted to step around her.

"I am going to marry Kaede," Sora yelled out.

"I see," Dain said. He turned to see Abel, she was in full armour with a claymore on her back, her Viper 2 was over her shoulder.

"Miss Li, please go to the waiting room. Dain, can you escort her please," Abel said.

"Isn't this your job?" Dain asked.

"I know you have important business, but Patya is with Lady Toshiko in his office still," Abel said.

Dain looked at Abel, who smiled. Dain looked at Sora. "This way, Miss Li." Dain over emphasized Li.

"I am an abandoned púca from Hashimoto House, and I know Li isn't my real last name, I don't have one, but the law does allow legal name changes, within limits," Sora said.

"I see," Dain said.

"Did you know I scored the most goals this last season for any player?" Sora asked, "I broke Abel's average of 1.3 goals a game. My average was 1.52 goals per game. I am getting a medal, and I am going to be a lady."

"No, I didn't that, girls football doesn't interest me," a confused Dain said looking at Abel.

"Sora, my brother, is not interested in girls," Abel said.

"This way to the waiting room Sora," Dain said, he glared at Abel, the headed down the hall.

"High Lord Dain, how do you feel about me breaking Lady Abel's record?" Sora asked as they headed down the hall. Dain groaned and went to the door of the waiting room and unlocked it.

Abel laughed and headed back down the hall. She messaged Kaede; "The Stag is out of the way."

Kaede came out of the toilets and headed to the throne room. Patya was on the throne, and Takahiro stood in the middle of the room. The only one missing was Dain.

"Prince Kaede now isn't the time," Patya said. He was a Field Elf in a black suit with a red tie.

"I have an appointment," Kaede said, bowing to the throne.

"Takahiro?" Patya asked.

"He wants a formal announcement for his engagement to Sora," Takahiro replied.

"The girl we are giving a sports award to tomorrow?" Maharajah Arjuna Desai asked. Arjuna, a Night Elf, was only 120cm tall, with jet black skin, his lips dark purple, dark purple hair, and violet eyes. Like the other lords, he sat facing the throne. He wore colourful silk robes with silk shoes.

"Yes, I signed her to play for the Galaxy Girls," Patya said.

"We should wait for High Lord Dain," Admiral Viktor Niemi said. Viktor, an Aquatic Elf, had ocean blue hair, bright blue eyes, and wore an Imperial Navy uniform with many medals.

"I have not received the report yet, but I fear I may have broken the Wealth cap. To fix this, I plan to give shares to the companies that provide the assets needed to mine my claims. Alard is downstairs, but I need my lawyer," Kaede said.

"Is Alard sober?" General Feygold asked. The general, at 210cm tall, was a Mountain Elf who was shorter than his daughter, Hilda. His blond hair was cut short, and it stood on end. He wore a grey guard's uniform.

"Yes," Kaede replied.

"Who is your lawyer?" Patya asked.

"Lady Toshiko," Kaede replied.

"She is my guest, and I have not finished questioning her," Patya said.

"Don't tell me. Tell Lady Toshiko. She is head of the Imperial Knights; she will have words with you as to why you are detaining her."

"What is this?" Dain asked as he entered.

"We were discussing what to do with the tens of trillions worth of mineral assets I have," Kaede said.

"Patya, what is going on?" Dain asked, sitting in his chair.

"Prince Kaede is richer than Takahiro, over ten times richer and counting," Patya said.

"Really?" Dain asked.

"It is true; I am well over the Wealth cap. My first problem is mining. To solve this, I offered you all shares in return for assets; to pay my taxes with mineral wealth. I will help grow the wealth base so none of you must sell assets. The I will sell plots in my claim. I also will establish an employee trust for the rest of the shares. But without my lawyer, we cannot conclude the deal. I can sue you for obstructing me and force you to pay my penalty for breaking the Wealth Cap. Czar, the penalty is ten percent of my assets, that comes to more than my grandfather is currently worth," Kaede said.

Dain laughed, "You cannot go from a few billion to tens of trillions overnight,", Dain said. But no one else laughed. He looked around.

Patya stood. "As Minister of Business, Finance and Economics, I can confirm Kaede Mining filed mineral claims asteroid fields in five systems. He has the largest collection of resources ever. The embarrassing part is that the largest find of Lonsdaleite is only four light years away in Alcyone Prime," Patya said.

"But that system only a dense graphite cloud," Dain said.

"The dense graphite cloud hides a dense asteroid field close to the star," Patya said.

"The gravity and radiation would make the system impossible to mine," Dain said to Patya.

"I have a plan," Kaede said.

"We can deal with Prince Kaede later. He is only a few billion over, the cap," Dain said.

"But he does have an appointment," Sky Marshal Rudolf Reinhart said. He was a Field Elf, in a Sky-Force uniform, taller than Dain, with short red hair and green eyes.

"Not billion, but many trillions over, there is 319 times the gold, methane, water, iron, and diamonds than in the current economy, we will be mining those systems for thousands of years," Patya said.

"We have a case of gross negligence against the Emperor; he should have arrested the spy. Not only did he not tell us about the spy. The spy escaped with a space plane that cost the Empire billions to develop. Our enemies will soon have advanced technology," Dain said.

"Patya, unless you have evidence, I demand my lawyer be released. If you all look at your phones, I sent you an agreement hours ago," Kaede said.

"What agreement?" Dain asked.

"Our phones are off, not that it matters, the room is shielded from radiation," Pharaoh Takis Alexandris, a Silver Elf said. Standing at 210cm tall, he towered over Kaede. His long silver hair flowed over his shoulders as he looked at Dain, his green eyes narrowed.

"You have a computer link," Kaede said.

"My business is a matter of Imperial Security," Dain said.

"So is mine. I found a couple of billion tonnes of Lonsdaleite. Which is a resource vital to the Imperial Fleet," Kaede said.

"How will you mine it?" Patya asked.

"I will have ships fly a path created by comets. As

they enter the system, they will grab asteroids with a set of four tractor beams that will land them in a forward-facing landing bay where an internal crane will place it into the ship's cargo bay. The ship will continue into the system and slingshot around the largest star, on a course to avoid the second star and return to space stations on the edge of the system," Kaede replied.

"Ships?" Viktor asked.

"I plan to a build a fleet of specialised class four mining ships. I call the design The Needle, it is a wedge-shaped ship using a new tractor beam, engines, computers, and two synchronised ultra-wave systems," Kaede said. He went to the main screen behind the throne. A picture of a long wedge-shaped ship appeared on the screen.

"Two synchronised ultra-wave systems?" Kenta asked.

"The Needle Class IV Transport has four of my engines, tractor beam, computer, and has two Ultra Drives. The ship's sub-light, and faster-than-light, speeds are faster than any Imperial Fleet ship. My tractors are stronger and have a longer range than any other gravity beam to date. I have four inside the forward bay, they work as one," Kaede replied.

"This is a working prototype or on paper?" Viktor asked.

"Yes, Hashimoto Industries has already tested the prototype," Kaede replied.

"I believe Prince Kaede is more than a few billion over the Wealth cap, but more important, with such wealth, he has a legitimate claim to the crown," Argon remarked.

"Which is why I have come to you today," Kaede said.

"What do you propose?" Viktor asked.

"I am offering you each a plot in the asteroid fields, each is too big for any one company to exploit and protect from illegal mining. You will not pay with gold, but with the resources needed for the mining operation. From building ships to space stations, to delivering asteroids to processing centres. Each of you will receive an offer depending on what you can provide. I am aware a find this large will lower the market value of Lonsdaleite. However, I need to deal with the Wealth cap. I will pay my tax in Lonsdaleite, but I will need a special waiver from the Senate to give more time to comply with the wealth laws, a month is not enough to arrange the sale of the excess wealth. It is within all your interest to expand the wealth base by allowing me time to arrange and sell small plots not just to the public but also private companies," Kaede said.

"I think he is offering us a bribe," Dain said.

"Did I ask you to do anything illegal?" Kaede asked.

"Prince Kaede has a point, a month is too short to determine how much he is over and how to dispose of this excess wealth. If any of you exploit the law to force him to face a penalty, I will come after you, because if one of us is over the Wealth cap, we all are," Patya said.

"I think it is best we grant a month by month extension, we will check the progress at the end of each month, then decided if to grant an extension or have outside auditors replace the team you have," Kenta said.

"Any objections to General Kenta's proposal?" Patya asked. He looked around, Dain didn't even blink. "Prince Kaede, use your time wisely and do not waste time. Do not abuse the extension, we cannot be favourable to you, nor as your competitors, use this to our advantage against you."

"I will do my best," Kaede said, he then walked to Takahiro and bowed. "Grandfather, I request you to plead guilty to a lesser charge of negligence causing workplace harm, which will require you to pay for the lifelong care of the injured party, pay compensation to the injured party and a fine to Empire. I request the Blood-Witches see to my father's medical needs."

"What?" Takahiro asked.

"I recommend charges of gross negligence handling of classified material resulting in immediate dismissal, but I agree, the Blood-Witches should care for Captain Hiro at Takahiro's expense," Rudolf said.

"But I will have to step down as Emperor for having a criminal record," Takahiro said

"You didn't tell us about the security breach, even now, it is suspected you deleted or destroyed data. You allowed someone you suspected of being a spy to pilot the craft he planned to steal to prove he was a spy, with your son in harm's way in a ship with inferior weapons," Dain said, smiling.

"Dain is right," Patya said, he walked over to Kaede and knelt. "Do you know what that means?"

Kaede turned to Takahiro. "Grandfather, the law is clear, the richest shall rule. As I am richer than you, I ask you step down as Emperor and hand me the crown," Kaede said. Then he faced the court. "Before coming here, I placed a bid to buy fifty-one percent of Hashimoto Industries. As Emperor of the Elves, I will grant my grandfather a pardon. As Emperor of the Flower Elves I will allow him to retain the title of Lord of The Inland Sea and keep his seat on the New Tokyo Council. Because I am still a púca, I offer him to remain as CEO. I propose the Senate accept this. My father was sceptical of Galen's guilt, willingly flew the chase plane and we have so little information on the Ogre pirates and who is aiding them," Kaede said.

"I find your proposal interesting, but we need rational debate before we accept the pardon," Chief Yaotl Belaúnde said. He was a Forest Elf with unbrushed, long, green hair and green eyes. He wore a deerskin vest, tight leather pants, and crocodile skin boots. He stood and said, "I think we can all agree that he should pay for Hiro's medical care?"

"You cannot seriously be considering this?" Dain asked looking at Patya.

"I am, and I agree, Takahiro needs to pay the bill, not just for Hiro," Rudolf said.

"I am," Patya said.

"We shouldn't be debating this," Dain said.

"Dain, I am touched that you want me to remain as Emperor," Takahiro said in a soft voice smiling. Before Dain could respond, Takahiro turned to Patya and said, "Patya, since I am the accused, I cannot vote. So, I shall leave the room, but the rules are clear, my accuser cannot be present for the debate. I will plead guilty and leave you to decide. Come, Dain, I let you insult me in my private office, while it is still mine."

"Takahiro developed a stealth fighter, with programmable missiles in secret, you know it is illegal to conduct research in secret from the Senate," Dain said.

Takahiro turned and bowed low to Kaede. He walked to the double doors, he held his head high and stopped at the Dain. "Come, Dain, you know the rules, your vote is locked in as the accuser, and I am the defended, this is now a trial, not a debate. My fate is in the hands of the jury of my peers."

Dain looked at Patya, then the other lords. They all

nodded, and Patya said, "Takahiro is right, if you stay for our deliberation it would a conflict of interest, you're the prosecutor. We know you will vote to remove and Takahiro will vote to remain in office. He cannot pardon himself but can call a vote for one. We will call you back for presenting Sora with Imperial Award for Sports. She broke Abel's goal record. Also, Prince Kaede is receiving the Imperial Award for Science," Patya said.

"Why?" Dain asked.

"The Artificial Organ," Patya replied. "Will you leave or will I have Abel come and put you in a headlock?"

"My company started that research, and I plan to appeal," Dain said.

"Dain, the Lilith Foundation owns the Artificial Cell. Before you say but Lilith was my mother, we all know that. She left all her intellectual property to Lady Toshiko. Kaede legally licensed the technology and conducted original research. You published no papers," Rudolf said.

"We have you on record abandoning that research. Are you saying since announcing the termination of research you have conducted research in secret from the Senate?" Kaede asked.

Dain growled and turned and left the throne room.

Kaede watched Dain leave, then turned to the Senators and said, "I will ask you all to keep the details of the business proposal to develop the mines secret from each other as I don't want you fighting or arguing over the offer. I know as public officials your holdings must be published, but you have thirty days to file with Treasury; I request you remain silent on the deal for as long as you legally can."

"If the deal is fair, but does it upset the order of houses?" Patya asked.

"Now this might be considered a bribe, but it does drop Dain from second place to thirteenth, his mineral scope is only good for dust, I don't need his ships, only the food he can provide. Czar Petrov if you need to examine the deal I am offering him, I will disclose to you if as head the Inquisition you present a formal request in a civil court. But I believe you will find he does have the least to contribute to the project. All of you remain in order; I saw no way to offer you equal plots," Kaede replied.

"That sounds fair to me," Prince Georgi Vlasov said. "But we need to discuss the deal in private." He was a Night Elf, a little taller than Maharajah Desai and spoke with a thick Russian accent. He had dark purple hair to his waist and had violet eyes. He wore a dark purple tailored suit. The jacket had gold trim and buttons, and his shirt was a light purple. He wore a silver headband.

"Of course, I know how important this is," Kaede said. He bowed to them before he left.

It was nearly 10 pm when Abel escorted Dain to the throne room. As he entered, he saw Patya and the other nine lords around a table of food and drink located behind the semi-circle of chairs. They parted as Dain approached. Kaede in the middle of the group continued watching Alard make sushi.

"Patya, how do I get a pardon for my grandfather and three exemptions for myself?" Kaede asked.

"You ask the Emperor to sign an official pardon," Dain replied.

"Dain, he is the Emperor," Patya said.

"You cannot be serious?" Dain cried out.

"Should I go?" Alard asked. A male Field Elf, he was taller than Dain but thinner. He was more a pale grey compared with Dain's pale cream skin. His hair was short and grey. He had a small, short, grey beard on his chin, but his face had no wrinkles. His three-piece suit and tie, down to his shoes and socks were white, except for a red handkerchief. Unlike most, he did not wear a smart band, but an analogue watch. It was gold with diamonds around the face.

"No, Lady Toshiko will return soon, and we need you to transfer the shares to Dain and witness him sign the agreement," Patya said.

"What is going on?" Dain asked looking around.

"Kaede is shedding his excess wealth. He is selling us plots in his mine. Then, in thirty days we all disclose our new holdings," Patya said.

"What if his wealth does not exceed mine?" Dain asked.

Yaotl snorted. Then Alard said, "We know you still don't believe it, but over a thousand samples taken. Emperor Kaede's holdings are so substantial, it will grow for at least the next thousand years. It currently stands at ten trillion, and it is expected only to go up as he brings to market new starship engines, new computers, new power plants and there are projects under commercial seal that are known to Czar Petrov and the security council."

"Excuse me, I need to write a pardon, and I need three exemptions," Kaede said.

"Exemptions?" Dain asked.

"After I pardon Takahiro, I will give myself an exemption to drive a car, fly a plane and operate a speed boat. I wanted five, but I promised my guardians I shall wait until I am older before getting a magic and a gun licence," Kaede replied.

"Is this before or after Takahiro pays the fine?" Dain asked.

"Dain, what does it matter when Takahiro pays?" Patya asked.

Dain looked at Patya. Kaede stepped between them. "He can afford it, he accepted my takeover bid," Kaede said.

"Who are his guardians?" Dain asked.

Kaede nodded to Patya, then went and sat on the throne, folded his arms, and slid his hands into his sleeves.

"I will appoint Lord Takahiro Hashimoto, Lord Takashi Iti and Professor Toru Yamane as my advisors," Kaede said. "I can bestow a title on Toru?"

"But Takashi is the Lord of Alcyone Three, why demote him?" Kenta asked.

"I will not be employing him directly, but his clan," Kaede said.

"You can bestow a title of Lord of a city or region, even for a planet if it is inside your kingdom, without requiring Senate approval. Other appointments are requests to the Senate. Your title is not as powerful as you think," Patya said.

"My Emperor, I call a vote; you do not have the training to run the Treasury," Dain said.

"High Lord Dain, you are not a banker, economist, accountant, or a farmer. We both have a few university degrees. I graduated school when most are starting. I am head of the largest and richest corporation, and I am the wealthiest Elf in the empire, that is all the law requires of me," Kaede said.

"By chance," Dain said.

"That is your opinion. I took a cunning and calculated risk-based on knowledge and now have the largest interstellar mining operation, far exceeding your carbon collection company," Kaede said. A long silence came from the other nobles all looking at Dain.

"I called for a vote," Dain said. "Do we vote or will you violate the rules of the chamber?"

"First, you pose a question to the Senate; then there is discussion time before a vote," Kaede said.

"Very well. I, High Lord Dain, request that the Senate appoints me as head of Treasury; regent and guardian of Emperor Kaede to protect him from being used as a proxy by Elder Takahiro, the former Emperor. His father is in a coma and permanently disabled, and the only other adults in the house are a Giantess and a Dwarf," Dain said.

"I accept the vote and call for the chamber to reject High Lord Dain's proposal. The Charter does not state age. I have many carers, including Czarina Katrina and hundreds of Imperial Knights and I, have tens thousands of relatives in my employ. Remind me later to tell Lady Abel her brother said she is incapable of protecting me, I am sure she and Lady Toshiko will want words with him," Kaede said. A few laughed.

"We cannot place the future of the Empire in the hands of a púca who made his wealth by putting a few pins on a star map and yelling mine," Dain said.

"If voting yes will give Dain two votes," Kaede said. "Second, didn't High Lord Dain put a crown on his head and yell mine when the previous owner was lying dead at his feet?"

"Allowing a púca on the throne without supervision would lead to the idea just anyone could rule," Dain said.

"The Charter did not specify age or qualification other than wealth," Kaede said. "Shall we vote?"

"Alard, sorry, but you need to wait outside," Patya said.

Alard left with a plate containing assorted cheese and pear in one hand with a glass of brandy in the other. The Knights closed the doors.

Dain sat and pulled up his screen. The others pulled up their screens, which all showed the question and a yes or no. Dain pressed Yes.

The names of the thirteen nobles appeared on the big screen on the wall behind Kaede. 'Yes' appeared on the screen beside 'Dain'.

Then General Yoshida, Maharajah Desai, Lord Alexandris, Lord Tikkanen and Chief Belaúnde voted no.

High Lord Dain, Lord Agrovar, Sky Marshall Reinhart, Prince Vlasov, General Feygold and Admiral Niemi voted yes.

Lady Toshiko sat in the chair behind the rows of operators in the control centre in sub-basement 11. On the main screen, she had split the display into four. Kaede was looking at Patya; Knights outside the room ready to charge in and defend him on the right; Dain grinning at Patya; the vote tally. Toshiko watched Kaede look at his panic button and sigh.

"Czar, surely you see the need for a strong leader," Dain said.

Kaede stood and bowed. "Some of you may know this. While the vote is incomplete, you can change your vote. I urge you all to vote *no*, so we can discuss why I called you here," Kaede said.

Dain stood. "Don't think I let you get away with buying votes again," Dain said with a snarl.

"You are charging the Senate with corruption, so you are free to return your shares, and I will find another source of food," Kaede replied.

"This is important, don't—"

Kaede interrupted Dain. "Yes, this vote is that Dain has stated he'd like to take over. Giving him control over my vote, my wealth, and my inventions, most of them vital to the security of the Empire, is making him Emperor. I fear he will not go when I am eighteen."

"What?" Dain objected.

"I suggest you all reject Dain's motion and sanction Dain for his unfounded accusations," Kaede said.

"Prove to me he doesn't control your vote. He needs discipline," Dain said.

"Czar Petrov, the Empire's highest ranked Inquisitor, and General Yoshiko, the highest ranked physician in the Empire, are my legal guardians. Do not give Dain unsupervised control of companies. They are in direct competition to his and he, less than a month ago, lost a ten billion gold lawsuit to Kaede Medical," Kaede said.

Dain stood in front of Czar Petrov. "Patya, vote now," Dain said.

"I have considered everything you said, Dain. I do agree

he that he needs a steady hand to guide him, I urge a no vote, and if Dain tries anything like this again, we will sanction him, but for now he can suffer a defeat of his motion," Patya said. He looked past Dain at the screen, smiled and pressed no on his tablet.

"The vote is officially 12-1. High Lord Dain, your motion has been defeated, please be seated," Kaede said, looking at his pad.

"Patya, do I need to pardon Lady Toshiko?" Kaede asked.

"I think it is safe to assume she didn't throw Lady Galené out an airlock. Likely Lady Galené left on a prison transport and deserted," Patya said.

"Can we consider her a rogue agent and not have her shot on sight?" Kaede asked.

"Unless she does harm to the empire, we can," Yaotl replied.

"What about the supply contracts?" Kaede asked.

"We need to prepare announcements for the ultra-wave broadcast before we meet with Alard and finish our business," Patya said.

CHAPTER 10

REACTIONS

December 20, 11574. Imperial Palace.

It was the first day of Yule, the last twelve days of the year, the festival of winter, renewal, and life. Yule was the closest event to a religious holiday in the Empire. At midnight, Freya and Masako had helped Kaede hang holly on doors, and decorate a pine tree in his room. They exchanged gifts of candy, hugs, and platonic kisses on the check. For most, it was time off work to spend with family. In House Hartman, Dain, Abel, and Abelard sang, drank wine, had a spit roast and at midnight danced with other field Elves around a bonfire wearing only long white tunics.

On the morning of the December 31, the last day of Yule, Kaede left the palace in a limo and headed East. Yuki drove, with Toshiko in the back beside Kaede. They stopped at a Japanese shrine on the shore of the lake, just off the eastern highway.

Lady Toshiko first checked inside, upon speaking briefly with the shrine maiden, Lady Hitomi. Toshiko then returned to the limo and waited with Lady Yuki outside as Kaede walked under the shrine's gate, known as a Torii, and up the stone stairs.

The shrine was large. It faced east and had many maidens of different ages on the grounds. All were dressed in the same white kimono with red hakama, white tabi and wooden shoes. All had a red caduceus on a black circle on the back of the kimono. Most had wands, and the rest carried a staff. They were not just working inside the shrine, but on the grounds also. Some were raking leaves, others tending the garden, and a group operated food stalls and souvenir stands.

The shrine was busy; most visitors were Flower Elves who bowed as the Emperor passed them.

Lady Hitomi bowed and walked beside Kaede down the stone walkway to the purification font. She washed his hands and took Kaede inside. He put his shoes beside hers and followed her to an office in the back of the main building. It had a sprig of holly on the door.

"Nice to see you again, Emperor. You have grown up so fast! I am so proud of you," Hitomi said as she closed the office door.

"Thank you, Lady Hitomi," Kaede said as he sat.

"I didn't expect to see you until tonight."

"I am on my way to see my father and stopped by to see how the approval for my marriage to Sora is progressing."

"I know Sora very well from my time at Hashimoto House. She is a remarkable girl with an attractive physique and is very athletic. I understand why you are closer to her, as she is only three years older than you, but Yuki would have been a better choice. She is smarter, stronger and is only eighteen years older than you."

"Yuki is already on the list of potential secondary wives. I want Sora."

"Yes, but do you love her?"

"I do."

"How do you feel about Yuki?"

"I do find her attractive."

"I see. I will recommend Sora accept Yuki when the time comes for her to choose additional wives. A male can have ten wives, but you will not be forced to do so. You can decide to do as your father and grandfather did. They both used a surrogate."

"I want to get married and have a family. Sora and I already agree on Akiko, Izanami, Mako and Miko as additional wives."

"Marriage is a social contract with expectations, and you need to understand that and them. Prepare for unexpected changes in your life."

"My grandfather tells me you're an excellent Blood-Witch."

"Yes. As a surrogate, I have anonymously carried four sets of twins. Two girls in 11557, another two in 11559. A boy and girl in 11562, and two more girls in 11569. Since then I have been preparing couples and performing formal weddings. In my free time, I help the Flower Elf Cultural Society by running this shrine. All the girls here are Blood-Witches."

"Anonymously? You never see them?"

"Only in my heart. We have our memory altered, so

we don't suffer the pain of loss. We know what we did for others, but not who. It is a very complex system."

"I see. Did you receive the list of potential brides?"

"Yes. Takahiro sent me the list yesterday. I was surprised to see Galené was not on it."

"It is complicated."

"Do you know a couple of weeks after she had disappeared she came to see me? She told me that she was on a mission and that no matter what I hear, she is not a traitor, then left."

"I know. But the truth is it doesn't matter how I feel about Galené, she is in love with my father. But, please keep that between you and me. Has she contacted you?"

"No, and I would tell you if she had."

"I was hoping she had."

"I know. Sorry, I cannot help you, but I have not heard from Galené in years."

"If she does, tell her I have a pardon waiting for her."

"If I hear from her, I will pass on your message. I know she means a lot to you. She is so beautiful and only eighteen years older than you. Do you want her on the list?"

"I do."

"Takahiro talks as if we have approved the wedding has already. Anyone can just live together, and every adult does have the right to have one púca. For you, that means a son because you're a descendant of the head of the clan. Marriage is an agreement to take care of each other. In your case, it is a one-sided since you can give them a lifestyle far more than what they can give you."

"I know that."

"All marriages need final approval of the Blood-Witches.

Takahiro has no power to stop you marrying Sora, you're head of the house now. But Sora can stop you marrying others."

"Izanami is a wonderful dance partner. We work well together. Sora is a great organiser, and the others follow her."

"You do love Izanami?"

"Yes, Lady Hitomi."

"Takahiro also believes Sora is a better leader and I agree. The marriage contract is complex, I will ensure Sora is prepared, understands the marriage contract and isn't jealous of Izanami."

"Thank you, Lady Hitomi. I have set aside funds so Sora can have lessons on culture, languages, cooking, dressing, walking, politics and law. If you have the time, I would like for you to teach her and Akiko, Izanami, Mako and Miko."

"Yes, I can do that. You do know some of your future wives might not want to carry their púca to term?"

"Yes. Would you be available as a surrogate?"

"No. I am not available."

"You are not that old."

"I am the same age as your father."

"I know that. You're perfect," Kaede said. Hitomi blushed.

"You want someone younger than me. Charming, beautiful, tall, and willing to undergo memory alteration."

"I would mind wipe you. I would let you raise the baby."

Hitomi blushed. "I will consider it."

"Thank you, Lady Hitomi," Kaede said standing. "I better go."

"I will see you out."

Kaede left her office, lit a stick of incense, and placed

it in the holder on the altar. He handed a gold coin to the shrine maiden.

"No need, the Hashimoto Corporation generously contributes to the upkeep."

"I feel better if I paid for the incense."

"Before you go, Sora told me you're interested in Lady Fukuhina?"

"Yes, but she is worried the age difference. But I don't understand why we live so long."

"What attracts you to Lady Fukuhina?"

"Like you, she is beautiful, strong, determined, hard-working and very smart."

Hitomi accepted the coin and bowed to him. "Next time let me know you are coming. We can have tea, and we can talk about girls your age."

"You're not coming over tonight?"

"I am still coming for third-meal, I will cook you something special and we can discuss controlling your emotions."

"I would like that."

"There is a matter of the fees. You have two hundred adults and over a thousand requests for arranged marriages from noble clans. Many of those are already married."

"We can discuss each application while you teach me to cook and I let you and Sora decide. Sora trusts and likes you, and that is good enough for me."

She smiled at him. He smiled at her, and she escorted him down the stone path.

She stopped at the top of the stairs and bowed to Kaede, he proceeded down the stairs, past many onlookers to Toshiko and Yuki.

Crisis

Kaede sat beside Yuki as she drove him down the Eastern Highway to Blood-Tower, 50 km away. The tower, north of the Airport, was in the heart of middle ring east of the Palace, surrounded by the various Imperial Security Agency offices.

Kaede sat beside Hiro in his hospital room. Hiro was still in a coma, hooked to life support in a hospital bed. Kaede held Hiro's hand, careful not to disturb the drip, one inserted into the back of each hand.

"I miss you, Father," Kaede said.

A knock sounded at the door, and Kaede went to see who it was.

In the hall, Takahiro stood with a couple of house guards.

"Emperor, I am leaving for Alcyone Prime," Takahiro said.

"Do you need to go?" Kaede asked.

"As the head engineer, I need to supervise the test of the Needle Ship. Viktor has ordered additional tests of the new tractor net," Takahiro said.

"I think Father is sleeping."

"Did you tell him yet?"

"That is embarrassing. What if a Witch walked in?"

"Nonsense, never be ashamed of having a penis. Trust me, one day you will be glad it is so big."

Kaede blushed. "But it is huge. Everyone keeps staring at the bulge in my pants."

Takahiro put his hand on Kaede. "The airport isn't far away, and I have time to talk to you while the shuttle fuels."

Kaede stood and bowed. "I apologise, Grandfather, but I already know about puberty. Did you forget I did medical training?"

"I didn't mean about the advantages you have, but about how you feel. I help if you talk to someone close to you about things like being stared at. I can help you gain control your emotions. As Emperor, you going to be judged every day, I cannot shield you from criticism for the rest of your life."

"Until now I felt like I was one of the girls; I could sit down, relax and talk with them. Now I feel like an outsider. In court, ladies stop talking when I approach. So many whispers behind my back."

"I know. One day you soon the girls accept you for who you are. You're not the first boy to feel this way. Your father was not handsome, but pretty in his uniform when he graduated from flight school. Girls flocked to him like bees to a flower. I am not an expert on girls or emotions. First time I meet Masako I was overwhelmed by emotions. Finally, someone who didn't jump on my lap because of my wealth or fame. I was wrong about Freya and regret not telling him."

"I miss my father so much."

"One day he will wake up. He is a Hashimoto, I survived a Dragon landing on me, Hiro is stubborn and a fighter, he is taking a well-earnt rest," Takahiro said, trying to sound confident.

"Of course, he will," Kaede said, attempting to smile.

"Before I go, you should know; Alard has valued your share of the first mine to be ten trillion. That was using the estimated market value of all the diamonds, emeralds, heavy metals, and the vast quantity of Lonsdaleite," Takahiro said. He saw the look on Kaede's face and put his hand on Kaede's shoulder. "Don't worry about the Wealth cap now. Once we sold of 125,000 allotments, paid out expenses, debts, bonuses, we can look at some once off non-asset expenses before even thinking about the cap."

"You were the first to have a million times a million, I guess it is proper a Hashimoto breaks that record."

"Go back in and tell your father how you redesigned my ultra-wave scanner to locate denser asteroids and designed an efficient, stronger gravity beam with more range. He is already very proud of you. As am I."

"Thank you, Grandfather. Have a safe trip."

"Kaede, I am glad you took the hint and replaced me."

Kaede smiled and watched him leave. He turned to Lady Toshiko. "Any word from Galené?" Kaede asked.

"None. I left messages. Because Galené failed to appear at the inquiry, Patya wants to issue a warrant for her arrest," Toshiko said. "I'd like to know how she disappeared, how she got back to Alcyone and explain to me why she refuses to report in."

"You did leave her my message?" Kaede asked.

"Yes, I spoke with her landlord, and all those she went to school with, as well as a voice message on her old number. A pardon in return for information," Toshiko said.

"I am going to sit with my father for a little while longer; please call Nori and see if he can come over tonight," Kaede said.

"Laser Tag is the hottest toy," Yuki said. Toshiko looked

at her and shook her head. Then Yuki said, "Don't forget to tell Hiro that, I am sure that will cheer him up."

Toshiko sighed.

Kaede's bedroom was the largest room in Takahiro's former residence at the top of the tower. His old futon lay by the fire pit the was in the middle of the room. He had awakened before the alarm went off. He walked over to the large set of drawers by the door and turned off the alarm. As he walked to the bathroom, he removed his night dress and tossed it in the laundry basket by the door. He went to take a shower, looked at the stream of water, sighed and stepped in.

Once he was dry, he returned to his bedroom and dressed in the large walk-in closet. Toshiko opened the vault in the back wall of the walk-in closet, removed the Imperial Seal and put it around his neck. She then escorted him to the private Emperor's office, a small complex west of his bedroom.

Toshiko looked inside the room, then stood at the door to the outer office. Kaede went inside.

The room was large, the desk a large computer desk with four additional screens on four arms folded up to the roof. A large bookshelf stood against the rear wall, and the door led to a private washroom. To the left was a paper door to a Japanese tea room.

Kaede placed his identification in the slot in his desk and put his palm on the screen. The computer resumed, he opened a browser and searched for The Stealth Incident of

11574. He saw a classified report from the official Inquiry and a group of images in the results.

He looked at the sender. It was Emperor Kaede. He looked at location tag. It was sent from the data centre, sub-basement twelve of the palace. The message was five minutes old.

Kaede looked at the images. They were of the interior of a room, cut into a grey rock. One series of images was a trail of three sets of large bootprints in dust that led to the wall. The wall and floor had no join, and the last imprint was only the back half of the boot and against the wall. The last series of images was of drag marks with smaller boot prints made by someone that had been walking backwards, the trail led to the wall. The last print was only a half of one, it was at the base of the wall.

Kaede put his phone on the desk and sent the pictures to his mobile and deleted the email. He checked the report, and it stated the tread matched boots only issued to Imperial Sky Force. He looked on the last page of the report. The last entry on audit trail was from Technical Support. They had sent the file to the Inquisition, addressed to Czar Petrov. It had no date of receipt.

Kaede picked his phone up off the desk and called Patya. "Patya, we need to talk."

"About?" Patya asked.

"I was bored, so I looked at the evidence from the asteroid again," Kaede said.

"Kaede, if you have another theory, build a model, and I come look at it later, I am headed to the race track," Patya said.

"I know you want to see my new sports car, but this is important."

"Will you let it go?"

"I believe the Goblins' claim that Galen's ship disappeared into the darkness."

"They are pirates, they will lie just to annoy us."

"Technically they are scavengers, the Goblins are guilty of illegal mining and repairing the Ogre's ship. The Ogre's did the piracy. But I have proof they might not be lying. Did you check all the photographs?"

"No. Agents examined most of them. I only saw those in the final report."

"Hold on. I am sending you some now," Kaede said. He then sent the images he had saved earlier.

Patya looked at the photos and stopped at the one of half a boot print against a wall, and he turned his car around. "Where did you get them?"

"I found them in my inbox."

"These photos do appear to be from the piracy case, but they don't have evidence tags."

"Which means what?"

"They never made it into evidence. A boot print halfway into a wall would have raised eyebrows. On its own, it means nothing, but it validates the Goblins' claim that the three Ogres came and went from that room. One of the Ogres was described as 240cm, rather tall for an Ogre, but not for a Titan. They said his skin was black as if it was burnt to a crisp, and that he had no hair. Mind readers were able to extract a clear image of his face, and it matched one of a wanted killer."

"Who did he kill?"

"Me. Before you ask, I don't know how. I was examining a warehouse used by an Ogre spy ring. We thought we had the whole ring. Then someone set fire to the building killing me, the spies and many agents. No one survived. But that was 300 years ago, and Ogres only have a lifespan of 150 years, and we do not share life expansion technology with anyone. Technical Support recovered one video from body cameras. It showed a 240cm tall black figure walking out of the flames. It was assumed then to be one of the Ogre spies."

"Could this be a different Ogre then?"

"We compared images extracted from the memory of more than one Goblin, and they each matched. Somehow this is the same, Ogre. They told us the Ogre calls himself Shade."

"The only being known to survive a fire is a Red Dragon."

"Officially, I survived the fire, because the Senate doesn't like drawing attention to our immortality. The case went to the cold case unit."

"They took samples of the dust, didn't they?"

"Yes, why?"

"Most dust is skin."

Patya turned east. "I am headed to the Inquisition building now."

"Can you investigate your death?"

"No, I need an agent with Omega clearance to investigate my attempted murder."

"Lady Naru."

"She is suspended."

"What if created a private security company and hired Lady Naru and her friends, then you hired my company which happened to employ only former agents with Omega clearance?"

"You know I hate coincidences?"

"You also hate liars, being wrong, the villain who got away and cold tea. Do you want a list of your likes?"

"I will check with the Inquisition's lawyers and get back to you."

A few hours later, Kaede and Patya entered a conference room. Seated around the table were Nadia, Hilda, Cerise, Naru, Fukuhina, Emi and Naru.

Naru stood. "Do we need a lawyer?"

Patya raised his hand. "None of you is under arrest or investigation. Lady Toshiko recovered data from a massive breach of security. The enemy had Imperial Fleet communications equipment, and had been receiving information from Alcyone Nine and a dozen ships in the local fleet."

"Then why are we here?" Emi asked.

"I am hiring you. I need each of you to fill out a request for extended leave to take a position at full pay equal to current rank with Kaede Investigations as private inquiry agent," Kaede replied.

"Why?" Nadia asked.

"I need you to investigate a 300-year-old case, the murder of Prime Inquisitor, Czar Patya Petrov," Kaede said.

"See Nadia, I was right," Emi said.

"Father, you lied to me," Nadia said slapping his face.

"I omitted facts due to secrecy. It is not the same thing.

Emi Niemi, you know better than to be discussing secrets," Patya said.

"It is Lady Emi Hagihara. You attended my wedding," Emi said.

"Right, sorry," Patya said. He noticed she was not wearing her ring.

"We are suspended, pending an investigation, so how can we investigate?" Cerise asked.

"Which is why I am hiring you. Officially the stealth plane and the cloaking device do not exist. I prefer you all take leave and tell no one outside this room the truth. We cannot charge you, but we can hold a formal inquiry into the missing communications equipment and data found in the hands of Goblin scavengers. But that will ruin you, and we prefer all of you to cooperate with us to locate the leak and the Ogre spies who got away," Kaede said.

"Who is *we*?" Hilda asked.

"In this case, it is the Senate. It was unanimous; we are not firing you, we are asking you to take extended leave to work for the Emperor," Patya said.

"I thought the only time you all agreed was what broth-" Cerise said, but she was cut off by Patya coughing loudly. "Bread you have with lunch."

"No, even then we argue, but sometimes we find something to agree on," Kaede said.

"You must tell me how you got my father not to smoke those awful cigars around the house. At least now he goes to a smoking room," Nadia said.

"Admiral Niemi used a fire extinguisher, and General Feygold reminds him it is illegal to smoke near a minor. We still working on him smoking inside the place, as it is illegal to smoke inside an Imperial building outside a smoke room," Kaede said.

"If we take extended leave, that will affect our promotion prospects," Hilda said.

"A charge of negligent handling of classified material will do worse. You will lose all benefits and rank while awaiting trial. Once found guilty you will be barred from court," Patya said.

"Are you blackmailing us?" Fukuhina demanded as she stood.

"Presenting the facts," Patya replied.

"Patya, let me handle this," Kaede said holding his hand up to Patya. He walked to the big screen, removed the remote from the holder on the wall and clicked it on.

"What is that?" Fukuhina inquired, turning to look. She walked to the screen. It displayed an image of a boot print halfway into a wall.

"Proof three Ogre spies vanished from an asteroid in deep space by walking into an empty room with no other exit," Kaede replied.

Hilda stood up and walked over. She towered over Kaede. "Who do we report to?"

"Lady Fukuhina will be the team's leader. She will report to me, Patya or Lady Toshiko. I will assign you Lady Yuki as your liaison with the Imperial Security Agency," Kaede replied.

"Count me in," Emi said.

"What will happen to the charges against us?" Cerise asked.

"When you find the spy, the Imperial Security Agency will claim it was an operation with your full cooperation, so the various branches will reinstate each of you to your respective departments with full-back pay. You'll get an off the record apology, but you will receive a commendation with an advancement in rank. Until then I pay you at your current rate," Kaede replied.

"Deal," Nadia stated.

"Good, I will provide you two armoured SUVs and later a car, body armour and a handgun," Kaede said. He turned to Patya, "Patya, are you still seeking a buyer for your artillery test range south of New Moscow?"

"Yes, it is too small," Patya replied.

"We can work on the details later, but I will buy it and build a training area for Kaede Security," Kaede said. He headed for the door, then stopped and turned. "Coming ladies?"

"Pardon?" Fukuhina inquired.

"Lady Toshiko is at the auto race track, I booked it for today to test my car," Kaede replied.

Fukuhina caught up with Patya as they headed out. "Is he serious?"

"We are. The spy who disappeared might be an immortal Ogre hiding on this world," Patya replied.

"I thought only the Senate lived forever," Fukuhina said.

"Patya, you know there is no such thing as an immortal," Cerise said behind them.

"Oh?" Fukuhina asked.

"A select group of Elves rely on Blood-Witches to keep them young and alive," Cerise said.

Patya stopped and faced Cerise. "Yes. It means our enemies have blood magic. We must contain and eliminate this spy. He is a threat to our existence."

"I know what it takes to appear unable to die. Like you, the Ogre will need cellular renewal treatment regularly. That is not the only technology required to extend his lifespan," Cerise told them.

Later, at the race track, Kaede, in a fire suit and racing helmet, drove fast around the track, the car limited to a top speed of 120 km per hour. The car, a low, sleek sports car, was made from plastic and had not been painted. He drove fast into and stopped hard in the pit stop. The car's door popped open, then slid back. Kaede got out as engineers checked the car, changed the wheels, fuelled the vehicle, and began to remove the oil. Another group in lab coats opened the rear hatch and connected a computer on a trolley to the engine and its black box.

A smiling Toshiko came up to Kaede as he removed his helmet.

"Now can I drive with a passenger?" Kaede asked her as she approached.

"You need to give Patya a turn behind the wheel," Toshiko said.

"He can drive his car anytime," Kaede said.

"Which is not as fast as yours," Toshiko said.

"He can buy one soon," Kaede pointed out.

"I will give you some high-speed lessons, but only if you give Patya a turn," Toshiko offered.

"No limit?" Kaede inquired, excited.

"First see how you handle a limit of 200," Toshiko replied, poking his nose.

Kaede raced up the stairs to the stand behind the pit stop. He passed Nori, who looked puzzled as Kaede went past him. He went and stood in front of Patya, who was sitting at the end of the row of the ladies, beside his daughter.

"I am taking a break. Would you like a turn?" Kaede offered.

"You know I would, Emperor," Patya replied. He stood and looked Kaede in the eye. Patya looked hurt.

"I am sorry," Kaede muttered.

"Did you say something?" Patya inquired, his eyebrows raised.

"I said, I am sorry that I used my rank to go first," Kaede responded in a soft voice, looking at his feet.

Patya lifted Kaede's chin and looked him in the eye. "Just don't do it again," Patya said with a smile.

Kaede sat beside Nori. "Nice car," Nori said, in a fire suit, holding a helmet on his lap and staring at the car.

"I know it is ugly, they are still working on how to paint it," Kaede said.

"Why can't they paint it?" Nori asked looking at Kaede.

"The paint peels off," Kaede replied.

"You never made a model, did you?" a confused Nori asked.

"Only models I am interested in wear bikinis," Kaede said with a grin.

"It is easy to paint smooth plastic; sand the surface, prime it, coat it, then clear seal it," Nori said after laughing.

"Before Lady Toshiko will let me take a passenger in my car, I must prove to her I am not going to crash," Kaede said, watching Patya race through the chicane.

"You can take him when I say so," Lady Emi said from behind, and she put her hand on Nori's shoulder.

"Mum!" Nori exclaimed, shrugging her off.

"Lady Emi, what if I took you first?" Kaede said looking at Emi.

Cerise laughed. Fukuhina leaned over to her. "Cerise, hush."

"Why are we still here?" Nadia asked.

"Because Lady Toshiko told you to stay," Kaede replied.

"Emperor, it isn't because I don't trust you," Emi said looking at Nori.

"After Lady Toshiko, it is your turn," Kaede said.

"All right," Emi replied. She looked at Cerise who poked her tongue out at Emi.

Patya pulled into the pit stop, and before getting out, he turned on the speed limiter.

"Set it to 200," Toshiko requested. She had a vest on and held a knight's helm.

"Do you think he is ready?" Patya asked.

"I will sit in the passenger seat," Toshiko replied, putting on her helm.

"Are you going to behave?" Patya asked, staring at Kaede.

"I know my patience needs work," Kaede said, looking Patya in the eye.

"Toshiko, do mind if I take him hunting tonight?" Patya asked, looking at Kaede.

Kaede's eye lit up, Toshiko's eyebrows raised and she looked at Patya then looked at Kaede.

"Have fun," Toshiko replied.

After driving around, the track twice with Kaede,

Toshiko got out. Emi put on a safety helmet and got in the passenger seat. Toshiko plugged the intercom into Emi's helmet. Kaede waited until given the green light, then drove off as fast as he could.

"Sora is an odd choice," Emi remarked, watching him.

"I know Izanami is smarter and prettier than Sora, but Sora is a better organiser," Kaede responded.

"But you love Izanami, and she loves you," Emi said.

"She has a temper," Kaede replied.

"What about love?" Emi inquired.

"This is marriage, not dating. The choice is about who will be Empress and the mother of my son," Kaede said.

Emi looked at him. "Is Toshiko telling you what to say?"

"No one is listening or telling me what to say," Kaede responded.

"They think I am a traitor," Emi said, looking out the passenger window.

"I don't believe the leak is you. But someone close to you and the others is helping the Ogres and has been for a long time. The question is why did they steal the stealth?" Kaede asked.

"Isn't it obvious? A plane that can sneak past our defences."

"We were not testing stealth. We know it works. We have many stealth craft. We were testing detection," Kaede said.

"Detection?"

"Yes. Please don't tell anyone. Even the others."

"Of course," Emi responded, smiling.

Kaede stopped in the pit stop, and Emi got out. Kaede

came around the car and hugged her. "Now, can I please take Nori around the track?"

"All right," a surprised Emi replied.

Kaede went around the track a couple of times with Nori in the passenger seat laughing and whooping with joy.

After the car, had been loaded on a truck, Kaede has the engineers promise to have Nori show them how to paint a model car. Emi took Nori home.

Patya and Kaede were flown north by helicopter to the edge of a park at a lake. Both wore camouflage with bright orange hunting vests. Patya unloaded a couple of packs and short spears, then checked Kaede's vest as the helicopter left.

"We will ditch the high-visibility vest later. First, I want to see how good your night vision is," Patya said.

"My night vision is excellent," a puzzled Kaede replied.

"Just because Elves can see in the dark better than other races, that doesn't mean we all see the same."

"You have read my medical records; both my low light vision and spectral range are excellent. Also, Dragons have better vision than Elves, they have better infrared and better ultraviolet than Dwarves," Kaede said. "Why are we out here?"

"I told you why. Now, just because you had a couple of tests in an optometrist's office does not mean you have great vision in the real world. Being able to see more shades of colours is different from seeing a detailed picture as I do."

"Are you upset about the photo?"

Patya went over to the two packs and picked up a short spear.

"But would you have seen it if it was not blown up?" Patya asked, holding the spear sideways. He tossed it to Kaede, who caught it with both hands.

"What are we hunting?" Kaede asked, examining the short spear.

"Frogs," Patya said, handing Kaede a pair of waders.

"Frogs?"

"Yes. Also, you are going to learn how to use your sixths and seventh senses."

"How is feeling electrical energy or movement around me going to help hunt in a swamp?"

Patya put on the waders, then picked up a pack. "You are not as smart as you think," Patya said, pointing the spear at him.

Kaede took a step forward.

"There is a spy inside the palace, and you think it is one of those women. I do not. Before you ask, Takahiro has books on spy-catching in the clan library. We have secret methods to catch spies. Before I took office, he was grooming me to run the company. My father had turned him down to be a career officer," Kaede said.

"Then who do you think the spy is?" Patya inquired.

"I can only speculate at this point, but it is someone close to them. I doubt it is a magic user skilled at Mind Probe, but it is taking too long to get information from inside the Ogre's high command. Currently, you rely on getting information from intercepted communications from inside the Ogres' military and gossip from many sources.

That is information filtered by analysists who are trained to hide sources," Kaede said as he put on the waders.

"Confidential informants tell me the Ogres know we are listening to them," Patya said.

"You have no idea who recruited Galen or when. Toshiko believes he is not the leak and I agree with her. I think he stole the plane to prove his worth to the Ogres, but he isn't working for them, there was no direct communication. We don't know who he is working for. A third party passed him information. Galené saw something when she was on the base, so Galen took her. He later released her, or he let her let escape to mislead us," Kaede said, picking up a pack.

"I am told the Ogres blame him for leading the Knights to the asteroid and are hunting for him. That doesn't make Galen any less a traitor, but you are right, we don't know who he is working for," Patya responded, heading for the shore of the lake.

At sunrise, there were three frogs skewered on one spear in the fire and only one on the other. A wet Kaede wrapped in a blanket sat by the fire.

"Feel better?" Patya asked, coming out of the tent.

"Yes thanks," Kaede replied.

"You need to work on your lying, you are terrible," Patya remarked.

"You're the most honest Elf there is, head of the Inquisition, the motto of which is Truth is Everything," Kaede replied, turning to face Patya. "Making you an expert on lying. The question is how can you sit in the Senate listening to lies?"

"To keep an eye on them. You can find the truth if you hear enough lies." Patya said as he sat beside Kaede. He put his hand on Kaede's forehead. "We can tolerate the cold, but we prefer and do better in the warmth. We rarely get sick, but our immunity can be comprised," Patya said. He cast magic hands and pulled a Frog off the skewer and offered it to Kaede.

"Why didn't you tell me my father is paralysed?" Kaede asked as he took the cooked frog.

"Kenta doesn't think your father will ever regain consciousness. I am sorry," Patya said.

Kaede put his arms around Patya and cried.

In the distance, Toshiko was watching and listening from a surveillance van. She took off the headphone, handed it to an operator and left the van. Yuki was one of a team of four on guard around the van. They wore black coveralls with a black beret, and each had one hand on a Viper 2.

She turned to Toshiko and asked, "Problem?"

"Maybe. Kaede knows about Hiro," Toshiko replied.

"He was going to find out eventually. He does know how to read a medical chart."

INTO THE ELVES' MOUND

CHAPTER 11

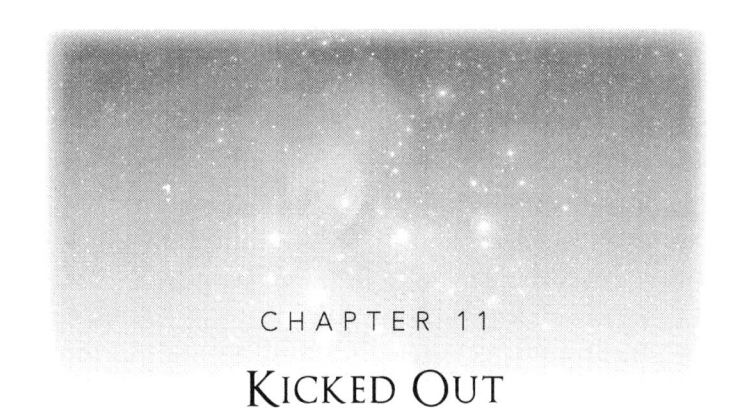

KICKED OUT

January 3, 11575. Imperial City.

Kaede woke five minutes before his alarm. His bed was a large, round futon many metres in diameter, covered with furs and quilts near a fire pit in the middle of the large room. He slid out from under the large quilt, a large pillow between him and the centre of his bed. He used a large red Makura with yellow trim covered in images of green Dragons for a pillow. In his night dress, he walked over to the north wall and tapped it, the screen appeared, and he turned off the alarm.

Kaede went to his bathroom. Instead of his shower cubical, he saw capped pipes and a notice on the wall, *No Hot Water*. He shrugged his shoulders and looked at his vanity. A range of hand creams, shampoos, body washes, bubble baths and grooming products covered the unit. He selected one of the bubble baths and started filling the tub. He had cold water only, so he stood outside the tub watching it fill. *My fault, I did ask them to install the mist shower.*

As he waited, one of the robot vacuum cleaners entered. It zipped around the room, almost noiseless, and stopped in front of him. Kaede leaned over to look at it, and then the light went off, and at the same time, he felt a surge of magic behind him. He reached for the panic button by the door, but a hand grabbed his arm. He kicked the person beside him and again tried to reach the alarm button. A soft hand was placed over his mouth and pulled him back, and he bit it hard.

He then headbutted the person behind him. His attacker caught his head, twisted his arm, turned him around and pushed him against the wall, a soft hand searched under his robe, then lifted him up and put him into the cold bath.

Kaede saw it was a female Elf, about his size. He tried to fight her off, but she kicked the back of his knees hard, this forced him onto his knees and held him in a chokehold. He struggled to escape and to breathe, but each time she slapped his hands for trying to grab her. She put her lips to his ear. She felt different, somehow cold. Even her breath on his neck felt cold.

"I don't have long," Galené whispered.

Kaede recognised her voice. "Galené, let me go. If you hurt me, Toshiko will make you suffer."

"I am not here to kill you. Shade has spies inside the Palace, and they are using your robot cleaners to watch you," Galené whispered, then let him go.

"Next time a simple note in my sock drawer would suffice," Kaede said, rubbing his wrist.

The lights came on, Kaede looked up, and Galené was gone. Kaede, soaking wet, stepped out of the bathroom as

Toshiko raced into the room. She looked at him in his night dress, covered in bubble bath. Kaede smiled and said, "This is embarrassing."

A short time later, Kaede was dry, dressed and went to the kitchen.

"Something went wrong with the cooling for the servers, and the crash caused the Palace power plant to reset," Toshiko said.

"I need to speak to Patya about staying with him," Kaede said.

"Why?" a puzzled Toshiko asked.

"While we have work crews to fix that, I am thinking of having a pool installed, and I am sure you would have issues with me watching you swim laps of your pool naked before sunrise."

"What makes you think I swim naked?"

"Why else put a transition cover over such a beautiful pool."

Toshiko stared at him then asked, "Why do you need to move out to install a new pool?"

"I want to raise the dome and put a large and deep pool on the under the dome. As well as a pool on the level below mine. While the workers are here, I will have them install a gym, salon, a fifty-seat theatre and many other changes to the layout of the residence. I already have a list," Kaede said, as he entered on his phone the message, "Inform Patya and Yaotl there are bugs in my robot cleaners," he held it up to Toshiko.

"Long list, you are going to need specialist engineers. But, what makes you think Patya will give you a room?"

"I don't mind living with you. I too like to swim in the morning. But Patya might be upset if I don't ask him first."

"I will talk to Patya." Toshiko laughed.

Kaede stood in the doorway, and he looked around the throne room. The other twelve Senators watched him. In the rightmost chair sat Dain with an angry scowl on his face. The room went silent as Kaede entered. The Imperial Crown sat on a pillow, on a stool beside the throne.

The Knights closed the door behind him. Kaede adjusted the jade seal of the empire around his neck on a gold chain and waved to Dain.

He looked at Patya Petrov, who sat in the leftmost chair. He wore a black suit, shirt, shoes with a gold tie with a White Russian Bear on it. Kaede nodded to him, and Patya nodded in return.

Kaede looked around the room, a large round auditorium. The twelve screens on the outer walls were all off. The double doors, the only way to enter the chamber, were sealed. *None of the air vents, on this level, are big enough to crawl in; when smaller I tried more than once.* He looked at the cameras, then back to Patya and nodded.

Kaede's throne was a large red leather reclining chair with gold trim, and the other twelve sat on black leather reclining chairs in a semi-circle around the three-layer dais beneath his throne. The throne was luxurious. On either side of his ears was a speaker. Each had a touch screen on a retractable arm on the left. Kaede pulled his up.

All eyes were on Kaede, as Patya stood without warning.

"Yes, Patya?" Kaede asked.

"Emperor, my inquiry into the missing Stealth has ended," Patya said.

"You have the floor," Kaede said.

"Galen crammed in the Ogres inside Stealth's empty missile bay while the Goblins were distracted with an illusion. They drifted out on lowest power side on and floated between Toshiko's shuttles outside; after that, he just waited for one to move and he left," Patya said.

"Two illusions," Kaede said.

"Pardon?" Maharajah Desai asked.

"If some Goblins saw three Ogres running for the empty room since there were only three of them in the asteroid, that would have to have been an illusion. The Ogres were not firing power bolts at Galen, they were scattering the Goblins," Kaede said.

"How come Goblins were not blown or burnt by the exhaust?" Dain asked.

"Goblins were to the rear, and he only needed minimum power to roll out. With the outer doors open and no gravity, he needed only a quick burst to drift out into space and disappear," Patya replied.

"Thank you, Patya," Kaede said.

"What about the fuss over boot prints in the empty room?" Dain pressed.

"A hoax by the Ogres to have us confused," Patya responded, looking at Dain.

"That concludes today's business," Kaede said, standing. The double doors opened, Kaede held a finger to his lips and went and closed them. He looked at his phone, opened the

Palace application, and zoomed on the red dot representing his location. Then he tapped the room, and on the menu selected security and camera status. Cameras were marked as off and cleaning robots disabled.

"Sorry everyone, that was a performance for the camera. I received an anonymous tip the Palace network has been compromised," Kaede said.

"That is not possible. After the theft of the stealth fighter, I personally checked the system. No one has been able to hack the Palace network in over a century," Yaotl said.

"Someone hacked one of the Palace servers this morning and sealed the cooling vent in the central column. That resulted in several systems crashing and a brief power outage," Kaede said.

"How is that related to the stolen stealth?" Dain asked.

"An informant told me they are related. Patya will have agents and Yaotl will send data security officers to the Palace undercover as work crews while I have remodelling done," Kaede said.

"How convenient," Dain remarked.

"I have asked Patya if I can stay with him. Two things. I am paying for everything." Kaede said.

"How long will this operation last?" Adalwulf asked.

"Until Patya and Toshiko think it is safe for me to return," Kaede replied.

It was nearly 7 pm when Kaede entered the elevator and went up. He strolled over to the kitchen and sat to dinner with Toshiko.

"I am sorry about this morning," Toshiko said.

"Any idea how she got in?" Kaede asked.

"None and I cannot identify the spell she used to leave your bathroom," Toshiko replied in a soft voice.

"We have an hour before I leave with Patya," Kaede replied, looking Toshiko in the eye.

"What did you want to talk about?"

"I know my busy schedule is a routine that you prefer I change and not be predictable, but there is a method to my madness."

Toshiko stopped eating and looked at him. "If they know where you are going to be it makes it easy for them to attack you."

"Yet they have not. I am building a following, and I already have many fans."

"I am worried about you."

"Enough to have me live with you?"

"Sure. I have a basement, a metal chair and duct tape."

"I need a whole floor at the Lilith Foundation. Rip out all internal walls. No security, no cleaning robots. Internal server and guarded 24/7. I will install a magic laboratory that will take up most of the floor. I need books on how to create spells, casting targets with force registers and everything on making wands, staves, cauldrons and brooms."

"You are too young to do a degree in magic. You learn how to make spells in advanced magic."

"I promise to behave, and you will not catch me watching you swim. I need to learn from the best."

Toshiko laughed. "I will talk to Patya and Kenta, and if they agree, you can do a degree in magic, but you need to qualify and then qualify for advanced magic."

Toshiko looked up, then Masako came in with Freya. Toshiko resumed eating.

Kaede ran over to Freya and gave her a hug. She lifted him up and said, "No tears, your father is fine and going to wake up one day."

"I know," Kaede said. She put him down.

"Masako tells me you're going away?" Freya asked.

"Remodelling. I am putting a dance floor under the dome, installing a pool, and the Empresses' private bedroom. I am going to need more bathrooms, a bigger gym, and a salon. Also, a dance studio for Izanami," Kaede replied.

"Will you be staying in your old room?" Freya asked.

Toshiko came over and said, "He is staying with Patya."

"Why?" a confused Freya asked.

"Because he is one of my guardians, and Kenta already has Sora, Akiko, and Izanami," Kaede replied.

"What about security?" Masako asked.

"He will have two Knights with him at all times," Toshiko replied.

"Is that enough?" Masako asked.

"It is," Toshiko said before she left.

"Freya, are you going to marry my father?" Kaede asked.

"What?" a blushing Freya asked.

"So, I can call you *mother*," Kaede said.

Freya kissed Kaede on the forehead and turned to Masako. "Don't you dare tell Takahiro."

"You can trust me. I am trying to get Takahiro to marry me," Masako said.

"What is his excuse?" Freya asked.

"He keeps going on business trips," Masako said.

"I'll find him a desk job, the rest is up to you," Kaede said.

"Maybe if I walk around in a wedding dress he will get the hint," Masako remarked.

"I have known Takahiro my whole life, and even that might be too subtle for him," Toshiko said as she re-entered the room.

Masako looked worried as Toshiko walked up to her. But then Toshiko hugged her and said, "I will help you even if I must drag him to the Blood-Witches by his ears."

"Wonderful," Freya said, holding her cheeks.

"Emperor, you need to change the law. I will draft a proposed marriage reform act which will allow two consenting legal adults who have already met the requirements of the bloodline law, to be free to marry each another. Best make it regardless of gender, species, or age difference," Toshiko said.

"What does that mean?" a curious Masako requested.

"It means my grandfather will have no excuses left. Toshiko is not only a brilliant lawyer, but he listens to her," Kaede responded.

"Exactly," Toshiko said.

A Knight entered and bowed. "Excuse me, Emperor, Czar Petrov is waiting for you in the Palace."

"Lady Toshiko, Lady Yuki with me. Freya, Masako good night," Kaede said as he left.

Kaede sat in the back of an SUV beside Patya, with Lady Toshiko in the front, beside Patya's driver. The rest of Patya's guards were in the SUV behind them, driven by Lady Yuki.

"Patya, why is Dain worried we would take funding from the Dwarves?" Kaede asked.

"Thirty years ago, the Dwarves had a disastrous war with the Orcs over a rogue planet. Both sides suffered heavy losses, and neither has recovered socially or economically. Fortunately for us, the Ogres are unable to take advantage of this, as they have their hands full with pirates," Patya said.

"The reality is we rule the Dwarves?" Kaede asked.

"Yes, over half the adult population works for Elves, mostly females in the service industry."

"We own over half of their heavy industry. I think we should annexe the Dwarves."

"The Ogres, Titans and Orcs would likely respond to that by declaring war."

"We are not going to invade them. We have no need."

"Why not?"

"Two years ago, King Weyland left his wife and moved in with Dain. Since then Dain has controlled the Dwarves for his own ends. This has lifted the Dwarven economy, but not by much."

"True. But that is not enough to persuade the Dwarves to end their independence."

"The rogue planet the Dwarves and Orcs fought over is now nearly mined out. We are sitting on a mine the size of 319 worlds. Patya, it is simple economics. We need the labour, and the Dwarves can be that labour."

"You think that is enough to get them to agree to join the Empire?"

"With wage reform, which includes unskilled labour, including…do you know what I mean by ladies in the service industry?"

"Yes, but you have a conflict of interest. Takahiro has many tea houses."

"A hurdle, I agree. But wage reform is needed, including lifting a ban on unions, because the Dwarves will never give up their Federation of Mining Workers. The other hurdle is immigration. We do not change the migration zones and guarantee the Dwarves we not moving in, completely."

"To annexe a member of the Dragon Council, under the terms of the treaty, first you need to have most members of the Dragon Council to agree. Then you need to hold a vote in both states. Then if the majority in both states vote yes, the smaller state will lose its seat and be considered a vassal state. It could be quicker if we invade because then it is automatic. It is very unlikely to pass the Senate given how expensive it would be to hold an election."

"Dain is an advocate of expansion. The vote isn't a problem."

"What is?"

"I know the Ogres will agree to our proposal. The problem is Caesar Giovanni, he wants to annexe the Orcs, who are weak from losing a war with the Dwarves."

"Another reason the Senate will not agree."

"Patya, we need to annexe the Dwarves. We must lift them out of poverty, or it will become an embarrassing propaganda tool against us. The problem is the female service industry; most of these workers are Dwarves who work for less. I think we need all non-Elves, not just Dwarves, on the same pay scale as Elves. I do not think it is a conflict of interest to give all adult workers the same pay."

"Your grandfather is the largest adult services provider in the empire, he will spank you for raising their pay."

"Wage reform is not aimed at prostitutes, but all unskilled labour. My system uses a rating from one to seven, with welfare at level 1, unskilled workers at level 2, with healers, managers at five, with specialists at 6 and the most highly skilled at 7. Of course, those wages at each skill level will only a minimum guide for private companies."

"You risk a backlash, Dain and Takahiro will join forces against you."

"We not increasing regulation, wages are already regulated, we reduce regulations, have minimum pay one each level, but reduce the cost of compliance. Patya, Imperial wage reform is key to internal peace. Wages are a key tool the Dark Elves recruit with."

"Many will oppose you because your clan is the largest employer of working girls and see this as a way of putting them out of business."

"If you do not mind answering, Patya do you hire any companions?"

"Takahiro didn't tell you? I retain the services of a Female Centaur."

"I thought that was Maharaj Desai."

"He regularly hires Centaurs and Dwarves. He likes the company of male and females."

"I am confused. I thought that was Yaotl?"

"No, Dain is a homosexual, he likes Dwarves, but he is having an affair with his personal assistant Roland, a Mountain Elf. Arjuna is a bisexual, he lives with a husband and a wife. Yaotl lives with a large group of females. There are his many wives, a female Centaur, and a few female Dwarves. They all live together in tents in the wildlife preserve on the southern edge of the city."

"I see. Not that it really matters, but most of those who oppose me equally have a conflict of interest to pay less and I rather not exclude anyone from the process, but see this as a chance to effect change," Kaede said as he looked out the window. He turned to face the front and said, "Patya, consider what the conspiracy against us do if we keep the Dwarves poor? At least with Annexing them, some opponents might support it or at the very least do nothing to stop us because they believe it might further their cause. I think they are not after wealth or titles, but power over government."

"That makes no sense."

"Patya, if all our enemies combined into one army, could they defeat us using direct force?"

"No."

"What about a vast conspiracy?"

"I would detect one."

"Like the New State?"

"Yes, it is the large radical group liked to the Dark Elves in the free states. They are focused on recruiting university students and hide behind free expression and free association to call for an end to the Imperial State."

"Professors radicalise students. These students become professors, teachers, and artists. They spent their life protesting, wearing society down. I believe we are at the tipping point. I have seen some students so obsessed with emotions and desire for power that they operate with no logic and attack anyone who opposes them. For decades, little was done about them because on many university campuses most of the professors and staff are members of the New State. They started off as harmless, but in the last ten years a consistent rise in protests and the level of violence. If we don't counter them, they will grow in the level of violence."

"What do you propose we do? We cannot jail them for life. We cannot jail them just because they oppose you. The charter grants all citizens freedom of association and expression. They are not a criminal conspiracy or in open rebellion."

"We need to defeat them ideologically before they are a large group, because if we do not, once the Empire is in turmoil, the Ogres will unite the others races and attack us. It will not be the first, second or third war that finishes us. It will be internal division and civil war."

"You are right. I don't like it, but you are right."

"Annexing the Dwarves is a necessary move, and wage reform needs to be part of that. I hope that you will see how it would shift people's focus and bring us much-needed positive attention from the public. But lifting the Dwarves out of poverty is only a start. It will not defeat the conspiracy that is based on envy."

"I do some merit, but I think you overstate the benefits."

"Even a slight change in opinions of us could help reduce their recruiting power and reduce the number of possible enemies we face."

"True Emperor, but many lords will oppose it, and that could be damaging to us."

"We need to give Dwarves equal rights and equal pay. So, we must work hard to reduce the opposition from within. The key to effective wages control is to also control prices and population. The Dwarves will need price, land, wage, and population control to fight poverty. They neither have the experts or infrastructure needed to do so. Possible opponents like Dain need to be sold on how much the Dwarves need us and how much we will lose if we don't embrace them as equals. Because the Dwarves could turn nasty like the Goblins have, and we lose the labour, we sorely need to continue building artificial fuel plants and mine asteroids."

"Yes, Dain will be furious, as he has many farms with cheap labour inside and outside the Empire."

"Yes, without his help, this will be a long process. Dain needs to see this is long-term, that it strengthens the Empire and secures our wealth. Cheaper to pay the workers now, than hire expensive security later, because the conspiracy will get the Dwarven workers revolt and if we don't annexe the Dwarves, the other Empires will eventually invade them meaning our fleet is permanently orbiting their worlds."

"Yes. I talk to Dain."

"Patya, you need to be clear to the rest of the Senate. The Empire needs wage and education reform. Not just the service industry. They are the largest offenders, they overcharge clients and then overpay workers for doing something that takes no skill."

"It is more complicated than that Emperor."

"Only to them. To me it is simple. These workers require no skill, and to encourage them to get a skill, they need to earn enough for basic living, but earn less than the average workers."

"How will they get an education?"

"To fund free education, we need to slash funding to the arts and use that to fund science, engineers, agriculture and trade schools. It is more complicated than that, as teachers wages in government schools and colleges will be only skill three wages."

"You will face a mass protests."

"Yaotl has information on some professors in the Imperial University. Until now he has sat on these scandals. If you arrest the head of the Association of Teachers and Professors for tax fraud we use that to shift public opinion that we don't go after the rich. Find a way for your inquiry to expand into the high cost of education, I am not telling you to just blame it on a few overpaid professors driving up the cost of education. But from my own experience with obtaining a degree, professors have many courses that pad the length of their courses."

"That could work in time. But in the short-term, it leaves us with an education system in tatters and a lot of distrust."

"We then open smaller private colleges. We need more trade schools and smaller colleges open day and night. A significant reform will be, instead of enrolling in one college or university, we have Árni as Minister of Education, Employment and Training implement a system where students all do an entry exam and receive one free degree based on results and projected vacancies. Then if they want to learn more, they can enrol in courses on any campuses, but pay for it themselves. Another change will the department will conduct all university exams. I plan to slash the cost of education."

"Are you insane? I cannot speak for Árni, but I doubt the education department has the resources or the budget to do that."

"No. Insane is doing the same thing we always do and

expect different results. The Treasury tells me no one reform can be done on its own. If we slash one budget, the money must be spent elsewhere immediately or face demands for tax decreases. The free market will feel threatened, as it needs to get something in return, we expand private education. That will also reduce the number of students in public education."

"You have spoken with the Treasury committee?"

"Yes. The committee believes it is possible to reform wages, education, and annexe the Dwarves, but done together, as a package. If we don't, we end up trying to tweak the budget as we try to introduce each measure."

"What about this security breach you claim exists?"

"I don't think the Ogre pirates are working for Caesar Giovanni nor King Chronos. Neither have youth and vigour. Chronos is in poor health fearing one of his sons staging a coup. Chronos wants out of the Ogre Alliance, but don't have the will or might to do so."

"I see my lessons are starting to pay off, but my money is on Atlas."

"We need to pick one and cultivate a relationship. I don't like Atlas or Zeus, but that is a war we don't want to happen soon. We want to split up the Ogres not tear them apart. Zeus would be a better replacement with one of Yaotl's cultivated agents in his ear."

"I have found it odd that the Ogres have exploited the information. They haven't even reduced the number of imports. I do not see any benefit to just gathering the information."

"I believe we use the opportunity to over the other Empires a new trade deal. One that protects non-Elven inventions inside the Empire as well as ours outside. I know many will be against it, I aim to reduce the possibility of war."

"You know Dain, and most of the others, just vote for what benefits them."

"I plan to annexe all the known worlds in 500 lights years and split them into fifteen provinces. To share our technology with them is only the first step."

"Now I know you are insane."

"No, what is crazy is the biggest threat to our people is our people. I have had Fukuhina search records for information on missing ships. She found out that a group will pilot ships from Freeport to the Utopia system. Many members of the New State come from the free states."

"Yaotl has lost many agents trying to infiltrate them."

"Our communication system is comprised. The enemy knows our every move."

"If that is true, I would have found out."

"No offence, but large volumes of secrets were found in the hands of Goblin Scavengers."

"They had some imperial systems and access codes, likely provided by Galen."

"This morning Lady Galené paid me a visit this morning in my bathroom."

"What?" an angry Patya asked, facing him, "I am going to spank you."

"Galené got into my room undetected. She could have killed me, but she didn't. She told me Shade has spies inside the Palace, and are using my robot cleaners," Kaede said.

Patya looked at Toshiko. Her face went red then she took a deep breath and looked straight ahead.

"Why use robot cleaners?" Patya asked.

"Not only do they go all over the Palace, but the computer that controls them is in the Data Centre," Kaede replied.

"I don't get it," Patya said.

"The Palace has many networks. But they are all connected to the Data Centre in sub-basement twelve," Toshiko said.

"Even the Imperial Command Centre in sub-basement eleven and Palace security in sub-basement ten?" Patya asked.

"Yes," Toshiko replied.

"Now I see. While I my focus was on the staff nearest to us, spies used our technology against us," Patya said.

"Right," Toshiko said.

"Patya, remember what I said about dust?" Kaede asked.

"Yes. You said it is mostly skin," Patya replied, looking puzzled.

"It has been bothering me for a while. The vents under some floors are dusty," Kaede replied.

"Why didn't you tell me?" Toshiko asked, looking in the rear-view mirror.

"I was little, it seemed to be nothing until now," Kaede said.

"Toshiko, please do not be angry at him," Patya said, looking at Toshiko, "I have seen him dusty many times. Back then I thought it was because the air vents were a low priority to the cleaning robots. Now I see that was due to robots spying on us instead of cleaning. We have to assume the cleaning staff is a spy-ring."

"You are right. I should be mad at you and Yaotl. You are supposed to find and arrest traitors, while Yaotl disrupts and breaks up radical groups. If agents have access to the vacuum robot server, they have access to all the others. I believe they would know and even use all the hidden cameras and microphones in the Palace. Worse, the Palace has records of every secret mission in the last one hundred years," Toshiko said in a soft voice.

"What now?" Patya asked.

"You and Yaotl need to spy on all the top officers who knew about stealth, try to link them to Palace staff, see who hired the robot cleaners, and revisit the Stealth case until we find a new threat. Now, by you and Yaotl, I mean personally, not agents. No official records, not mission reports; the only help you get is Toshiko," Kaede said.

"What if your friend Nori is an agent?" Patya asked, looking at Kaede.

"I am sure he isn't. I do not think Lady Emi and her friends are spies. I don't know how, but they are being spied on. But to answer you, I would put Nori in prison. I will not kill my friend, even if he has betrayed me. But many are going to die for betraying their oath of office," Kaede said, looking at his phone. He texted Izanami. "I want you to catch the vacuum robot in my room, replace it with the broken one from the workshop and take it home. Only tell Kenta."

"Just issue it orders," Izanami texted back.

"No time to explain. The cameras are off. Work crews come tomorrow to rip it all out. Just do it."

"What about dance practice?"

"You can afford one night off. The show doesn't start for a couple of months."

"I know I can, but you need the practice."

"You are hilarious 'Nami. I need you to do this for me."

"All right, I can afford to be late for dance practice, just be there waiting for me."

Kaede put his phone away.

Inside Kaede's room, he had a massive walk-in closet, and on the back of the door was a tablet with a menu system. Staff were taking clothes off the rack in the room, scanning them, sealing them in plastic and putting them on mobile stands.

Masako led an engineer to the bathroom. "He designed a new hot tub and toilet. You need to remodel the bathroom and install another bathroom behind his bedroom with a set of concealed stairs to the bedroom below."

"What about the mist shower unit?" the Engineer asked.

"He still wants that installed," Masako said.

"What can do you with a toilet? You know gold seats don't come cheap?" the engineer sneered.

"It is not gold, but a gel cushion with a soft, warm cover with an electric warmer. The Emperor added a bottom washer, dryer and a dual flush to save both paper and water. It has many features including a Smart Screen, such as an auto seat closer, perfume release with big flush and music. Remember he owns the designs of the mist shower, the luxury toilet, and the super-hot tub. He wants them installed them in all bathrooms in the Palace, many of his hotels and other places," Masako said.

"I need the original plans if I am going to knock out a wall," the Engineer replied, looking at the far wall.

"My office will provide you with all the information you need to knock out walls, pull up tiles and install new pipes, cables and so forth," Masako said.

"I am going to need a bigger work crew," the Engineer said, looking at Masako.

"All you need to do is make sure it is all done before his 18th birthday," Masako said, glaring at him.

"Relax, the stairs to the room below, a bigger bathroom, a second large bathroom, a gym, salon, game room and pool will only take a year, maybe two," the Engineer replied.

"The residence will be divided into four wings. The bedrooms on the east side, the kitchens and dining on the north, the offices on the south and the entertainment on the west, with the central foyer replaced with a pool on each floor with a walkway over it, around the inner and outer edge."

"How big is the crawl space?"

"The crawl space between each floor is three metres."

"You have very high ceilings, so what is the gap between floor and roof?"

"The roof is five metres from the floor."

He looked up and around. "The internal diameter of the tower?"

"Five hundred metres…are you writing a book?"

"Trying to work out the size of the area to know how many to hire."

"You will have hundreds working on everything from a balcony facing the sunrise on solstice to a salon with massage chairs, to a game room able to keep a boy busy for years. Others have done all the planning. You will manage those teams."

"I prefer to do the hiring."

"Come," Masako said. She left the bedroom and walked across the foyer to Kaede's office. "This will be the entry to

Crisis

his offices. It will be an entirely self-contained three-storey building inside the residence with toilets, washroom, and break-room with kitchenette. Like the other sections, it will need to have stairs, and an elevator installed."

"I have nothing to make notes with."

"I will give you the details later," Masako said as she walked through the foyer to the west door. "In the west wing will be a small theatre, relaxation centre, yoga room, gym, dance studio, a large salon and toilets, large washroom, hot tubs and massage centre."

She walked around the central column to the kitchen. The engineer looked at the group of Knights at the Central Column. They were looking at him, and each had one hand on her slung Viper 2. He raced up to Masako.

"…and in the north wing, an entirely new kitchen on each floor and one under the dome in the service area. Three different dining rooms and a large entertainment room. Most parties will be under the dome, which needs to be raised, to fit in the pool and add three storeys.

"Any questions?" Masako asked, turning to him.

"At this height, how will you raise the dome?" he asked.

"Workers will remove the panels. A transport ship will use its Tractor Beam to lift the frame, move it, then later put the frame of the dome back. I don't need you to do a cost estimate, I have experts working on the budget. All I need to know from you is do you want to take the job on, or go back to making roads?" Masako asked, with the tips of her fingers pressed together, smiling, and staring at him.

"I will do it," he replied.

Masako escorted him to the lift. After he had left,

security notified her Izanami was coming up. Masako waited to see what Izanami wanted.

Izanami left the elevator with a wire trap and a stun baton. She entered Kaede's room, followed by a curious Masako. Izanami put the cage outside the exit to the vacuum bot. She wore a headband covering an earpiece. Mako and Miko were in the security room listening.

"I am in place," Izanami said.

Mako and Miko sat in Toshiko's office. They shut off the cameras, lights, and recording and the power to the top level. Then they activated the cleaning bot.

Inside the bedroom, the round robot came out of its concealed bay in the wall, into the metal animal trap. It sprang shut. Izanami stood beside the metal cage, holding a stun baton against its side. As soon as the door snapped closed, she pressed the trigger. The robot shorted out.

Masako called in a couple of Knights to carry the cage to the elevator. The power restored, Mako and Miko deleted logs. Outside, Kenta was talking to the guards.

Sora and Akiko came out of the elevator and handed her a robot.

"Found this one in recycling," Sora said.

Izanami looked it over.

"I found it in recycling, it has a burnt-out motor," Akiko said.

"It will do." Izanami sighed, taking it to the kitchen.

"Where are you going to?" Sora asked.

"He keeps a toolbox under the sink. I am going to change covers, so the replacement has the right serial numbers," Izanami said.

"We will be late for dance class," Sora said.

"I will change the covers and get the one you captured to you," Masako said.

"Good, 'Nami, we need to go," Sora said.

"What if she gets it wrong?" Izanami said.

"Izanami, how dare you. Now apologise for your assumption, and hand her the robot. Explain what you want. I am sure she can swap cases, send you the one you shorted and put the one Akiko brought you in his room," Sora said.

Kenta received a text, "On the way stop off at the store and buy the same model vacuum robot, and bring it to me, please."

After dancing with Sora, Akiko, Mako and Miko, Kaede practised a lively dance routine with Izanami. Toshiko watched them while Patya went outside with Kenta.

Patya lit a cigar.

"Do you know how unhealthy those things are?" Kenta asked.

"You prefer we sit in silence in a smoke room wondering who is listening?" Patya asked.

"Used to be we knew who was listening," Kenta replied.

"Maybe we should retire," Patya said, looking up at the stars.

"We knew we would never get it right every time," Kenta said.

Patya was about to say something, but a town car pulled up. Patya turned to look. Abel got out the driver's seat and walked up to Patya.

"Lady Abel, Toshiko is inside," Patya said.

"Freya called me and asked if Dain will come to meet the Emperor here," Abel replied.

"Dain asked his big sister to protect him from the bullies?" Patya asked.

"Yes," Abel replied almost laughing.

"Does he honestly think we are going to assassinate him?" Patya asked.

"Something like that," Abel replied.

"As much fun as it would be to scare him," Patya said removing his gun from his shoulder holster, "this is serious." Patya handed the gun to Abel and walked over to the car and tapped on the passenger window.

Dain rolled down the window. "You were asked to come speak with the Emperor without drawing attention to yourself."

"I summoned by the Emperor to a car park behind a studio in the dead of night," Dain hissed looking forward.

"You're early. Kaede is still dancing," Patya said, "Now that you are here, come in out of the cold."

"I have seen him dance, and I admit he is an excellent dancer. He does not have the power to summon me out of my home like a junior officer," Dain said.

"Yet you came, hiding behind your big sister," Patya said. Dain glared at Patya. "Dain, you are in danger, but we all are," Patya said, then he leaned in and said, "Get out of the car before I drag you out."

Dain got out of the car and looked Patya in the eye. Dain was about to say something, then he saw Kaede exit the building. Kaede walked up to and bowed to Dain. "Dain, thank-you for coming on short notice. I heard you're ahead of me in artificial intelligence."

"Abel!" Dain bellowed.

Kaede kicked Dain in the shin.

Crisis

Dain looked at Kaede then Patya grabbed Dain. "Shut up you idiot, we are having a clandestine meeting," Patya growled.

"You have all gone mad?" Dain asked.

"Never mind how I got the information, the point is I am going to sell you all my research," Kaede said.

Dain raised an eyebrow. "Why would you and why should I be interested?" Dain asked.

"Because I can trust you. You are a hero of the Empire, a patriot. You will do it because the Empire needs you to do it."

"Are you serious?" Dain asked Kaede, then looked at Patya. "I cannot trust you. You dropped me from second the thirteenth, secret meetings. You arrest spies, let some go, jail others on minor charges unrelated to spying. Now you expect me to buy your research?"

"Patya, please, give me a moment alone with Dain," Kaede said to Patya.

Kaede watched Patya head over to Abel. He then turned to Dain. "I want you to be able to trust me. In the last hundred years, a secret organisation has grown powerful. They have been able to select candidates, beat sophisticated encryption, and in turn communicate with better encryption than us. What can beat a room full of players at any game?"

"A computer."

"Right, but not just any computer."

"No. One that can apply every known theory and learn from losing."

"High Lord Dain, I do apologise to you. Accept my sincerest apologies. I was not personal, I made a business decision. Now I need your help."

"To do what?"

"You have an AI. I will sell you my research. I need you to build a new central command system. Not just any AI, but one that is incapable of leaving its host, unable to copying itself onto a new host or be copied over. It also must be hosted on a portable device. I will licence to you the solid-state memory system that uses atoms. Each memory node is 700 MB and is the size of a pea. I designed a series of safeguards. We are far from complete. But the AI is designed to detect patterns, break codes, study tactics, find links between events and predict outcomes of events. However, until it is finished, the AI will need to remain a secret."

"How are we going to fund a secret project when our financial matters are public record?"

"Leave that to me," Kaede said heading back into the studio.

Abel grabbed Dain and looked him in the eye.

"You know I will do it. I am loyal to Empire," Dain said.

"I know, but don't use this project to topple the Emperor," Abel said.

"Abel, you're in love," Dain said.

Abel kicked Dain in the shin, then headed to the driver's side door, "Get in," Abel said.

Kaede, Patya, Kenta and the girls left the dance studio. As Kenta led the girls to his SUVs, Kaede ran up to Izanami. "It just occurred to me it isn't enough we identify the parts and find a way to track down who made the vacuum robot spy."

"You don't have a plan?" Sora asked.

"My original plan was to track down the group using the parts they purchased to modify my cleaning robots. But it occurred to me that might not get the whole ring. Nor will a dead one be able to tell us the strengths and weaknesses of their surveillance equipment. We need to capture one that is operational," Kaede said.

"I want to compare the parts in the robot you captured to those we found on the pirates' base," Toshiko said standing behind Kaede.

"We need a robotics expert," Kaede said.

"Me," Izanami said.

"You're not a robotics expert," Sora said to Izanami.

"I know electronics and computers," Izanami said.

Without turning around, Kaede said to Lady Toshiko, "I will hire someone to teach Izanami what she needs to know, as Izanami and I want to start a Robot Toy company. I planned to start with two models. A Land Dragon and a Cat Sìth. They will fetch a toy ball and perform other tricks. It is important that she hires Nori as a consultant."

"Why?" Kenta asked.

"Keep him busy, keep me close to him and see what he does," Kaede replied.

"I see, but why a robotics toy company?" Kenta asked.

"Other than a robotic toy cat sìth to sell? Our own range of spy robots. Only we will also have a model to hunt for spy robots as well," Kaede said.

"One condition," Izanami said behind Kenta.

"Oh?" Sora, with hands on hips, turned to Izanami.

Izanami ran to Kaede and said, "I want to work on the super wand with you."

"Super wand?" Toshiko asked.

"We can talk about it later Lady Toshiko, but it is still only in the design stage," Kaede replied looking at Toshiko. He then turned to Izanami. "The wand is one of many projects I manage. You can stop by the workshop, but the robot is more important than a new wand."

"But—" Izanami said.

"Izanami, it is late, we need to go, and Kaede has given you a task," Sora said.

"Lady Toshiko will come see you to form a company and work out a rights agreement. I am investing billions, Izanami, so if you are not up to the task, I will find someone else," Kaede said.

"Kaede, maybe you should find an adult to do this?" a concerned Kenta suggested.

"Izanami is smart, and I am hoping the enemy will just see it as a harmless toy," Kaede said.

"Just don't make flying drones," Patya said.

Kaede looked at him. "Yes, almost every flying drone has a camera. The robot company can expand later into spy toys for the Imperial Intelligence Agency."

"We are—" Mako began.

"—graduating soon," Miko ended.

"Good, have you decided on what you are doing?" Kaede inquired.

"Medicine," Kenta said.

"Of course, Kenta you can bring them to the medical research centre," Kaede said.

Kenta nodded and turned to the girls. "All right, in the car girls, we need to go."

The girls waved to Kaede as they got in the car.

Kenta came to Kaede. "Do you think it is wise?" Kenta asked.

"You know, if they cannot handle seeing blood or organs they will not be able to become healers," Kaede replied.

"Yes, but we are working on arousing coma patients," Kenta said, looking at Patya.

"I am aware some things might be of concern to you, such as the organ growth tanks. Then there's the study of the brains of coma patients by removing the top of their skull and the cadaver display of various races to teach advanced anatomy. It is up to you of course what they see," Kaede said.

"Kaede, that is not it. You should have spoken with Kenta alone and given him a choice," Patya said.

"Oh, I am sorry." Kaede bowed low to Kenta.

"You're right, to study medicine you must be able to deal with blood, be able to cut someone open and not be squeamish about internal organs. However, sometimes your father is brought in for tests and is naked on the table," Kenta said.

"Naturally, you control what they see. Again, my apologies. I need to go now. Goodnight," Kaede said.

As Kaede turned, he saw a light out of the corner of his eye. He turned to look, but all he saw was the cars in the parking building. He got in his vehicle.

A small winged figure, an Archon, hid behind the beam of light from the street lighting. It was 15cm tall, made from a slightly bluish light. It watched Kaede get in the SUV. The Archon tried to follow but was too slow. It slowed down and then stopped. It then faded into darkness.

CHAPTER 12

AWAKENING

In the early hours of the morning, Kaede, wearing yellow overalls, was in the back of a meat van driven by Toshiko also in yellow overalls and cap. The meat was cold, but not frozen, and blood dripped from some. The van entered the underground parking and drove down to the bottom to the loading dock.

Toshiko got out to meet a group of Knights waiting by the roller door. While they went inside and opened the roller door, Toshiko opened the back of the truck, and Kaede got out.

While workers loaded the sides of beef into carts, Toshiko escorted Kaede inside the loading bay to the cargo elevator in the back.

"Takahiro didn't want you to meet the Dragons until you turned eighteen," Toshiko said.

"We don't have a choice," Kaede said.

Toshiko nodded and opened the cargo elevator and took Kaede down in the dark to sub-level sixteen.

Adjusting to the darkness, Kaede followed Toshiko

out of the elevator and down the large, wide tunnel to a cavern. They passed a large feeding tray on the shore of a large lake. Kaede saw the shadow in the water move. It was like a massive snake, and he felt something creeping up on him. Kaede turned to see a Red Dragon sniffing the air behind him.

"Hello," Kaede said.

"Have you come to tell us the real reason Takahiro stepped down?" a soft voice asked from behind Kaede.

Kaede turned to see the head of a Green Water Dragon. It had the body of a serpent, but a large reptilian head with four short horns that protruded from the ridged skull plate. Kaede looked at the Dragon's large reptilian eyes. It did not squint, for it could see him clearly in near darkness and looked right at him. The sound of her voice was coming from the device on a collar behind its head.

"Amaterasu, he did not lie to you, my grandfather kept secrets, too many secrets. Officially was punishment for my father in harm's way, but really, he hurt the feelings of the Senate by not trusting them with the security breach. That is not why I have come to see you. I need to discuss an urgent matter. We are working on a new treaty with the Dwarves, one that will annexe their worlds," Kaede replied.

"Do you want war with the Ogres? Many Giants depend on cheap food and labour from the Dwarves, and they too may side against you. The Green Dragon Riders are the only Giants whose support you can count on," Amaterasu said.

"I have many intelligence reports outline different attacks on the Empire, namely aimed at removing the Senate from power. The Ogres cannot win an open war, so they plan for the many corrupt lords to fight over the Empire while they annex worlds around them. To prevent this, I plan to invite all the leaders to trade talks and kept them here for as long as possible and find ways to turn the Orcs and Goblins against the Ogres. But the sore point is the Dwarves, for too long have we let their economy crumble under the weight of drunken, corrupt, and inept leaders," Kaede said.

"The Dwarf king is not dead, he is Dain's lover. Why annexe their worlds when you just need to have Dain whisper in his ear?" Amaterasu asked.

"His wife sits on the throne and has surrounded herself with Dark Elves. She is angry and bitter with the Empire. Many lords no longer recognise Weyland as their king. I fear her advisors will have the Dwarves siding against the Empire. I need to remove them, uncover the threat and defend the Empire from all enemies, not just the external threats, with covert actions without killing leaders if I can help it, better the enemy we know, we don't want entire worlds seeking revenge," Kaede said.

"I see," Amaterasu said.

"I need your cooperation," Kaede said.

"We would like time outside," Amaterasu said.

"Your meal is coming, I will consider how to comply with your request, then work on a deal to suit us both, but as you know, Dragons naturally inspire fear," Kaede said.

Amaterasu blinked and nodded.

It was nearly midnight when Kaede sat to the fourth meal with Freya in his private dining room. Just as he sat down, his phone rang.

"Excuse me, Mother," Kaede said standing. He bowed and went from the dining room to the sitting room. Saw caller ID was Nori, he pressed answer and said, "Hello Nori."

"Sorry to bother you," a distressed Nori said.

"What is wrong?" Kaede asked.

"My father hates me," Nori said.

"That is a bit harsh Nori," Kaede said. "What is wrong?"

"He is always fighting with my mother—"

"Take a deep breath, Nori. It isn't my business to interfere," Kaede interrupted.

"But he wants to send me away to boarding school. He says I spend too much time on robots and other stuff."

"Did you get bad grades again?" Kaede asked.

A long pause. "I got a C-plus on my mathematics assignment," Nori murmured.

"Your father doesn't hate you. He wants you to do your best. As do I," Kaede said.

"I don't want to go," Nori said.

"Relax. Put your mother on," Kaede requested.

"Oh," Nori said and handed the phone to Emi.

"Emperor, I am sorry," Emi said.

"It is no bother, Lady Emi. Nori doesn't understand, just because his father works for the Imperial Navy, it doesn't mean I can tell him what to do all the time. Technically he works for your father," Kaede said.

"I told my husband that my father would never let him send Nori away. It is not that Shinji hates you, he is worried that you're a bad influence on Nori," Emi said.

"I know how much Viktor loves you and Nori," Kaede said.

"It is complicated," Emi said.

"Is your husband home?" Kaede asked.

"Do you want to talk to him?" Emi asked.

"Is this a bad time?" Kaede asked.

"Shinji went out," Emi said.

"I don't see why Shinji is upset. Nori is a C average student, a C plus is a good result," Kaede said.

"I tried telling him that, but is complicated," Emi said.

"Lady Emi, did he hit you again?" Kaede said.

"Please don't interfere," Emi asked.

"If he hurts you I will," Kaede said.

"He is under a lot of pressure. My mother and father believe he should have more wives, but he only wants to get his third star," Emi said.

"He needs to relax, and socialise more with the other command staff. How many wives he has will not get him a third star, Viktor must go by performance reviews and qualification to fill vacancies," Kaede said.

"I know," Emi said.

"I cannot give him that promotion, but if he sends Nori away, then I will do everything I can to make his life a misery. As an incentive to keep Nori at home, I will give him a good deal on a cabin cruiser and a berth at the marina," Kaede said.

"Thank you, Emperor," Emi said.

"Have him bring Nori tomorrow if he wants that third star. He needs to be on better terms with the high command," Kaede said.

"I will try," Emi said.

"Well, next time he raises his fists, tell him the next time you show up for work with so much as a broken fingernail, every hand-to-hand-combat-ready evaluation will be with Hilda," Kaede said.

Emi giggled, then said, "That isn't fair."

"No such thing as a fair fight," Kaede said.

"But she is a heavyweight boxing champion, and he is only a lightweight black belt in Karate."

"Fine, you can have options. Choose from Yuki or Toshiko to do it, they know Karate," Kaede said.

"You know what they would do to him," Emi said.

"Then I expect to hear no more talk of Nori going to a military school on Merope and Shinji to show up tomorrow with Nori at the Karting Track," Kaede said.

"You're a tough negotiator," Emi said.

"Goodnight Lady Emi," Kaede said. "Don't hang up."

Emi handed the phone to Nori. "Yes, Kaede?"

"I will see you tomorrow and stop worrying, you are not going to get sent away," Kaede said.

"Thanks," a cheerful Nori said.

"Goodnight," Kaede said.

"Goodnight," Nori said.

Kaede ended the call.

In the early hours, Kaede in stood in the dark in the gardens beneath that Palace. He wore a Gi with a black belt with two red bands. He held a wooden training sword.

"When will my sword be ready?" Kaede asked.

Toshiko's voice echoed around him, "It is ready now, but you are too young to handle the effect magic has."

"I can control my emotions," Kaede said turning, studying the dark.

"Night vision works in low light, there is no light in the caverns, you must relax and feel with your sixth and seventh senses," Toshiko said running past him. She tapped him on the shoulder, and Kaede turned, but she disappeared into the bushes.

"You're using magic," Kaede said slashing at a shadow.

Toshiko put a wooden dagger to Kaede's throat and said, "In the real world there is no fair fight."

"The only fair fight is one where both live or both die," Kaede said bowing to Toshiko.

The lights came on, and Takahiro clapped, he was wearing a pair of glasses that had round bluish lens. "Amazing, casting Night Vision spell onto an item and letting mana discharge sustain the spell," Takahiro said.

"I found similarity with the cauldron of everlasting with the loop in the guard. It is a sustaining loop. In short cast a spell on it, then as long as you have mana, the loop will drain it and sustain the spell. You can hold it, or use a mana battery," Kaede said.

"How small can you make one?" an excited Toshiko asked.

"A loop can be as small as a ring," Kaede replied.

"You were wrong about the spell trap?" Takahiro asked.

"No, loop sustained the Absorb Magic Spell. Kaede worked out the tree inside the blade was the trap. It fed the mana it collected into the gap between the hilt and guard, which must have housed a mana battery," Toshiko said.

"You can make new cauldrons?" Takahiro asked.

"Thanks to Kaede, I have successfully made an everlasting loop," Toshiko replied.

"Well done, I will let him practice magic, only for one hour, once a week," Takahiro said before she left.

Toshiko bowed. Kaede grinned.

The next night, at the go-kart centre, an Archon sat on a powerful light bulb at the go-kart track as Kaede and Izanami raced around the track. Nori watched them with his father, Shinji Hagihara, in the stands. It moved closer, but then a shadow moved. The Archon stopped. Someone underneath the stands was watching Kaede, a dark shadow hung over that figure, the Archon floated back into the beam of light.

Shinji stood. "Our turn soon," he remarked seeing Kaede and Izanami near the finish line.

"Thanks for coming," Nori said.

"No problem, son," Shinji said with a smile.

The shadow looked around and looked at Nori, and the darkness stirred in Shinji.

Excited, Nori grabbed his father's hand then pulled him to the track. The shadow gazed at Kaede. Kaede got out of the kart.

"All yours," Kaede said and offered his kart.

"Nori can have it. I don't want him screaming unfair when I win using the loser's kart," Shinji said.

"Hey!" Izanami exclaimed.

"Relax 'Nami. I don't see why you complain. You come second often," Kaede said, running over to the stands.

Izanami stomped her foot and ran off after him.

"Dad?" Nori asked.

Shinji looked down at Nori. "Ready?" Shinji asked as he put on a helmet.

Shinji beat Nori, making his son crash on purpose. Nori took a corner too wide, and Shinji nudged him into the tyre wall and didn't even stop to check if Nori was all right.

Shinji went into the male toilets. Galené went to follow him, but he turned, looking her way, so she walked past him. He watched her go into the eatery.

Kenta came up behind Shinji and asked, "Coming or going?"

"Sorry," a startled Shinji replied, and he went in.

"Old shipmate?" Kenta asked, following.

"I am not sure," Shinji replied.

"Ah, the life of a sailor. A girl in every port," Kenta remarked, heading for the toilet.

Shinji went in. A short time later when he came out, he looked around. He saw Toshiko with a tray of ice creams. She was alert, but not looking his way. He walked towards the group, then felt a prickle of energy. He stopped and looked around, and then Nori came up yelling, and the feeling went away. "Dad, I was looking for you."

"I was busy," Shinji said, pointing back to the toilets.

"You're always busy," Nori said.

"Some of us have to work for a living," Shinji said, shooting a glance at Kaede.

"I know that. Izanami has offered me a job," Nori said.

"Is this like the time you showed a group of engineers how to paint plastic?" Shinji asked.

"Izanami is going to be making toy robots. I will be testing a robot pet," Nori said.

"Interesting," Shinji said, as he looked at Kaede.

"Not joining the navy?" Shinji asked.

"'Nami and I both have an interest in robots. It is a gift to my future bride, a company of her own," Kaede said.

"I want a dress company," Akiko said.

"Hush," Sora said to Akiko.

"What about you, Sora?" Kaede asked, facing her.

"I want to build the largest stadium in the Empire," Sora said.

"Lady Abel has already done that," Toshiko said.

"I cannot build one bigger?" Sora asked.

"I am afraid not, princess. Many have tried, but the structure fails," Shinji said.

"I am not a princess," Sora said.

"I am sorry, but you are going to marry the Emperor," Shinji said.

"It is Lady Sora. She has to earn the title of Princess," Kaede said.

"I am going to be a Knight," Sora said, looking at Lady Toshiko.

"You have to qualify first," Toshiko said.

Shinji smiled and said, "I better go now, it is a long drive, and you know how traffic is on the bridge." *No, you don't. You put on your sirens or fly over us ants.*

Kaede said goodnight to Nori, who left quietly with his father.

Galené followed on a big Hashimoto road bike. After crossing the bridge over the lake, a small group of bikers on the same Hashimoto bikes saw Galené and cut across traffic in front of her.

Then a couple of bikers more pulled alongside Galené. Then two more. Then five more. They swarmed around her. She lost sight of Shinji. She took the next turn off the main road, at the last minute, tightly. They followed her.

She smiled at the lead biker and started to unzip her top.

He stared at her as she reached inside her jacket. He stared at her lace crop top. She put her hand on her wand and cast *Quickness* and then *Haste*. The world slowed down. She then cast Aether vision. The world was now mostly dull grey. She looked around, and none of the bikers glowed. "None of them magically active," Galené noted to herself. "The first rule of combat is to bring a magic user. The second rule of combat, kill the magic user first." Galené recalled Toshiko addressing a line of Knights in uniform.

She pulled out her wand and pointed it at the biker.

"Seven seconds before my mana has recharged my wand," Galené thought. She recalled Toshiko showing her the wand. "Use it too often, and you pass out, so always count to ten for the casting fatigue to go away. Always track your mana. But should you find yourself tired, you are going to pass out if you keep casting."

One...

He freaked out, and on ten she then pointed it at the front wheel, he engaged the brake. Galené cast *Blast*. The spell shattered the front wheel, the bike flipped over, mangling the bike and the biker.

The others pulled out chains and handguns. They took shots at Galené.

Galené cast the spell *armour*, and it covered her in a

slight glow. *I am protected from any fast-moving projectiles while I can sustain it. That was my fourth casting, so I have twenty-one mana remaining, so twenty-one minutes before armour ends unless they break the barrier first. Must avoid getting hit more than once.*

Galené looked around and leaned left. The gang went to turn left, so she quickly shifted and spun the bike around and raced into them, so they scattered. She cast *Stun* on the lead biker as she shot past. Four managed to avoid the crash. The rest did not. Traffic stopped, and many got their phones out. *Only a few minutes left on armour, but worth it.*

Galené tapped the button on the side of her helmet. The transition plastic faceplate turned black. She turned her bike into an alley, and the gang followed.

Galené cast *Jump* and stood up on her seat. She pushed off her bike and was propelled up. She landed on a balcony on the second storey of a building with a clear view of the alleyway. She ended the *armour* spell. She pointed her wand down, and as the bikers entered the killing zone, she cast an *Aether Ball*. The invisible ball of aether expanded around them, and as it was seven metres in diameter, it caught them all. She felt a surge of energy and pain. It was a surge of energy like the inside of a powerful microwave oven. The blood boiled, pain surged through their body, then the light in their eyes went out as blood poured from their eyes, ears, mouth, and nose.

Darkness enveloped Galené as the wail of sirens approached.

Later Fukuhina and the team arrived. She walked up to a uniformed guard. "Point out who is in charge," she said holding up her identification.

Good for a bluff, bad if they run it. Should have called Yuki, she thought. But the guard didn't question her, just pointed out a pair of plain-clothed officers with their badges around their necks.

"All dead?" Fukuhina asked as she walked up.

"Who are you?" the lead detective asked.

"Admiral Fukuhina, I work for the Emperor," Fukuhina replied.

"We all do, lady. This crime scene is for authorised personnel only," the second detective said. He knelt and looked at the dead, blood in the ears, ears, nose. "Magic."

"Obviously. You need a magical forensics team to arrive within minutes of casting. You are contaminating the scene and making it harder to detect the spell used and record the caster's signature," Fukuhina said.

"Look, Admiral, maybe in your starship you have all the resources of the universe at your fingertips, but down here in the real world, we don't have teams of magic users waiting around to polish our boots and untangle our panties for us," the first detective said.

"Which is why you should take your rubber gun and leave," the second scoffed.

"I have a team," Fukuhina said.

"Make like a leaf and blow me," the first said.

Fukuhina pulled out her phone.

"Who are you calling?" the first detective said, going to grab her arm. Then he noticed Hilda, who was at the entrance to the alley, had taken a step towards them. He saw she had arms with more muscle in them than he had in his entire body. So, when she took another step forward, he pretended it was a wave and turned to his partner.

"Hello?" Adalwulf replied to his phone.

"Sorry to bother you General Feygold, but I am at a crime scene and need you to explain to a couple of City Guards to get out of my way," Fukuhina said.

General Feygold left the family room, looked at the caller id, then said, "Put them on."

A short time later the detectives walked out of the alley and waited. Fukuhina and Emi walked around with wands out. Hilda examined the crashed bike further down the alleyway. Cerise ran her staff over the bodies, while Nadia talked to witnesses.

Fukuhina looked around, then up using *Aether Vision*. She saw the spell residue on the building. She cast the spell *Levitate*, then used a *Push* Spell to rise, then used the *Pull* Spell to move her closer to the building, where she cast *Magic Analysis* on the residue. Her wand transmitted data to her tablet, which was in her handbag. She then lowered herself by using the *Pull* Spell aimed at the ground.

They gathered around. Fukuhina said, "I will compare the signatures at the foundation with past readings, but I am sure it was only one caster."

"None of them was a Sorcerer. The group in the alley were all killed by magic. The others crashed, and two of them should have lived. I don't understand what happened, but they did not die from their injuries. They died of heart failure soon after the collision," Cerise said.

"Yuki is on her way. I will ask her to send the bodies to the foundation medical centre so you can perform an autopsy," Fukuhina said.

"They were members of a small biker gang, nothing but punks who harass customers. A couple of them do have records for dealing marijuana without a licence, a few speeding fines, nothing major and never clashed with other gangs before," Nadia said.

"We need official status; we cannot just keep looking for odd events and showing up," Hilda said.

"I will speak to the Emperor again, but he will tell me that the agency is against it. He has enough trouble with many commanders complaining we are interfering in ongoing cases. Some officers have filed complaints with your father," Fukuhina said to Hilda.

"I will talk to my father," Hilda said.

"I know this is strange, but they all have the same spider tattoo on the back of their necks," Emi said.

"Of course, they do, they are in a gang," Nadia said.

"Yes, but look at their jackets. The gang symbol appears to be the kanji for fire. Also, since when do we have Flower Elf biker gangs in an Aquatic Elf suburb?" Emi said.

"You live nearby, don't you?" Fukuhina asked.

"Yes, but I am closer to the lake, and I assure you we don't have any gang problem, most of the units around the bridge house Palace workers, which includes house Guards and Knights," Emi said.

"We can only investigate further if it becomes a cold case. We need to check if the spell used to disappear was the illusion spell invisibility. But this one appears to be an alteration spell," Fukuhina said.

"But they don't know that we have no authority," Hilda said.

"They soon will. Word is spreading fast. Some already call us the rubber gun squad," Fukuhina said, she looked around and leaned in and in a low voice said, "Last guy to compliment me was the Prince."

"I haven't had sex in years. My husband doesn't even look at me," Hilda said.

"My husband refuses to touch me," Nadia said.

"My husband insults me, sometimes in front of my son," Emi said, almost in tears.

"Really?" Hilda asked, "He was always polite to me."

"Hilda, he fears you, not me," Emi replied.

"Really?" Hilda asked.

"Hilda, you're the tallest Elf, a heavy weight boxing champion, almost everyone fears you," Fukuhina said.

Hilda frowned. "I am so sorry, I didn't mean it like that," a worried Fukuhina said.

"We love you," Emi said, hugging the huge, muscular Elf. Hilda smiled.

"Yuki is here, so we'd better get to work and match this to a cold case, or we must leave this to those detectives. I don't think they could solve a mystery novel if we let them read the last chapter first," Fukuhina said.

On Sunday night Kaede hosted a dinner for King Weyland. The king sat at the head of a table in the imperial ballroom beside Kaede. Another chair beside him was empty. Guests filled the rest of the room. Dain sat down the other end of the table.

Many reporters were at the event, and most of them had a camera crew, ranging from the large professional team at

Hashimoto, Dain, and Petrov Media, down to a couple with a single camera operator following them.

Around the room were ambassadors from the six different nations of Giants, who were supposed to be Democratic Federation. One table was just for the Titans, who were technically part of the Ogre Alliance, but they sat apart from the other Ogres, who were a mix of Russian, Asian, African and Mayan. Two more tables were for the red and the blue Jötunn, another breakaway group from the Ogre Alliance.

The brown, green, grey, and orange Orcs sat as far apart from each other as possible. While all the Goblin leaders sat around the table glaring at each other.

The artificially created races had an alliance, but no central government. The Centaur and Daemon sat at a table with the Rabbit people, Fox people and Cat people. The Minotaurs, however, sat behind the Dwarves. There was no table set for the Dragons.

The most divided group were the Dwarfs. There were tables for every group. The Trolls insisted on being at the front. The Persian and Japanese Oni sat on different sides of the room. The Eurasian, Chinese, Germanic, African, North and South American Dwarves each had a table, and their various delegations took up most of the second floor.

Then all eyes turned as Queen Clíodhna of the Red Dragons was announced. Everyone but Kaede stood. She was a Western Fire Dragon, only one metre long. She kept her bat-like wings folded by her side. She had a leather cover over the hook on the end of them. She took each step slowly, but she wobbled as she walked. She wore fitted boots and gloves.

Many gasped as she walked past them. Two Knights escorted her to Kaede. He stood and said, "Lords, Ladies, other dignitaries and guests. Queen Clíodhna will represent the Dragons."

Clíodhna sat on the chair beside Kaede, resting her head on the table.

Kaede waited for the cameras on him. "We are gathered today to start talks that will create new treaties, see a lift on trade restrictions between the various state, foster more peaceful cultural exchanges, and changes to the Dragon Treaty," Kaede said.

"Emperor, quick question," a Field Elf, wearing a white t-shirt, blue jeans and sneakers put in.

"I know the media want details, and we will make announcements, but at the appropriate time. Then after the meal, you may request individual interviews," Kaede said and sat. A pair of Knights stepped towards the media, bowed, and pointed to the empty tables at the back. The media went quietly to their seats.

Staff served a large variety of meals to every table. A waiter placed an acid proof bowl in front of the Dragon, then pointed out a trolley with several different hams. As he ran his hands over the hams, she wagged her tail and nodded. He placed that leg in the large bowl. Clíodhna licked it with her tongue, then swallowed it. Then she looked at the waiter like a puppy begging for more.

After dessert, the journals came back to the front seeking the Emperor, but Kaede already was sitting with the Orange Orc Chief, Henrik von Wessely. Imperial Knights kept the media away.

"Why are minor states involved?" Henrik asked.

"My trade deals will affect them and the six independent Elf worlds, especially Freeport," Kaede replied.

"But Freeport does not have a position in the Dragon Council."

"That is true, but Freeport is an unofficially an Elven world and is a trade hub between our Empire and everyone else."

"You are offering us two new worlds, but we will want three."

"Each world takes hundreds of years to terraform."

"So, you say," Henrik said, his eyes narrowed.

"Of course, I will let the Senate know your terms," Kaede said. He looked around and leaned in. "Will you asking us for assistance to prevent the Ogres annexing you?"

"Your spies must be blind. Our military is not weak."

"It is not our opinion that you are weak. Our informants tell us that is the Ogres' judgment of you."

"Those flat heads could not even provide us with a decent skirmish, let alone a great war. You are not very skilled at deception. Hurry up and bring out the real Emperor. Tell your grandfather the joke is no longer funny."

"This is no deception. Look at the Titans, they pretend to hate their northern cousins but sit near them. They avoid any contact, but the Titans and Ogres show no contempt for each other. The Titan ambassador is eyeing the wife of the black Giant Chief, and she is exposing her neck to him. Would you care to make a wager?"

"What is your bet?" Henrik asked, looking at them. He wondered if they were looking at each other. She was smiling and leaning on her hand. Then he looked at Kaede.

"If the Titan ambassador meets in secret with the wife

of the black Giant Chief, you will acknowledge I am the real Emperor. I will present to you a peace treaty. No screaming, yelling or leaving. You can ponder my offer at your leisure. I do not ask for agreement, only that you withhold the details from everyone and negotiate the details with King Argon Agrovar."

"If you are wrong, then you must acknowledge and support me as the High Chief of all Orcs in the Dragon Council, and in your meeting, it is you who will be listening to my proposal," Henrik said, leaning in.

"Deal."

Henrik looked at him then nodded. Kaede headed to the balcony, and Toshiko stood behind him. "Bold move, Emperor," Toshiko whispered.

"Yaotl is going to be angry. He planned to use the affair to force their vote," Kaede said.

"We still can. Have Yaotl follow them. I am sure it will not be long before they dance with each other again," Toshiko said.

Dain and the other lords sat around the main table. Clíodhna cast a make-sound spell. "We do not get out much. Thank you for the invitation."

"You are welcome," Patya responded with a slight bow.

"I like ham," Clíodhna said, looking at the empty trolley.

Patya grabbed a waiter, and soon another ham was in her bowl.

Argon looked around. He noticed Kaede stand and bow to the Orc Chief. Argon got up and intercepted Kaede before he could get to the Titans. "Emperor, we are off to a bad start," Argon observed.

"What is wrong?" Kaede queried.

"As Minister of External Affairs and External Trade, I should inform you that putting all our enemies in one place to talk with you was a bad idea. It has them talking with each other," Argon replied.

"Yes, and Yaotl has agents listening to everything. There is much to learn."

"Are you aware if one group walked out the humiliation could ruin you?"

Kaede looked at the Mountain Elf, who was tall, proud and appeared to sincere, "What do you suggest?"

"You leave the negotiating to me. I will present to the ambassadors the trade deal, arms reduction, cooperation against pirates, and your annexation proposal in my office. Then, once we have a treaty, the Senate will vote on it. Your job is to host a celebratory dinner and congratulate the ambassadors and Senate. Summoning their leaders creates resentment of us all."

"You are aware the idea of having the leaders come was to stop them from going to war with us?" Toshiko said from behind Kaede.

Kaede lifted his hand. "Toshiko is right. However, Argon, I will let you talk to them, please focus on trade and how it will benefit them. I will issue official invitations to my formal coronation and wedding to Sora. I did promise to hold talks with Chief Henrik, but you may sit in."

Argon leaned in and said, "Thank you."

Kaede pondered the Titans as Argon left, then Chief Yaotl came.

"Tag teaming me?" Kaede asked.

"Whatever do you mean, Emperor?" Yaotl asked.

"Argon has already given me the *this is my department*

speech. Have you come to give me some technical support or inform me my refurbishment of the Palace is doing harm to the environment?"

"Well, as Head of Technical Support that is my job, and as Minister of the Environment that would be my duty, but I want to talk to you about my collection of cloaks and daggers." Yaotl led Kaede to the outside balcony. He went to close the doors on Toshiko, but she placed her wand in his nostril and her foot in the door.

"Emperor, please call off your cat sìth," Yaotl said.

"You know I cannot," Kaede said.

"Watch it, Yaotl. I know everything you think before you think it," Toshiko said.

"Be careful of her. She is the reason most of the old gods are dead," Yaotl said after taking a step back.

As Toshiko closed the doors behind her, she said, "The Old Gods we charlatans who used parlour tricks to prey on the weak-minded."

"I didn't know you were a believer, Yaotl. I do not recall removing the ban on organised religions," Kaede remarked. "Should I call Adalwulf to arrest you? I am sure Patya will enjoy investigating you."

"It is not illegal to have an opinion. I believe spirits exist. It is illegal to build a temple to them or preach in public," Yaotl replied, looking at Toshiko.

"Don't look at me, provided you and your crazy cult are not plotting to overthrow the Empire, you can smoke as much marijuana in the forest as you like," Toshiko said.

"Yaotl, belonging to a cult is illegal," Kaede said.

"He doesn't belong to one, he runs one," Toshiko said with a giggle.

"I don't care if you mock me, but spirits are real. That is why I need to speak to you alone, Emperor. One of our Spirit Talkers has come to see you," Yaotl said.

"I will meet with him—" Kaede said.

"Her," Yaotl said.

"I will meet with her tomorrow after I see my father," Kaede said.

"She is waiting for you at outside Blood Tower," Yaotl said.

"Yaotl, he cannot just leave," Toshiko objected.

"Please?" Yaotl begged.

"Toshiko, tell Patya and the others I am ending this early to please Argon," Kaede said. Yaotl appeared to be happy, but Toshiko was not hiding her displeasure.

Kaede headed around the room, greeting, and thanking guests, then as he went to King Weyland, Dain stood between them. "I'd like to discuss the Annexation Act with you on behalf of the King," Dain said.

"I'd rather discuss the passing of the revised marriage act," Kaede said.

"It is my right to delay my vote to investigate the merits of the proposal," Dain said.

"What do you want?" Kaede asked.

"This isn't what I want, it is what the Dwarves want," Dain replied, pulling Kaede away from Weyland.

"What does he want?" Kaede asked.

"Too much," Dain replied.

"That is vague. If you don't want me to talk to Weyland, just say so, and I will ignore you," Kaede said.

"I heard you're reforming the marriage act so an Elf can marry a Dwarf," Weyland remarked behind Kaede.

Kaede turned to see Weyland coming towards them. "Yes, we are," Kaede responded, then looked at Dain.

"When can we marry?" Weyland asked as he stood beside Dain.

"It is complicated, ask him," Dain said looking at Kaede.

"Spoken like a politician," Weyland remarked, he had his hands on his hips and shook his head. He looked at Kaede and asked, "Why won't you sign the new marriage act into law?"

"Dain is aware I am waiting on a report from the lawyers to make sure it will not conflict with any existing legislation, such as our immigration control act, on the day the ink dries, you can marry," Kaede said.

"I see," Weyland said, also looking at Dain.

"It should be passed soon. Dain is so eager to have the bill pass he told me he has been going to the law library every day to help. You should go with him," Kaede said.

"Wonderful idea," Weyland said.

Dain was red-faced.

Abel said, "Now little brother, now is not the time to bother the Emperor with private business."

Dain looked at her, Abel took him by the arm and dragged him off to the balcony. He tried to pull his arm free, only to be released as she closed the doors.

Dain barked at her, "Sister, you have gone too far, embarrassing me in public."

"You will call the law library in the morning, do what it takes to pass that bill and marry King Weyland, or I tell him it is you who is holding up the vote," Abel said.

"Abel, never mind the fact the average Elf lives for 1500

years, and a Dwarf has a lifespan of about 500 years. I am not going to age, but he will," Dain said.

"Everyone knows you, I, Abelard, Toshiko, and the Senate, except Kaede, are immortal. Other than Patya, none of us has died," Abel said.

"Never known a fire to be too hot for a cold spell. Patya must be too embarrassed to admit he didn't have his wand," Dain said.

"Only one too embarrassed to admit anything is you," Abel said.

" All right, I'll sign the act, come out publicly and marry Weyland," Dain said, looking away.

"Good. Now the Emperor told me how he plans to pay us," Abel said, tapping his nose. "I bet you will never guess how?"

"Let me guess. The Emperor will skim from Takahiro's casino?" Dain asked with a sneer.

"No. The same way Takahiro built his wealth. He will use gold, silicon, and other precious metals from his recycling plants. You need to grant him a waste recycling contract so his trucks can deliver as they remove waste," Abel said.

"After I depose him, I know who the next Triad boss is," Dain said.

"Yakuza, he is Nipponese, not Qing," Abel said as she went to leave. "Just for that, you are going to buy him a very expensive gift. It has to be something he wants, and you will do so this year."

"You know I cannot give him what he wants, that would be illegal," Dain said.

"Give him two of your Formula 500 racing cars,"

Abel said. "Though I am sure he would prefer ones from a winning team."

"Are you kidding me?" an outraged Dain asked.

"You can afford it. I will inspect the cars, so you had better have them both in racing condition and packed in time for the Emperor's 16th birthday. I will provide him with helmets and fire suit," Abel said, leaving.

Kaede was standing in Hiro's room. Hiro was bald, with a scar on his crown from a recent operation. He was in a gown with breathing tubes, drainage tubes, waste collection, two drips in his arm, a heart monitor, and a stimulation mat.

The Spirit Talker was old, her face wrinkled and her green skin pale and broken like caked mud. Her hair was grey and thin. On her scalp, there were a few patches of exposed skin. Her eye teeth were long and pointed, and the top pair sat on her bottom lip. Her green eyes were warm, but her hands were cold and hard when she grabbed Kaede by his upper arm and pulled him closer. She was stronger than her appearance suggested.

"His spirit is weak, he is standing on the shore," she squawked in a hoarse voice.

Kaede looked around. It was dark, and they stood on the shore of a calm lake. Hiro stood in the water. It was up to his knees.

"Father?" Kaede cried out. He tried to move towards Hiro, but the Spirit Talker tightened her grip on him.

"He cannot hear you. He only hears the voices on the far shore."

"This is an impressive illusion."

"This is no illusion," she said, and she pushed Kaede in the chest with one hand.

Thinking she was old and weak, Kaede did not block or dodge. He found himself pushed back hard, landing on his bottom. She had knocked all the breath out of him.

He went to stand, but he then saw her enter the water. She took the beads from around her neck as she approached Hiro and put them on Hiro. She then turned him around. She pointed to Kaede. Hiro saw Kaede and took a step towards him. The old lady smiled and waved then stepped behind Hiro and pushed him onto the shore.

Kaede woke up, and saw he was sitting beside Hiro, and holding his hand. He saw Hiro was awake and staring silently at the ceiling.

Kaede hit the call button. Toshiko came charging in with her wand out. She looked around, and then she saw the beads on Hiro's neck. It was the beads the old lady was wearing.

Kaede saw Yaotl smile and not to him, then put on his hat and coat and leave.

CHAPTER 13

ACQUISITION

"Water," Hiro mumbled.

Kaede put his hand on Hiro's chest. "Don't move, you have been in an accident, Father."

"Kaede is that you?" Hiro asked, turning his head.

"Relax, don't talk, the healers will be here soon," Kaede said.

Toshiko pulled him back as Blood-Witches entered the room. They pulled the screen around his bed.

Kaede looked around, but Yaotl was in a car leaving the centre.

Kaede called Patya. "He woke up!" Kaede exclaimed.

"Emperor?" Patya asked, wearing only socks and boxers, on the edge of an enormous four poster bed.

"My father woke up. I don't know what Yaotl did, but I will explain later," Kaede said.

"Yaotl is a traditional healer. Be careful, some of his powders are powerful stimulants, the kind you find peddled in alleys behind nightclubs," Patya replied.

"I am sorry to wake you," Kaede said. He saw out the window the sun on the horizon.

"No need to apologise. I meant it when I told you I was here for you."

"I want to bring my father home."

"He is Takahiro's responsibility."

"I don't want him in an institution."

"What are your plans?"

"To get him home as soon as possible."

"That is a desire, not a plan."

"My grandfather's ship is already in the system, I will talk to him about a home care plan, even if I have to pay for it. I want to spend time with my father."

"That is a plan. Will you be moving out?" Patya asked. A muffled moan sounded behind him.

"I can sleep in my old room."

"I am not kicking you out."

"I know that. I do have a favour to ask."

"Oh?"

"Argon thinks I made a mistake. I beg to differ. I am of the opinion the intelligence gathered was worth ruffling a few feathers, even Argon's."

"Yaotl tells me he was able to update in detail the files on everyone and has some strong indicators of trouble in the Ogres we can exploit as well as some juicy blackmail material to win key votes in the Dragon Council for years to come."

"I think we can have a rough draft of the trade deal in a week, instead of months. But the favour I am asking is to talk to Argon. I need you to pull the Senate together. They don't see me as the team's captain, but as a player on loan."

"You need to step up your game. Argon is a close supporter of Dain."

"A captain is only as good as his XO."

"I will have a chat with them."

"Thanks. Say hello to your wife and sorry for interrupting. Bye for now," Kaede said, ending the call.

Patya put his mobile down and turned to face his bed, where Katrina, bound and gagged, lay in bed looking at him. "Hiro woke up," Patya said.

Katrina replied with some muffled sounds.

"Of course, we will stop by the hospital," Patya said, getting into bed. "After."

Hiro lay in bed looking at the ceiling. Healers told him the injury was not that bad. The healers took Hiro away from tests. He was brought back hours later. An old Witch stood beside Hiro.

"Look on the bright side," she said as she read his chart.

"Which is?" Hiro replied.

"It says you still have use of your arms."

"When will you fix my legs?"

"You have partial paralysis of your legs. You have a tear in your spinal column that disrupts the signal. We cannot fix that. Elves do regenerate, but not all wounds. You survived wounds that would kill an Ogre. You were very lucky."

"So, I will never walk again?"

"Your test results indicate you have some feeling in your feet. No loss of bladder control and able to be aroused. But

I think it is unlikely you will achieve more than a few steps without means of a frame."

She looked at Hiro and left. Kaede came and stood beside him.

"How tall are you now?" Hiro asked.

"150cm," Kaede replied.

"The same as me," Hiro remarked, eyes still looking up.

Kaede sat and said, "Much has changed."

Hiro looked at Kaede, and he went to say something, then he saw the Imperial Seal. "I know you want to be Emperor, but you are too old to be playing pretend. If my father saw you wearing the seal, you will be lucky if he only spanks you."

"That is one of the changes we need to discuss; he is no longer the Emperor and has not been for the last four years."

"Is this a joke?" Hiro asked, trying to sit up.

Kaede put his hand on Hiro's chest. "No. Dain charged him with negligence. If convicted, he could have spent ten years in jail. I took control and pardoned him."

"How did he take it?"

"Grandfather cried in his room for a week, then spent a few weeks in the tea house until Patya pulled him out. Since then he has worked for me. Since then he has thanked me and is living with his girlfriend, Masako, whom I made a Lady, and who is still employed as head of housekeeping at the Palace."

"Did you find Freya a new job when she left?"

"She has not left you. She does have a new job, as Masako's assistant. She stays in your room and waits for your return. In her spare time, she had completed a degree in nursing and has visited you regularly."

"I am not in a hospital, am I?"

"You are in the coma ward in Blood-Tower."

"What did you do?" Hiro asked, feeling his head. All his hair was gone. He lifted his gown and saw a pinch of skin on his right side; it was less than a centimetre long and looked like a tiny vagina.

"Kenta removed the top of your skull more than once to try direct stimulation of your brain."

"What is this?" Hiro asked, distressed, pointing to the lump.

"That is the passage used to clean your artificial organ. You squeeze it to open, then slide a specially designed syringe all the way in and inject the cleaning solution. Then wait a few minutes and suck it back out with the same device."

"What is an artificial organ?" a shocked Hiro asked.

"It is called the Liver Assistant and is made by my biotech company. It is a toxin filter, located beside your gall bladder. It is to get rid of the chemical produced by cell decay and other toxins. It needs cleaning at least once a week. Freya already knows how to do it. Someone will show you how to do it yourself."

"Why would you do that to me?"

"I was against it, but your father, not me, is your legal guardian. Kenta thought maybe toxins from your injuries prevented you from waking."

"Well, it worked. Now that I am awake take it out."

Kaede went and closed the door. "That isn't what woke you."

Kaede sat and recounted the events of Yaotl and the Spirit Talker. When Kaede finished, Hiro laughed. "Son, it is common knowledge Yaotl smokes a powerful drug that would knock out an elephant."

"He wouldn't dare drug me."

"Didn't my father tell you about Technical Support?"

"I know Yaotl is head of Technical Support, and that includes the Imperial Intelligence Department. Ogres put out memes of him in a cloak and dagger calling him the lie master."

"Do you know what Imperial Intelligence do?"

"Please do not treat me as if I am still twelve. It is bad enough that everyone else does. My guardians will not let me read some reports because of what they call the rough stuff. I have sneaked a peek. Patya and Yaotl get into such a lot of dangerous stuff. But they should be in an office, not out in the field."

"Yes, but you should be outside, enjoying life, not in an office."

"I know," Kaede said trying to smile.

Hiro started crying and put his hand on the brake. "I cannot live like this," Hiro said, looking at Kaede. Kaede wiped a tear off Hiro's check.

"Please don't give up. My company can grow skin, lungs, kidneys, and livers. We can keep organs alive for weeks before transplant. We are working on a blood substitute."

"How does that help me?" Hiro asked.

"It is all building up to repairing the tear in your spine."

"Until then?"

"Until then I want you to make sure your father makes your life worth living," Kaede said, wiping the tears off his father's face.

Hiro smiled and asked, "Do you have a girlfriend?"

Crisis

"Many, but Sora is my favourite. In a few years, we will marry, and my son is going need a grandfather to look up to."

"Are you still dancing with Izanami?"

"Yes. You should see the lines outside the studio. We are very popular."

"Have you kissed her yet?"

"Dad!"

"I take that as yes."

"I don't want to discuss that; too many eyes and ears about."

Toshiko came in. "Nice to see you awake Hiro," she said.

"Father, soon I will officially make you a Lord, low rank, but equal to Grandfather. When you are ready, I want you to be one of my advisors," Kaede said.

"Emperor, Kenta and his medical team have arrived, and they need to see Hiro alone," Toshiko said. She leaned over Hiro and looked at him. "Your son never gave up on you. So, don't you quit."

"What can I advise him on?" Hiro asked.

"Be there to talk to him," Toshiko replied.

"He has you for that," Hiro said.

Toshiko whispered, "I can do the heavy lifting, but he needs his father."

Kenta entered. "Hiro glad to see you are awake."

When Kaede returned with Toshiko to the Palace, he went to his old room and flopped on the bed. His crib was in the corner, with a doll inside and an old stroller beside it. He looked at the stroller. It was the one Izanami was pushed around in on his first birthday. Then as punishment, she had spent a week pushing the Sora and Akiko around in turns.

A cleaning robot with a mobile phone on top entered the room. Kaede picked up the phone. As soon as he did, the robot went back into the hall, and the phone rang.

He looked at the phone. It was an old phone with a single line LCD, which had 'blocked' displayed. He clicked the green button and put it to his ear.

"Don't talk, just listen and please remain behind the door. Cough twice if you understand," Galené said.

Kaede closed the door, turned around and looked up. He saw that he was under a tiny camera facing his bed. He then coughed twice.

"They can hear if you talk. Are you alone?"

Kaede coughed twice.

"Galen plans on using the stealth to assassinate you and the rest of the Senate at your coronation. I heard talk of a shadow army, but I have no other details. Do you understand me?"

Kaede coughed twice.

"They will detect the phone soon, so after I end the call, go and put the phone down the nappy chute and stop trying to find me," Galené said and then she ended the call.

Kaede walked to the nappy chute and put the phone in. He closed it, and the phone dropped down the waste collection chutes inside the walls. It fell all the way to the recycling centre.

Galené picked it up, walked into the ladies' room, pointed her wand at the wall and walked into the dark portal.

The door opened, and Kaede turned to see Lady Toshiko with a security team.

"Where is the phone?" Toshiko asked.

"I heard the elevator open and the sound of many boots in the hall, so I tossed it in the garbage chute," Kaede said.

"Excuse us," Toshiko said to the team. The security team left. She walked up to him, "Your guardians can limit some of your activities. You have a phone. Tell me, when and how did you get an unauthorised phone?"

"Turn the cameras off, and I will answer you," Kaede said, pointing to the camera in the top corner of the room over the door.

"Wait a minute," Toshiko said, looking up at the camera. She took out her phone, and said, "Turn the cameras and sound off."

"Yes, Lady Toshiko," an operator in the security room replied. She tapped control on her console and said, "They are off."

Toshiko turned off her phone and looked at Kaede. "Well?"

"Galené called me," Kaede said.

"What!"

"She didn't tell me much, but she said Galen plans on using the stealth to assassinate the Senate, along with me, at my coronation. Then she mentioned a shadow army but no details."

"Is that all she told you?"

"It was a short call, and I know you detected it. So where is Galené?"

"The exchange in New-Shanghai was all we got."

"Her information tells me three things."

"Like what?"

"First it tells us we have time, second it tells me the conspiracy is not as big as we first feared."

"How can you be sure of that?"

"It is public knowledge I have a concert at this Founder's Day parade. They could plan an attack then and kill some of us. But they plan to kill off all of us. That means no one inside the Senate or at the very top of Imperial Security is part of the coup."

"That makes sense—go on."

"Second, if the shadow army were big, they would not need to steal a stealth fighter."

"The third thing?"

"They could hit us on any day we are all in one place. So, something special occurs on my eighteenth. The only thing I can think of is the opening of my vault."

"You are going to learn to shoot."

"Patya and Kenta need to sign off on that."

"They will."

"When do I see the spell data?"

"Later. Fukuhina tells me they have a new case."

"Oh?"

"You were with your father, I had your phone, so I answered it. Shiori Iti, Lord Iti's daughter, was dragged off by wolves in the wildlife sanctuary, north of Foros on the south coast."

"Of course, help, but why is it a case?"

"There are no wolves in that or any park on the peninsula. There are only a few foxes."

"Give Lord Iti all the help he needs to find her."

"You already have."

"If you continue speaking for me, you must marry me one day."

"Ha. I am too old for you. Soon you will have Sora and a whole harem of young ladies to entertain."

"I am serious. I am intoxicated by your beauty."

"Do you believe the enemy will be waiting for coronation day?"

"There is one way to find out."

"Have Patya chat with Admiral Hagihara?"

"I doubt he is involved. He hates his wife and loves the Navy too much to be a traitor."

"What do you suggest?"

"We kick the bee hive. Put the Palace on lock-down, bring in Izanami's robot spy hunter and robot traps. Capture all the robot vacuum cleaners. Arrest anyone trying to leave. Root out the spy network. But make it look as if the information came from a defector from the Ogre embassy. Find one Yaotl and Patya would like a chat with and invite him over for talks. Have the Ogre first seen by the media shaking hands with him, and then take him inside the Inquisition Building."

"In the middle of talks with all our neighbours?"

"You are right, inform Argon, Patya, Yaotl and Adalwulf. If they agree to the operation, they can tell the rest of the Senate while you secure the Palace and island; no one except Knights in or out."

"That will take too long, I will call them after."

"After what?"

"This," Toshiko said as she walked over to the panic button and pressed it. Alarms all over the Palace went off. Guards raced to their posts. Officers made calls. All over the city, many Knights and guards descended on the Palace. "Oops!" Toshiko said, then took Kaede by the arm and left the room.

Outside the Palace, Dain was driving to the gate when the shutters come down. All the ramps on the highway around the island were sealed. Traffic was still able to cross the lake. Around the lake, patrol boats headed to Imperial Island. Ahead of them flew helicopters. At Camp Bravo, two pilots scrambled to fighter jets.

On the bridge, all the lane lights went red, and all traffic stopped. Roller shutters sealed the ramps to and from the island. The gates to the Palace grounds shut. Dain was in the back of his SUV when the driver stopped, even the express lane had closed. Dain took out his phone and called Abel.

"Not now," Abel answered her phone.

"I am outside the Palace, and they have closed all the gates," Dain said. "What is going on?"

"Sorry brother, all I can tell you is there is an emergency."

"Inside the Palace?"

"Yes, the island is now on lockdown."

"I am an Imperial Senator. Let me in," Dain demanded.

"You're the Minister of Agriculture, so no."

"Abel, I demand you have them open the gates."

"Only Knights and authorised members of the Imperial Security Agency are allowed in during a crisis. You are a spare wheel. Your authority is over the plants. Go home and water my roses."

"Was he caught with a girl to his room?"

"I hope he was. Back off and leave this to the professionals."

"I cannot, they sealed all the exits."

"I know, just wait. Guards will be checking all the cars and clearing traffic soon. Sorry, but I have to go now."

"Abel!" Dain yelled, but no reply, as she had already hung up on him. He tossed the phone to Weyland in the seat beside him. "What?" Dain snapped.

"You are so cute when you lose your temper," Weyland said.

As Kaede sat in the panic room, he bounced a small rubber ball against the wall and caught it with his right hand. A couple of Knights watched him, and one of them was Lady Yuki.

"Must you?" Yuki asked.

"I am bored," Kaede said.

"Relax, watch the screen."

"Nothing on."

"There are over a hundred channels on the network."

"I don't watch shows. I find them boring and repetitive."

"Listen to music. There are thousands of songs in the database."

"Will you dance with me?"

"I beg your pardon?"

"I am missing dance practice, and it helps me relax. Will you please dance with me?"

Toshiko was in the command room with Patya. He ended a call and turned to her, "Yaotl has the Ogre."

"Begin arrests, I will check on the Hatchling," Toshiko said.

She went down to sub-basement 13, through a maze to a large double door with two fully armed and armoured knights on duty. She walked up to a stand with a palm scanner, scanned her identification, then put her hand on the pad. She walked up to the door and keyed in a code on a keypad beside the door. The door opened.

She stepped in and saw Kaede dip Yuki. He stared into her eyes. Kaede pressed his body against Yuki. Toshiko coughed, and Kaede looked at her.

"Am I interrupting?" Toshiko asked.

"No. Lady Toshiko, would you like the next dance?" Kaede asked, still staring into Yuki's eyes.

"Some of the cleaning robots were wired with a micro audio-video recording device. We also captured an odd device. It had legs and dug into the data line like a tick. The robot tried to run from a robot cat, but it was caught by a modified squirrel trap," Toshiko said.

"Can I see it?"

"Later, the device is headed to the forensic laboratory."

"Did Patya and Adalwulf like the cats and cages?"

"Yes, they will soon be placing orders for toys to conduct sweeps of the Imperial Command buildings."

"Did you explain the reason behind the lock down?"

"I told them I received an anonymous tip to observe the cleaning robots. I found one watching you."

"Are they onboard with grabbing an Ogre spy chief and

blaming the bots on gossip media after photographs from inside the residence?"

"Yaotl and Patya liked the opportunity to snatch, but they want to pin the bots on an Ogre inside the embassy."

"Both. I want to paint the Ogre's spy rings as gangsters leeching of Ogre traders and that the Ogre leadership is inept and selfish. We need to weaken, not destroy them."

"Those are games Yaotl likes to play."

"Good. Do you mind if I make a palace-wide announcement?"

"Go ahead," Toshiko said. She took her phone off her belt, tapped the screen a few times and handed it to Kaede.

"This is the Emperor. I am distressed to learn some of you are engaged in spying on me. You have one hour to surrender to the nearest Knight. If not, Inquisition agents will find you. If you make us find you, it will be unpleasant for you, your family, and friends. If you do not surrender, Lady Toshiko will execute you in public. If you surrender now and confess, you will go to the plastic jail on Alcyone Two.

To my loyal staff, I apologise, and after this is over, you will enjoy a meal and drink on me. I thank my loyal employees for your honesty and hard work," Kaede said. He pressed end and started a countdown timer. He turned to Toshiko, "Walk around tapping your Viper 2, and hold up this up, he offered her the small clock. "Start with the staff who maintain the cleaning robots. Check all workers in the data room. Go room to room in the security centre with Patya, as someone didn't do background checks or no follow up checks on staff. Check payroll for anyone not here today and find out why."

"I will get on that," Toshiko said.

"We should build our own."

"Emperor?"

"Spy robots. Ask Patya if engineers from Izanami Robotics can study them. We need to develop counter measures. I am sure he will pass on data to his own robot company."

"I'll see what I can do. Now can I have my Knight back?"

Kaede let go of Yuki's hand, and he bowed to her. "Thank you for the dance, it was very satisfying," Kaede said.

Toshiko grabbed Yuki and pulled her out of the room, then looked at Kaede. "Behave."

Toshiko sent one of the other Knights in and closed the door.

Hours later Kaede was in the gym when Abel brought Dain in. Abel knocked on the open door. "Excuse me, my Emperor," Abel asked from the door. Dain waited in the hall, with a Knight standing guard on either side of the door.

Kaede was lifting weights, with Freya over him. He stopped, got up and towelled his face and hands. "Yes, Lady Abel?" he asked.

Freya went outside the room.

"My brother would like a word," Abel said.

"Now?" Kaede sighed.

"Only a couple of minutes of your time please?" Dain asked.

"Lady Abel, give us a few minutes. Come in Dain," Kaede said.

Kaede sat on an exercise bike and started pedalling. Dain came over and said, "Lady Toshiko told me what happened. It was an outrageous abuse of power."

"What if it was a bomb and not a camera in the robot?"

"Well, it wasn't."

"The perpetrators have confessed to spying. The Inquisition continues to make arrests. The official story is the Inquisition discovered a group within the Palace spying to sell information to the media. We leaked some photos of me doing crunches with no shirt on to the media, and it has had the desired effect, it distracted everyone from the shutdown, as my physique is the lead story. I did well out of it a book deal and some appearances on fitness shows. Nice to have some pocket money without worrying about the Wealth Cap."

"Isn't that a rather lame cover story?"

"I know this is a cliché, but if something works, don't question it. Other than Argon, most do not care the Palace closed for a few hours. Unless it affects them personally, the public does not care. The Ogres have staff go missing from their embassy all the time. There is a defection every week, Caesar Giovanni will send the usual threats to our ambassador, who will send on the next transmission. The Ogres will watch the outgoing ultra-wave transmissions and smile. But it is words not deeds. The Ogres lost in the last ten years have had over a few hundred ships lost or damaged. Many of their naval ships suffered damage. We manage to force into port over a quarter of their warships using long-range tactical weapons, we found and destroyed over a dozen pirate bases."

"Why release a photo?"

"I told you, it was a distraction. It worked. Even your news network is running the photo as the lead story. The story on the Ogre who disappeared from their embassy, the shutdown, and the Ogre's accusation that we behind attacks by pirates on their ships has been replaced by leaked photos of me."

"I agree it is a very flattering photo. But it is true, you have had covert operations pay Dark Elves, Orcs, Goblins and other pirates a bounty to conduct hit and run raids on Ogre warships. In return, you have released many their comrades with payments, the Ogres will retaliate. You cannot trust the pirates not to talk."

"Flattering? It is awesome, and it looks like I have a party going on in my pants."

"What about the Ogres?"

"Covered. An agent in Freeport brokered the deal. We have lawyers all the time brokering the release of pirates. The fleet trades captured pirates for fresh meat, wine, and fresh fruit all the time. The bounty and payments are not paid to released pirates. It is a bounty posted by a pirate group known as the Space Spiders who hate the Ogres. In return for not attacking us, we turned over to them some of the captured Ogre's ships, weapons, and provided them with the locations of Ogre's secret bases. We don't give them gold openly. But I do not trust them. I am closely watching them. My scouts have spread out over the free states, Utopia appears to at the centre of the conspiracy. Messages originate from Freedom Hall, their planets government centre. It is a collection of a dozen anarchist and anti-Empire groups."

"Now about these spies arrested today, why are you not charging some of them with treason?"

"I told them if they confess, I will not have them killed."

"You should plan operations with the Senate, not make them up as you go along."

"It was a security matter, and the security agencies handled it. Lady Toshiko is my head of security, and she coordinated with Patya. You know, him, he is the head of the Inquisition. He kept Adalwulf, head of the Imperial Guard, in the loop."

"The Ogres claim you kidnapped one of their staff."

"That was Yaotl. I asked him to bring in someone who Caesar Giovanni will miss. One of his errand boys who is a go between for their pirates, merchants, and gangsters. Right now, he is strapped to a chair in one of the Inquisition's confession rooms."

"To what end?"

"Caesar Giovanni will have to cut ties with some groups, find new cat's paws. He has been looking for someone to blame for the loss of pirate bases. We need an Ogre who can give us details on the most loyal Ogres. We then frame Chronos. Caesar Giovanni will purge his government of some Titans. We must grow the divide between various factions."

"Yaotl has not shared his plans with me, what do you know?"

"We are working on having Caesar Giovanni kill those close to him who are funding and building ships for the pirates. One plan is to have the pirates believe Caesar

Giovanni sold them out for a trade deal. Another is to leak some of the Ogre's demands to the Titans, Orcs and Goblins to make it appear that Caesar Giovanni is blaming them for the pirates while seeking a trade advantage over them, including providing information to us in return for anti-ageing treatment and life-extending drugs."

"What about the pirates turned merceries you hired? Could they not sink the plan and go public?"

"We cannot hire the Space Spiders indefinitely. But my plan is they fade into the background. We give them new identities and a licence to trade opium. We include them in the trade talks as representatives of the Free States. We turn our enemies into legitimate trading partners. Our ties to the Space Spiders cannot be proven, and it is in the leader's best interests to make sure their crews don't know they took gold from me."

"Who is going to do the killing?"

"Depends on who is going to die. Chief Belaúnde will be creative. Domestically Czar Petrov can bring traitors to trial and have Lady Toshiko do the beheading."

"You are popular as an artist, but as Emperor, the public sees you as weak. The Orcs know that we know that the Ogres fleet was preparing to attack us. They pulled out only because they expected to see our fleet attacking the Ogre's forward bases."

Kaede stopped pedalling. "Lady Abel?"

Dain turned to see Abel come in.

"Yes?" she asked.

"We have an execution scheduled for tomorrow?" Kaede asked.

"Yes, Emperor," Abel replied.

Crisis

"Make sure you are doing the execution and have your brother in the front row when you take off the head, nothing too fancy, and have the head land at his feet," Kaede said.

"He will whine if get I blood on his suit," Abel said.

Dain was red with rage.

"Next time someone calls me weak, they are insulting the Senate, and it is your duty to defend the honour of the Senate, not score cheap political points," Kaede said to Dain. Furious, Dain turned to leave. "I am not finished." Abel stood in Dain's way.

"Dain. We don't want the worker ants. The only thing we learn from them is how weak they are. If they confess, the rest scatter like bugs when the light is shined on them. We don't want the strong to get away and have the weak suffer in jails. When the weak get out, they return to crime. I want to jail the strongest of our enemies. Have them wither and suffer. Then when they are weak, threaten to release them into the general population of the prison. They will sing, because not only are they weak but have many enemies and no friends. This war we not going to fight with our weapons, but our minds. We want to demoralise the enemy. We do not to drive Chronos mad but instil just enough fear to have him come to trade talks begging for a deal, once he does, he cannot walk away, he will need sort of deal he can use to hold power with. Yaotl will have Ogres who are working for us in place to feed him a fall guy Chronos can blame for the attacks. Yaotl has only hinted it will be a close ally, but someone he will believe to be a traitor because so many Ogre Lords are double-dealing opportunists," Kaede said. He got off the bike and faced Dain.

"Just like that?" Dain inquired.

"Dain, there is no point in defeating him on the field of battle. If we bomb him, his people resent us more. If we remove a fanatic with violence, we make a martyr and fuel the fire. We must douse the fire by destroying the idea of going to war against us. Not by attacking them with weapons of mass destruction, as that will only fuel the idea in them to use such weapons on us. No, those who talk of war must be made to look foolish, selfish, and seeking to profit from war, we use their politics of class warfare against them," Kaede said. Abel clapped.

"Brilliant!" Abel exclaimed. "The Emperor is right. We could bomb their world to ash, but that fear does not last. It has always turned into anger against us. The Ogres rallied everyone against us using the idea our wealth is based on theft."

"We cannot just move in and bring them trade, peace, and prosperity. Dain, we can do so for the Dwarves, but not the others, especially the free states. However, we offer all groups a place in the Dragon Council and make it not just a forum for talks, but a trade forum. Longer we keep the leaders talking with Argon, the further we move away from war."

Dain, red-faced, turned to Kaede. "I came today to inform you that our little project is not progressing. We have hit a hurdle that I fear we may never jump over," Dain said.

"Do you need more resources or more funds?" Kaede inquired.

"The program has many bugs. The Alpha program can find and analyse data, but it is slow and needs a supercomputer to do so. The beta program is a more annoying version of you."

"Is that with the two-core or three-core processor?"

"The Alpha program is on a three-core quantum computer."

"I am working on heating issues with the core five. I want the Alpha in the Data Security Building, I will pay you for the beta. Don't deny it, just tell me how many you made?"

"I designed two models, beta finds ways around the safety parameters. I cannot make the program obey and retain problem-solving ability. It is portable or safe, not both."

"How smart is the second system?"

"It is not about how smart it is. I asked it what it would do with an army of killer robots. It replied it would eradicate the enemy. In some wargames, it would commit genocide to win. It would bomb any enemy back to the stone age."

"Find a balance. If you cannot make it fully compliant with each of my rules, then try to make aware of them all and no stronger than the average Elf. Patya and I are working on anti-robot weapons."

"What if we cannot?"

"If you cannot control it, then confine it. We need to study AI. The enemy has a name, The Chosen. The leader's name is the Grand Vizier. They are cultists of Moloch."

Dain gasped, looked at Abel, then said, "You only have a suspicion they have an AI."

"No. We have images of an army of killer robots. They have command ship in orbit controlling them. The other free states don't want to publicly acknowledge that Utopia is no longer a theocracy. If we can get the other free states on our side, then the Ogre's only have Utopia, a few thousand anarchists, and a couple hundred pirates. I hope you agree that trade is the key to buying off the other worlds and help get all the leaders here for talks?"

"Yes, you have my support."
"Goodnight High Lord Dain and thanks."
"Goodnight Emperor."

Kaede was in his room, preparing for his sixteenth birthday party. He put on a black suit with a red shirt and no tie. When he left his room, he found Toshiko waiting with Sora and Akiko, all three of them in uniform.

"Hello ladies, looking very professional," Kaede said.

"Hello, my Emperor," Sora said.

"Thank you, my Emperor," Akiko said.

"Emperor, they have proved themselves to be splendid Knights," Toshiko said.

"I understand you just completed space training?" Kaede asked.

"Yes," Sora replied.

"Eight kinds of fun," Akiko said.

"Good, I am looking forward to it," Kaede said.

"Two more years," Toshiko said.

"I would like to stand here all night looking at the three of you," Kaede said.

"The girls only have the night off, at 11 pm they return to Camp Bravo," Toshiko said.

"Then I shall not waste it talking in the hall, allow me to escort my fiancée to my party," Kaede said, offering Sora his arm. Sora put her hand on his arm, and they headed to the elevator.

Kaede danced first with Sora, then Akiko. When Kaede

escorted Izanami onto the dance floor, the rest cleared a huge space for them.

Izanami and Kaede were electric. He finished the dance by lifting her into the air by her hips and spun slowly, getting down on one knee, holding her up, with their eyes locked. They were given a standing ovation as he put her down. Many in the room were excited, lining up to dance with Kaede.

Lady Abel grabbed Kaede first. "Are you poking Dain in the eye?" Kaede asked as they danced.

"I am considering your offer," Abel said.

"I made many proposals to you," Kaede said.

"The two space stations."

"Name your price, as I want them both."

"Why should I sell them to you?"

"I need to assemble my Quantum Three CPU in zero gravity."

"We launch a high precision automated factory that can produce a couple of dozen quantum processors per hour and is the size of a cargo container."

"It is not just to make processors. It will be printing cars, chips, reactor parts, ultra-drives, and a range of new weapons in a high security, zero-gravity laboratory."

"My stations don't have a zero-gravity laboratory."

"I have modified the Lilith-Toshiko to generate zero-gravity."

"Did you say print cars?"

"Yes. Would you like to be one of my product testers?"

"What will I be testing?"

"The Hashimoto Sports Plus. It will be faster, lighter, cheaper and better armoured than a Knight's cruiser. I hear Dain's outrage. But the truth is, he will benefit. He can sell the cruiser to other agencies. I will be selling the Hashimoto Sports Plus to the rich with a model for my Knights and a third model for the extremely wealthy. I am also launching a range of shoes, boots, and sandals next month. I love to see you in knee-high boots."

"Do I get to keep them?"

"Yes."

"A dozen pairs?"

"Yes."

"Did Izanami design them for you or did you hire someone else?"

"I designed them. My shoes are in high demand. The soul is a new super-gel that last longer, decreases impact and increases comfort. We have expanded the range of colours and styles."

"I want a pair of those platforms you made Sora. The pink ones with the triple overlapping toe strap with the wide ribbon tie around the ankle."

"I will make you a pair."

"No need to hand make them?"

"I handmade all of Izanami's shoes."

"Somehow I don't see you making women's shoes in your spare time."

"I am looking for the balance between thinking and doing. I am going to run out of things to think about. So, I do things. I even learnt flower arrangement."

Abel clapped as the music stopped, and the band took a break. Kaede went to sit with Mako and Miko.

Dain came up behind Abel. "Getting rather cosy?"

"Jealous?" Abel asked.

"What were you talking about?"

"Shoes."

"Fine, if you're not going to tell me."

She stepped close to Dain and said, "If I say we talked about shoes, then we talked about shoes. To be precise he told me he made Izanami's shoes, and he offered to make me a pair. I accepted."

"Don't you have enough shoes?"

"What a horrible thought."

"Abel, you have a room full of shoes."

"What can I say? I like shoes."

"Understatement of the year."

Kaede danced with Lady Fukuhina. "How do you like working for me?"

"Some days are better than others," Fukuhina replied.

"Problems with the team?" Kaede asked.

"No. Even after saving Shiori from the wolf, many in the ISA still treat us as intruders."

"It is not your fault."

"We never found where the wolves came from."

"Likely an animal smuggler had some escape. It is not your fault Shiori nearly died. In fact, Adalwulf told me, it was Hilda who tracked her, and then Cerise saved her life."

"Not much of one. Poor Shiori will be in bed for the remainder of her life. She lost an arm and both legs. The wolves tore most of her skin off, a kidney was punctured, her liver was ruptured, and they had to remove her uterus."

"Would it help knowing that I established a fund for

her care, education and made sure púca from Hashimoto House will visit her?"

"It does."

"Nothing on Shade?"

"Anyone who knows him must be dead or missing. After the lock down, Shade stacked up bodies and put out word anyone who snitches on him will be buried alive."

"You solved a dozen cases and helped uncover a massive spy ring. Along the way, you discovered a smuggling ring and an illegal brothel. Excellent work for private investigators with no powers to obtain warrants."

"Not good by my standards. We should not have to push mud uphill to prove our innocence."

"Shade has spent his life in hiding and moving. I know it will take you time to discover the one place he returns to the most. It will be a well-guarded secret, a place only a few will know about it. I know investigative work is hard. Please keep pulling at those threads until one is left."

Fukuhina nodded. Lady Toshiko cut in.

"I must warn you. I am a great dancer," Toshiko said.

"Then let's tear up the floor," Kaede said.

Izanami stood, jaw dropped, as Toshiko and Kaede danced. Together Izanami and Kaede were great. But Toshiko was near perfection with each step. In the end, they spiralled around, one arm in the air, eyes locked, arms around each other's waist, and when the music cut he pulled her in and dipped her. Then he raised her, and she stepped back, panting. He bowed to her as the audience cheered, and girls pushed past Izanami.

Toshiko escorted Kaede to a balcony and closed the doors.

Crisis

"I ran the program you wrote," Toshiko said sitting on a bench.

"Results?" Kaede asked sitting beside her.

"What was the bet with Patya again?"

"He has to wear a kimono to court for a month."

"With Hakama?

"Everything, even Tabi socks and wooden shoes."

"Deliver them to him. You should have had him wear a Kabuki mask. Only you are too young to drink Sake and sing songs about war and love."

"What were the results?"

"First off, where did you get all that data?"

"I asked Yaotl for all the spell fragments from the archives."

"Your program processed the library of fragments and combined them with mystery disappearance fragments to produce a complete spell. However, the spell's code is not like any I have seen before and contains waveforms not in the existing spell library."

"Did you cast the spell?"

"I did. You and Patya need to see it, and then we can decide the next step together."

"What can you tell me about the spell?"

"The spell is an alteration spell, but it didn't cover the caster in darkness, it was a ball."

"It is a gate to another dimension, right?"

"Yes."

"Did you test my spell, *Sound Barrier*?"

"Yes, and it is brilliant. No sound from inside the barrier can be heard outside, but you cannot hear any sounds from outside. Audio devices pick up a buzz from the barrier."

"Good. I will licence it immediately to the various security agencies."

"I am using it now."

"I didn't even notice."

Toshiko stood looked inside. She saw Patya and Katrina dancing. Toshiko ended the *sound barrier* spell, "Let me tell Patya about the Shadow Dimension."

"What?" Kaede asked. Toshiko smiled and returned inside. She made her way through the crowd to Patya.

Kaede went to follow, but Yuki grabbed his arm. "Time to open your gifts," she said, putting a heart-shaped box of chocolates in his hand.

Kaede followed her to a table stacked with items.

On the table were a range of different-sized boxes and many gift baskets with towels, shampoos, soap, body scents, shoes, socks, and underwear. Kaede opened various boxes to find handguns, body armour, and electronics.

Dain and Abel escorted him to the parking lot where two trucks were parked. Inside each was a formula-500 racing car. One was blue with matching flame suit and helmet, with a large matching bag. They had 'Hatchling' on them. The other racing car was red with matching gear that had 'Hot Head' on them.

Kaede laughed and handed Izanami the red helmet. She glared at him. "Who else can I race?" Kaede asked.

"True, I am only the one you cannot beat," Izanami replied.

A week later Kaede, Patya and Toshiko entered a large laboratory in the Lilith Foundation building. It took up

Crisis

most of the floor. Outside the entry, armed Knights stood in armour. The white room was almost empty. It had a large clear blast screen in the middle. An observation window beside the airlock and a control panel beside the door.

Toshiko sealed the airlock, flipped a couple of switches on the control panel. The door sealed, and the shutters closed.

"I feel like we surrounded by energy," Kaede said.

"We are. The walls have three layers of Orichalcum mesh, on full power, it is rated at Force 30," Toshiko said.

"Why so high?" Kaede asked.

"When powered the mesh will deflect any spell half its rating," Toshiko replied.

"Interesting," Kaede said looking at the walls.

Toshiko walked to the middle of the vast room. Kaede and Patya followed. She stood behind the clear blast shield.

Toshiko took a deep breath and cast the gate spell, and a dark ball appeared in front of her.

Patya looked at it, Kaede started a stopwatch, and seven minutes later the sphere vanished.

"Have you used it yet?" Kaede asked Toshiko.

"Used what?" Patya asked.

"I made a robot with cameras, a remote arm and big bright lights on the front. I sent it to Toshiko yesterday. We should send it inside. It has a recording device in case we lose the signal. I will set it to it reverse after six minutes," Kaede said to Patya. "You have some Aether vision cameras?" he asked Toshiko.

"Yes. I have everything," Toshiko replied.

"Send for three goggles, four cameras with stands and

the robot. We will send the robot in, watch and record for the sides, top and bottom if possible?" Kaede inquired.

"Yes. I have professional camera stands," Toshiko said.

"Robot arm?" Patya asked.

"Yes," Toshiko replied.

Toshiko drew a large circle on the floor while staff set four cameras on robotic arms were set up around it. Toshiko directed them to set up two more, one over the top, then the last camera on the ground angled up.

Staff handed them goggles then left. Kaede brought in the robot.

Toshiko closed the door and turned on the energy field. "Get ready," she said.

"Where did you get all the Orichalcum to shield a room this big without making significant withdrawals?" Patya inquired.

"By recycling old wands," Kaede replied.

"So, you are sitting on more wealth than you report," Patya commented.

"Waste is not wealth, Patya until it is processed and you can only tax it if I sell it," Kaede responded.

Patya pondered his answer.

"Ready," Toshiko said.

Kaede leaned over to Patya. "I know you want to audit me, but you have already seen the mountains of waste outside New-Shanghai," Kaede said, turning on the robot.

"Interesting robot," Patya said.

"Work in progress. It is for bomb disposal, but it is not ready for testing yet. Working on adding attachments such as a shotgun, Freon sprayer and a projected water disruptor," Kaede said.

"A water disruptor?" Patya asked.

"A small directed blast of water to shatter the bomb, making it a wet firecracker," Kaede replied.

"Interesting, I would like to be the one to conduct the trials," Patya said.

"Quiet," Toshiko said.

Kaede nodded to Patya.

She turned on the cameras and started recording, then stood back, and cast the spell.

A seven-metre round black cloud formed inside the circle on the floor. Kaede used the remote to send commands to the robot, which was a medium-sized six-wheeled kart with a single arm on top, headlights up front and cameras front and back on turrets. It went in, and it disappeared. The controller was a small notebook computer.

On screen the image was black, the lights came on and did not penetrate far, and then there was static. Six minutes later the robot drove out.

Kaede downloaded the video to the controller and then played the footage. At first, it was the dark, and they heard what sounded like static. Then the laboratory appeared, only it was dark, lit by the light from the robot.

All four cameras worked. Most of the laboratory was dull grey, except anything with energy, which had varying degrees of a yellowish glow. The walls, floor, and roof were dim. The light around the door at the seal was like a halo, and the door had only a faint glow. The light bulbs were bright but did light the room. The cameras had a dull glow. The three Elves had a glow that had moving swirling patterns and some red.

When the robot moved out, the screen went black briefly and displayed a colour image of the room.

"I saw the robot until it entered the cloud," Patya said.

"Did you use Aether Vision cameras on the robot?" Toshiko asked.

"No," Kaede replied.

"I used Aether Vision, you can see anything inside the ball, but not beyond," Patya remarked.

"I suspect the cloud is a spell to Shift Dimension of the target," Kaede said.

"It is like Shadow Walk, but is not an area version of that spell," Toshiko said.

"Shadow Walk displaces an individual into the Shadow Dimension for the duration of the spell. But I suspect Shift is an instant spell. All the mystery disappearance spells have similarities. The last one, bothers me the most, we have so few pieces of the spell, and no one has seen it in use. So, unless we can image what the spell does and try many combinations of the formula, we not going work out the missing parts," Kaede said.

"If we get enough readings we will work out the spell. Like we did with Shadow Walk," Toshiko said.

"Every spell has the same structure. How come trying combinations of symbols will not work?" Patya asked.

"Every spell has the same structure. Now force, type, shape, and duration are basic symbols the computer understands. But the symbols after that are keys to the database of waveforms and patterns. There are far too many combinations we don't know. Most combinations do not produce anything. The most important waveforms are the ones that define what the spell looks like. Also, every caster leaves their unique energy signature created by their personal energy like a stamp over the spell, which we need to filter out, to know the formula," Toshiko said.

"How did you create spells?" Kaede stated.

"Lilith and I took almost a hundred years to create the known spell library, we just tried imaging spells and running combinations against all the readings of energy we took," Toshiko explained. "I don't think you understand how complex magic is."

"My understanding is this the wand charges the Orichalcum in the bulb to draw aether from the wielder and traps it in a glass vacuum tube, covered in orichalcum, in the stem. The computer in the bulb then matches symbols from the spell formula to a waveform in the library and sends that to a signal generator at the base of the bottle. Then when the excited Aether reaches its peak, the computer opens the containment bottle at the pointed end, and the aether shoots out. A lot of computing power just to turn off and on a wire mesh," Kaede said.

"Yes," Toshiko replied, smiling at Kaede. "What is your point?"

"My point is I get how the mystery of magic is best not understood."

"Yes, takes all the fun out of casting when you know how it works. Most of that computing power is for processing thoughts of the caster to know when to activate."

"I took it a step further. I have been watching spells form. What you call light, and dark aether are light grey and dark grey. Illusions, Healing and Detection spells use light grey aether. The combat spells Stun and Stun Ball also use light grey aether. But the spell Power Bolt, Power

Ball, Aether Bolt, and Aether Ball are made using dark grey aether. Alteration spells also use both light and dark grey," Kaede said.

"What do you mean, watching spells?" Patya interjected.

"I had a special high-speed camera made with an Aether Vision lens," Kaede replied.

"Can I borrow it?" Toshiko asked.

"Yes, but it is one of a kind so if you break it, you bought it," Kaede replied.

"I know light aethers appears in aether vision as light grey, and dark aether is dark grey. What's the point?" Toshiko asked.

"The reason you could not match spell fragments or turn them into spells before now is there are four types of aether, White, Light, Dark Grey and Black. That is why I wrote you a new data matching program for spell fragments; your program was dismissing too many fragments as degenerated," Kaede said.

"How did you come to this conclusion?" Patya asked.

"Most of the spell fragments are from three formulas, I sorted them and gave Toshiko only one set. Those fragments have never been matched to a spell before because the old data matching system was comparing the whole wave to the known spell library. My program is set to look for partial matches within the various fragments, eventually cleaning them up into a complete waveform. Using that I found some did have partial matches to parts of the Power-Bolt and Heal spells. From that, I found the waveforms for isolating White and Black Aether."

"You got all that from the data your teams collected?" Patya asked.

"Combined with the unknown spell fragments collection from Yaotl. I managed to isolate and identify three not in the spell library. They are *Black Bolt*, *Gate* and *Advanced Heal*," Kaede replied. "The rest I believe are from a spell for which we have not enough data to make a complete formula."

"Did you try them?" Toshiko growled.

"I had researchers try them for me," Kaede replied. "That is why I had the laboratory built. I had my researchers test them when you too busy watching me. I left you the black cloud fragments in hopes you would independently confirm my discovery of Black Aether."

"Tell us about these spells," Patya said.

"First is *Dark Bolt*, which is not a physical impact like *Power Bolt* or a mind killer like *Aether Bolt*. *Dark Bolt* acts like a lethal poison. Second is *Gate*. It goes to another dimension. You can see the energy from ours. It has an atmosphere because of the tiny little tears that open and close around energy. They think that is how magic users get aether. A magic user is a living mana battery. In this dimension, my researchers have seen lights move in the distance. The last spell I call *Conceal*, and it is how they hide from mind reading. It is an alteration spell that uses Light Aether to create a barrier that absorbs Detection spells, like Mind Probe," Kaede said.

"Why has no one heard of Dark Aether before?" Toshiko asked.

"Forget that, I need to see this conceal spell," Patya said.

"I need to know; how did you get all this?" Toshiko persisted.

"I told you. I have been gathering spell formulas,

comparing them, breaking down the waveforms like sheet music. I have a lot of video of casting taken at thousands of frames per second to confirm. Unfortunately, the frame rate far exceeds data capture rate, so in slow motion you see gaps. I have teams working on improving both the data rate and size of video storage. I have all the data on the spells and research done so far on my private server in this building, and I will give it all to you today," Kaede said.

"Good."

"A few changes are needed to spell books. First, is renaming the category Combat Spells to Force Spells. You only need to look at the spells Push and Pull. They have what you call combat spell headers. As well as spells to add to the library, there are the new waveforms for the new forms of Aether. I also have a new waveform for the shape of the spell, cloud. But I am not finished with the data. I am on the verge of creating a new magic program that will customise spells," Kaede said.

"We better call the others; they need to see this too," Patya said.

"I want to see this data," an excited Toshiko stated.

"We need to set up a proper Demonstration of *Gate*. To do that I need to get my high-speed camera out and I will have support change the robot to carry it," Kaede said.

"Good idea," Patya remarked.

"Just do not blow up my building," Toshiko scolded them.

CHAPTER 14

Seventeen

August 31, 11579. North-side of the Imperial Palace grounds.

It was just after sunrise, and Kaede was pushing Hiro in the Japanese gardens.

"Son, you haven't asked for a wish, is something wrong?" Hiro asked.

"I have all that I need. I want you to get well, Father," Kaede said.

"Son, you going to be eighteen next year, once you marry Sora and have púca of your own, then you will not much time for me."

"Father, you once promised me to make my wishes come true if they were reasonable and in your power. I want to do something for you. Do you have a wish?"

"You know I'd do anything just to be able to walk again."

"I am working on that. I am working on ways to use stem cells to repair the damaged tissue, I have a project that uses robotics in an external frame, and working on magic to regenerate the body," Kaede said, his voice flat.

"I can tell, something is bothering you."

"There is no easy way to say this. Freya is upset with you. She told me she has demanded you marry her and you have refused. Grandfather married Masako last year, and they are talking about having a púca. If you are worried about money, I will pay for the wedding."

"Son, I do appreciate your offer. But I am going to outlive Freya by a very long time."

"One of my companies makes anti-ageing drugs. They do not do much for Elves, but they can greatly extend the lifespan of a Giant. It is a powerful drug, and very expensive. I will pay for your wedding, honeymoon, and I will provide Freya with a lifetime supply of life extension drugs."

"Son—"

"Father, please marry her. I think of her as my mother, and she wants to be your wife."

Hiro put his hands on the wheels. "I do have a wish. As a wedding present, can you have a sailboat made, one I can sail on my own?"

"I will, and I'll give you a berth at the island's marina."

"I am told you are opening a shoe store in Hashimoto Mall?"

"Yes, I started Kaede Fashion with shoes. We now have socks, stockings, pantyhose, dresses, bags, a huge range of accessories and beauty products for males and females. We have a unique order system. A customer is scanned by the full-body scanner and can see how they look in our products. They can choose patterns and styles from a huge catalogue. We then make and deliver within two days. Our research shows a shift in male fashion with demand for more colours and style options."

"I heard you increased the staff at your research centre?"

"Yes, I have many projects old and new. Our biggest is expanding the economy, so grandfather doesn't have to sell so much as one block of land, or he will find ways to ruin me."

"Why haven't you marketed your two-core processors? The company report says you developed three-core processor and are working on a five-core processor."

"It is a software issue. The almost complete. We developed a new virtual reality program that is amazing in detail. We use the mind reading interface to allow users to create their own avatar. We hope to install it soon on Exodus ships to make life better."

"I am concerned you spend too much time with Lady Abel. You know she tells Dain everything you do."

"Abel works for me as an automotive engineering consultant. Fancy way of saying she is building my car and teaching me to drive. However, lately, she has been doing modelling. She has been promoting my shoes, clothes, and makeup. There is a revolution in fashion. Many do not like it, but you cannot deny many heterosexual males want to look and smell nice."

"Just be careful, please. I am worried if you keep starting new projects, the Senate may believe you're abusing the long-term agreement to slowly grow the wealth of the people to hide the fact you are expanding your power and wealth to a level they can never reach."

"Remember the artificial cell project?"

"Yes."

"Lady Toshiko wanted a spray-on sealant for space suits because patches were not always sticking as the glue often they froze before been applied. Well, spray seal gave Mako and Miko the idea of doing the same for skin. A Spray-On Bandage that is made from artificial cells that stick together and it dries quickly. The body absorbs them as it heals."

"I saw the Iti girl in the Palace clinic last night. Are paying for her treatment?"

"I am. Shiori has our latest in replacement skin and has signed on for research into bone growth. We are studying how she grows up with her injuries, how her healthy bones act compared to other bones. I know it seems cruel for her to spend weeks at a time in a hospital room been poked by needles and then placed into an isolation room, but she is getting an education and medical care."

"Am I only a test subject to you?"

"Of course, not, Father. I am hurting because you are hurting. I want you to live a happy and healthy life. I cannot be involved in your care because I made the device implanted in you. Your father is your guardian. I do not see you as a test subject. I only want you to receive the best medical care."

"Dain claims you're just making clients by putting artificial organs into everyone, so we have to spend a lifetime buying your cleaning solution."

"Once a patient has recovered, the Filter Device can be removed."

"Kenta wants to me to trial the second-generation filter."

"The first-generation artificial organ needed a custom cleaning fluid, but the new one is flushed with water and has a second chamber for fluids to be absorbed into the bloodstream, such as long-term drips, a birth control solution, liquid medication or even vitamins."

"Kaede, all of that is impressive, but has any progress been made with the walking frame?"

"The new model is stronger than the previous one, and we renamed it the exoskeleton. Unfortunately, walking is still slow, and it needs an umbilical cord for power and hydraulic pressure. We sold the first couple we made to the fleet as heavy lifters on space stations. Viktor, Rudolf and Adalwulf have asked for more to be built, and they want a couple of different models, such as one to be able to load launch tubes."

"You are so much like your grandfather, always trying to find a way to make a profit. At least you are making things."

"We are trying to develop a better battery, and we haven't given up on the exoskeleton. It needs to be user-friendly and easy to put on and off. We have a lot of interest in them for use in construction, loading trucks and ships, as well as other heavy lifting tasks."

"Son, we cannot expect technology to meet our expectations; there will be limits. Look at engines, any faster and cars will fly off the road, and only a few can handle a speed of 300 km/hr or more."

"Yes. All new cars are required have a speed limiter installed. The device requires the driver to insert their licence and speeds over 100 will only unlock if they are licenced to do 200 or 300 based on tests and experience."

"What about trucks?"

"All trucks and buses already have a speed limiter, it will take time to get long hauliers doing two hundred kilometres per hour. To try and ease fears we will first add black box recorders to all trucks, and to all new vehicles. We are working on driver-assist technology such as auto parking, collision detection and even an autopilot. But automation laws will make sure professional drivers do not lose their job. Automation will be limited."

"After developing the compact fusion reactor, most will have retired."

"We are developing new models of reactors, propulsion, shields, scanners, long-range communications, and ultra-drives. We going to use a modified ultra-wave radar to send and receive a communications signal."

"That is good. Before I forget, can you tell me why is Dain suing you over two space stations you bought from Abel? I heard it is because you paid only one pair of shoes?"

"I bought two zero-g laboratories from her. I use one to make hundreds of Quantum Two CPUs. The other I use one to produce cars, six-wheel jeeps and trucks. It has six automated factories, and each one assembles a car or a six-wheeler in four hours or a tank in eight hours. Dain is upset because he believes she should have given him first right of refusal. But he doesn't use zero-gravity space stations, which is the reason Abel sold them to me. She used them to buy more shares in Artificial Oil Plants, and she is now richer than Dain. I delivered to her on the day of signing the deal a pair of handmade shoes."

"Wow, Dain must be livid."

"Abel said he nearly choked on his bratwurst when she saw her ahead of him for the first time since the markets opened."

"I heard you reached the Wealth Cap and yet you started construction on fifty new oil plants?"

"The Wealth Cap is the combined wealth of the Senate. Patya, Arjuna and Yaotl are selling off shares using my wealth creation program to get us below 50% of the total shares on the Fortune 5000."

"Then why is Grandfather so against it?" a puzzled Hiro asked.

"He thinks I should only sell shares to other Fortune 5000 listed companies and end the employee share trust that pays a share of the profits to top employees."

"Son, from what I have seen, I am proud of you. You have done a lot, not just for the clan, but for the Empire in the four years."

"He has more now than he did as Emperor. He has a mountain of gold in the bank. But he is upset with me because wage reform has prostitutes on minimum wage, medical drugs cheap, I banned interest on interest, no more variable interest, introduced a flat tax and other changes. Soon you will have a new identification card and licence. They have a hologram and other protections against forgery. But no more gun licence and your licence to drive, fly, operate a boat or a starship will all be on one licence. Lose one for any reason, lose them all."

"Grandfather will not be the only one upset. I am with you, though. I don't know about other changes, but I remember the flat tax movement, Grandfather called them dangerous radicals."

"You remember the little robotics company I started with Izanami?"

"I like the Cat Sìth robot."

"Many did, it was the toy of the year."

"I like that fact you include your girlfriends in your projects."

"Izanami is great at design and programming. She has

expanded the range to a dozen robots. A big seller we have is the robot trolley. It can be programmed to perform tasks or follow the wearer of a RFID badge. We will have them in all Hashimoto shopping centres on thirty worlds and with new partnerships, we soon to be all over the Empire and beyond. The fleet has ordered a model to be used on automated supply shuttles, on ships, and space docks. But I had an idea; it just occurred to me, what if I made you a wheelchair you can drive?"

"I cannot believe no one thought of that before, yet the idea is so simple. I have seen the trollies in the Palace many times moving about on their own. Still, it's weird when a maid tells a cleaning cart to stay, and it beeps twice. If you do make me a wheelchair like that, don't use the Cù Sìth robot brain."

"Why not? You can whistle, and your chair will come to you. At least let me add an arm so you can lift yourself, and design an SUV you can drive. I know you would rather walk, but it may take twenty years, or we could have success tomorrow."

"All right, go wild, just make it easy to use and comfortable. Maybe add a back massager, a phone holder, and speakers. I have my good days and my bad days. But days like this, talking with you like this, it gives me hope, son."

"We are no longer making helicopters. The new VTOL will replace all rotor blade craft within twenty years. The first model has only 19 seats, but it has twice the range of a helicopter and is much cheaper to run. The power supply is a hydrogen fuel cell, and the fuel is a compressed liquid binary explosive. Another ten years and they will be micro-fusion powered. We have designed and are testing a variety of models. I will be replacing my helicopters with a 47-passenger model. The new flight controller is hands only. But it has not been given approval for use for disabled pilots."

"Why not?"

"Rudolf said it was a safety issue and he got enough votes in the Senate. So, the disabled pilot program is on hold, for now."

"So just like that, they shut the project down?"

"We have to respect his vote. That doesn't mean I cannot work to improve it, but until then it can only be used in a flight simulator. I have experts reading his report and working on the legal issues. He does have some valid points. We cannot provide controllers for every disability and must provide a report defining who is able enough to use it."

"That is better than nothing."

"His company will be the principal contractor, but we have revived the Banshee Two program as a two-seat, two-engine, ground to space plane. We will be using the Banshee One design. But it will be made with materials from the prototype. It will have the nose cannon, internal missile bays, engines, armour, and electronic warfare systems from the prototype. It will have the improved micro ultra-wave detector from the Banshee Plus that you flew."

"I miss flying, and with luck soon we will have disabled controllers in real aircraft, not just flight simulators."

"I look forward to seeing you in one of my VTOLs."

"Me too. Now that you are seventeen don't forget to enrol in either medical, fleet or the Knights. If you don't do military service, the crown goes back to the previous owner."

"Relax, I know Grandfather was hoping I would forget. I know how to keep my title. As does Sora, but she will take maternity leave to stand in for me. I am required to do seven tours. But she and the others will return at some point to active duty. At some point, Izanami will be on the throne."

"Seven? Some Admirals have only done one tour!"

"I know. I have signed up for two years as a Knight and then two as Sky-Force. That will count as one tour of duty. Then I will transfer to the Imperial Navy as a pilot and enter the shuttle program. Hopefully, by then, we will have new ground to space shuttles. But at the rate, the Senate wants to introduce new technology I will learn to fly a chemical rocket orbiter and pilot the slow gravity drive shuttles while Rudolf tests the new shuttles."

"Are you going to be flying a suborbital?"

"Yes and no. The suborbital was to be retired and replaced by long-range missiles. Instead, the current planes will undergo a refit. They will get my inline fusion engines, my compact fusion plant and new electronics. There are going to be two production models, both will be V/STOL. The prime contractor will be Reinhart Aerospace but will be in conjunction with Kaede Enterprises and Hashimoto Defence. The first model will be high-speed, long-range interceptor, able to break orbit and remain in space for days. The second is a larger, wide-body, versatile, V/STOL craft for cargo, refuelling, radar or carry large numbers of passengers to and from space. Soon we going to build gravity beam launch sites to lift shuttles to and from orbit, but new shuttles will be able to self-launch to and from the world using contragravity technology and fusion propulsion."

"That sounds better than the suborbital I flew."

"Yes. The new engines are quieter and much faster than the old model. They still glide down to flight level, then land like a regular jet."

"Son, always make sure you have enough promotion points before transferring, or you will be demoted to Cadet each time you transfer. Every opportunity you get to do a course, you do it. You earn more points by having more skills than you will by completing missions."

"Thanks, father."

Hiro stopped and turned the chair on his own. "I will marry Freya this Yule, and not because you are giving me a yacht. I want to call her mother, and if my father objects, you confront him. She may not be the one who gave birth to you, but she thinks of you as her son."

Kaede poked Hiro on the nose. "I look forward to sailing rings around Viktor with you soon."

"We will."

"If you have time, maybe later we can go to the simulator in the workshop, and you can show me the cockpit of a sub-orbital?"

"It is not a complicated craft, which can make it more dangerous to fly. You don't do a lot of steering or even stick work in a sub-orbital. That is because they climb so fast most of the work is automatic, but you must watch your instruments like a hawk. The fun part is cutting the engines and gliding. You go from pilot to passenger until landing."

"Sounds fun. But the new model has more in common with a shuttle than the rocket with wings you flew."

"I see."

"I will be fun learning together."

"Great... Later, son," Hiro said, waving to Freya as she waited for them on the path ahead.

It was noon. Kaede stood in the indoor firing range and lined up on the target with the Viper 2. Abel adjusted his stance.

"Balance, you always be ready to move," Abel said.

"Yes ma'am," Kaede said.

"You out rank me and are familiar, you can just call me Abel."

"Abel, have you ever dated?"

"Not for a long time. Why?"

"You're hot. I mean you know Toshiko is beautiful, but you light up a room."

"I am here to train you, not date you. What are the four rules of gun safety?"

"Always treat the gun as if it was loaded. Never point a gun at something you do not intend to shoot. Keep your fingers away from the safety and the trigger until you are in position and ready to shoot. Always be aware of what is around and behind your target."

Abel went to push Kaede, he stepped to one side.

"Now today I am going to teach you to shoot long-range, only all the targets will be moving slowly to you. You need to shoot them all. You must be able to switch from long-range shooting to short-range, to switching from rifle to gun. It sounds easy, but over time you will tyre, need to reload and not always land a kill shot. What are my special rules of shooting?"

"Count your shots, so you know how many bullets I have left without looking. Don't stare at the target, be aware of the surroundings. Two in the chest is better than one in the head. Don't stare at your chest or bottom."

Crisis

"You break the last one often. I am going to have to put you in a cold bath. I swear you're worse than Abelard."

"I hope not, I want to do better with women than him."

"Then learn to look at my eyes and not my curves," Abel said in Kaede's ear. She then stepped back. "Get ready."

"All six targets?" Kaede asked glancing at her then at the targets.

"All six will move towards you. Then six more and so on for an unknown number of waves each time," Abel said putting on ear muffs and blowing a whistle.

The targets started to move, Kaede started to shoot.

Six hours later Kaede dragged himself into his room.

It was 7 pm when Kaede sat at the head of the table in the ballroom. The room was full of clan members, nobles, and the Senate. They had their prime wives with them. Weyland sat with Dain.

Abel came in wearing a white leather cap, vinyl dress and a pair of large strap white platforms with a red K on the side.

"These are such great shoes," Abel said she leaned over. "How did you make a dress that fits perfectly without taking my measurements?"

"I looked at your record and used the measurements from your last dress uniform fitting," Kaede said.

"Naughty boy, the next time you want my measurements, ask, don't look them up," Abel said as she softly poked Kaede's nose with her finger.

"My first best seller. How to not impress a beautiful girl by Emperor Kaede."

Abel laughed. "I give you a C minus for the effort. At least you didn't look up my age," Abel said with a gentle tap on his arm.

"You don't look a day over 21."

"Careful, Dain may be my brother, but he is very protective of me."

"Since I cannot ask you to come up to my room, I have to settle for asking you to enjoy my party."

"I can take you to the firing range."

"Where are Dain and Abelard?"

"I couldn't care! All they do is arguing. Each wants the other to move out. They forget the fact I own the mansion."

"What happened?"

"Abelard entered the kitchen in Dain's wing to speak to him, Weyland was wearing only an apron.

"Oh. How is the car?"

"I want to buy it from you. Can you paint it pink and change the interior to cream?"

"That is a test model. The Hashimoto Sports Plus is not finished, but I will take a pre-order."

"Why? Are you mad that I copied your order system?"

"I am aware that Abel Fashions now has a made to fit option. But, I welcome competition. I only patented the technology, not the idea."

"How refreshing, my brother would be furious even if it was me who used one of his ideas without discussion. What did you think of my new site?"

"I like your panties," Kaede said with a wink.

Abel saw Dain enter. "Call me in a year." She winked at Kaede and walked off.

Kaede was looking at the gifts when Sora arrived with Akiko. She bowed. "My apologies, I forget that I am speed limited."

"Just in time," Kaede said as Izanami, followed by Mako and Miko, raced up. Izanami went to take Kaede by the arm. Sora slapped her. Lord Yasuo Iti stood and tapped his glass. Kaede turned to face them.

Lord Yasuo Iti raised his glass. "Emperor, Happy Birthday," Yasuo said.

Beside him was Shiori in an electric wheelchair.

Kaede walked up with Sora beside him, with Akiko pulling Izanami to walk beside her. Mako and Miko followed.

General Feygold stood as Kaede approached with the group. "My daughter, Hilda, wants me to legitimatize your little private army."

"I will, but they know I cannot legally do that until they have resolved some legal issues and that case is closed," Kaede said.

"I keep telling her that," Adalwulf said, looking at Hilda.

"I am told you put the *Owl* back into Spacedock?" Hilda said.

"It will be the first ship to use the new missiles, drives, shields, deflectors, detection package and electronic warfare system," Kaede said.

"I am interested in your new VTOL; a single pilot tank-killer," an excited Adalwulf said. "When is the next evaluation trial?"

"Tomorrow. If Hilda is up to the task, I can have her flown to the proving grounds. The controls and other systems are the same as our standard attack helicopter," Kaede said.

"Not much she cannot fly, but what about size?" Adalwulf said.

"No problem. The Aggressor comes in the scout, standard and the super aggressor. The first two are for smaller Elves, but the third is more tank than aircraft and built for Mountain Elves," Kaede said, winking at Hilda.

"Great," Adalwulf said.

"Thank you, General," Kaede said.

Walking away, Sora punched his arm.

"What?" Kaede asked.

"That is for flirting with her," Sora said.

"Careful, hitting the Emperor is a crime," Kaede said.

"I saw nothing," Toshiko said.

"She is a fine woman," Kaede said.

"Do I need to dunk you in an ice bath?" Toshiko asked.

"No ma'am."

"You are seventeen, not twenty-seven, so behave, or I will put you in a bath full of ice, again," Toshiko said.

After greeting more guests, Kaede headed into the Palace and to the entrance. A crowd of fans waited on the field on the other side of the road. Kaede stood on top of the stairs and waved.

Most of the group were young girls who screamed and waved signs that read, "Marry Me" or, "I love you."

Kaede looked at Toshiko and said, "I want to shake some hands, and sign autographs."

"Stay by my side, and do not get in arms' reach of them. If the mob surges, Yuki will drag you to the safe room and leave you in a bath full of ice for a year," Toshiko said.

A line of house guards formed between Kaede and the crowd along the tape line as Toshiko checked Kaede's vest. When they walked past the group, many screamed with joy and held up cards, or held out their phones screaming "Friend me.". Any girl that even looked like lifting her top was stopped and taken the back of the group.

A girl went to throw flowers, and Toshiko stepped in front of Kaede as the guards pulled her aside. Then Toshiko noticed the crowd pushing forward, and she pushed Kaede inside as the guard started dispersing the groups.

Out of the corner of his eye, Kaede saw Galené standing at the end of the line. He looked at her, and she disappeared into the crowd, as Knights rushed him inside. The iron doors closed and the shutters came down. Outside, the group was told to disperse and go home.

Toshiko looked at Yuki, then Kaede. "The parade tomorrow is going to be a nightmare."

"I forget the Founder's Day Parade. I told Adalwulf the VTOL test is tomorrow morning," Kaede said.

"I will contact him, and due to a security issue, we moved the test to later," Yuki said.

"Lady Toshiko, did you see the pink-haired girl at the end?" Kaede said.

"Hey!" Izanami said, running up.

"Relax 'Nami," Toshiko said to Izanami, then to Kaede, "I saw her."

"Hey, only Kaede gets to call me 'Nami," Izanami said.

"Did you say something, cadet?" Toshiko asked. Her eyes narrowed, and she leaned in close to Izanami. "Well?"

"I came to tell K—" Izanami said.

"The Emperor," Toshiko interrupted.

"I came to tell the Emperor, it is time to get ready," Izanami said.

"Right, Toshiko, start letting them in, and I will go get ready," Kaede said.

"Are you sure about this?" Toshiko asked.

"It will be fine. While the crowd heads to the mall, we will use the tunnels," Kaede said.

"It is not getting there that worries me. It is you leaping off the stage into the arms of a thousand teenage girls," Toshiko said.

"I did consider a stage dive," Kaede said.

"You would not last five minutes alone with them."

"It would be a glorious death."

"Naughty boy."

"I should slap you," Izanami said.

"Izanami, are you jealous of those vixens?" Toshiko asked, hand on Izanami's shoulder.

"Me jealous? Of them? Please, don't make me laugh. I bet they are now screaming at sailors on the docks. I am worried my K-K will catch something from them," Izanami said.

"What would you know about that?" Toshiko looked down at Izanami.

"I know about mouth infections. You should give K-K a shot of penicillin," Izanami said.

"An antiviral drug is used to treat the kissing disease, 'Nami, not penicillin," Kaede said.

"Whatever," Izanami retorted.

"Izanami Li, you and I are going to have a chat about jealousy very soon. Kaede, I do not care if you chase streetwalkers and groupies when you are eighteen, but dare touch one now, and I will make your life a misery for tossing away the crown for a cheap hussy," Toshiko said, tapping Kaede on the chest.

"Yes, my lady," Kaede responded in a hushed tone as he bowed to Toshiko. Behind Toshiko, Izanami poked her tongue out at Kaede.

"Good. We will go down to the kitchens and leave via the north side tunnel. If the crowd is well-behaved, then I will escort you and Izanami to the centre stage of the mall. After you sing, meet a few selected members of the crowd, and then it is back to the Palace."

Kaede responded with a nod. It was not long before Kaede was dressed as a pop idol and on stage with Izanami.

They sang:

"Do you feel like your flame had gone out?
Do you feel like a flightless bird?
Do you feel like you are trying to fly into the wind?
Do you feel like starting again?

Do you feel that everything just caved in?
You try to scream, but nothing comes out.
Do you know there is always another chance!
Do you know you can always change your life?

Baby spread your wings, ignite your flame, go light up the sky!
Own your life and fly away. Leave behind all that pain.

You are a Firebird; you can fly again.
You can soar on wings of fire and own the night.
You can make them go Oh, Oh, Oh
You can make them go Ah, Ah, Ah
You can be Yeah, Yeah, Yeah
You can be a colour burst,
You can light up the sky.

Do not let them feel you are a waste of space.
Do not let them be in your face.
Take control, spread your wings, and fly away...
Everything will be all right.

The reason they make you cry
The reason they shut that door
They do not see what you are worth!
They do not see you are so much more...

Baby spread your wings, ignite your flame, go light up the sky!
Own your life and fly away. Leave behind all that pain.

You are a Firebird; you can fly again.
You can soar on wings of fire and own the night.
You can make them go Oh, Oh, Oh
You can make them go Ah, Ah, Ah
You can be Yeah, Yeah, Yeah
You can be a colour burst,
You can light up the sky.

Boom, boom, boom
You light up the room

You fly so high
You soar over the moon.

Baby spread your wings, ignite your flame, go light up the sky!
Own your life and fly away. Leave behind all that pain.

You are a Firebird; you can fly again.
You can soar on wings of fire and own the night.
You can make them go Oh, Oh, Oh
You can make them go Ah, Ah, Ah
You can be Yeah, Yeah, Yeah
You can be a colour burst,
You can light up the sky.

You are awe, awe, awesome.
You are boom, boom, boom
You are yeah, yeah, yeah
You are a Firebird, SHINE!"

The crowd screamed and cheered. Kaede held his hands up and said, "I love you all."

Toshiko looked at the crowd, as Kaede signed autographs and posed for photos. Not all were teenage girls trying to get near Kaede.

Kaede and Izanami were taken back to the Palace via the tunnels under the island, up the elevator, a stop to change, then in formal robes to be flown north to Abel Mall.

Kaede sat in a box with Abel.

At the front of the parade was a marching band from the Academy, a local private school owned by Abel. Various floats followed it, schools, different local businesses, and small sporting groups.

"I hope my brother doesn't offend you?"

"No. I actually like Dain, he is an impressive character and is a patriot. His bluster is not the ranting of a madman, but a carefully constructed act. Sometimes he is right."

"Really?"

"Not that you get my grandfather to admit, but he is fond of Dain."

"Yes."

"I have a question about Abelard."

"Oh?"

"I want to understand Dain. The records state Dain and Eve had a son, then his father married Eve. Was Eve Dain's wife?"

"Our mother Lilith was queen, she had a son with Adamos when they got married. Dain and I were a born on her one-hundredth birthday. She found out her Dain, was a homosexual, and she was angry. It was illegal then, and the penalty was death. Our eldest brother, Abelard, had died in the war. Dain was eighteen, we don't know why Lilith left him alone with her assistant Eve, but later we learnt Eve used magic illegally on Dain to well—you know. What we also did not know until a Demon possessed later Eve. As soon as Eve was with child, she got Adamos to kill Dain's lover, banish Lilith, marry her and she sent Dain and me south to a fortress. Eve used magic our father, she ran society into the ground with stupid laws that worked against us. Social programs sounded great, but over time, people became lazy, unmotivated and dependant on the state. No one wanted to live beyond the walls where Wolves, Ogres and Ice waited."

"It must have been a terrible time."

"Many refused to have púca. Eve founded the

Blood-Witches to force pregnancy. The Witches were both Inquisition, Blood-Witches, and Eve's private security. They were backed by female knights known as Amazons. All our father cared about was his next meal."

"Why would anyone not want to have púca?"

"Many felt the end was near, others just wanted to party, and take drugs. Many people would drink until they fell, and sink to new levels of depravity. The reaction to stop self-destruction was just as bad. Mind control magic was used to force people to join the military and was even used to forced marriages. But if you really want to understand Dain then know this. Dain was always happy as a little boy, he was never angry, and the three of us always played together. Then one-day Adamos put Abelard into uniform and sent him to the wall. He died that day. Lilith was no longer interested in developing magic, she wanted the king to fund her research into space ships. We were raised by Eve's Witches who treated Dain poorly just for being a boy."

"I am sorry."

"Dain loves his son, but he doesn't want to talk about Eve. She warped his view of females. She was a Devotees."

"Devotion to what?"

"They were secret society who worship the Goblin Moloch who resided in Babylon. They were spoilt brats who always had to win. They engaged in market manipulation, nepotism, murder, and blackmail to get their way. They were always finding new ways to suck the fun out of anything with regulations and taxes to have the state fund their charities, which were a sham. They held fundraisers that spent more on them than helping the victims of war.

They were depraved and were selling arms and secrets to the Ogres, via the Goblin traders."

"Traitors have not changed."

"No, they are always the same. Tell me, can you accept losing?" Abel stood and looked at Kaede.

"My father once said, if the red carpet is rolled out, he will never strive."

"If you can lose gracefully, I will like you a little more than very much."

Sora and Akiko were leaving cooking class in the Palace kitchens when Hitomi came up to Sora and said, "Got time to talk?", then looking at Akiko, "Alone?"

Sora looked at Akiko and nodded, and Akiko headed to the elevator.

Takahiro came out. "Everything all right, Ladies?"

"Lord Takahiro, I have a couple of private questions for Sora and the files on two girls, twins, whom I think she should consider."

"Great cooking as usual Lady Sora," Takahiro said, returning to the kitchen.

Hitomi lead Sora down the hall until they come to an empty break room, took her inside and closed the door.

"You could have just called and had a courier bring me the files," Sora said.

Hitomi took the files out of her bag. "I know the Dark Elves have some robot thing on your data lines. I don't want to get mixed up in security operations."

"The names will leak soon; the media are watching me.

It is so hard, what with almost every qualified lady either a Knight, married or over one hundred."

"He can still marry them; it's just that they do not get extra child support or paid leave."

"Yes, but they don't qualify to have a third púca either."

"He can hire surrogates. Trust me, there are more than enough Blood-Witches who would do it."

"I know there are enough Blood-Witches who do it with him. I am sure most would prefer the *do it with me in my bed many times* method."

"Yes, my desk has a pile of applications. Most of the Blood-Witches are more than willing to offer their services if conception is natural."

"So why do I need to consider these two?"

"Fumiko and Ume are identical twins. They are genii in both recalling facts and problem-solving. They scored higher than Izanami on all tests."

"Is that why you didn't want to leave the files on my desk in case she tore them up?"

"Something like that."

"She isn't that jealous of other girls. She is worried about gold diggers. You know the smarter they are, the longer it takes to find them out."

"What about you and Hilda?"

"That is different. Kaede is turned on by her physique. I do worry he might run off with a bodybuilder one of these days."

"I do not think so. Yes, Kaede will stray, but he will always come back if you keep providing him with a place where he can be himself."

"We would be a perfect match for him if I was one dress size and two cup sizes smaller."

"No. Izanami is too volatile to be Empress, and besides, there are different kinds of intellect. You are far more cunning and calculating than her."

"Are you suggesting I am a gold digger?"

"The right kind. You want to stand by Kaede and propel him to success."

"I do."

"Does Kaede know Akiko does more than wearing your clothes?"

"Yes, he knows about us."

"Will Akiko get between you and Kaede?"

"No. I know how to handle relationships within the harem. Akiko knows to show Kaede more physical and emotional attention than me."

"Good. I brought the girls with me. I would like you to consider inviting them to the wedding as your flower girls."

"I'll have Mako and Miko take care of them."

"The girls live at Hashimoto House. They already on scholarship to the Academy. They formed friendships with other girls and don't want to graduate early."

"I will arrange extra security."

"Also, they are magically active, rare at that age, since it usually appears during the last stage of puberty."

"Any other problems?"

"What do you want me to do with the applications from the married women?"

"Keep them. Now, this is between you and me. Kaede has a problem. A too-much-wealth problem. The price of many commodities was expected to fall, but it hasn't. That is due to the high demand for resources driven by exports to the many worlds beyond the Empire."

"He has many problems. According to my calculations, he can support 108 wives each with a dozen púca."

"That is far more than he can legally wed, and then there is the population cap."

"The Senate is considering expanding the number of legal marriages to twenty."

"Not enough, but over thirty and many will not receive enough attention."

"Some applications you added have with the words 'he can do anything he wants to me', and some of the photos are very candid.

"Do you want to remove them from the list?"

"No, but with all the leaks, hacks and security agents reading my emails, best we only discuss them in private and not scan those photos into the system. After the honeymoon, I intend to start interviews. But the only one I want him doing anything with and everything to is me."

"After the wedding, you best let me discuss fetishes with him. He is at the age when males are in a rush to do anything and everything."

"Yes. As for Kaede's púca, I insist they all be raised in the Palace. If I need to, I will hire a plane load of wet nurses."

"That might not be a good idea. You know Kaede still drinks breast milk?"

"I know. I plan on being Kaede's morning tea."

"After signing the marriage contract, it is traditional for the couple to be witnessed making love. Do you consent to this?"

"Of course. I want a weeklong celebration of love to

surround my wedding. Not only do I want to have all the ladies watch us, but I want to watch him make love to them. I will do anything for him."

"That is something I will bring up with the female guests. I will have some of the more eager ladies meet you. Legally, he needs your approval, but he must have a say in whom he impregnates, marries or just dates."

"I know. I do not mind whom Kaede chooses, so long as he comes back to me."

"Even Hilda?"

"I used to fear he liked her more than me because she is more masculine than me, but now she is like a sister to me, and I trust Kaede."

"Yes, I notice you have no adultery clause for him, in fact, you do not expect much from him."

"He can have anyone he wants so long as he comes home to me."

"It will take me a long time to interview all the woman. He has paid for 1,500 interviews. After I am done, you must meet them as well."

"We can use that to our advantage, as it will take years to go through the list. You can stay with us, and we can house fifty in the top residence. Give them five private meetings in the Palace, and that gives time for the others to come of age. He will only be able to satisfy between five and ten a day. As per our contract, one day a week he is all mine, and Kaede has every Sunday off."

"Do you know where Kaede will be training?"

"He will be training at different stations, but most of his training will be in the Palace. We have a security training centre for the Knights stationed here and for them to train the house guards. He will also attend a couple of private training facilities, but after we have married, he will be going to the Academy to learn magic. Why?"

"He will be with Nori for most of that time away."

"Nori will do anything Kaede tells him to do. You don't have to worry about Nori. He knows when to fade into the background."

"Yes, but the question is how attached will they get on long missions?"

"Emi is in love with Kaede. I thought Nori was the only one who doesn't know."

"He knows, in fact, he loves the idea of his mother running off with him. My question to you is about Nori, not his mother."

"Well, if you know Nori likes Kaede that much, then you know Nori would never hurt Kaede."

"Kaede needs to prove he is the alpha male."

"I know, but I think your plan goes too far."

"At least consider it?"

"I haven't thrown it out. I just think Kaede has so many things to worry about, that proving he is the leader of the pack will come in time."

"He needs to establish himself."

"He is confident, competitive and has swagger."

"He needs to get the girls. I think he has to steal a bride."

"He has."

"Lady Cerise and the others don't count. It must be a tough challenge and generate a scandal. He has to handle family drama, public outcry and paranoia from the lords in court."

"I will find someone."

"There are plenty of married women interested in him."

"Why?"

"He has to stand out more, but at the same time try not to be everyone's friend. He needs to dominate his peers. Right now, Kaede popularity is high, but as an artist. As a leader, the people see him as weak. Leaders need to do what is right, not what is popular. Also, he lacks flaws to set himself apart."

"I am working on him been a strong, decisive leader. He prefers to be minimal in his public announcements. He comes up with ideas and relegates to others. He sees the noise and bluster of public debate as time wasting."

"You come off a little too domineering. You need to let Kaede dominate you, at least in public."

"I am not."

"Sora!"

"It isn't my fault he backs down."

"So, next time I see him stand up to you, you're not going to make a scene and scream until he walks away?"

"I don't do that!" Sora exclaims looking away.

"Goodnight Lady Sora, if you going to be like that, I cannot help you," Hitomi said in a soft voice, standing up to go.

"Wait. Please!" Sora pleads, she bowed and said, "I have to be tough too."

"To the other wives, to the staff, not to him. It is your place to mop the floor with any gigolo that winks at you. It is your duty to stand besides, complement and defend your husband in public. Whenever you disagree, you do so in the privacy of your office. You organise his life according to his wishes, not to colour coordinate his office and private space with your shoes."

"Oh."

"Will you leave his private space alone and not argue with him?"

"Yes, ma'am."

"If you don't, then I will put you over my knee."

"Yes, ma'am."

"Good. Sleep well Sora. There is hope for you yet."

"Goodnight and thank you, Lady Hitomi."

CHAPTER 15

LAST WEEK OF FREEDOM

August 25, 11580. Imperial Palace.

Kaede was in his Palace office when Freya and Masako came in.

"Emperor, have you seen Izanami?" Masako asked.

"She left with Sora, Akiko, Mako and Miko. They are flying to New Tokyo to go shopping," Kaede replied.

"She asked me to make major changes to her wedding dress, I told her to meet me in my workshop," Freya said.

"The Palace dressmakers have a mannequin of her," Kaede replied.

"We need her, they are using it to finish her bridesmaid's gown," Masako said.

"I have one in my workshop," Kaede said.

"Why do you have a mannequin of Izanami?" Freya asked looking concerned.

"It isn't like that, Mother," Kaede said.

"It isn't that big a secret. Everyone knows you make Izanami's clothes," Masako said.

"Really?" a surprised Freya asked, "I thought hand made by Kaede was just bad marketing."

"No," Kaede replied, "I am hurt you think I would do that."

"I am sorry," Freya said. "Is that what you do in your workshop?"

"No. I don't make clothes and shoes often, but I make all our competition clothes," Kaede replied.

"Really?" Masako asked.

"Every year I have designed and then made dresses, shoes and stocking for Izanami and then after Yule, they go on sale in my store," Kaede replied.

"In a way, it is rather romantic," Masako said.

"I hope you will not get upset with me, but I never have been to your store," Freya said.

"The Kaede Shop is a unique fashion experience; we don't sell off the rack, we will make clothes to fit anybody regardless of gender, race, or shape," Kaede said.

"How?" Freya asked.

"You step into a body scanner and follow the prompts. You see how you look on a full-size display, then pay and order, then we deliver," Kaede replied.

"We better get going, or he will tell us all about the body scanners and order system later," Freya said, heading for the door, she turned and asked, "Oh, can you have a guard less us in your workshop?"

"Sorry, but I cannot allow you inside my workshop," Kaede replied.

"Will you come down soon?" Masako asked at the door.

"Yes," Kaede replied.

"Good," Masako said, closing the door.

Kaede entered the dressmakers' workshop pushing a naked, poseable, lifelike mannequin of Izanami. On the workbench, Freya was cutting the white dress in half while Masako was laying out a bolt of white embroidered silk.

"What are you doing?" Kaede asked.

"She wants a Two-Piece Gown with three different styles of detachable skirts, each to have three different three-layer lace, folded and layered lace petticoat," Freya said.

"I know, Nami just messaged me she needs a pair of red open-toed pumps for those, a pair of black heeled sandals for the black three-layer ruffled petticoat and a rose pair of heels," Kaede said.

"Will you make them?" Freya asked.

"Yes," Kaede said, "I have the time."

"Do you have time to help us?" Masako pleaded.

Kaede spent hours in his workshop laying out material, cutting, and sewing. He assembled the shoes on a pair of feet. He picked up the stop watch, clicked it off, went and opened the door and went back to Masako and Freya.

Masako was adjusting the hem of a white knee-length skirt, while Freya was trying different clip-on straps on the topless dress top.

Kaede made a couple of calls, soon a dozen dressmakers entered. He walked around the room assigned them to a project as more arrived in small groups, some pushed sewing machines with them.

Soon all the skirts, petticoats, panties, bras, stockings and other articles of clothing had a trio of female Flower Elves cutting out patterns, trimming hems, fitting to the dress mannequin or sewing.

"You're not tired?" a tired Masako asked.

"I am fine," Kaede replied.

"Must be wonderful to be young, I have never seen you tired, you disappear for an hour, and come back fresh," Masako said.

"He naps in his office, workshop, and I would not be surprised he has a cot in his private office behind the throne room," Freya said.

"Mother!" Kaede exclaimed.

"Oh relax, I am not teasing you," Freya said.

"You and Izanami are so alike," Masako said, adjusting the top of the dress.

"I am not. 'Nami has a temper!" Kaede said as Izanami entered the workshop behind him.

"What!" Izanami squawked.

"Now you show up," Masako grumbled.

"I told you I was coming back early," Izanami replied. She saw the wedding dress and screamed, "What have you done to my wedding dress?"

"Izanami, calm down, you told us to split it," Masako said.

"Not *my* wedding dress, my bride's maid dress!" Izanami cried. She ran out crying.

"I will go take care of this," Freya said running out after her.

Masako looked at Kaede. Kaede stood on a chair and called out, "Everyone, third and fourth meal with drinks are on me. I will pay to have you all do the same for her bride's maid dress tomorrow."

Freya ran after Izanami, who was pressing the call button on the elevator. She put her hand on Izanami's shoulder, Izanami turned, and Freya put her arms around Izanami. "It is my fault dear; you said the dress for the wedding."

"You don't understand."

"I know the dress is plain. Sora just wants to shine in her wedding kimono."

"I don't mind that. I have huge breasts, and they jiggle. Sora, Akiko, Mako and Miko have perfect breasts that don't even jiggle as they walk, then Sora puts me in a strapless gown," Izanami said, then cried loudly.

Freya patted her on the back. "I know, having big breasts is not all that great."

"Easy for you to say. You are big."

"Oh, trust me I would love to have breasts like you. My shoulders ache, and they feel like swollen udders. I am wearing a sports bra. Most bras don't last a week."

"I wear sports bras. Sora makes them."

"I like to be able to wear a bikini without having my breasts flop out."

"I know, took me ages to make one."

"You should sell them."

"What?" Izanami asked.

"I would buy them."

"Really?"

"Yes."

"You're not just saying that?"

"You're a very talented and beautiful girl," Freya said, she turned Izanami around and said, "We are going back. You going to apologise for the mix-up and thank everyone for their hard work."

"Must I?" Izanami asked in a loud, high-pitched shriek.

"Yes, you must," Freya said, looking at Izanami.

"It doesn't bother him."

"He hired a team to get the dress ready. The least you can do is help finish the job."

"But—" Izanami said, but Freya put her hand on Izanami's lips.

"Too late to unmake all the changes to the dress now. You're going to be a princess, act like one. You should be in control of your emotions."

"But-"

"I know it is your wedding dress. You can wear the long skirt to get married, then the short skirt when you are walking around the room, then dance in the asymmetrical skirt. So, do whatever you need to do to put both dresses on sale because image how many are going to rush to buy one soon as you walk outside in it?"

"Wow, that is an excellent idea. Come. We have a lot of work to do, we need to put out an evening dress to go with," Izanami said racing back towards the workshop.

"Don't forget to apologise to everyone," Freya called out.

Izanami stopped and turned. "Can I call you mother too?" she asked playfully.

"I would like that very much," Freya said.

August 30, 11580. New Shanghai.

An Ogre entered a Super K hardware store, grabbed a cart and headed to the rear. He walked past a male holding at a hedge trimmer as a sales representative spoke fast in Mandarin of the virtues of a chainsaw.

A dark-skinned girl with pink hair blew bubbles while stacking batteries. The Ogre went to grab a lantern battery. She took it, stood, and faced him. "You don't want that one," she said in Mandarin.

The Ogre looked puzzled. "I want that one," he said in slow Mandarin.

"Your Mandarin is terrible," she said in Germanic, putting the battery on a trolley full of batteries. "These batteries no good."

"What do you mean?"

"Double life battery," the girl said in a thick Asian accent while holding up a large lantern battery which had the brand 'Hashimoto Energy'. Over the stand was a sign, 'Hashimoto Energy: Twice the power or twice your money back.'

The Ogre looked at the battery. He heard nothing, he looked around. The store was nearly empty, the sale representative was escorting the man out the door. Galené saw a handgun sticking out the back of his pants.

The Ogre reached for his gun under his jacket.

"Looking for this?" Galené said, putting the Ogre's nine mm handgun to his back.

"Lady, you have no idea who you are messing with," the Ogre snarled, turning to face her.

"Non-Elves get ten years just for illegal possession of a firearm," Galené said, ejecting the clip, then the bullet in the chamber. She tossed him the gun.

"Is this the part where you tell me if I rat out my friends, I get a reduced sentence? Well fuck you, I ain't no rat," the Ogre sneered.

Galené took off her cap, pulled out a 13mm five shot revolver and put it to his penis.

"No, this is the part when you tell me where to find Galen or the only masturbating you will do will be for your cell mate," Galené said.

"A 13mm handgun! So, you are a Knight. Well, the joke is on you; he is not part of our crew," the Ogre said.

"Tell me where to find him, and I will let you walk away with your battery. I don't care about Shade and his smuggling operation, I just want my brother," Galené said.

"Hurry," the nervous male by the door called out.

"Haven't seen him since the raid on our asteroid hideout," the Ogre said.

"Try again. I know you sold Galen rocket fuel," Galené countered and pressed the gun hard against the Ogre's penis.

"That was the Chosen, they sent him to pick it up," the Ogre said.

"Who are the Chosen?" Galené asked.

"We're out of time. I think the security guard has noticed us," the salesman yelled as he was running from the front door to the rear exit.

Galené looked to see two security guards looking in the front double clear plastic sliding door.

The Ogre took advantage of her inattention to him. He grabbed and twisted the gun out of her hand. He then tried to headbutt Galené.

Galené backflipped, and kicked the gun out of his hand. It skittered under the shelves.

The Ogre ran at her and swung his fist.

Galené ducked under his punch and hit him in the gut.

The Ogre swung his arm like a club at her head, clubbing Galené on the side of the head, and knocked her into the shelving.

Outside, one of the security guards tried to open the doors while the other was on his phone. The guy with Galené ran out the back. The guards upholstered their 9mm pistol and ran to the side of the building.

The Ogre leaned over, grabbed Galené's hair and said, "You hit like a girl."

"I will," Galené said. She poked the confused in the eye and then kicked him in the testicles. The Ogre dropped to his knees, growled and let go of her.

"I am a girl," Galené said as she picked up two large lantern batteries as she stood. She then clubbed him on the temples with the batteries, one in each hand.

Dazed, the Ogre tried to stand. Galené kicked him in the forehead, leaving a mark of her heel. He fell face down. She pulled his top over him, then fished her 13mm out from under the shelves.

Galené's accomplice ran out of the building, and around the corner came the security guards. They pointed their weapons at him and yelled, "Freeze."

"Don't shoot," the male said with his hands up. "An Ogre came in, he acted crazy and tried to rob us. I got the other customers out, but he is still inside. I think he has a hostage."

The guards went to look, and the male ran off. Galené heard them coming in. She ducked down took the Ogre's identification, keys and phone.

Galené put the store cap back on, make a crying face and ran sobbing towards the guards, "Help me please."

Soon Galené was wrapped in a blanket, and they left in the back of their security patrol car. The guards left her alone and went inside.

Galené ditched the blanket, got in the front of the vehicle, tapped the screen on the centre console and selected run identification. She swiped the Ogre's Identification card over the computer screen in the car's centre console, selected alert another agency then sent it Office of Emperor's Security. Are clicking yes on are you sure, she got out of the car, left the store cap, reversed her jacket and walked away.

Kaede got a call from Adalwulf. "Emperor, I have a security matter to discuss, which involves Galené Fey."

"What are the details?"

"A dark-skinned Elf with bright pink hair knocked out an Ogre in a hardware store in New-Shanghai to prevent a robbery. The City Guards arrested the Ogre for illegal possession of a handgun. A clerk fleeing claimed he pulled the gun and tried to rob the place. Simple enough you think? Well, it is not. The female was already in the store wearing a store uniform when the Ogre came. She was well-spoken and fluent in Mandarin, so they left her alone in the back of a patrol car because they thought she was a witness to a robbery. But then she ran the Ogre's identification and tried to send it to the Palace. The message was flagged and routed to Guard command. By the time they raised the alarm, she had left already. The Ogre claimed she attacked him and that he was there to buy a lantern battery. They still charged him with illegal possession of a firearm. Technical Support gathered many clean prints from the gun. When they checked them, they got immediate security alert on the girl. The fingerprints they took from the cruiser's console, a couple of batteries used to beat the Ogre and those on the gun belonged to Galené Fey. She was impersonating a store clerk. We don't know why she was after the Ogre, but the Inquisition has him now. The store's real staff were found locked in the back unharmed. Galené had pulled a gun on them, but then gave them a 100 gold each. She had used lawn chairs and zip ties from the garden section to tie them up. She had help, a local pickpocket she hired to lift the store manager's keys. Her accomplice was caught a couple of blocks away still in the store uniform. He is cooperating but appears to have no ties to Galené. He claims she found him the night before picking pockets in a bar. He was also handed over to the Inquisition. That is all I have for you."

"I am going to get my investigation team to New-Shanghai. I hope we are not going to have any trouble?"

"None, Emperor."

"Good. I'll save you the trouble, and I will send a recording of this conversation to Patya. Prepare the Ogre to be transported to Inquisition HQ."

"HQ?"

"I am told Patya gets cranky if he goes for more than a week without a friendly chat with a suspect in the interrogation room."

"Yes, Emperor, he does."

On the top of a hotel, East Lake Luxury Apartments, on the east side of the lake, a figure in a black flight suit and helmet stepped out of the dark. He walked up to a female Silver Elf. She was dressed in a long black, tight, revealing, cotton dress, with black fishnets and ankle boots. She had a black kabuki mask on with solid red lens.

"Hello Gomorrah," Galen said.

"Here are the latest security codes," she said, handing over a memory stick.

"What does this get me?"

"Access to all the defence satellites, including live feeds of the city from Sky Watch. Using the IFFs provided on your missiles, it should give them five minutes of flight time. Anti-missile is on full alert, so you have one shot at this."

"Only five or maybe five?"

"Maybe. If we test it, the Imperials will reset the access codes, and we risk the Inquisition finding our operation. They have increased patrols, but other than missile defence, I don't know what the Navy and Guard are doing, but all

Knights not on duty in the wedding crowd and on active duty in full armour."

"Not going to help them when four mini-nukes go off around them."

"Once you launch, dimension shift and meet The Adamos at the arranged coordinates, they will only wait an hour for you."

Galen pocketed the memory stick, held up a clenched fist, and she responded with the same salute. He turned, took a step and vanished in a flash. She went to the stairs and went down a flight.

Galené drove the Ogre's car to an apartment building, it was a small room, toilet and a shower at the end of the hall. She found a couple of tins of cheap marijuana on top of the refrigerator and put them in her jacket pocket. No food inside the refrigerator just bottled water and take away menus on the door. She looked under the mattress, she found only used condoms. In his desk, she found pay stubs for Shady Lady Imports and Exports.

Galené drove to the industrial park. She parked and walked down the street carrying a large black backpack and motorcycle helmet. She stole a large pickup with a large metal push bar on the front, from a building centre. She drove it a couple of blocks to the warehouse. She parked down the block from a small import-export business near the airport.

'No time to be subtle,' Galené though.

Galené checked her vest, a small machine pistol, her

13mm revolver and wand. She put on her backpack and her motorcycle helmet. She drove fast towards the warehouse, she put her hand on her wand and cast *Quickness*, *Haste*, *Armour*, and *Shield*.

Galené drove fast into the loading area of the warehouse, crashing into the shelves, as it did, Galené cast the spell *Levitate* and then jumped out of the vehicle.

The Ogres scattered, and inside a couple of Ogres came out of the offices on top of the main office. Armed with light machine pistols, they ran to the car, as they did, they took shots at it. Galené ended *Levitation* and took cover until they stopped firing.

Galené rolled under the car and opened fire at them. She sprayed them with her machine pistol in her left hand, three of the five scattered. With the 13mm revolver, she shot an Ogre in the forehead, blood sprayed, and he collapsed in a heap.

The other Ogre went to shoot her with his machine pistol, and it jammed. Galené raced over, took cover behind some containers and reloaded. She saw the fuel drum behind her, it was marked 'Fuel danger: high explosive'. She looked at it.

"*He was just here,*" she thought to herself.

"*But he needs liquid hydrogen to make plasma, not liquid fuel,*" she thought.

Galené went to take a closer look at the drum, she went to touch it and stopped. No noise. She listened, the Ogres tried to sneak up on her.

"*I really should tell these idiots Elves can hear a rabbit's fart, but I rather kill them,*" Galené thought.

Galené crouched waited for one to show his head, soon as one did, she shot him in the head with her pistol.

They resumed fire, and she returned fire and killed another one.

Galené then heard a beep in her head. She closed her eyes and concentrated on her wand, and saw the words Armour spell flashing with '30 s' beside that.

"No need to check your mana, you're low," Galené thought.

"No shit," Galené thought.

"Roll out the barrel," Galené thought.

Galené went back at the drum, she tapped the sides. Empty. She rolled the drum out. They watched it roll to the middle of the room, then they laughed.

"It is empty," one yelled.

"No shit," Galené thought, *"Now what?"*

"Shoot," Galené thought.

Galené shot it.

The Ogres laughed again.

"Only in movies do they exploded," one taunted her. They headed towards the shelves.

Galené sniffed the air, the vapours of the liquid explosive spread fast. She put her hand on her wand, and it was slightly warm, *"Fully charged, renew armour?"* Galené thought.

"Produce Flame," Galené thought.

Galené drew her wand and pointed it the drum. A flame appeared over it. The explosion was not big, but it scattered the Ogres and set off a fire alarm. It had not set fire to anything.

Galené saw Shade and another Ogre leave the upstairs office. She came out shooting with her machine pistol the remaining Ogre guards. Then raced behind the stairs.

When the guard had reached the bottom, she stepped out and shot the guard in the back of the head and pointed her gun at Shade. "Where is he?"

"Fuck you!" Shade replied.

Galené shot the other Ogre in the forehead, and then put the revolver to Shade's penis.

"Where is Galen?" Galené asked.

"You just missed him, he left an hour ago," Shade replied.

"Tell me about the fuel? Why does he need it?" Galené asked.

"*Missiles,*" Galené thought.

Galené looked puzzled. Shade laughed, and made a rude gesture with his middle finger at her and said, "Bye bitch."

Shade faded into darkness laughing. Galené pulled the trigger, but Shade was gone.

Galené took one of the dead guard's phone and keys. She ran out to the car park and clicked the alarm on the keyring, then raced to the car that beeped, and it out of the city until it was out of fuel. She pulled over and got out. As she walked into the nearest residence, she dialled and number on the stolen phone.

"Imperial Palace, how many I direct your call?" the operator answered.

"Put Toshiko on," Galené said, walking through a park.

"Lady Toshiko is busy; who may I say is calling?" the operator said.

"I am sure all calls are screened and that you have run the number, know it belongs to an Ogre, where I am, and you're waiting for Voice Print Identification. Tell *Lady* Toshiko that Galené Fey is calling. Soon your system will confirm that and inform you that I am a wanted fugitive. I am calling from New-Shanghai from the phone that I just borrowed from an Ogre gangster. She will want to take my call," Galené said, as she walked up stairs and out onto the roof.

"Please hold," the operator said. She looked at the screen and image of Galené with *wanted* flashing over the image, alert Lady Toshiko. The operator pressed a button and a senior officer came over and looked at the screen.

Galené stood near the edge of the flat roof, her wand at the ready. In the distance sirens from patrol cars wailed.

"Galené," Toshiko said on the phone from the middle console of the command centre, looking at the big screen with a satellite zooming in on Galené.

"I just missed him. He bought liquid fuel from a couple of Ogre smugglers. Shade was there, but he vanished. Did you find the Ogre at the hardware store?"

"Yes."

"He is a bomb maker for Shade. You going to find bodies in Shady Lady Import and Export her in New Shanghai."

"What is your brother planning?"

"I told you, he plans to kill the Emperor."

"We do not have time to play games. Do you know what Galen is planning or not?"

"He keeps changing his plans. He is constantly on the move. I am sorry, he is still one step ahead of me."

"We know about the dark dimension. I need you to send me your spell book."

"No time to explain, there are many spells."

"Yes, and we three of them."

"Then you don't need my help. I have to stop my brother."

"We never see him appear or disappear and his spell residue is different from Shades. Galan can disappear, and a short time later he appears on the other side of the city."

"I don't have that spell."

"Did he hire the bomb maker?"

"I was trying to find out if he did and why before I was interrupted," Galené stepped on the ledge.

"Why do you have to stop him? Tell us how you are tracking him, and we will capture him," Toshiko said in a soft voice looking worried at the screen.

"Galen and Hiro were in Sky Force together, and something happened. Galen tried to get Hiro and me together. Hiro was his co-pilot. Something to do with a failed training mission and Hiro was promoted and transferred to the fleet as a starship pilot."

"Let us help you."

"Galen's new friends are using him, they're from outside the Empire, the attack is a just a distraction. The Free States are not going to attack without the backing of the Ogres. They want something from the vault. Something to do with a sword Lilith made. They have the spells, but not the casting device."

"Is that all you got for me?"

"Shade works for the Shadow Mafia. Shade just left New Shanghai, and this phone is one of his employee's. I will leave it here for you."

"Where is the plane Galen stole?"

"He enters the dark dimension, the Shadow Mafia and other pirates travel inside it."

"They can Gate a ship?"

"Yes."

"How can we block them," Toshiko asked, looking at the main screen, on the side screens cars and helicopters approaching her.

"I am sure if you look around the Shadow Dimension you will soon find what you can and cannot pass. They tried and found they cannot use it to enter the vault. Shallow water is like mud, so is UV light. Large bodies or water and thick metal walls have enough energy to block anything from moving through them. There is air in the shadow, but not the outer dimensions."

Galené saw the City Guard helicopter getting closer to her.

"Does anyone else have Galen's spell?"

Toshiko saw Galené stand. "You will figure it out, you're almost there. I am sorry, but I must go now."

"Stop playing games and come in."

"I cannot."

"Tell me what is going on right now, or I'll come find you, and when I do, I will rip every memory from your head until you beg to tell me to stop. I will Mind Probe you until your ears bleed. If you think the spell hurts when used once, then wait until I have used it a hundred times on you. You're not twelve anymore, so stop playing *I know something you don't know* and tell me what I need to know."

"You are going to kill me anyway. What does it matter?"

"Not if you tell me. The Emperor is offering you a full pardon."

"I must stop my brother. It is the only way I can be free of it. Galan put it in, he can take it out," Galené said, tossing the phone into the alley. She then ran off the roof.

Toshiko watched Galené dive, about half way down she disappeared, darkness enveloped her.

Patya entered the small office to find Toshiko and Hiro drinking sake.

"Celebrating early," Patya said.

Hiro drove his chair around to Patya. "If someone came and told you there was an organised plot to kill your son, what would you do if all you can is watch?"

"We are going to stop them," Patya said, putting his hand on Hiro's shoulder.

"I don't want you to stop them, I want you to kill them," Hiro said between his teeth, his fists clenched.

"Tell me what happened with Galen on the training flight, Rudolf said the file is sealed, and I don't have the time to pry it out of him," Toshiko said.

"I almost forgot about that. It was our first flight in a suborbital with the instructor, a simple training mission or so I thought. Galen was always the better pilot, I was his co-pilot. The mission was to fly a suborbital out of New Moscow and just as we exited the atmosphere we were to roll over and launch an anti-ship missile at a target in orbit. It was a tight arc, we were to complete the roll and re-enter. Our destination was to be New-Vladivostok. The flight was fast, we rolled, when on our back when Galen pressed open on the launch bay, it jammed. Galen just looked at the mission screen, frozen as well spiralled. He looked as if he was waiting for orders. Before we bounced off the atmosphere, I cut the engines, stopped the roll and levelled us out. I reset the system, but we were in a low orbit and too low on fuel, so I ejected us. He said nothing as we floated in orbit," Hiro said.

"Nothing?" Toshiko asked.

"At the hearing, Galen blamed the equipment. You know Rudolf, he believes only a bad pilot blames the plane, but the Inquiry cleared Galen, the plane crashed, but they found the flight recorder and enough wreckage to determine a short in the weapons bay," Hiro said.

"What happened next?" Toshiko asked.

"I was accepted into next stage of training, shuttle flying, and Rudolf assigned Galen to fly cargo planes. We were three bar officers then, but in Sky-Force rank doesn't matter, what does is what you fly. I went up, and he went down, we never saw each other until New Ghana Space Centre in August, 11574," Hiro said.

"Toshiko, is this relevant?" Patya asked.

"It seems Galen got hold of fuel and a bomb maker in New-Shanghai. I want you to take over the interrogation. We know he might have four EMP missiles, but my guess is replaced the four he used," Toshiko said.

"Disablers are useless against ground targets. They are homing missiles, they lock onto a ship's radar image. Galen's only chance is to try and come in low, and fast, then drop retard bombs and disappear over the lake. He knows the plane is almost invisible to detection over 1000 kilometres. Even if you shot the bombs, they are low and will explode.

If you move the wedding indoors, he has no target, but he could target the parade later," Hiro said.

"Could he launch them at a starship in low orbit and have it fall on the city?" Toshiko asked.

"Yes, but missile defence will most likely hit them first," Hiro replied.

"A low run is the only option?" Patya asked Hiro.

"Only if he has iron bombs," Hiro said.

"If he has missiles?" Patya asked.

"Two options, we know he has disablers, if a ship is low over the city, dropping it will cause massive devastation, but if he has nukes, he will fire them into the base of the Palace," Hiro said.

"Thank-you captain," Toshiko said as she stood. "Patya, I need you inside that Ogre's head, find out what weapons Galen has."

Toshiko left, and Patya followed her out.

As they walked down the hall, Patya said, "He could be anywhere, we need to activate the planet's anti-missiles systems."

"Shut up. I am trying to think. We are ready to do that, but we don't know what Galen will do. He might decide it is too hard now and drop the craft on the parade or worse, he has a ship killer, we need to give him an opening to attack," Toshiko said.

"If we move the ships on the south coast and move the one in the lake closer to south west lock, he might not see it as a trap," Patya suggested.

Toshiko called Kaede. "Emperor, we do not have much. Galené could be planning anything from a bombing run to using the last missiles to drop one of the orbiting ships on you. Patya thinks if we leave a corridor open in the south, he will use it given a fast and low bombing run is the only approach," Toshiko said.

"Unlikely, but all he needs to do is trigger a state of emergency. Assume he knows everything Galené does, including the locations of the panic rooms and the emergency exits," Kaede said.

"Galené said it had something to do with your father. I spoke to him, and he told me about an incident on a training run to fire a cruise missile at a target in orbit. Something went wrong and because of that Hiro was accepted into the Fleet as a pilot and not Galen. Instead, he was assigned to fly cargo planes. I am sure he wants the Senate and your father, not just you."

"Yaotl has intercepted a lot of chatter from a group called the New State, a splinter group of The Chosen. Hundreds of members have disappeared without a trace over the last month."

"We should move the coronation of Sora inside, but he could target the parade."

"We know the weaknesses of the spell. I already have a plan, we will hold the ceremony in the underground grotto where I was born and broadcast it live."

"What!" Toshiko exclaimed, "Your grandfather will never allow it."

"Grandfather has no choice, but I hope he will agree. It is the only place we know that is sealed, and it has independent power. When we installed mesh inside the outer wall, he used some to line the caverns and electrified it to keep out rats. He has a large lake full of fish and an elevator in the north wall to bring the Dragons down in. If I need to escape, I will head for that elevator. The mesh is new, so I doubt they will know about it. There are UV lamps already in the roof. We can hide some Knights and house guards in the compound during the broadcast, we station most of the Knights around the Island."

"He might not bomb the Palace. We know he has EMP missiles, your father thinks he could try and disable one of the ships in low orbit as it passes the city."

"We need a plan to make sure he attacks the Palace. I am sure you are aware the Palace was located in the middle of the lake in case of a nuclear attack."

"Do you think it is possible to ensure he attacks the palace?"

"If we leave a couple of holes in our defences so that he approaches from the south so once he attacks, he has a long turn over land, making it easier to track him and we can have mobile SAMs hidden in both New Ukraine and New Russia."

"What if he drops a ship on the city?"

"We make sure a Frigate is over the Palace, and I proclaim Sora to be my wife and crown her at midnight. We show the crown on display in the vault to the media, we show off Sora's dress and rings. We know they monitor the media. If they know soon after the wedding the vault will be sealed, they will want to attack, this will give them no time to see the trap."

"We don't have much time to plan."

"Send for the heads of the branches of the Imperial

Security Agency and send out a leak we are expecting light rain, ruining the possibility of a wedding at sunrise."

"Yes, Emperor."

Kaede then ended the call.

"We are going to the throne room Patya, send for the security chiefs, including Yaotl," Toshiko said to Patya.

August 31, 11580. Imperial City.

The Banshee Two prototype sat in the Dark Shadow Dimension, inside an empty cave in the mountains, in the nature reserve in the south of Imperial City. Just after the sunset Galen suddenly appeared inside the entrance of the large cave and cast *Dimension Shift*.

Inanimate objects were shades of grey, the floor was glowing a dim shade of yellow, Galen walked up to the spacecraft. He pulled opened the bottom hatch and entered a code on a keypad. The inner hatch slid open and once inside the craft, loaded the memory stick. Placed his hand on a black box beside the pilot's chair, and cast *Dimension Shift*. The plane left the Dark Shadow Dimension. He connected communications system to the Imperial Security Agency Network.

On the primary display was a satellite view of Imperial City. Galen zoomed in on Imperial Lake. There were some aircraft on patrol around the island. Galen changed the view to a news broadcast, which showed different marching bands around the city.

Galen changed the view to a satellite view of base north of the city. The view panned over the base, showing hundreds of tanks and mobile SAM launchers parked in rows.

Galen changed the view on screen to Camp Bravo, west of the lake. Then he zoomed in on the airfield where there were cargo planes on the runway. Galen zoomed in on one plane until he saw on screen the ground crew unloading. He zoomed in closer and could see they were unloading fireworks from the aircraft onto trucks.

Galen then flipped television channels until Kaede was on screen. Kaede, dressed in full Imperial Regalia, with the seven-leaf crown on his head, stood in front of a wooden house, a red H on a green dot in the corner of the screen. Behind Kaede sat the twelve Senators in a row. The camera panned to the top of the stairs. Takahiro, in traditional Japanese clothes, stood beside a platinum tiara covered in pink diamonds, and behind him were two Knights in full armour.

Galen changed the view to Imperial Island, then zoomed in on the park and panned to a stage in the middle. On stage was a rear projection billboard-sized screen. He saw a Dain News van and a crew beside it.

On the communications screen, the information network appeared, and Galen selected the Dain News Network. He selected live news broadcast.

"The stage behind me was initially setup for the formal coronation of Lady Sora. However, Lady Masako, the event organiser and wife of Lord Takahiro, has informed me that due to concerns about the weather, the event has moved into the Palace. From midnight, the coronation will be broadcast live and displayed on screens, like this, in parks around the city," the reporter on the screen said.

Galen made a fist and hit the armrest a couple of time. He accessed space traffic control, flipping view screens until he found a frigate in low orbit that would pass over the city. He checked the flight plan. It was due to descend at 11 pm over the sea off the coast, and proceed over Imperial Palace and fire twenty-one fireworks from its rear missile port. Galen pulled up an image of the ship on screen.

Galen pressed the ignition button. The engines came to life. He checked the data link.

"Buckle up you are about to experience a bumpy ride, for we are going to play a game I call Topple the Tower," Galen said to the image of the ship on screen.

A house guard drove Hiro to Camp Bravo, to the command bunker. Hiro sat in the back of a car as Rudolf came to the car and leaned over. Hiro lowered the window.

"Captain, the Emperor, feels you will be safer aboard a ship and can help find the stealth," Sky Marshall Rudolf Reinhart said, handing Hiro a licence.

"I know my son asked you to do this. But I am asking you, no begging you, when you wake up tomorrow, advocate for the disabled to have the right to drive, fly or boat with the hand controller. I don't mind if I need pass a test," Hiro said in a sharp voice.

"I will."

"After we calibrate the scanner on your stealth craft, land them," Hiro said, pocketing his licence.

"Why?" Rudolf growled.

"We don't want to shoot them down, I want to be the only thing cloaked over the city."

Hiro was driven to a shuttle and helped aboard, waiting was his uniform, with a note, "Take care, father."

September 1, 11562, Imperial Palace.

It was just after midnight and Sora exited the elevator on sub-basement 20 with Akiko, Izanami, Mako, Miko, Fumiko and Ume. Toshiko and Yuki greeted them.

Sora wore a three-layered kimono; the top layer a short, red kimono with green trim. It had long, wide, sleeves, and the symbol of Hashimoto House on its back. The second layer was slightly long, it was pink with white Anemone flowers. The third layer was slightly longer again and it was white. She had a broad red sash wrapped around her waist and in a large bow at the back. She wore light pink silk, lace top, stockings with pink suspenders just visible. She had short white lace gloves with wide lace trim around her wrist. Her shoes were wooden wedges with pink leather straps.

Akiko, Izanami, Mako and Miko wore her pink bride's maid gown, it had puffy shoulders. Each wore elbow long pink gloves, pink stockings with pink leather shoes and two earrings in her ears.

Akiko walked beside Sora's and held a held a paper umbrella over Sora's head.

Izanami was behind Sora, with Mako and Miko just behind her.

Fumiko and Ume were behind Mako and Miko. They wore long white kimonos with white socks and wooden shoes. They were holding baskets of red, white and yellow roses.

Toshiko and Yuki wore Knight's uniform, and they lead the procession to Kaede.

Kaede stood with Nori at the base of the stairs to the front of the house. Lady Hitomi stood at the top of the stairs.

The Senate, Knights, House Guards, Takahiro, Masako, and Freya stood on one side. Freya held a video camera. Seated on the side of the path was Emperor Jimmu of the Koropokkuru, King Weyland king of the Dwarves, King Amos of the Goblins. Behind them was King Eric the Red of the Jötunn, King Sargon of the Oni, King Henrik von Wessely of the Orcs. In the next row sat Emperor Taizhong of the Beast-Man, Kaiser Frederick Grimm of the Trolls, King Chronos of the Titans, Chief Mpande of the Giants. Behind them was Queen Clíodhna of the Dragons, Queen Zola of the Daemons, Chief Jason of the Centaurs, Caesar Giovanni of the Ogres, and King Midas the Minotaur.

Fukuhina operated a camera with an antenna from the balcony, Naru stood in the middle of the path with a camera, it too had an antenna. In the Imperial Command Centre, an operator sat at a video control console with many camera feeds, she selected different feeds. The wedding was broadcast live onto screens around the Palace, Island, and large screens in parks, guarded by groups of heavily armed City Guards. Many in homes, hotels, bars, even in ships in orbit, watched the wedding live on wall screens, tablets, phones, or computers.

Sora knelt before Kaede, Akiko remained beside Sora,

Crisis

the umbrella folded. Izanami stood behind Sora, then Mako and Miko, then Fumiko and Ume.

"Lady Sora Li, do you take Emperor Kaede Hashimoto from this day forth?" Hitomi asked.

"I do," Sora replied.

"Emperor Kaede Hashimoto, do you take Lady Sora Li to be your wife from this day forth?" Hitomi asked.

"I do," Kaede replied.

"Should anyone doubt their union, or have any reason they should not wed, speak now," Hitomi said.

Kaede looked at Takahiro. Abel looked at Dain, Toshiko looked at Takahiro.

"I declare you husband and wife," Hitomi said.

Nori in a suit stood beside Kaede, he held a red pillow with a wedding ring on it. It had two wide gold bands in the shape of a dragon, both had two tiny emeralds for eyes. One had a large pink diamond on its heads, with a line of pink diamonds set into the ring.

Kaede took the ring with the pink diamonds and slid it on Sora's ring finger.

Kaede kissed Sora on the lips, she put her arms around him and slipped her tongue in. Many cheered.

Takahiro came with a black lacquer box, it had the symbol of House Hashimoto on the lid and gold inlay. Takahiro opened the box, and Kaede removed a platinum tiara, the front was a pattern of seven leaf Lotus and had 108 pink diamonds set into it.

Kaede slid it on Sora's head. Sora's ears wiggled.

"I, Emperor Kaede, bestow the title of Empress of East Hyperborea and the title Empress of the Elven Empire of the Pleiades, to my wife, Lady Sora Hashimoto," Kaede said.

In Petrov Football Stadium in the north of the city a large crowd watched the wedding on the jumbo screen and cheered, some wore a half pink and white football shirt shirts with Hashimoto All Stars on the front with Sora and a big red '1' on the back.

Hiro and watched the wedding on the small screen of the captain chair. He was strapped into the captain's chair of his starship.

Then as the stealth craft approached the rear of the *Unicorn*, the detection officer's console in the *Night Owl* beeped.

"We have a possible contact, contour mapping has begun," the detection officer said.

"Signal the *Unicorn*, launch another batch for decoys," Hiro said.

Small iris hatches sprang open and then launched decoys. The pilot's finger hung just off the keypad. The decoys exploded into confetti and fireworks.

"Confirmed, a Banshee Two, not broadcasting an Imperial IFF," the detection officer said.

"On screen," Hiro said turning off the wedding.

The main screen switched to a view of the south, overlaid over the distortion was an outline of a Banshee Two.

"Tracking a Banshee Two, it has engaged the image distortion and radar deflection field," the detection officer said.

"I have a data link via satellite, the craft is receiving mapping data," the communications officer said.

"I have weapon lock," the weapons officer said.

"Open a channel on that frequency and patch it to me," Hiro said.

"Aye captain," the communications officer said, she tapped on her computer and said, "Link established."

"Galen, we have a lock on you, surrender now or we will open fire," Hiro said into his headset.

Galen opened the weapon's bay and fired the four EMP missiles towards the *Unicorn*. Then the *Night Owl* decloaked. It was above but to the side of the *Unicorn*.

"Weapons, take out his missiles first," Hiro ordered.

The small gun turrets on both ships tracked and fired a short burst in front of each missile. The stream of lead smashed each missile. As did, the *Unicorn* launched a combination of decoys and fireworks. All over the city fireworks were set off.

The Banshee Two banked hard and headed for the Palace. A large cruise missile sat ready in the bay.

The *Night Owl* grabbed the Banshee Two with a tractor. Galen tried to bank away hard and tried to launch the missile. The craft exploded, and the ejection system was engaged.

The tractor beam grabbed the cockpit pod and lifted it near the large top rear hatch, locked the landing beam on it and brought it inside. When the cockpit was inside the outer hanger, the ship engaged shields and rose above the clouds.

"Good work, Detection," Hiro said.

The officer stood and saluted Hiro. "Could not have done it without you, Captain," she said.

"Thank my son; his ultra-wave scanner makes stealth obsolete," Hiro said.

"At short-range," the officer remarked.

Inside the cockpit, Galen tried to cast Gate, but nothing happened. The tractor beam had surrounded the cockpit with energy. Galen was kicking and screaming, "No" before he passed out.

The cameras were off, Hilda escorted Sora and her group to the elevator. Hilda wore a Knight's uniform and armed with a Viper Two, a massive Claymore on her back.

Toshiko said, "A Banshee Two was detected, and a short time ago groups of Elves on motorbikes approached the south side of the lake in the dark. Estimate to be a thousand of them armed mostly with light automatic rifles."

Takahiro flopped down on the steps. Abel gathered the Senate and many Knights, she sent them inside, Toshiko went up to Takahiro.

"Sora was so beautiful," Toshiko remarked.

"This was my private space," he moaned, but Toshiko was not paying him any attention.

Then Toshiko heard in her earpiece, "This is scout nine, they split into two groups is now at the lake."

"Get ready they are about an hour away," Toshiko yelled.

The Senators followed by most Knights entered the house. The regular House Guards and Knights remained on duty. The remaining house guards escorted the lords, ladies, and other guests to the elevator. The guests included foreign ambassadors and leaders, including the Titan King, who was closely followed by two Knights.

Kaede went to Masako. "Lady Masako, please have the

kitchens prepare a tray of Yubari King Melons, wines, beers, and spirits for them. Keep them in the Palace," Kaede said.

"Yes, Emperor," Masako said.

Kaede turned to Toshiko, "Tell security if any try to leave stop them, but if they panic and run, stun and detain them."

Toshiko nods.

"This is outpost twelve. I followed about half of the group underground, they entered the subway tunnels that run on the bottom of the lake," an invisible Witch said while she floated over the lake on a broom.

A Dark Elf in a subway tunnel took a blow torch to the fire alarm. The subway trains running in tunnels under the lake to the Palace stopped.

In the Dark Shadow Dimension, a large mixed group of Elves raced on bikes down the tunnel, the world around them dark shades of grey. The tracks and lights glowed a pale yellow, the water around the tunnel appeared as a dark grey fog swirling.

They saw a large yellow object in the water, it swallowed a couple of smaller yellow objects before it swam off.

Toshiko was in a room with female Knights, they stripped off and put on padded underwear. Then they put on full-body armour. The Knight's armour was a full-body suit made of a triple weave Kevlar, with a hood, boots and gloves. They helped each other don the armour and then pulling each other's ears through the slit in the hood.

Lady Emi came in with Sora and Akiko.

"I refuse to sit this out," Sora said.

"We're Knights," Akiko said.

Toshiko pointed the four bags, "Empress, your new armour awaits you."

Mako and Miko entered. Sora removed her kimono, revealing a shoulder holstered 13mm over the pink kimono. Akiko helped Sora out of her pink then white kimono. Then Akiko stood behind Sora and under tied a pink corset with lace trim. Sora stepped out of her shoes, removed the pink suspenders and the light pink stockings while Akiko was folding Sora's clothing. The white kimono was not lace, but a weaved material like the armour.

"Izanami and the crown are secured in the kitchens," Mako said to Sora.

"With Fumiko and Ume," Miko said to Sora.

"Suit up, you will find your armour in the bags," Sora said as Akiko passed Sora a white padded bra and panties.

After donning the body suit, they put on a solid plastic torso, shoulder pads, elbow pads, upper arm and forearm guards, upper leg armour and solid knee-high boots. The left upper arm guard had the symbol of the Empire on the side, and the right upper arm guard had the outline of a unicorn's head on the side.

They each put on combat webbing with a belt and a backpack. Each Knight loaded equipment onto their belt, then put on the helmet with nose mouth, chin guard, with a gap for their ears. Then donned a pair of large clear goggles with a dial on the left side. They pulled out and turned the dial, the lens went from fully clear to fully polarised back to auto and pushed in to lock the dial. The helmet had a speaker, microphone, with a phone plug.

"My fellow Knights, this is what we train for. Empress, you will take a Viper 2L to the North-East tower with Akiko, Mako and Miko in the North-West, Abel will be in the South-East tower, I will be in the South-West tower. The rest of you will line up around the wall and sit, and await orders," Toshiko said then stood to attention and put her left fist to her chest. The group of twenty-four knights returned the salute.

"No grenades, we want to keep damage to a minimum," Toshiko called out as she circulated, checking everyone.

Toshiko took a Viper 2L of the weapons rack and handed it to Sora and then handed one to Mako. A long-barrelled sniper rifle with a large scope, they inspected the weapons. Akiko and Miko slung their Viper 2 and were given a tablet with a cord, and an electronic scope on a small tripod.

The Knights performed communications checks and examined each other's armour sections. Then clipped each other's rank onto the collar, then lowered their partner's faceplate.

Those without a rifle grabbed a Viper 2 off the weapons rack and split into pairs.

Everyone loaded their partner's backpack with a couple of rifle clips, pistol clips, a couple of speed loaders, then attacked a claymore to the pack.

Toshiko, in full armour, inspected them, then sent them out. She shouldered her rifle, then a bullhorn, a scope and grabbed a leather wrap with two swords and a naginata. She walked out of the house and found Takahiro in a combat vest and helmet. She handed him a scope and bullhorn, then said, "You're with me."

The second group of Elves reached the lake, they stopped and split into small groups of ten, they fanned out. The fifty groups headed towards the island.

Their bikes appeared to be dark grey, the exhaust was swirls of grey, red and yellow. Most appeared to each other grey with a dull yellow glow.

In another room, the Senate put on fatigues, a combat vest, helmet, and given a Viper 1 from a rack on their way out. Except for Dain, he had a Viper 2L, and Patya had his 9mm in a shoulder holster and wore his long black armour coat over his combat vest.

Kaede was in the main room of the house, he put on Knight's Armour. He slipped into padded underpants. Put on the mesh pants, they were held up by suspenders, slipped on the shirt, which clipped to the pants. He slipped into the mesh socks, then slipped on the mesh hood. He popped his ears out and wiggled them. The armour looked like metal but was soft fabric and was easy to move about in.

Patya came in, Kaede stopped flexing in the mirror.

"It is a bit tight," Kaede said.

"It is very light for heavy armour," Patya said as he helped Kaede put on the mesh gloves.

"Thanks for the rush order, I had hoped after all the

surgical strikes, the Dark Elves would give up, I mean the Ogres got the hint."

"The group are the hard-core fanatics, they are after something your Grandfather is hiding in the vault, they believe Lilith is a now a divine entity," Patya said as he handed Kaede a Viper 2.

"Technically I am hiding it, but legally belongs to Lady Toshiko."

"Tell that to Dain, Lilith gave it to him."

"Patya, we both know the sword does not work, and it was abandoned. He didn't find it."

"It will get out that you have it," Patya growled.

"It doesn't matter now. Had we revealed it when it was found, we would have been bogged down by a legal challenge from Dain instead of studying it."

"That is an assumption."

"He launched many cases in the past against Toshiko over ownership of Lilith's patents, then her tools, then her notebooks, then tried sue for a share of the foundation."

"We finish this conversation later over a drink. The enemy has left the subway via the emergency tunnels.:

Kaede put the on his belt. He noticed the wand holder was empty and there was no wand box. There was a box with a 13mm pistol.

"No wand?"

"It takes years to train in combat magic. I cannot afford to have you pass out from mana loss. The plan is to have them surrender, not gun them down."

"I would feel better if I had one."

"Ready?" Patya asked checking Kaede's armour.

Kaede flexed the glove a few times. Then he nodded to

Patya. Patya put an arm band with a gold star on Kaede's left arm. They headed downstairs, Dain was on the outside balcony. He saluted Kaede. Kaede returned the salute.

Outside Abel, Toshiko and Yuki were waiting. Abel escorted Dain to the South-East tower.

"Wait here," Toshiko said, then she pulled Kaede aside and helped put a wakizashi and a katana on his belt. Toshiko pressed the mute button on her microphone and lifted her faceplate. Kaede did the same.

"Do not use them if you have to, I rather you not reveal the Sword of Light yet. But if we are overrun, I want you to use them and cut a path to the exit, I will cover you," Toshiko said.

"I see you have yours," Kaede said.

Toshiko handed him the Naginata and said, "I combined the blade weapon with my staff. Now clip it on me blade down, you will see clips on my webbing."

As Kaede clipped the Naginata on Toshiko, he said, "Patya knows we have the original."

"That doesn't matter now, I will deal with Patya, and if need be Dain, later," Toshiko said.

"Why are you giving them to me? I thought I wasn't to use magic?" Kaede asked.

"Only use them if anything goes wrong. Make your way to the top of the tower, your father has a shuttle on standby ready to collect you. Don't wait for Sora or me. She and the others will be on a helicopter," Toshiko replied.

"I want you to come with me," Kaede said.

"I am immortal, so are the Senate. You are not, I rather you be alive to be in trouble for using magic than listening to Hiro yell at his father for losing you," Toshiko said smiling.

"Sorry I didn't get the new armour to you sooner, I hoped Patya would have had them ready a week ago," Kaede said.

"It doesn't matter, it is lighter and less restrictive than the old armour. Patya tells me this is the stuff you make your car out of?" Toshiko asked.

"The faceplate started as a clear cockpit canopy for the V/STOL scout, the top coat of the armour was the protective coat on my car, the inner core was the structure of my hydrofoil, and the Kevlar weave was designed originally as storm sails for my father's boat," Kaede replied.

Toshiko saw Patya coming and put a finger to her lips and said, "Thanks, Emperor, I mean Cadet Hashimoto."

Toshiko unmuted his microphone and put his faceplate down, then did the same to her phone and faceplate.

"Come with me," Patya said putting a hand on Kaede's shoulder. Kaede turned to face him.

"Keep your head down," Toshiko said.

Kaede turned back to Toshiko. She was walking over to Takahiro.

Kaede turned and followed Patya. Yuki followed Kaede, Patya lead them to the east wall. Kaede saw Dain and Abel climb into the South-East tower. Abel and Dain flipped a coin. Abel handed Dain the rifle, he handed her the spotter's scope and screen. Abel put the scope on the edge of the guard box and hung the tablet and plugged it in the scope.

Abel and Dain sat, Able got up and grabbed the scope and sat.

Toshiko set up with Takahiro in the South-West tower, Takahiro sat, Toshiko clipped the rifle on the overhead rack and took the bullhorn and waited.

Guards made sure everyone set their phones to a group, and after the communications check, there was silence in the cavern. The lights went off. Knights sat behind the wall, while the few visible guards walked a patrol. They listened to reports from scouts who sat on a broom in the Dark Shadow Dimension. As each scout saw the Dark Elves approach they would cast *Dimension Shift* which moved them out of Shadow Realm to the normal dimension. Then they would report their position to the operators in the Palace command centre.

In the shadow dimensions, many Archons came to the Island. Most were in the light shadow dimension, and they moved about the crowd. The world was dull grey to them, but the living had a pale-yellow glow. When one found one with a bright glow, it would latch them, and the Archon's glow would increase, then once it glowed bright, it would drift off.

The Palace was radiating energy in both the light and the dark shadow dimensions, and that kept the Archon out. But when the barrier around the Palace went off, many entered the Palace.

In the power plant control room, a technical support officer, left the power room, inside all the fuses smashed. A pair of Inquisition agents were outside waiting, the stunned the Dark Elf and left. A team of technical support officers entered the electrical room. While in the control room power was switched from the local grid to the city grid.

The barrier wasn't turned back on, the lights left off, but elevators turned on, and the air flowed from vents. The doors to the vault closed and the shutters to the entry room closed.

The Archon saw the bright figures of the Dragons stir in the Dark Shadow Dimension, inside the lake and most fled. Inside the Palace, an Archon went down the elevator shaft.

A kilometre from the island, the small army of 500 militants, stood on the swirling energy where the water was in the Prime Dimension. They were all dressed in a makeshift uniform of green fatigues with red berets and black lace-up boots. They were carrying an assortment of weapons, mostly 7mm automatic rifles. Some put on red scarves to cover faces, others had a badge of a clenched fist on their berets, some had wands.

The group checked and ready weapons, then saluted each other with fists clenched in the air, then got on their bikes and continued towards the Island.

The group of militants reached the station, they had to get off their bikes and walk them around the people on the platform and push their bikes up the stairs. Those who collided with people didn't affect the people, they were immovable objects. In the station, they went to a pair of locked sliding doors at one end. It had House Guards either side of the door.

The leader pushed the bike wheel in, then proceed to walk through the door. They went down a long tunnel and passed through doors at the end into the car park under the mall. As they rode through the car park, one militant was knocked over by hitting a parked car.

"Idiot, anything glowing or too dense like water, or walls, you cannot pass through," the group leader said to the militant as she stood.

The militants drove fast down the tunnel and passed through another set of guarded doors into another tunnel. They passed through another set of doors into the car park on the north side of the palace. They went down the ramps to the bottom and passed through the checkpoint unseen by the Guards in the prime dimension.

They followed the road that spirals around the outside of the palace to the bottom. At the end of the road was a large door in the inside wall of the Palace. They pushed through it and the other at the end of the short tunnel.

The militants entered the huge artificial cavern. The leader of the first group called out, "We need the Emperor alive to open the vault, kill the rest."

Around the cavern near the roof, invisible Witches floated on a broom. One saw them and waited until all the militants had assembled into groups and started running on the "water". The witch cast *Dimension Shift*. "They are inside the cavern," she spoke into the microphone on the cord from of her phone.

"Security, turn on the mesh," Toshiko said.

"Yes, my lady," the operator in the Palace Security Centre replied, then tapped her screen.

"Why?" Takahiro asked, he stood and place the scope on top of the wall of the guard box.

"We are going to trap them in here with us," Toshiko replied, setting up her rifle. "Turn on the lights over the compound!" Toshiko said into her microphone. Over the house, the sun lamps were turned on.

The militants saw the glow of the mesh behind them, then glow around the walls on the island ahead. Unable to push closer to the walls or open gates, the militants' wizards opened Gates around the edge of the Island. Groups of Elves charged out of them

"Wait!" Toshiko said, "Everyone stay down."

The Archon followed the group of attackers. No one appeared to see the tiny dim bluish light dart about.

On the walkway behind the palisade, Kaede waited, hiding with Patya and Yuki on either side of him, as the group ran towards the walls. Other than a few guards and Toshiko, the rest remained hidden.

A scout in dark shadow dimension saw the wizards leave. The last one stepped into the gate in front him. From the Dark Shadow Dimension, a Gate appeared as a hole with a yellow rim, she could see the prime dimension inside. As he walked into the Gate, he went from an outline with a halo to just a glow. She cast dimension shift and appeared in the cavern, in the prime dimension, the Gate appeared as a Black Sphere, she saw the wizard.

As she spoke "All out," into her microphone on her headset, she flew on her broom to the compound. She was invisible, but the Guards on the wall used *Aether Vision* which allowed them to see through illusions. The Witch landed, in the compound, armed guards approached her, she pulled out her identification as she ended the illusion.

"Now turn on all the lights," Toshiko said into the microphone.

In the command centre, the operator tapped her screen.

"Why?" Takahiro asked Toshiko. All the overhead lamps in the cavern came on. The militants stopped and looked up.

"Powerful UV lights will stop any gates from forming," Toshiko said. She picked up a bullhorn and stood up. "We have you trapped, you will find it impossible to open a Gate or Dimension Shift. We hold the high ground, we outgun you, and we can send thousands of reinforcements. You cannot escape. Surrender now."

Some of the militants fired at the overhead lights, others fired at the few guards on the wall.

"Stand and fire!" Toshiko said into her microphone.

Takahiro stood and used the scope, and aided Toshiko to shoot at those with a wand.

Kaede flipped the safety to burst, stood and took aim, then pulled the trigger. *Just another day at the range. Aim for the centre of the chest and squeeze.*

The Viper 2 had almost no recoil. Each time Kaede squeezed the gun fire three rounds. He shot a militant in the middle of her chest. Blood oozed out of her wounds, she took a step and fell face forward. The look of horror was frozen on her face as she collapsed in a heap. Kaede felt a pain that was like a kick in the chest.

Kaede went to stand as he stared in horror at her lifeless body as it lay face down in a bed of flowers. Then as bullets whizzed past his head, he was pulled down by Patya.

The Archon floated about, then saw a huge powerful glow on the wall, and headed towards it.

"Keep down," Patya growled.

Kaede knelt and took aim at the closest attacker, and shot him in the face. One by one Kaede aimed and shot at the Dark Elves, who didn't appear to be well trained because they didn't take cover, they rushed in tight groups, and most had poor aim. Most didn't get to fire their weapon before being shot.

Patya stood. Kaede was reloading, Yuki took aim and watched, waited.

Akiko stood in the guard tower beside Sora. She looked at the incoming attackers with a digital scope that displayed bearings. The scope on Sora's gun was attached to a screen hung on the wall in front of Akiko.

"12 degrees left, 200 metres. The smug female field elf with her fist badge upside down, she is kneeling beside her pack, she is preparing a rocket launcher," Akiko said.

"Not for long," Sora said as she adjusted the gun.

Akiko looked at the screen, saw the head of the elf on the screen. Sora aimed at the badge on the Elf's beret. It was a black metal badge of a raised clenched fist in a circle.

"That's her," Akiko said.

Sora squeezed the trigger, the bullet hit the badge, continued into the skull and obliterated the back of her target's head, the female fell over, eyes wide open, part of her brain hung out.

Akiko used her scope and saw one of the militants bend over to pick up the launcher.

"Another is going for the weapon," Akiko said.

Sora put a bullet in that Elf's head, then one into the barrel of the launcher as the militants scattered.

Abel watched Dain shoot a Field Elf in the left shoulder, she dropped the wand, as crawled for the wand, Dain shot it, and it smashed into two.

Mako was in the other tower. Miko looked at the crowd, saw a militant wizard. He had a red scarf half covering his face and a wand in his hand.

"310 metres, back of the pack, a wand bearer, easy to see, he has a red scarf on his face," Miko said.

Miko looked at the screen as Mako put a bullet in his head, the wizard fell over as blood oozed from the deadly wound.

It was not much of a battle, in less than an hour, most of the Dark Elves were dead or dying.

Most lay dead or dying. A few hid behind trees. "Cease fire," one of the militants hiding behind a tree yelled. She tossed her rifle aside and got down on her knees.

The knights looked at Lady Toshiko.

"Cease fire," Toshiko called out.

No one fired.

The Toshiko said, "Team One go out and disarm them, any resist, only stun them. Witches get ready to go out treat the wounded, the rest of you cover them."

Toshiko went to the gate as a team of four Knights at the gate, in full armour, slung their Viper 2 over their back. Each picked up large clear shields from the rack with their left hand and drew their wands from their holster in their right.

Other Knights opened the gate.

Most of the militants had dropped their guns and waited

nervously on their knees. After the team left the compound, the gate was closed. A group of Witches waited with medical bags and staffs near the gate.

The Knights fired *Stun Bolts* at a few of the militants who were still standing.

One militant tried to ambush the Knights by stepping out from behind the tree, he fired his rifle, hit their shields, the bullets scratched the shield, but were deflected. The Knight was shocked but fired a *Stun Bolt* at him. The bluish bolt hit him, he convulsed and fell over unable to move.

Toshiko went around, apart from a few bruises, most hits left a scratch on the armour. Toshiko looked at Kaede's helm and said, "You're lucky that was a single 7mm fired by an amateur."

Patya looked at Kaede's helm, a bullet had scraped the side.

Kaede said nothing as Toshiko looked at Patya, then continued her inspection.

In the Dark Shadow Dimension, the Imperial Lake was a swirling dark pool of energy. A group of five hundred militant Elves pushed motorbikes to the edge of the lake. The surface rippled but they did not sink.

The group rode their motorbikes over the lake. As they neared the island ahead, they could see the bright dots of the living on the island.

"Kill them all!" the head biker said.

High above the lake, Witches on brooms floated, and as the militant Elves passed their position, they left the Dark

Shadow Dimension to report. When the last one left, the group were about 100 metres from shore. After she had left the Dark Shadow Dimension, around the island powerful UV lights were turned on. The lamps formed a ring around the island. Most stopped before hitting the glowing wall, which formed around the island and grew to form a thick dome around the island. The lead group hit it. It was like mud; the impact did not hurt them but was sufficient to stop them pushing forward. As it expanded, those caught inside were pushed out. It expanded to 100 metres around the island. It was slow, but those caught inside could pull themselves out of it.

The groups looked around. The patrol boats in the lake moved to 500 metres offshore and turned on UV lamps.

In the lake, Raijin, a three-metre Dragon turtle, swam in the energy pool. The Dragon was now beneath the group.

Most of the group only had a very faint glow, except the few with a wand.

Raijin rose out of the lake amongst a group of the Dark Elves, most of whom were pushed over. Raijin cast a fourteen-metre round *Aether Ball* at another group. They died instantly. Others fired at the Dragon, but most their bullets bounced off his hard shell before he sunk into the lake. Screaming in fear some tried to gate out. A patrol boat shone a lamp on the Gate, which broke up and faded away.

Amaterasu, a six-metre eastern water Dragon, also at ease in the water, hunted down another group. Like Raijin, she rose out of the energy, cast a fourteen-metre round *Aether Ball* at a group, the ball landing on a group, all

Crisis

those inside the ball collapsed dead, then she slid back into the lake.

Chou, a six-metre eastern winged green flew overhead and swooped down and killed several Dark Elves by regurgitating acid on them. Some tried to flee by racing towards shore. Venus, a six-metre western winged Dragon flew around the edge of the lake, and killed many, with a combination of magic and regurgitating acid onto them. After a few passes, she switched to using stun.

Clíodhna, the one-metre western red Dragon, flew very fast and went after the Dark Elves who headed toward the shore of the lake.

Groups of fifty Knights entered the Dark Shadow Dimension, formed into two lines, those in the front had large clear shields. Over them flew witches on brooms.

Fewer than fifty radicals were alive, and most of those immediately surrendered, casting aside weapons, and heading with hands on their heads towards the Knights on the shore. Some tried to shoot at the Knights. Some shot other radicals in the back. The witches and Dragons cast *Stun Bolts* at those who did not disarm.

In the cavern under the Palace, Knights led prisoners in small groups, to the elevators. The captives had their hands zip-locked behind their backs, and wore hoods over their heads. Other survivors were on their knees watched by trigger-itchy Knights while Guards disarmed them, zip-locked their hands and put hoods over their heads.

Kaede removed his helmet. He stared at the bodies below.

"Emperor, are you, all right?" Toshiko asked.

"I feel great," Kaede replied.

"If you're going to throw up, go to the bathroom."

"No. It is hot in this armour, and my crotch guard itches," Kaede said as he watched Knights checked and disarmed the dead and dying. Blood-Witches came with medical pods to collect the bodies of the dead, while healers tended to the wounded.

He looked up, only some of the sun lamps were still on.

"Emperor, no one will hold it against you if you need to vomit. Nothing prepares you for the first time you take a life," Yuki said.

Kaede took Yuki's hand and headed down the ramp, "Toshiko, I will be inside if anyone needs me, please make sure no one needs me," Kaede said.

Yuki turned to Kaede and asked, "Are you feeling all right, Emperor?"

Kaede pulled the cord from his phone, then Yuki's phone and lifted his face plate. Then hers.

"Would you give me a bath, honey?" Kaede whispered to her.

"Yes Emperor," an excited Yuki replied.

Patya sent a message to Toshiko, "Fifty says he vomits."

Toshiko looked at her phone and grinned. She replied, "You're on."

Takahiro looked at the smashed lights, the holes in the roof, at all the trampled plants, then as he walked around, he found Dain look at the state of the Elf.

"Yes, that is a young Toshiko," Takahiro said.

"I wonder if anyone else noticed the irony. A place that seen so many births now has seen so many deaths," Dain said walking away.

Toshiko having changed into her uniform found Kaede in the bathroom of the master bedroom. He in the bath, with Yuki. They were both naked, Yuki was behind him, he was leaning on her, she had her arms around him, and was stroking his penis.

"You were right; any group planning an attack on the Palace would not surrender," Toshiko said.

"It was bold of you to dare the Senate to stand on the wall with us, I didn't think they would."

"Early reports are none of them aimed high."

"I was worried they are too cosy in their office. Apart from Patya, they need to do more field work, but first I need to change the structure of bureaucracy."

"How many do you think you hit?"

"Five dead, ten wounded."

"It is just after 3 AM, you like to rest before the wedding?"

"Yuki, honey, let's continue this conversation in the bedroom," Kaede said standing.

Yuki blushed, Kaede took her arm and headed towards the house.

"You're getting married soon," Toshiko said as she followed them out of the bathroom.

As Kaede walked passed Toshiko, he kissed her on the

lips, his hard penis up against her hand. "I have always loved you too."

"*Nice dick*," Toshiko thought, she did not know Kaede heard that. She just smiled at Kaede, and he smiled back at her.

Kaede rubbed his penis against Toshiko as he kissed her on the cheek. Then led Yuki to the bed. Toshiko turned and watched the wet, naked Kaede lower the wet, naked Yuki onto the large futon.

Kaede closed his eyes. On his phone the message application opened, a message to Sora, *"Honey I want to fuck Toshiko and Yuki,"* appeared and was sent.

Kaede's phone beeped. As Kaede put his head between Yuki's legs and began to tease her clitoris with the tip of his tongue, Toshiko went to the pile of armour and clothes and read the message to Sora and her reply.

"How did you do that?" an astonished Toshiko asked stepping towards Kaede.

"You will find out later today," Kaede replied, he leaned over and licked Yuki.

Sora was in the salon, holding her nails under a lamp, and Akiko stood beside her, holding her phone. Akiko showed the message to Sora, who read it to herself.

"Text back, *save some for me,*" Sora said.

"What is going on?" Izanami asked.

Akiko sent the message and closed the message application. "Yuki was asking if we are on schedule for the wedding feast sunrise," Akiko said.

Sora looked at Izanami, she was wearing a red dress,

Crisis

"You need to go put on your bride's maid dress for the first meal, we are expected to in the Dining Hall in an hour," Sora said.

"It is hideous!" Izanami exclaimed, "I want to wear my dress."

"You are my bridesmaid, not a model. You will wear the dress I gave you until noon today. You will wear it again tomorrow for Akiko. You can wear your wedding dress on Wednesday, but on Thursday you will be wearing the bridesmaid dress I gave you when Kaede marries Mako and Miko," Sora said.

"Must my gown be light pink?" Izanami asked.

"Yes, and you will wear the pink elbow length gloves, pantyhose and shoes. Don't you even think about wearing your tiara until your wedding day, or I'll crown you with my fist," Sora said.

"Does everyone have to watch you and Kaede have sex?" Izanami asked.

"If you want to be his wife, not only will you watch, you are going to be watched by a large group of ladies with me beside you," Sora said.

"It sounds so exciting," Akiko said.

"That is the plan," Sora said smiling to Akiko.

"I don't want everyone to see my vagina," Izanami said.

Sora turned to face Izanami and said, "It might not be as beautiful as mine, but you are going to be a dutiful and traditional wife. You are going to kneel beside us and on your wedding day you going to let him bend you over and take you in front of us or pack your bags."

Izanami red-faced, bit her lip, then bowed and left.

Kaede kissed his way up Yuki's body to her mouth, he caressed Yuki's breasts, and she shuddered as he penetrated her with two fingers. He still had one hand on her breast with her nipple between his fingers. Her heart raced with each thrust. They locked lips again, and his tongue probed her mouth. As they kissed, she opened her legs and moaned. Eagerly Kaede shifted his position and guided in by Yuki; he penetrated her.

Toshiko watched as Kaede made love to Yuki. Yuki moaned in pleasure and wrapped her legs around Kaede. Together they moved, panting with excitement, as Kaede faster and faster moved inside her.

With each thrust, he looked at Toshiko. Yuki moaned and then cried out. Kaede moved inside her until he orgasmed. As he did so, Yuki looked at Toshiko. Toshiko was excited and licked her lips as Kaede withdrew.

"Emperor, you need to get ready for the first meal, you many guests, your wife is waiting for you, and we need to leave at 11 for the parade," Toshiko said.

"We have plenty of time, Sora isn't ready yet," Kaede said. He got off the futon and went into the bathroom. Just as he entered the shower, Toshiko looked in.

Without looking, Kaede said, "Yes, I want you too," then he turned on the shower. Toshiko turned around blushing.

Yuki lay on the bed, looked at Toshiko, she asked, "Are you waiting for me to leave?"

"What?" Toshiko asked.

"He just said he wants you," Yuki said standing.

"I am too old," Toshiko replied.

Yuki put on a pair of panties, walked over to Toshiko, and put her hand on Toshiko's shoulder. "A naked young hot male just said he wants you. Do you want me to leave so you can fuck him?"

Toshiko shiver as she removed her armour and clothes. Toshiko was fit, and her body did not immediately betray her age. Nevertheless, Toshiko clearly was much older than Yuki. She had a grey streak in her fringe, her eye teeth were longer than Yuki's, her breasts sagged a little, and her vagina was hairy and mostly grey, whereas Yuki had only a light patch of pink pubic hair.

Kaede washed. He did not rush. When he returned. Toshiko bit her lip and looked to Yuki. Kaede took Toshiko in his arms and kissed her on the neck as he felt her vagina. She rubbed his penis, it was hard and he just as passionate with her as he was by Yuki.

Up close Kaede saw Toshiko used makeup and creams to hide the crow's feet and age spots, her hair was dyed, and her breasts were soft and drooping. As they kissed, she stroked his penis, and he was eager as he felt her vagina. She clung to him tightly and pulled him down to the futon. She wrapped her legs around his waist and arched her back. He was quickly inside her, she rolled him on his back, got on top of him and rode him fast. He tried to make it last, but soon he could no longer hold back and orgasmed inside her.

Toshiko sat on his lap until he was no longer hard, then got up. She helped him up, then put on her panties. As Kaede washed, Toshiko called Sora.

Kaede came out and found the room empty. He dressed and left the room, and went downstairs and out the front door. He found Takahiro sitting on the front porch, he smoked a kiseru. He turned and frowned at Kaede.

"I know it didn't go as I said it would, Grandfather,"

Kaede said, bowing. "I apologise and accept responsibility for the damages."

"Nothing I cannot fix, I am glad you are all right," Takahiro said.

"Thank-you for your cooperation. You may want to keep some of the bullet holes and blood-stained rocks. It adds character," Kaede said.

"In the old Empire, he would add even more character by placing the severed heads of his dead enemies on pikes at the front gate," Toshiko said coming out. She was dressed in her Knight's uniform. Her hair was still wet. Patya handed her a fifty-gold note. She smiled and took it.

"Scouts have checked, it appears we got all of the Dark Elves," Patya said.

"After the Inquisition has interrogated the survivors, they will get a fair trial," Kaede said.

"Kaede, you will have to make an example of some," Takahiro said standing.

"I will personally behead those who are sentenced to death, but Patya needs to hold his inquiry before Rudolf has his trial," Kaede said.

"Yes and no heads on a pike, Takahiro, you know it distresses the púca in the school tours," Patya said to Takahiro, he turned to Kaede, "I suggest you get lots of practice with a large axe, gory hacking with a sword gets bad ratings. You'll have a live audience, and it will be broadcast live."

"Kaede, I recommend the Naginata for beheading," Takahiro said.

Kaede went to say something. "I will have him ready," Toshiko said.

"You have time. It will take weeks for me to process them all," Patya said.

"How come I was the only one in the Senate with solid body armour and a Viper 2?" a curious Kaede asked.

"We only issue the Viper 2 Rifle and Solid Armour to Imperial Knights," Toshiko replied.

"Patya, you didn't offer anyone an armour jacket?" Kaede asked.

"These are only issued to the Inquisition," Patya replied.

"I see," Kaede said, he turned to Toshiko, "I almost forgot. How are our guests?"

"Livid, but unharmed. Many of our guests have complained about been locked inside the palace. They claim doing so placed them in harm's way," Toshiko replied.

"Patya, send Argon to go speak to them but have him remind them the fact they are nobles, and because of that they were in danger, and we protected them," Kaede said.

"Yes, we saved them the embarrassment of dying at the hands of the fanatics they armed," Takahiro remarked.

Kaede took Patya aside. "Excuse me a moment; family business."

Patya nodded and left.

Kaede sat beside Takahiro. "Grandfather, I know you are angry, but I am handling this."

"Yes, you are handling things very well by getting my retreat shot up. You have many other open areas."

"Sub-basement six has many rare plants, the matsutake and shimeji farm, and would have taken a lot of work to completely seal the area."

"The barracks on 13 or the training area on 14."

"They a max of small buildings, bunkers, storage, and

not only the walls, but we also need to seal the floor and install high UV lamps. The energy expands slowly in the shadow dimensions. Sub-basement 20 is the only level with a large open body of water."

"The Dragons' habitat has water," Takahiro remarked in a low growl.

"It doesn't cover almost the whole floor. Maintenance will come and fix everything. The place will be spotless," Kaede said.

"You are the Emperor, not a foot soldier," Takahiro said sounding worried.

"Grandfather, the public gave you and the rest of the Senate a free pass from continued military service because you are one of the founders," Kaede said.

"Doesn't mean you get into a firefight in my home," Takahiro snapped.

"Toshiko?" Kaede called out.

"Yes, Emperor," Toshiko replied stepping out of the front door.

"Put the Empress's crown on display in the main hall, make sure every knows my Grandfather made it. Get the other jewellery ready to present to Sora."

"Yes, Emperor," Toshiko replied.

Kaede turned to Takahiro, "Lord Takahiro, I apologise, but we have no other venue. Given the threat posed by dimension crossing, I will be forwarding you all the research I have. To help prevent such intrusions in the future we need to build buildings with doors Dragons cannot pass through. We need a new standard on all light bulbs in government buildings to have high UV. I will need you to build me a new

Palace and help build many other government buildings, here on the Island."

"Will you continue putting yourself in harm's way?" Takahiro asked standing.

"Soon Sora will be carrying my son, I want him to have a home that is not facing the constant threat of attack. We will redevelop the island, and you can relocate your home to a new Hashimoto Building on the Eastern Shore," Kaede said.

"You want me to move out?" a shocked Takahiro asked.

"We as a family need to move out," Kaede answered, "The Palace should only be an office building. We will live in our own tower. One I will pay for you to build. I haven't finished the plans for the redevelopment of the Island and city, but I will let you finish them. But my vision for the island is thirteen office builds, hotels, three resorts, six fun parks, two of them aquatic parks on the shore, a cruise ship terminal, a large marina on the south side, lots of ferry terminals. The island will need roads, north-south bridges and subway tunnels. I want to expand the tube train to four in, four lines out with a station and put the main station under the island. We going to need massive underground parking, a massive base for the Knights, and the Guards. We need to provide many electric taxis."

"What about the mall?"

"Add a second building."

"What about the park?"

"A two-kilometre wide park around the edge. You expand the rim of the island underwater so we can build some beaches and an underwater walk way around the island on and top, with a fine anti-shark fence."

"Can I expand the marina?"

"Yes. We going to need some long docks, because we going to have submarine rides, and let the dragons out on weekends. We will have Guards watch them, as púca will want to come see them."

Takahiro considers this, he rubs his chin. Then said, "I noticed you have new armour, another project you didn't include me in?"

"Patya developed the armour with the carbon nanotubes I developed for my car. The soft armour it is a triple weave. The hard armour is made from a triple weave of a high-density polyethene set with resin. It is coated with a layer of ultra-high-density polyethene. The material is stronger and lighter than metal. It is stronger and lighter than the ceramic plates we currently use, and this material can take multiple hits from a rifle round."

"How come you are not wearing an armoured undershirt?"

"I am wearing armoured clothing. I have a soft armour kimono on underneath. Like all vests, it is stab and bullet resistant. It has pockets on the front and back for protective plates. The plates are the same material as the solid armour."

"Who makes it?"

"We make the material, Kaede Arms will make custom armour such as clothing and civilian armour coats. Petrov Arms will continue to make vests, armoured coats, and hard armour for the Imperial Security Agency. Our clothing will be on the market soon, but before we can sell it, Takis needs to do his own health and safety checks. I will make sure you get fitted soon as we can."

"Next time you need an arena, use Petrov Stadium," Takahiro growled.

Kaede bowed to Takahiro. "I love you too Grandfather."

Takahiro smiled and returned the bow, "You did well today." He lit his pipe, then turned and headed inside smoking.

Kaede walked over to the Gatehouse, he saw Emi.

"Lady Emi, will you come with me?" Kaede asked.

Emi followed him to the Elevator.

In the Inner Hangar of the *Night Owl*, an Engineer with a cutting lance cut the door off the cockpit ball. Then others pried it off. It walloped the deck, and the crew pulled it out of the way quickly as Knights moved in and pulled the tray back, revealing the pilot unconscious in the pilot's seat.

Hiro sat in the captain's chair watching on the big screen. A Knight removed the pilot's helmet. Hiro watched and waited. An Inquisition officer took the pilot's picture and prints while Knights removed the wand, stripped him, put him in an orange jump suit and chained his hands and feet to a collar and belt.

The Inquisition officer came racing down the hall from the Hangar to the bridge door. She was immediately let into the bridge. She whispered to Hiro.

"Communications, send a priority message to the Palace and tell the Emperor. We have captured Galen," Hiro said.

Kaede closed his eyes as the elevator rose, *'Are you a Demon?'* he thought to himself.

'No, I am Aizen-Myoo' a voice replied. It sounded like an elderly Nipponese Flower Elf.

'That means nothing to me.'

'I am the God of prostitutes, landlords, singers and musicians. Your ancestors worshipped me, offered their bodies to me in orgies. Priests would sing my praise as worshippers filled cauldrons in my shrines with gold.'

'I don't believe in Gods you vile Demon.'

'I am not a Demon or a Wraith. I am an Archon.'

'What is the difference?'

'I do not possess, I inform.'

'Power?'

'Yes. I am a god and I can I grant you power.'

'Gods are a myth created by the Demon possessed to delude the weak-minded. I shall have you removed.'

'A god is any being of supernatural ability. I have the power and knowledge to make you the greatest singer, warrior, poet, and brothel keeper in the Empire. Or I can leave.'

'I already am a popular singer, dancer, and I own the largest brothel in the Empire.'

'With my help, the most beautiful and powerful witches will lay at your feet, and your magic will be more powerful than a Dragon's.'

'Oh really?'

'Yes, I can make you a Sorcerer.'

'What is a Sorcerer?'

'The possessed only gain mana and an increase in force rating. A Sorcerer merges with the entity and gains powers.'

'Powers? Like what?'

'Each Archon gives you increased mana, but I can give you the ability of passive mind reading without a wand and knowledge. Each entity is different. I gather knowledge on property, lust, sex, singing, and music. As an example, I can give you the memory of the 17 Naturally Erotic Scents to arouse a woman, so you can cast the Illusion, Produce Smell with near perfect results. I can improve your singing voice or play many different instruments like an expert.'

'What about the other entities?'

'All Demons give you the ability to influence others, the power of gnosis and its ability. A Wraith can give you the ability to summon and control different entities.'

'What are the differences?'

'Archons value knowledge, Demons value power and Wraiths value harmony. But all entities will help increase your force rating, increase resistance to possession and mind control spells. Do you want to be a Sorcerer? If I possess you, you need to talk to me or to use my powers you need to let me control you.'

'How can you make me a Sorcerer?'

'We merge.'

'What do you mean?'

'I will swirl about in your mana. Once we merge, I have all your memories, and you will have mine. I will exist, and you still risk losing me in an exorcism.'

'Does it take long?'

'No.'

'After that can you still leave me?'

'I can, but I am bound to you. For every hour I am gone, I weaken and eventually fade out. Without me, you will lose the powers I grant you, the increased mana I provide and the

higher force rating you gained. However, you will retain the knowledge you gained from me.'

'*Higher force?*'

'*Yes, the more entities you host or, the stronger I become, the higher force rating you can achieve. It is better if you merge, then you will know what I know and don't have to stand about looking as if you are daydreaming.*'

Kaede raised an eyebrow and pressed his hand to the panel. The elevator stopped, and he got off at sub-basement six. He showed his ID card to the security desk and headed towards the Tea House.

Emi followed him to the tea house when he stopped at the front door, she stood behind him.

"Wait here, I need a few minutes alone," Kaede said looking at the Tea House, the cavern was empty except for a traditional Flower elf gardener in the distance.

"Emperor?" Emi asked.

"I need a drink. My grandfather keeps the bar stocked, ensure I am not disturbed," Kaede said.

"Yes Emperor," Emi said.

Kaede entered the tea house and went upstairs. He poured a drink and stood on the upstairs balcony drinking it, below he saw Emi looking up.

'*Nothing is free, what is the cost to me?*' Kaede asked himself.

'*You take on our goals, needs, desires, and habits. You need to feed us.*'

'*Tell me yours.*'

I am a sex god. I feed on the emotional energy given off during coitus.'

'*Is that it?*'

'Sort of.'

'What do you mean by sort of?'

'If a woman looks at you and I am hungry, I want you to take her, even if she is married. I am greedy and needy when it comes to sex. It is my food, and without food, I weaken. If I am weak, that makes you weaker.'

'I am ready' Kaede said looking out the window at Emi standing in front of the Tea House.

In the forest near the coast, four teams of Knights descended on a small hotel on the side of a mountain. It was a plain, two-story, white building, with boarded up windows.

On the grounds, some Dark Elves were on guard with small arms.

The knights surrounded the place, in unison, they advanced on the building. Each had suppressors on the barrel of the Viper Mini.

They advanced fast in a slightly crouched posture, guns at the ready. On the edge of the forest teams of snipers surrounded the Hotel and moved into a firing position.

The guards were caught unaware and shot by the snipers. They watched as the Knights run towards the building. There were many teams of Knights, Guards, and Inquisition agents in the woods.

A team of four Knights raced to the back door, while another raced to the side door to the kitchen and two teams on either side of the front door. Two teams run up to the side of the building and floated up to the top of the building and went to the roof door.

One of the four Knights in each team pointed her wand at the door, while the others took cover behind her.

The Knight cast *Blast*.

The boards against the inside of the doors were blown off, the knight behind her then tossed in a flash bang.

"Surrender, don't move!" the Knights yelled as they raced in.

They disarmed the Dark Elves, as teams of Guards moved in behind them the Knights moved ahead, going room to room, in the large dining room was a command centre. A group of a dozen Dark Elves shredded documents, one female was burning paper in a bin, another smashing mobile phones with a hammer, another watched screen as a program was counting percentage. While the others emptied filing cabinets. Each put their hands up and stepped back as the Knights entered guns at the ready.

One Knight checked the bin, tipped it on its side and stomped it out the fire while another covered her, a knight moved towards her and grabbed her and checked her for weapons. Another looked at the screen, the percentage was rising faster, no cancel button, the Dark Elf smiled, the Knight yanked the power cord out.

On the roof Knights raced in, and down the stairs. They shot the guards as they went room to room.

As more members of the Guard entered the building, members of the Inquisition moved prison transport vans up to the doors. Others went inside with a portable fingerprint scanner.

Armed Dark Elves in the stairs shot at the advancing

Knights. The wounded Knights were pulled back as others shot at the Dark Elves guards. Knights came down the stairs behind them and shot the Dark Elves.

In the basement, chained to a pipe, a team found Galené beaten and naked against a support column with her hands bound by a chain behind the column.

Galené was covered with a blanket and raced to one of the waiting vans, the team jumped in with her, an officer closed the door behind them, and the van raced off.

Roads were blocked, media helicopters kept back by a couple of Sky Force gunships. In the forest teams in camouflage patrolled.

A team of Inquisition investigators stood in the car park, a burnt area was tapped off. Forensic officers in Technical Support Uniforms took pictures of the scorch marks and tire marks.

In the lobby of the hotel, the surviving Dark Elves were photographed, fingerprinted, tagged, stripped, and examined by a healer. Then the prisoners were put into orange jumpsuits, gagged, their hands and feet shackled. Last a hood was placed over their head, and the cord on the hood pulled tight. The prisoners chained in groups of six, then a guard led the group by pulling on the chain. Each group handed to Inquisition, who loaded them into prison vans.

An unmarked truck entered the underground parking of the Palace and drove down to the delivery dock on the bottom level. The back opened, and a group of Knights in full armour led Galené out. She wore an orange jumpsuit.

Kaede came up to her.

'*She is possessed by a cat Demon,*' Aizen-Myoo thought.

"We have captured your brother alive," Kaede said. Galené looked relieved.

"What will you do?" Galené asked in a soft voice.

"I have to hand you over to the Inquisition, but first Lady Toshiko wants to talk to you. If you cooperate, I will give you a pardon," Kaede said.

"Please don't kill my brother," Galené pleaded.

"If you get him to talk to us, it will help secure a pardon," Kaede said

"Where is her? Can I see him?" Galené pleaded.

"Come," Kaede said.

Kaede took Galené to his office.

"Wait outside," Kaede said to the Knights. After they left Kaede kissed Galené on the lips.

Galené fell backwards, Kaede sat her on the chair.

"Emperor!" Galené exclaimed.

'*I am Nekomata, a powerful God. Obey me and wealth, riches and power will be yours,*' a female Nipponese voice in his head thought.

'*The Nekomata is weak, and it can only grant you the ability to control cats,*' Aizen-Myoo thought.

"Relax Galené, I know you love my father. I took the Demon out of you, don't tell Patya, but you can tell Toshiko after I tell her about removing it," Kaede said.

Galené nodded.

'*Do not underestimate me or the power that comes from being able to understand and control cats,*' Nekomata thought.

'*Merge with me Nekomata,*' Kaede thought.

'But her power only works in the line of sight,' Aizen-Myoo thought.

'That is the same with mind reading. If our host uses the spell mind-link, then he can see, hear, feel, taste and smell for the duration of the spell, even if the cat is out of sight,' Nekomata thought.

'You are both weak, for now, but I want you both,' Kaede thought.

'If I absorb her I will be more powerful,' Aizen-Myoo thought, in a deep voice.

'Galen is host to a powerful Demon, once that can summon and control other demons. Please don't let Aizen-Myoo absorb me. I can help you,' Nekomata thought.

'Don't listen to her, let me absorb her. There are more powerful demons than her,' Aizen-Myoo thought.

'True, but no demon has the power to control everything,' Nekomata thought.

'Demons will try to control you,' Aizen-Myoo thought.

'Yes, but I know what you know. If we merge, she is bound to me and a domesticated Nekomata will be handy to have, I will host her,' Kaede thought.

Kaede concentrated, his mana swirled and turned, the normally bright yellow was not blue, yellow, and red swirls of energy, like a hurricane. The colours merged and the swirling stopped. Kaede saw a little blue entity shaped like a tiny elf and little red entity horned cat person with bat wings. They bowed to him, he smiled and bowed slightly to them.

Kaede opened his eyes. 'It is done,' Kaede said blinking. The knocking on the inner door was loud and rapid.

"What is done," Galené asked as Kaede opened the door.

"What took you so long?" Patya asked as he stormed in, "Toshiko told me, you have my prisoner."

"Yes, I brought her to my office to offer her a pardon, she has agreed to talk once she sees it. What took me so long is I was looking to see if we can restore rank, privileges and employment," Kaede said heading around his desk.

Patya stood beside Galené and asked, "Is that so?"

"Yes," Galené said as Kaede sat in his chair, "Czar, please consider it. I know I acted irrationally, but I thought I could convince my brother to surrender."

"I will soon know the truth," Patya said tapping his wand.

"I will be asking Lady Toshiko to monitor your interview with Galené, and I ask you not to use Mind Probe on her," Kaede said.

"Are you telling me how to do my job?" Patya asked Kaede.

"It is a request. I expect Galené's lawyer will make it a formal request in court on medical grounds. She has valuable information, not just the spells in her device. I know you still can use passive mind reading spells to record faces or help her when her recall is vague. But I want her to recover and return to work as one of my Knights, not be traumatised by being subjected to a Mind Probe," Kaede replied.

Patya was about to say something when Lady Toshiko entered the room, she had a cord from her phone to her ear, "I agree with the Emperor. I will represent Galené. I need time with my client. Patya, the helicopter bringing Galen from Camp Bravo is almost here."

Crisis

"Patya, I need to speak to Lady Toshiko. However, I ask you to keep Galan in my cells, because we have electrified mesh. You can interview him after the Witches have seen him, I will be offering him a pardon. I shall do so in front of you. I want to give Galené a chance to convince him to cooperate," Kaede said.

"I notice you have already put many in your cells," Patya said.

"You can have a private office in the cells, but my guess is many will be executed, this saves them a trip to Inquisition HQ, and to Court and back here. Rudolf has the authority to hold a trial on the sixth floor. You can hold your inquiry into today's attack here too," Kaede said.

"I am going to install mesh in my cells," Patya said.

"Save yourself the time and expense. I am working on a field generator to secure buildings cheaper," Kaede said.

"Do I get to speak with my client?" Toshiko asked.

"Excuse us please Patya, I will not come with you, I need to negotiate a pardon and her client," Kaede said opening the office door, "Will you house Galan and the others here?"

Patya looked at Kaede, he sniffed him and replied, "Yes," as he left.

In the distance, a helicopter raced towards the Palace inside Galen chained, bound and gagged sat hooded surrounded by Knights watched by Hiro as Patya rode an elevator up.

-= The End =-

GLOSSARY

Aquatic Elves

One of the five races of Light Elves. These Elves have pale light blue skin with webbed fingers and toes. Most have pale blue hair, while a minority have dark blue hair. Eye colour is predominately blue with some green.

Most are Greek with some Germanic, Celtic, Nordic (Zealander), Chinese (Gobi Inland Sea), Viet (Mekong River People), Okinawan and Pacific island tribes.

They weigh less than and are thinner than field Elves of the same height. These Elves have an average height of 150cm.

Archon

A race of small energy beings also known as Will-O-Wisp or Angel. While most do appear in the form of a transparent blue generic humanoid with butterfly wings, the precise form varies. They also vary in shades of blue and brightness.

An Archon is unable to do physical harm in the real dimension, they are, however, capable of possession. Each can confer magical abilities to their host, most only have one ability. Each entity adds their mana to their host's mana pool and increases the host's force rating. Archon value knowledge.

Most only have a magic force rating of one. Over time they do increase.

Beast-Men

Twelve hybrid races the Ogres created by combining animal DNA with Giants and Dwarves. While appearing mostly human, they have animal eyes. The animals used were Rat, Ox, Tiger, Rabbit, Lizard, Snake, Horse, Goat, Monkey, Chicken, Dog, and Pig. While most have black hair; Rabbit people have blonde hair; Horse, Monkey and Dog have brown hair; Pig and Rat have grey hair. The snake people were also known as The Naga. The Naga not only have the eyes of a snake but also retractable venomous fangs and a snake tongue.

They have an average lifespan of 80 years.

Beast-Men have a natural maximum magic force rating of five.

Blood Witch

The Elves' population police, they part of the Imperial Security Agency, thus part of the military. They are the only branch of service that is entirely female. Like the Knights, they report to the Emperor. The Witches are all magical and non-magical healers. They have many medical roles in the Empire.

They perform a range of services. Each Witch is train

in Blood Magic, magical and non-magical healing. The agency runs the blood bank, arrange organs transplants, tissue bank, breast milk bank. The agency issues licence to have children, prostitution, and registers births, deaths, and marriages.

Witches are not just healers. Some are midwives, surrogates, marriage brokers, and marriage celebrants. Only Witches perform organ transplants, they collect organs from the deceased.

The agency runs the Empire's immortality program. A specialist team make and administer a cocktail of drugs and use magic to extend the life of individuals and to boost their cellular regeneration and immune system. They also keep an electronic record of memories and a DNA record of each immortal.

Should an immortal die, the witches produce a clone, and at eighteen give the clone the memories of its predecessor.

They are the only agency with the technology to manipulate DNA. They maintain a database of all DNA. Not just every Elven family line, but all non-Elves, including plants and animals.

They maintain the population and should they need they have an artificial birth chamber to produce offspring in.

They are the only ones allowed to know and use blood magic. *Oxygenate*, will infuse blood with oxygen. *Blood Cleanse* is a spell to cleanse the blood of disease, bacteria, parasites, and other contaminants. *Purge Death* is a spell the cleans the subject of death, it required blood. *Resurrect* will bring back someone who is dead, but capable of living, it needs blood. *Rebirth* will turn a corpse into an 8-cell embryo, needing blood and a surrogate.

Due to force and time required for the process to complete, a Coven usually casts blood magic.

Cat Sìth

A large black wild cat with a white spot on its chest.

Highly intelligent, they learn quickly and can instructions. They are not kept as pets. Instead, the cat chooses a home, and the homeowners leave out milk and often keep fish ponds stocked to keep them around.

Elves allow them to roam and fend for themselves.

Centaur

Created from DNA from an Elf and a Unicorn. They have the torso of an Elf with the body of a white horse. The majority are a field Elf hybrid.

A male is called a Centaur, the female a Centauress.

They have an average lifespan of 80 years.

Centaurs have a natural maximum magic force rating of five.

Cù Sìth

A wild dog the size of a young bull with the appearance of a wolf.

Its fur is shaggy and dark green though sometimes white.

Its tail is long and coiled up. Owners often plaited (braided) the tip of its tail. Its paws are the width of a large hand.

It is strong and can be ridden like a horse by Elf it is close to.

Coven

A group of Witches, usually three to five. They combine magic to cast a spell at a higher force than they could individually, up to the sum of their total force. It also enables to them to share mana. Unlike traditional spell casting, where the caster will lose mana equal to force and gain fatigue, in ritual casting, the group loses an equal portion of the mana, and fatigue equal to the average of the force of the spell.

Daemon

A hyper-intelligent hybrid race created from Elves. They have wings of a bat, the tail of a stingray, and instead of hair, they have horns. They can control their tail and use it like a whip. The end of the tail is barbed.

Their horns vary, one tribe may have a pair of small horns on their forehead, another a ridged skull crown with many small horns on the rim, another tribe may have a pair of large long twisted horns on their head.

There are Aquatic, Field, Flower, Forest, Mountain, Night, and Silver Daemon.

They have an average lifespan of 500 years.

Daemons have natural maximum magic force rating of six.

Dark Elf

A Dark Elf is not a species of Elf, but a term for Elves who are frequently hysterical, distraught, angry, or aggressive to others with little provocation. They range from the slightly unbalanced criminal to the psychotic killer. Many are capable of self-control and function on the fringes of Elven society, most leave the Empire for the Free States.

Whereas magic tends to make most races calm, sexually aroused, even slightly delirious, but generally in a good mood, a Dark Elf is not. They are left feeling disappointed, and even more short-tempered than usual. They can only experience joy from the suffering of others.

Demon

They are a race of small energy beings. While most do appear in the form of a transparent red generic humanoid with horns and bat-like wings, the precise form varies. They also vary in shades of red and brightness.

A Demon is unable to do physical harm in the real dimension. However, it is capable of possession. Each entity adds their mana to their host's mana pool and increases the host's force rating and grants the possessed the ability influence others, gnosis. Only some have other abilities. A rare few have multiple powers. Demons value power.

Most only have a magic force rating of one. Over time they do increase.

Dragon

A hyper-intelligent hybrid race created by Ogres. They are the result of manipulating the DNA of modern era creatures with various dinosaurs.

The Eastern Dragons are mostly serpents, while the Western Dragons are mostly reptilian.

All Dragons have strong stomach acid, which they can regurgitate on command.

Most Dragons are carnivores, except the Land Dragon, which eats grass, some leaves, such as ferns and soft fruit.

The Black Land Dragon is a three-metre long black and yellow tiger striped wingless bipedal reptile with a long tail, short arms, and long powerful hind legs. It is a cross between a Gold Tegu and a couple of herbivore dinosaurs. Unlike other Dragons, it was bred primarily to be a mount, not a weapon. It has excellent hearing and vision.

The Black Dragon Turtle is a three-metre long land turtle with large spikes on its shell. It is an eastern Dragon, a cross between an alligator snapping, a giant sea turtle and an ancient sea serpent. It is black with large snake-like eyes. There are three species, the Golden and the Green. The Golden Turtle is a freshwater pond turtle, while the Green is a sea turtle.

The Western Green Winged Dragon is a six-metre long dark green skinned winged dinosaur with scales. It has a long reptilian tail, a long narrow jaw with conical teeth, long rear legs with claws and small forearms with claws. It has huge bat-like wings. It has huge yellow eyes with the pupil a vertical slit like a gecko.

The Eastern Green Winged Dragon is a six-metre long blue-green skinned winged snake with a large head, with an elongated snout. It has four short legs, it can grip equally with all four claws. It has feathered wings like those of a giant eagle. It has the eyes and fangs of a Mamushi. The bite is very venomous and can be lethal.

The Eastern Water Dragon is a six-metre long black banded sea krait with spines down its back. On top of their head, between the eyes is an armoured plate that has thick ridges and lined with two protruding horns on either side. A frilled neck like a frilled neck lizard. It retains the fins of a krait but has four short gecko legs. It also has both lungs and gills like a lungfish. It has fangs with venom ten times stronger than that of a cobra and a large long forked tongue. Unlike most Dragons that are hunters, this Dragon is an ambush predator.

The Red Winged Dragon is a one-metre long red skin winged dinosaur with a short reptilian tail, a medium-sized jaw like an alligator, and its short arms and legs are the same length and have three-toed claws. It is a 1m carnivore the feeds on fish and small animals. It has bat-like wings. It can walk upright but is faster on all fours.

The Blue Winged Dragon is a 40cm tall winged dinosaur with pale grey skin covered in bright blue feathers. It has feathers with wings and a tail like a bird, a short beak that has a jiggered razor edge on top. It has two short legs with sharp claws with a long sharp spur.

All Dragons are unable to speak without magic. They need a casting device attached to them to use magic.

They have an average lifespan of 2000 years.

Dragons have a natural maximum magic force rating of twelve.

Dwarf

A race of people that range in height from 90 to 120cm tall. There are four distinct groups, Caucasian, Mongoloid, Negroid and Australoids. There are over 5,000 tribes of Dwarves. Trolls are largest Caucasian group and Oni are the biggest mongoloid group.

The Koropokkuru are a Japanese Dwarf with dark brown hair, large round dark brown eyes, and a child-like body, with a large head. They average 100cm tall.

All Dwarves have an average lifespan of 500 years.

Dwarves have a natural maximum magic force rating of six.

Elf

A race of thin, androgynous people. There are seven races, Aquatic, Field, Flower, Forest, Mountain, Night, and Silver, with common features.

They have dense muscles with soft and flawless skin. If their hair is not cut regularly, it will grow to their feet. Their nails will grow into sharp claws if not filed down.

They a heart shaped faces with a high forehead, high cheekbones, a narrow round chin with a wide mouth and thin lips. They have slightly longer canine teeth, all their teeth are sharp.

They have pointed ears, but each tribe a distinct ear pattern. All Elves have long tongues averaging 12cm, small noses and long fingers.

Males do not have facial hair until over 1000 years old. Adults have fine body hair, including pubic hair. Their pubic hair doesn't thicken until middle age.

All Elves have exceptional senses, some better than other. Forest Elves have a better sense of smell, capable of telling each other apart by scent within a metre. All Elves can see in the dark, Night Elves can see in the dark the furthest.

All Elves have seven senses. The sixth sense, known as electrical detection, which comes from special sensing organs, called electroreceptors, on their palms of their hands, the base of their soles and on both sides of their necks. They are too small to be visible. They can detect the small electrical fields generated by most animals.

The seventh sense is linked to the sixth, vibration detection. The seventh sensory organ is also on the neck, a lateral line either side of the neck. It is a thin visible line down the side of the neck. It is used to detect vibrations and changes in pressure around them.

Both the sixth and seventh senses work better underwater and in the cold. It makes Elves vulnerable to pulses used to repel sharks. Elves are vulnerable to sonic weapons that stun or incapacitate.

All Elves are stronger, smarter, more agile, and healthier

than Dwarves and Giants. Most adult Elves can complete a marathon without shortness of breath. Having higher tolerance to heat and cold, Elves rarely perspire. They have only a faint body odour.

Elves can digest raw meat, bird, fish, mushrooms, nuts, and vegetables. Elves can eat some mushrooms that have a mild toxin with no ill effect.

Elves are completely androgynous, that is they have no difference in average height, weight, strength, appearance between male and female from the same tribe. Male even have the same facial, skeleton frame, hand, and foot size as a female Elf.

Elves are just biologically comparable with other races, able to breed with, Dwarves and Giants, even Ogre, Orcs, and Goblins. Unlike other races, they can breed with Daemon and Centaur. But they unable to share their blood, organs, or skin tissue with other races, but can do with other Elves. Elves all have the same blood type. Their blood has a higher salt content that taints their plasma blue.

All male Elves are born appearing female. Males do have a Y chromosome, they have a vagina with no uterus. The ovaries are testicles and remain internal. Usually, for a male, the clitoris will grow into a penis at puberty. On average occurs between the ages of twelve and fifteen. Sometimes males will develop small breasts. Rare, but sometimes a male will not develop a penis.

Elves do not have genetic defects. They engineered out genetic diseases and defects except for the deficiency that causes males to be born with a female appearance. They do not see this as a defect, nor are they ashamed.

Females outnumber males ten to one. Thus, males can

marry many females at the same time. Females once ruled society, but went too far, and enslaved the males. Adamos led a revolt long ago and established the Amazon accord that gave males positions of power.

Elves have a high tolerance to heat, and cold, with a low perspiration rate.

Female Elves usually experience menopause around 900 years old. Their period ranges from 28 to 84 days apart. Infertile females are rare. Pregnancy lasts from eighteen to twenty months, with twins been exceedingly rare, and most twins are two females. Most twins are not identical.

Elves health is beyond that of other races with most mental illness rare. Elves are immune to almost all virus and bacteria, except influenza and powerful bacterial infection.

Elves age at the same rate as other races until 18, then age at a very slow rate, with an average lifespan of 1500 years without the use of magic. Most Elves have children between 18 and 30, they call púca, and prefer to live in a close family group.

All Elves have a high pain tolerance and can survive wounds that would kill a Giant. Elves can regenerate most light wounds to any part of their body. An average adult can pull a broken tooth with no pain and within a day, regrow a replacement. Elves can fully regenerate a mildly broken bone, some nerve damage and mild organ damage, even to the brain. Most moderate wounds Elves can recover quickly from but are scared for life. A severe injury, such as the loss of limb is permanent. Some injuries that would kill others do not always kill an Elf, but will not an Elf fully recover from an extreme wound. When an Elf dies, their body does not decay for at least a week, while most races can't be revived after minutes, Elves can be revived easy within hours of death, and days using magic.

Elves are the most advanced race technologically, they also have a very tolerant society. They have a moral code based on liberty, free speech, and justice. However, these rights come with limits. While they restrict political freedom, they are not as restrictive on personal liberty. Elves accept homosexuality and other consenting adult relationships, but the majority live in groups of one male with many females. Elven females are rarely adulterous, but an abusive relationship can break the emotional bonds. Hypergamy is rare. Males rarely abandon their wives, but some will only marry a few. Most males don't have a brother, but many sisters.

Elves rarely divorce, but divorce is easy. All adults must keep a register of assets. Most land and homes belong to clans. Wives have no community property rights, and children belong to the clan of their father. Divorce is a matter of going to the Blood-Witches, signing a declaration, and settling any jointly owned property. The female must then vacate the family home with only her property. Joint banking is rare, and the female is expected to contribute to the household. The average wage can support a male with three females each with one púca.

Elves are protective of their species and bloodlines. They limit all breeding with non-Elves. It is not illegal, but Elves are discouraged from having children with members of other tribes. It is discouraged to breed with non-Elves.

Birth control is mandatory for both males and females. Having children is licenced. Having a child without a permit, the parents are neutered and the child raised by the state.

Most Elves live in clans, that is a group of three or more related families.

A house is a term for the top single richest families.

Elves have a natural maximum magic force rating of seven.

Field Elf

One of the five races of Light Elves. These Elves are tall, slender Elves with blonde hair with a minority having red hair. Eye colour is predominately blue with some green, grey, or gold eyes.

The second-largest ethnic group, most common language is Germanic. Their languages combine to form a common Elven language.

Found in all over Scandinavia, Europe and Ukraine, Middle East and all the way to Central Asian Highlands to the western side of the Gobi Sea.

Field Elves average height is 180cm. Their ears are about human size, but instead of a round arch at the top, their ears come to a point.

Flower Elf

One of the five races of Light Elves. These Elves have purple, cherry red, pink, blue, or green hair and vary in shade. Eye colours are violet, yellow, blue, green, or gold.

A distinct feature of flower Elves is their longer than average fingers and ears. Flower Elves ears differ from other Elves as their ears are narrow and longer than other Elves.

Also, their ears are double joined, able to move up and down and from perpendicular to their head to back against their head. Flower Elves ears typically sit perpendicularly. Often flapping ears when excited.

Flower Elves have a sweet body odour like a flower.

Flower Elves have an average height of 165cm.

Forest Elves

One of the five races of Light Elves. These Elves are tall and muscular Elves with pale light green skin, light green hair, a minority have dark green or blonde hair. Eye colour is predominately green with some blue, violet, or gold eyes.

Forest Elves have an average height of 190cm.

Free States

The Free States is a group of worlds not under control of the Empire. Populated by rebellious Elves, there are many ports with pirates.

There is also a group of worlds populated by Dragons.

The largest Free State is Freeport, halfway between the Elves and Ogres, it is a hub in the middle of all the Empires. It is a large dry world with a few large bodies of fresh water. Central City is massive and is large than Imperial City. Located inside a 500-kilometre round depression near the equator, the city fills the depression. Transport is a mixture of roads, canals, trains, subways and an elevated magnetic levitation train system. It is home to pirates, traders, smugglers, assassins and exiles.

Giant

A race of tall people with a rounded head, broad shoulders, and range in height from 180 to 220cm tall.

There are six races of Giants, Green, White, Red, Yellow, Brown, and Black. The Green and White Giants are both Caucasian, but one has green hair with green eyes, the other has white hair with pale blue-grey eyes. The Red, Yellow and Brown Giants each have dark brown hair and brown eyes but differ in skin tone. The Black Giants have black skin, black hair with yellow eyes.

They have an average lifespan of 200 years.

Giants have a natural maximum magic force rating of six.

Goblin

A race of people with dull, pale grey skin, a flat head, long narrow faces with a square chin, large round ears, pointed teeth, a long hook nose, and large round eyes with large pupils. Goblins can see a short distance in the dark. Goblins are greedy and mischievous pranksters.

They have an average lifespan of 80 years.

Goblins have a natural maximum magic force rating of five.

God

A god is a being with supernatural abilities. Possession by an entity on its own is not sufficient, the entity needs to merge with the host to convey its supernatural abilities.

Hakama

A traditional Japanese garment, based on Chinese trousers. Hakama are worn over a kimono, tied at the waist, and fall to the ankles.

There are many kinds of Hakama from Formal to Field Hakama worn by farm workers.

Jötunn

A race of highly intelligent Ogre with pale white skin and greater strength than an Ogre of the same weight. Males average 220cm and females 190cm.

Two tribes the Red (Fire) and Blue (Frost) Jötunn. A Red Jötunn has dark red hair with hazel eyes. Blue Jötunn have pale white hair with grey eyes.

Kazoku

Japanese for the family. The Flower-Elves view family as the ideal relationship, a bond of love, forgiveness, honour, and duty. Setting aside selfish goals to have a common goal. The core belief is that sexual love, the giving of gifts, and spending time alone together is special, but should rare, not be the goal or foundation of the relationship, but family harmony with the husband in charge. Another part of this belief is sex should be regular and not based on mood swings or desires but seen as a marital duty. The prime duty of a husband's wives is to him, then the family. The husband's prime duty is the clan. The clan's duty is wealth and prosperity to its member. That all púca are raised by the whole clan.

Kimono

A traditional Japanese garment, a T-shaped straight-lined ankle length robe with long, wide sleeves. They are wrapped around the body left to right and secured by a sash.

Kiseru

A traditional Japanese pipe typically used for smoking Kizami tobacco.

Kizami Tobacco

A finely shredded tobacco product. Traditionally it is prepared without any additives and very finely chopped.

Magic

The highest level of technology. No one knows why some races have a higher force than others. But anyone can use a casting device, which is though controlled by a nano-etched quantum computer, which typically found in the bulb at the end of a wand.

The technology is simple, a casting device gathers Aether from the wielder using charged Orichalcum mesh, which then traps the Aether inside the vacuum tube, then the nano-quantum computer translates the spell formula in radio waves and then releases the charged Aether.

An Aether battery is a device that traps Aether inside a glass vacuum tube until the charge in the mesh runs out.

While magic appears to defy logic, it does follow the laws of physics. Force governs how powerful a spell is. A caster can try to cast over their magic rating, the feedback causes physical harm to the caster, unless they cast in a ritual.

Using more force means more fatigue to caster and more time wielder needs to charge the casting device. The more fatigue, the harder it is to cast spells. While small fatigue takes seconds, a moderately fatigued caster takes minutes to recover, then as the casters fatigue grows, it takes hours to recover. Risking loss of consciousness if they continue casting spells without pause.

The small amount of electricity needed to power casting devices comes from a thermocouple and is stored in a micro-sized zero-point energy system. Only some electricity is to power the computer in the bulb, and the interface, which is a device that can detect the wielder's thoughts and transmit data to the wielder. The casting device can connect to tablets, phones, or computers wirelessly, but needs the casters mana and will to cast spells. Most of the electricity is used to draw, store, and change Aether, which is powered by mana from the caster.

Supernatural beings, such as Archon, have the natural abilities considered magical.

Makura

A small round pillow filled with buckwheat.

Mana Pool

The amount of energy in a user. The maximum amount of mana a caster has is equal to seven times their force rating. The amount of Mana consumed depends on the spell and force of the spell. If a spell can be sustained it will drain additional mana based on force, if unable, the spell ends.

It takes one second to transfer one mana, and after charging a device, mana then recovers at the rate of one unit per second. Transferring mana causes fatigue. Magic users practice tracking their mana pool so they know how much they can transfer without passing out and learn to count seconds between casting.

Waiting for the number of seconds equal to the spell force between casting is a common practice to reduce fatigue.

Reaching mana zero will cause pain and fatigue to the caster.

Mountain Elves

One of the five races of Light Elves. These are Elves are tall, muscular Elves with blonde hair, a minority have an assortment of red hair. Eye colour is predominately blue with some green, grey, violet, or gold eyes.

Most are Celtic with some Germanic, Norse, and Greek tribes.

Mountain Elves are the tallest and the strongest of all Elves with an average height of 240cm.

Night Elves

One of the two races of Dark Elves. These Elves have black skin with purple hair, the majority have dark purple. Eye colour is predominately gold eyes with a small number having violet eyes.

Most are Hindi with some Slavic, Aramaic, Persian, Russian and Mongol tribes.

Night Elves are strong as a Field Elves with an average height of 120cm.

Naruko

It is a wooden clapper used in Yosakoi. It originated as a device used by rice farmers to scare away birds.

Oni

One of the Ogre races. They have a distinctive pair of large conical eye teeth that protrude from the top row, which average 3 cm long. Oni have black hair and large, upturned, almond shaped eyes.

There are two tribes of Oni. The Red or Japanese Oni average 190cm tall and they have red skin with red eyes. The Blue or Persian Oni average 220cm tall and they are very thin and have sky blue skin with light blue eyes.

Ogre

A race of people with common features that distinguish them from Giants. They have a protruding forehead, a flat crown, and a square jaw. Internally they have large thicker bones than a Giant. They are known for their aggression and are typically stronger than a Giant of the same size.

Unlike Giants, Ogres are far more diverse. Ogres break down into four distinct groups, Caucasian, Mongoloid, Negroid and Australoids. There are over 5,000 tribes of Ogre.

While male Ogres average 210cm tall, with females averaging 180cm tall, the Titan and Jötunn are taller and stronger than the average Ogre.

Ogres have an average lifespan of 150 years but are elderly by 70.

Ogres have a natural maximum magic force rating of six.

Orcs

A race of southern Germanic people. There are four tribes of Orcs, the brown, the green, the grey, and the orange. They all have flat heads and dense muscles. Their long arms reach their knees and large hands with claw-like nails. They all have a protruding jaw with large bottom fangs. The rest of their teeth are spaced and conical.

Males have hairy chests. The average height of a male Orc is 180cm. The female Orc has an average height of 160cm. Orcs are much stronger than a Dwarf but not as strong as an Elf but are they stronger than most Giants, except Titans.

They have an average lifespan of 80 years.

Orcs have a natural maximum magic force rating of six.

Púca

A term Elves use to refer to Elven children. In the old Empire, before labour laws, púca would sleep in the day and be left to guard cattle at night, chase rats with sticks or lay under bushes to watch for bandits or as lookouts for bandits.

Pureblood

An individual whose ancestry only consists of a single type that is unmixed with any other tribe, race, or species.

While most consider it a racist term, Elves do not, they see having the majority pureblood as a duty. The Elves see purity as a mean to avoid extinction. It is not just cultural practice but expressed with laws on migration, and population control.

Ritual Casting

Some spells need to be cast at a force too powerful for one user, so they need to be cast as a group. A ritual casting is when a group of magic users share mana with to the caster using a ritual casting device.

The maximum force is the combined force of the members of the group. Originally started as three witches holding hands. It was discovered using a standard wand or quarterstaff they could use Orichalcum thread to connect them.

A cauldron (a giant pot) was originally designed for a coven of three, later five, to do blood magic. A ritual pole (a giant quarterstaff) was designed for a coven of seven.

Silver Elves

One of the two races of Dark Elves. These Elves are tall, have black skin with silver grey hair. A minority have pale blonde or pale red hair. Eye colour is predominately red with some having violet or gold eyes.

Most are Egyptian with some Greek, Semite, and Zulu tribes.

Silver Elves are stronger than field Elves and have an average height of 188cm.

Tabi

A traditional Japanese ankle- high socks with a separation between the big toe and other toes.

Titan

A race of Ogre that is 240cm tall with massive chests, arms, and legs. They have olive skin with brown hair and brown eyes.

Trolls

One of the largest races of Dwarves. They are a Germanic people with brown hair, brown eyes, a thick skull with a flat head, squarish jaw with a protruding forehead. They have slightly grey skin. They appear youthful and childlike until 100, then they age quickly, both males and females have thin grey hair.

Trolls will often live apart with males raising daughters, and mothers raising sons.

Unicorn

They are an ancient species of horse. Only the male is white and has a single spiral horn in its forehead. The female is brown with white spots.

The original breed is small. The male is 50cm tall, and the female is 40cm tall.

The modern breed of Unicorn is an improved cavalry horse, the size of a large riding horse. The breed combines intelligence, speed, and aggression.

Unlike a regular horse, the modern Unicorn have an average lifespan of 80 years, the miniature Unicorn is short lived.

Wild Cat Sìth

A cat bigger and stouter than a Cat Sìth, with longer fur and a non-tapering bushy tail, it is ginger with a striped coat.

Highly intelligent, they learn quickly and can

instructions. It is illegal to keep them as pets. They hunt small rodents, rabbits, and birds. They usually sleep outdoors.

Unlike a Cat Sìth, milk and fish do not interest them, they prefer rabbit. They often seek out magic users.

Elves allow them to roam and fend for themselves.

Wraith

They are a race of small energy beings. While most do appear in the form of a transparent grey generic humanoid, the precise form varies. They also vary in shades of grey and brightness.

A Wraith is unable to do physical harm in the real dimension, they are, however, it is capable of possession. Each entity adds their mana to their host's mana pool and increases the host's force rating. A Wraith can grant the possessed the ability to summon and control different entities. A rare few have other abilities. Wraiths value harmony between forces of good and evil. They believe one cannot exist without the other and that no being is pure good or pure evil.

Most only have a magic force rating of one. Over time they do increase.